Song

of the

Wolf

T.C. Smith

This book contains the following content which may be distressing to some readers:

Alcohol, Animal Death, Anxiety, Blood and Gore, Bones, Death, Decapitation, Racism/Xenophobia, Graphic Depictions of Violence, War

This book contains mentions of the following content which may be distressing to some readers:

Child Death, Harm to Children, Forced Experimentation, Genocide, Kidnapping, Terminal Illness

"A true leader has the confidence to stand alone, the courage to make tough decisions, and the compassion to listen to the needs of others. He does not set out to be a leader, but becomes one by the equality of his actions and the integrity of his intent."

Douglas MacArthur

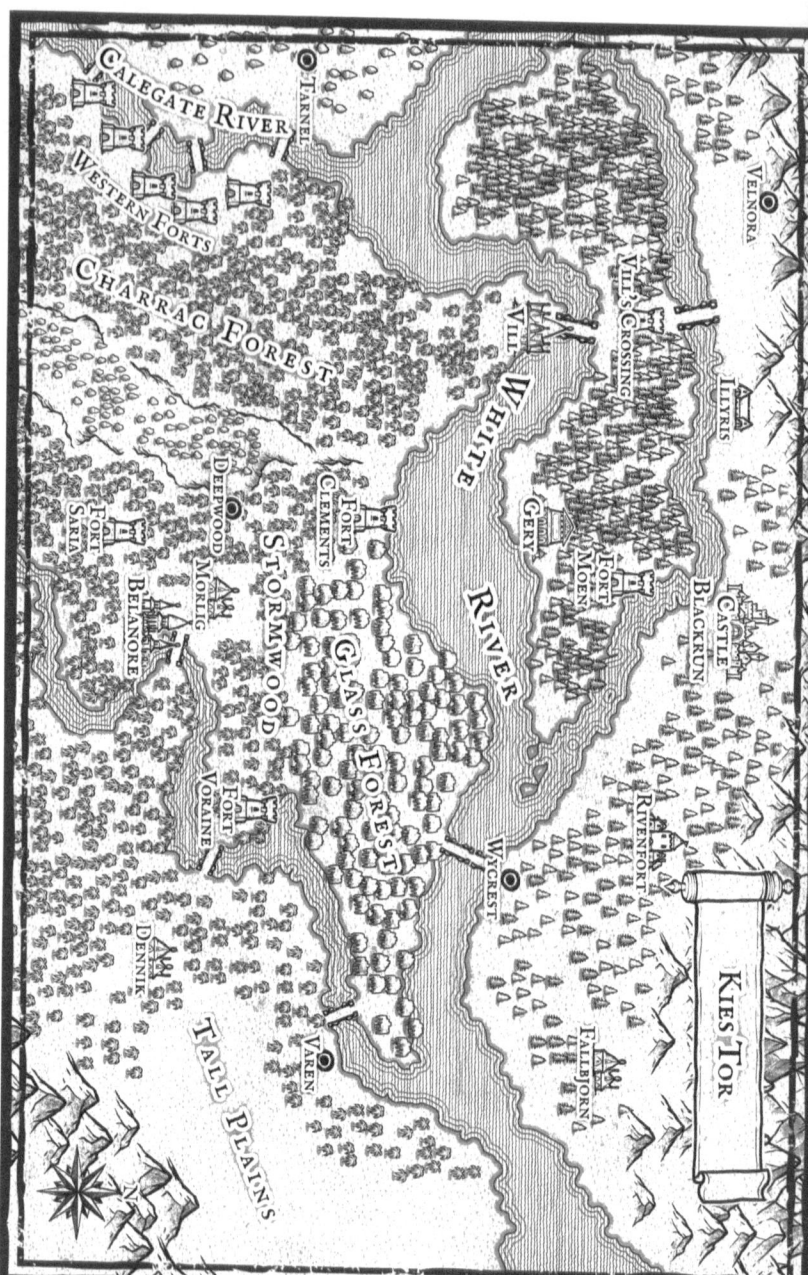

N

Ed'Sarr

Ed'Kharned

Ked'Tald

Ed'Nehill

Ked'Kivane

El'Dravo

El'Vane

White River

Northern Desert

Set'Dhinn

Draconian Lands (North)

Set'Valdor

North Draconian Bay

Valdor Lighthouse

Isle of Trees

R ed Wolf could feel a shift in the energy of the gathered crowd when he stepped onto the balcony.

It was an odd feeling, to be sure, and he had no idea how he could even feel such a thing, but there was no denying that the animated crowd below reflected his feelings today. Eagerness. Hope. Excitement for their new queen.

He could feel a slight unease, too, nagging at the back of his mind. Despite whatever else he might have told himself all morning, he knew this was far more than a simple coronation. The moment that crown was placed on her head, their struggle against the invading Hellhounds would fall upon the shoulders of Talin Zylvaris, second of her name.

Red Wolf had the feeling that she wasn't prepared for any of this.

"Big turnout," Golmin said, appearing on the balcony beside him. He'd already changed into his ceremonial armour, the polished metal glinting in the morning light as he rested his forearms against the banister. "Last time I saw a crowd this big, you and the king had just ridden back from a victory north of Wycrest. A shame that it was all for naught in the end."

"Hmm. I told the princess she need not worry about a crowd," Red Wolf said. "It appears that I was wrong. Rufus, do me a favour and let her know she's about to receive quite the warm welcome. I'll be with her soon."

"Aye, I'll do that." Golmin straightened and vanished through the balcony doors. Red Wolf watched the crowd for a few moments longer, scanning for any sign of trouble. When it became apparent that nothing was amiss, he turned away, heading back to the armoury to don his gear.

Ashera had finished polishing his armour by the time he arrived and looked pleased with her work. Red Wolf examined the metal and found it flawless, as he'd expected from his squire, despite her youth. He smiled and struggled into his gambeson and mail.

"This might be your best work yet," he said. "Once we're done here, you should change into something for the occasion. You'll be accompanying me outside after the ceremony."

The girl's eyes widened. "I'd be honoured, sir."

"Well, if you're to join the Royal Guard, you need to know what to expect," Red Wolf said. "Think of it as...gaining work experience."

"Pfft, just admit you're bending the rules," Ashera said and stuck her tongue out.

"Ah, you know me too well." Red Wolf pulled on his tabard and turned so she could fit the plate armour over his shoulders and arms. She handed him his sword and scabbard, allowing him to unsheathe the blade to check that it was sharp.

"I sharpened it earlier this morning," Ashera said.

"Oh? Excellent work," Red Wolf said. He turned again so that his back was to her, and she pulled up a stool so she could reach up and fasten the rich blue cloak of the Royal Guard. Emblazoned in its centre was the white raven that marked the royal crest.

Why a scavenger bird? he'd once asked Arnas. *Why not something grand, majestic, like a lion or dragon?*

What's freer than a bird who can soar across the open sky, untethered by the world? the king had replied.

He banished the thought.

"Will the princess really let me join the Royal Guard once she's crowned queen?" Ashera asked.

"Of course. I was a nobody from nowhere when I was a squire, and I was allowed to join the Royal Guard," Red Wolf said. "Look at me now. About to be Lord Commander of the Royal Guard under two sovereigns." He grinned.

"But you squired for the *king*," Ashera said.

"And you squire for the royal bodyguard." Red Wolf shrugged. "Where you come from doesn't define who you can become." He buckled his sword. "Now get yourself changed. It's going to be an exciting day."

The girl darted off eagerly. Red Wolf made his way back to the palace's upper levels, weaving through the maze of corridors and hall-ways, dodging guards and palace staff as he passed them. He reached the princess' chambers just as she stepped out.

"You look stunning today, princess. Happy birthday," he said, his boots drawing to a brisk halt on the carpeted floor. It was true; Tal-in looked every bit a queen as she stopped in front of him. Her waist-length chestnut hair had been fixed in a complicated array of locks and braids, falling down her back like a ripple and throwing her face and pointed ears into stark relief. Gold and silver threads wound through her white robes like vines, glinting in the morning light. 'Stunning' didn't do her justice. Talin gave him a smile and thanked him for the praise.

"Walk with me," she said, and he fell into step beside her.

"Captain Golmin might have told you about the crowd," he said.

"Yes. He was quite excited about the fact that half of Belanore is gathered outside the palace gates." Talin didn't quite meet his gaze. "I never imagined I'd be celebrating this birthday with a coronation."

"I can sense your unease," Red Wolf said. "Relax. All will be over and done with soon enough. We've gone over the proceedings before."

"This isn't a rehearsal," Talin said.

"No. But that doesn't mean it will run any differently. Just pretend the crowd isn't there. You'll do fine."

"I'm not ready for this."

Red Wolf shrugged. "If you felt ready, I would say that you are not ready to be queen."

"What do you mean?" Talin asked.

"You do not seek this power," Red Wolf said. "That's a good thing. Far too many heirs are eager to rule and abuse their power once they sit on the throne. The promise of such power can do terrible things to a person. Remember that this is a privilege, not a right."

"What if I do mess it up?" Talin asked.

"You won't." Red Wolf offered her a smile. "Or if you do, you'll fix it. You're a good person. I know it. The crowd outside knows it. You'll be a fine leader. It's in your blood." He halted outside the throne room. "I'll be waiting right here when you step out."

Talin turned to face the doors. The two guards standing there moved, ready to open them. "Red Wolf, come with me."

"You know I can't." Red Wolf remained unmoving. "I may have been lord commander under your father's rule, but unless I am sworn in again under you as the queen, I cannot accompany you inside."

"Damn the protocol, we both know I'm not going to find a new lord commander," Talin muttered under her breath.

Red Wolf huffed a laugh. "Be brave, princess. Whatever happens, remember that this is your duty. When you step back out of these doors as queen, you will have the power to make the world a better place. Stay true to yourself. Do the right thing. Always. I have faith in you, I know you'll not fail."

"I..." Talin glanced at him, then at the doors again. "Thank you."

At Red Wolf's nod to the guards, they pushed on the doors, letting them swing open into the room beyond. Talin spared one final glance back at him; then, taking a deep breath, she squared her shoulders and strode forwards.

"The gods be with you, my queen," he said softly.

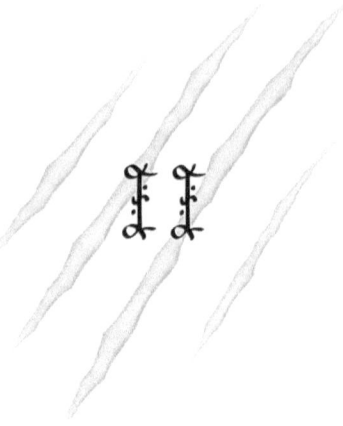

Illyris was taken, according to reports from the northern front. Castle Blackrun, their strongest fortification in the Highlands, had fallen to the Hellhounds. Enemy cavalry now rode for Vill's Crossing. In the west, the Hellhound horde invaded and plundered villages where they saw fit, turning the place into a hunting ground and death trap for any who tried to cross the Western Forts.

Talin supposed the only good thing to come out of her father's defeat in the White Forest was the destruction of the bridge at Wycrest, which had cut off the Hellhounds' advance in the northeast and forced the northern hordes to reroute to the heavily fortified crossing at Vill. Reinforcements from Fort Voraine had cleaned up the few Hellhounds who had made it across the bridge and into the south.

But they weren't enough to save Father and his cavalry.

She shook her head. With Illyris now under Hellhound occupation, Vill's Crossing would fall next unless they sent reinforcements.

We have nothing to send.

The floorboards creaked. Talin jumped and cursed under her breath when Red Wolf's towering form appeared at the war-room doors. The visor of his helm was down, as it usually was, concealing his face and golden eyes. His sword hung at his hip, the hilt glinting silver in the candlelight. Below the neck, he wore mail and a tabard, with steel plate to protect his shoulders and arms.

"If you're here to give counsel, speak," Talin said. "Otherwise, you should sleep. The hour is late."

"You can't hold the north," Red Wolf said, ducking through the doorway.

"As my entire council has told me," Talin said. "Still, I wouldn't mind hearing your opinion."

Footsteps rang through the small hall as Red Wolf strode forward, resting his gauntleted palms on the map spread in front of her. His eyes darted across it momentarily before he jabbed a finger at Vill's Crossing. "The Hellhounds have the Crossing and its fort under siege." His hand moved to Illyris and its surrounds. "With Illyris gone, you've lost a significant portion of Kies Tor's agriculture and food supply. It won't be long before the food shortages start. With the destruction of the Wycrest bridge, your father has unfortunately taken away any opportunity you might have of flanking the Hellhounds. Your nearest barracks are here." He pointed at Fort Moen. "You could send out what's left of their garrison, but it will only delay the inevitable. Vill's Crossing *will* fall, and once it does, nothing will be left standing between Belanore and the Hellhound horde. They will rip this land to shreds."

Talin huffed a short exhale. "That's not comforting."

"I only speak realistically, my queen."

She sighed. "I know. Lord Wormwood said the same. He's of the opinion that we should start thinking about siege preparations."

"You agree with him?" Red Wolf asked. There was a slight edge to his voice that she couldn't quite place.

"I don't know," Talin confessed. "Half my council says one thing; the other half says another. I've no idea who to agree with." She straightened. "Either way, I suppose the only thing we can do now is try to delay the Hellhounds as much as possible. Buy ourselves time."

"To do what?"

"Find allies, find the Hellhounds' weakness, *something*." Talin shook her head. "Get some sleep, Lord Commander. Captain Golmin has posted a guard around my chambers already. I'll be protected enough."

"As my queen commands." Red Wolf bowed. "Though, if I could be so bold, perhaps she would allow me the honour of escorting her back to her chambers."

"Very well." Talin let him fall into step behind her.

"You're certain you won't be needing me tonight?" Red Wolf asked.

"My answer remains the same, Red Wolf."

Talin had been asked that question every night for the past month, ever since an assassin had slipped into the palace. If it had been anyone other than Red Wolf posted outside her door that night, she was certain she would have been killed. Her bodyguard, thankfully, had emerged unscathed. The assassin hadn't been so lucky.

"You'll be holding another war meeting tomorrow, then?" Red Wolf asked when they reached her chambers.

"I must. General Virion will be forging a campaign towards Vill's Crossing in two days' time. I cannot delay him if we are to hold the Crossing."

"Then I suppose you'll not object to my attending."

"My objections never seem to have any bearing on your attendance, so let us presume you are correct."

Red Wolf bowed again. "Then I take my leave here and bid you goodnight, my queen."

"Same to you, Red Wolf." Talin opened the door to her chambers and stepped in. Behind her, his footsteps faded down the hall.

She drew the curtains across the windows silently and changed into a nightgown. Outside, thunder rumbled, and a flash of lightning lit the sky.

The storm season is on its way.

The storm season was good in a way, she supposed. The Hellhounds weren't acclimated to wet weather, being from the frozen wastelands in the far north, whilst her troops were used to the storms and heat of southern Kies Tor. The rivers running through the kingdom would rise, and the waters of the White River would turn into the foaming rapids that gave it its name. Maybe there was hope yet for holding the north. Talin climbed into bed and blew out her candle, willing sleep to come.

She was woken sometime in the night by a sudden breeze and the nagging feeling that something was wrong. Slowly, she sat up, turning her head towards the open window.

That window hadn't been open earlier.

A flash of lightning illuminated the room, allowing her to glimpse the stranger standing by her window. Steel glinted in the waxing moonlight.

Oh, gods.

The door to her chambers crashed open, and something launched itself into the darkness. The silhouette went down. She heard a *thud* and a scream.

"Stay down. You won't win." Red Wolf's voice. There was another *thud*. Talin fumbled for a match in the dark and managed to light a candle.

Red Wolf was crouched at the foot of her bed, his armour shining gold and silver where the light hit it and red where his visor was splattered with fresh blood. Pinned beneath his hulking frame was a black-clad man with a thin face and lanky hair, whimpering as he clutched a broken wrist. His nose looked more of a ruin where the front of Red Wolf's helm had smashed into it, gushing blood down his chin. Evidently, her bodyguard hadn't gone to bed as she'd asked. He must have sent her guards off duty instead and taken their place outside her chambers.

Perhaps for the best, Talin thought. Had he retired to the barracks, she was certain she would have died at this assassin's hand.

"Red Wolf, how did you know..." she began. She hadn't heard a sound from the man as he slipped inside, and yet Red Wolf had rushed in at exactly the right moment.

"With your permission, my queen, I'd like to take this *abiyo* down to the dungeons for questioning," he said, ignoring her remark.

"R-Red Wolf?" The assassin's eyes widened. "You weren't supposed to be on duty tonight—"

Red Wolf scoffed and grabbed a fistful of the man's shirt, lifting him off the floor with one hand. Compared to the lord commander, he looked fragile enough that Talin was afraid her bodyguard might accidentally crush him in his iron grip.

"Gods-forsaken assassins these days, they'll believe anything."

What?

Things began to slot together. If Red Wolf had been asking to guard her ever since the first assassin had slipped in, he must have suspected there would be another attempt on her life soon. And this time, it seemed, he wanted the assassin alive.

Talin glared at him. "Was this all a ruse?"

"I'll question this assassin and see what he can tell us," Red Wolf said, ignoring her again. "Apologies for the blood. I'll find someone to clean it out of the carpet in the morning."

"Answer me, Red Wolf," Talin commanded.

Red Wolf hesitated. She wondered if he might elect to ignore her order too.

"Yes," he finally said, and disappeared through the doors with his prisoner in tow.

Talin pinched the bridge of her nose. It wasn't as if she could fault him for organising something like this in complete secrecy, given how easily information seemed to travel in Belanore, but she wished that he'd at least informed her of his intentions beforehand. Either way, she doubted that she'd be getting back to sleep tonight. She threw on a coat with a sigh and headed to her study to finish her outstanding paperwork.

Talin didn't expect to see much of Red Wolf the next day, given the prisoner he was no doubt entertaining in the dungeons, though she still felt a pang of disappointment when she saw no sign of him at her war meeting. Despite whatever else she might have told herself, she did miss him a *little*; his constant presence by her side was a reassurance, if nothing else. She left the meeting to prepare for court and longing for his company.

Honestly, I don't know why I bother holding these meetings at all. She was half-tempted to let the Hellhounds sweep through the kingdom and tear it all to shreds. But she knew they couldn't simply give up; her father had fought so hard to keep control of the north and had given his life to keep Belanore safe.

Talin spent most of her afternoon dealing with the usual complaints from the townsfolk, sorting out petty disputes between neighbours and granting permits and whatnot. Nothing particularly exciting, if she was honest with herself, but it had been almost two weeks since she last opened the palace gates. The war effort made it far too difficult to hold court every day.

You should pay more attention to what your people need.

She admitted two more merchants looking to gain a trading permit in Belanore and granted it to them, then called for Lord Karl to usher the rest out. She made her way down towards the cells alone.

"I must say, my queen, I'm impressed by how long you've managed to put this off."

Talin didn't turn. "You're making a habit of sneaking up on me."

"What can I say? I have a light tread." Red Wolf stepped out of the shadows at the top of the dungeon steps. He was still clad in his armour from last night, she noticed. Dried blood painted the front of his helm where he'd headbutted her assailant, a smear of crimson across his otherwise shiny visor. Talin took a torch from its socket in the wall and descended the stone steps.

"You certainly do have a light tread—for a giant," she said.

"I am no giant." Red Wolf fell into step beside her. "Your would-be assassin has told us nothing. Perhaps you'd like to see him."

"Why do you think I'm going this way?"

"One could presume you were up to something devious."

"You know I'm not that sort of woman."

"And yet you come to me seeking answers."

Talin rounded on him. "You have an obligation to tell me, Red Wolf. I am your queen. Do not forget that."

"Of course, my queen," Red Wolf said. "But all I do, I do in your best interests."

"Including withholding information?"

Red Wolf said nothing.

Talin tried a different tactic. "Why did you allow the assassin to scale the walls?"

"We needed a man for questioning." Red Wolf took the torch from her at the bottom of the steps and led the way onwards, past endless rows of black-barred cells. She could see some were occupied, though none dared come close to them in Red Wolf's towering presence. A straggly youth with rags for clothes spat on the ground when they passed. Her bodyguard slammed the bars with a gauntleted hand, and he jumped back, eyes wide.

"You and Captain Golmin set this up?" Talin asked.

"The plan was my idea. Captain Golmin only helped because he had an obligation to his lord commander," Red Wolf explained. "We organised a new night shift that left blind spots on the walls and allowed the assassin to observe the pattern. We also leaked false information that I would not be guarding you at night. I had been asking you if you required me to guard your chambers only because I did not want to go against your word, but you refused each time. We were running out of opportunities."

"You mean to say that I was bait," Talin said.

"Not the word I would use, but in a way, yes," Red Wolf confessed.

"Why?"

"You have been on the throne for less than a *year*. If someone wants you dead this quickly, something is amiss. I'd like to find out what."

They rounded a corner and halted. Red Wolf gestured to the cell on their right, and Talin turned, trying to peer through the bars. She glimpsed Golmin's bearded face and the assassin on his knees in front of him.

"What has he revealed?" she asked.

Golmin turned and bowed. "Nothing yet, Your Majesty. Though I'm hoping that will soon change."

"Continue, then."

"You'll stay?" Golmin asked, sounding surprised.

"I want to hear what he has to say."

"Very well." Golmin dipped his head. Beside her, Red Wolf slipped the torch into a bracket on the wall and unlocked the cell, joining his captain.

"Let's try this again. Who sent you?" Golmin asked, crouching in front of the man. The assassin responded by spitting on his armour.

"I don't have time for this," Red Wolf said. He grabbed the front of the man's shirt and dragged him up with one hand. "Who sent you?"

"H-he didn't give his name," the man stammered, trying to wriggle free.

"You'll have to do better than that." Red Wolf slammed him into the bars. Golmin passed a dagger into his free hand. "Here's what's going to happen. The good captain and I have been awfully generous with you today, but you've now worn my patience *paper-thin*. I'm going to give you to the count of three, and if you don't give me anything by then, I take your right ear. Still don't give me anything, I take your left ear. Keep resisting, and I'll start removing your fingers, one by one. We understand each other, yes?" He lifted the blade and rested the edge against the top of the man's ear. "One."

The assassin gasped. "I never got a name, I swear. We met at the Dragon's Inn. I was to go back there to collect my payment."

"Why were you sent after the queen?" Red Wolf growled.

"He...he said...she wasn't supposed to be on the throne. Told me everything. He's working for the rightful king." The man squirmed as Golmin came forward again. "The Crown doesn't belong to her. You have to believe me!"

Talin felt a chill going through her. Only one person would have cause to do something like this.

"He's telling the truth."

Red Wolf and Golmin both turned their heads simultaneously.

"Your Majesty, with all due respect, this man is spitting nothing but lies at us, trying to shake our loyalty. There is no evidence to support what he says," Golmin said.

"He's telling the truth," Talin repeated.

Red Wolf shoved the man hard, sending him tumbling backwards into the wall. "Rufus, clean up in here and have Corvan sent down. I believe we're done." He stepped out of the cell without another word and pulled Talin away, taking the torch from the wall.

"You know something?" he demanded.

"I...have reason to believe that Ettrias is the man we're after," Talin confessed.

Red Wolf was silent.

"Your brother?" he said, after a beat. "He's been exiled for...what? Ten years? Why suspect him now?"

"Because we both came of ruling age a few months ago," Talin said, "and he wants the throne."

"I don't understand. The High Court stripped his claim to the throne when he was exiled."

Talin shook her head. "That makes no difference to him." She sighed. "Ettrias is my twin, and older than me, if only by a few minutes. I'd wager he never truly accepted the loss of his claim."

"I knew Wormwood shouldn't have granted him leave to attend your father's funeral," Red Wolf muttered. "He must have remained in the kingdom afterwards and vanished into Belanore, plotting your downfall."

Talin winced. "You know what they say. No good deed goes unpunished."

"Either way, we must track him down," her bodyguard said. "He should not even be in the kingdom, let alone in Belanore." He shook his head. "I don't understand. It's been ten years. He's been content with the loss of his claim for *ten years*. Why plot this now?"

He was never content, Red Wolf. You, of all people, should know that.

"I don't know," Talin said.

"Then we'll need to find out exactly who hired these assassins. I hope you won't mind if I take my leave of you tomorrow."

"You're going to visit the inn?"

"I must." Red Wolf lifted his visor and eased the helm off his head, revealing the tuft of dark hair he always kept trimmed. What always drew her attention, however, were his eyes—glittering golden yellow. *Wolf eyes*, she'd always thought.

"Then see to it that you find some answers," she told him.

"I'll certainly try, my queen," he said.

"And..." Talin began.

"Yes?"

"Be careful."

F or an inn located in the poorer half of Belanore, it was surpris-
ingly well-furnished; the place was well-lit and kept clean, and the
attached tavern downstairs was packed full by dusk. Red Wolf watched
the patrons and barmaids mill about from his table at the back. He'd
swapped his usual guard's uniform for a simple tunic and had donned
a cloak that concealed his face from passers-by. He had left his sword,
too, despite Talin's protests; such an expensive weapon would draw
unwanted attention in this part of the city. Instead, he wore his dagger
at his belt, tucked away beneath his cloak. If it came to a fight, this was
all he would need.

The innkeeper had been reluctant to disclose any information about
his patrons at first but quickly changed his mind when shown the silver
brooch of the lord commander. He revealed that a long-term lodger

named Vinters had signed in shortly after the king's funeral. Red Wolf had traded two yarii for the innkeeper to signal when Vinters returned.

But it was now almost sundown, and his suspect had yet to show himself. The inn was growing rowdier and more crowded by the minute. Red Wolf tried his best to drown the background buzz but only succeeded in amplifying it.

A helmet would be useful about now.

Perhaps coming here had been a bad idea. Perhaps the assassin had lied about his contact being here. Red Wolf flagged down a passing barmaid and ordered another cup of ale in a final attempt to dull his senses with alcohol.

Who am I kidding? It's never worked before. He glared at the empty mugs on his table.

He should leave. This place was too loud. There were too many people. Too many scents.

"You sure drink a lot, even for a giant," the barmaid said, returning with his drink.

"I'm no giant." Red Wolf tipped her a copper and resolved to return to the palace after he finished his ale. He'd left Talin unguarded for far too long already.

A dark-haired elf with blue eyes strode in as he stood, ready to depart. The elf paid for his room without missing a beat and continued upstairs while the innkeeper gave the smallest of nods.

Red Wolf followed the elf up to the guest rooms soundlessly.

"You're a damn traitor, Red Wolf."

He felt the cold bite of steel against the back of his neck and raised his hands slowly. "Prince Ettrias. Your sister sends her regards."

Ettrias scoffed. "She sent you to arrest me. It doesn't take a genius to work that out. I take it that means she survived the assassin I sent after her?"

"You tried to kill her twice. That's it? No remorse?" Red Wolf scowled.

"I should kill you for helping my own father exile me," Ettrias said. "I looked up to you once. But you chose to protect Talin over me."

You know why I chose her. He didn't voice it out loud.

"Kill me, and you'll be found guilty of murder again. And exile won't be an option." He shrugged. "A personal opinion, but I feel you would look more dashing with a noose around your neck... I wouldn't risk it, my prince." He wrapped a hand around the hilt of his dagger. "Besides, you know what I am. Threatening me with a pointy piece of steel serves no purpose."

The blade disappeared from his neck, and he turned to face Ettrias. The prince certainly looked less elegant than he remembered, dressed in woollen trousers and a cheap tunic with an old sheepskin coat to keep him dry in the storm season. He'd trimmed his hair a few inches and wore it loose to partially hide his ears. Red Wolf was impressed by how much effort he'd taken to disguise himself; he was barely recognisable as the former Crown Prince of Kies Tor.

"You're a disgrace," Ettrias spat. "A disgrace to the uniform. A disgrace to your own damn knighthood."

"Perhaps," Red Wolf said. "But when all is said and done, you are the one convicted of murder, not me."

"You're a cruel man, Red Wolf," Ettrias said.

Red Wolf scoffed. "Do not talk to me about cruelty. You do not know the meaning of that word."

"Were you not cruel when you betrayed me? When you stood by and *allowed* my exile for something you knew I never did?" Ettrias hissed.

"That no longer matters. The High Court has marked you as a murderer and exiled you for life."

"All thanks to you."

"My duty was to the Crown. As it always has been. As it always will be."

"Your duty had no bearing on the situation, and you know it."

There was a beat. Red Wolf lowered his gaze.

"I'm not proud of what I did," he said, "but the past is in the past. I cannot right this."

"You can right it by letting me go," Ettrias said. "We both know the throne should be mine."

"The throne is Talin's now, whether you like it or not," Red Wolf told him. "I will not help you commit *treason*, Ettrias."

"Is it treason if I'm the rightful heir to the Torrian Crown?" Ettrias countered.

"Talin is the rightful heir," Red Wolf said.

"Oh, please, we both know I was born first," Ettrias said. "The claim is mine."

"You no longer have any claim to the throne, Ettrias," Red Wolf said. "Any rights you may have had were stripped ten years ago."

"I was always the outcast, wasn't I?" Ettrias laughed bitterly. "Just like you."

"I am *not* an outcast." Red Wolf felt a rush of anger and pushed it down reflexively.

"No? Giants have been extinct in Kies Tor for a thousand years, and you're not nearly old enough to come directly from their bloodline. You are not of this kingdom," Ettrias said.

"I am no giant."

"Yet you stand a foot taller than most."

"Perhaps my mother was cursed by a witch when she was carrying me."

"Jest all you like, Red Wolf, but you will not leave this inn with me in tow."

Red Wolf lifted his brow. "And how are you planning on getting away? Even if you escape now, you know I can track you through the entire city. It would be easy."

"Arrest me, and I will reveal the truth to *everyone*." Ettrias held up his hands. "The whole palace will know, and soon, the whole of Belanore. Everyone will know the truth of the crimes *you committed*."

Red Wolf hesitated.

Everyone will know. Talin *will know.*

"So be it," he said. "I will let you go today. Leave the city by tonight. I will report to my queen in the morning. If you're still in Belanore by then, the city will be put under lockdown, and there will be no way out."

"Leave?" Ettrias demanded. "Abandon my pursuit of the throne? No. I will not stop until that crown rests atop *my head*! It is my birthright!"

"Rulership is not a birthright," Red Wolf said softly, turning away. "It is a duty. Your sister understands that better than you ever will. Do not make me regret letting you go tonight, Ettrias. Leave the city. Give up this foolish quest."

"I will fight for the throne until my dying breath if I must. Think of it as revenge."

"Then the honour you have is worth as much as mine."

He brushed past Ettrias and headed for the front doors.

Night had fallen by the time Red Wolf reached the palace. The streets were mostly empty now, save for a black-clad worker lighting the lamps along the side of the road. Red Wolf gave him a nod as he passed.

Ettrias will be arrested eventually. And then he'll tell everyone the truth.

Perhaps it was time. He had spent far too long running.

"I take it that Ettrias escaped, then?" Golmin said, meeting him at the palace gates.

"He gave me the slip," Red Wolf said, trying to brush it off as a stupid mistake. "How are *you* so certain it was Ettrias, is my question."

"Nobody gives you the slip unless you let them," Golmin said icily, keeping pace with him as he made it through the front courtyard and up the steps into the throne room antechamber.

It was worth a try.

"It's a long story," Red Wolf said.

"Red Wolf." Golmin stepped into his path neatly and barred him from continuing forward.

Red Wolf sighed. "Rufus. It's been a long day. I want to sleep."

"You know he's innocent," Golmin said. "You knew he was innocent ten years ago and said *nothing*. Is that why you let him go? Guilt?"

"How would you know anything of the sort—" Red Wolf began.

Oh, by the gods.

Golmin averted his gaze.

"You and Ettrias..." Red Wolf said. "That's who I saw you with before the trial. You...confessed your feelings for each other. Why didn't you tell me?"

Golmin, for his part, had the decency to look a little embarrassed. "Ettrias didn't want you to know. I told him that was a tall order, given our relationship, but he insisted. I suppose he wasn't ready to tell you then."

"And I suppose you also wanted to avoid confronting me," Red Wolf said.

"I wasn't sure that he was innocent," Golmin said. "I trusted you to do the right thing." His expression shifted into a hard glare. Red Wolf found himself staring at the man's neatly trimmed beard. "But I also know you. If you let him go tonight, then—"

"You're right—he is innocent," Red Wolf said softly. "I'm sorry. I can't say more. There are some secrets best kept from my queen. But if I had...known...about the two of you..."

"What, you would have told the Court the truth?" Golmin scoffed. "You've convinced yourself you're doing this for the queen, exactly like you did ten years ago, I'm guessing. You have no *right* to decide what secrets should be kept from her."

"I have every right to keep her safe. As is my duty." Red Wolf shoved him aside and made for the stairs.

"Your duty is to the Crown, not to her!" Golmin called after him.

Red Wolf paused on the bottom step. "I *am* doing my duty to the Crown."

"Keep telling yourself that."

He expected that Talin would already be asleep by now, and that Golmin would have already posted guards outside her chambers, but still, he made his way to the upper levels to ensure that nothing was amiss before returning to the barracks. Ashera had probably returned to the women's barracks too—if not to sleep then to chat to the off-duty guards there. He passed the soldiers' lines without looking for her and continued down the hallway to his chambers. There, he stripped his cloak and tunic and pulled his boots off without bothering to light a candle.

Who are you doing this for? The queen...or yourself?

Red Wolf banished the thought and tried to sleep.

Red Wolf was still having breakfast in the soldiers' mess when Talin found him, coffee cup in hand, chatting to some guards. No doubt he hadn't learned anything of value at the inn yesterday; he hadn't yet returned by the time she retired last night and would have woken her had he apprehended someone. She suspected that whoever had hired those assassins had simply fled as soon as they realised their second attempt on her life had failed.

"Stand fast. It's Her Majesty!" a guard yelled. Every soldier stood and turned towards the doors in half a heartbeat. The hall fell dead silent.

"As you were," Talin said. She made her way between the tables to Red Wolf.

"My queen." He wiped his mouth and rose, taking a knee before her.

"Walk with me," she said.

"As my queen commands." He stood once more and followed her from the mess hall.

"I take it your trip yesterday proved unsuccessful," Talin said.

"Unfortunately," Red Wolf said.

Something about his tone gave her pause.

"There's something you're not telling me."

"I'm not sure I understand, my queen," Red Wolf said.

"Red Wolf." Talin fixed him with a glare.

"…your brother was there," Red Wolf confessed. "He slipped away before I could get close. I believe you were right—he was the one behind those two assassination attempts. He signed in at the inn under an alias just after your father's funeral."

Talin let out a long breath. Much as she had hoped her brother wasn't involved, the evidence added up. Ettrias knew the palace layout by heart and would be able to advise the assassins on which entrance points were best. And if Red Wolf's intelligence from the inn yesterday was accurate, then…

She huffed a humourless laugh. "He used Father's funeral as a means to re-enter the kingdom. I thought he was better than this."

"What would you have me do?" Red Wolf asked.

"Relay my orders to Hesar to lock down the city," Talin said. "Nobody leaves without a permit until Ettrias has been detained. Put out wanted posters at every noticeboard, inn, and tavern. I want him found."

"As my queen commands." Red Wolf inclined his head and moved to leave.

"Once you're done, join me in the small hall," Talin said. "I could do with your advice, truth be told."

"Of course." Her bodyguard vanished down a different hallway while she continued towards the small hall.

She had no doubt that Hesar and his Chained Owls would find Ettrias eventually, given the time; Belanore's City Watch was one of the most effective in the kingdom, and its commander had served since her father took the throne before her. But with the growing threat of Hellhounds in the north, *time* was not something they had in abundance.

The only way we can win this war is by finding an army from somewhere past our borders.

The Royal Council had assembled by the time she made it to the small hall. The Master of Coin and former Lord Regent, Felix Wormwood, sat directly to her left, with the elderly Healer and Records Keeper, Master Corvan, beside him. General Virion sat to her right with the Highett brothers, Lord Karl and Lord Cassius, further down. The latter two served as her head of civil affairs and intelligence, respectively.

And Red Wolf, of sorts, she thought. Though her bodyguard was not officially part of her council, his position as Lord Commander of the Royal Guard meant that he was present at most of her meetings anyway, and she had yet to think of a good reason for him *not* to be in attendance.

Besides, his suggestions were, admittedly, better than most of the suggestions her council made.

"Thank you for gathering, my lords," she began. "As you may have heard already, my brother Ettrias, who was allowed to return to Belanore for our father's funeral, has outstayed his welcome in Kies Tor. He is currently hiding in the city and seeks to usurp the throne."

Her council was silent.

Lord Cassius finally spoke up. "If he's plotting against you, then finding him must be a priority. My spy network may be able to turn up something of value—with your permission, Your Majesty."

"Make it happen," Talin said. "I've ordered the city locked down. There should be no way out for him."

"It may also be worth informing the High Court of the situation, Your Majesty," Master Corvan said. "If all else fails, you will need to procure search warrants from Judge Branweyn."

"Lord Karl?" Talin said.

"I'll speak with Judge Branweyn after this meeting."

"Good. Let us move on—" The side door creaked open before she could finish to reveal Red Wolf, now with his helm on. He bowed to her, then her council.

"My deepest apologies for the interruption, my queen," he said.

"No matter, you're just in time," Talin said. "The Owls have been alerted?"

"They have," Red Wolf said.

"Good." Talin stood and unrolled the map of Kies Tor while Red Wolf took his usual position behind her left shoulder. "As we all know, Hellhound cavalry continues to advance in the north. Vill's Crossing will not last much longer. General Virion will ride out tomorrow to rendezvous with the two thousand soldiers marching from Fort Voraine. It's my hope that this will buy us the time we need to round up sufficient reinforcements to hold the Crossing."

"And where do you propose we get those reinforcements?" Lord Wormwood asked. "Even if the Crown had the coin to hire mercenary groups, there *are* none still operating in Kies Tor. There have not been mercenary groups in this kingdom since the establishment of the Torrian Royal Army."

"Then we must find our reinforcements from outside Kies Tor," Talin said. "Travelling south puts us in Astaria. Fae country. What's the situation there?"

"The Fae will be no help to us," Red Wolf said immediately. "From what I hear, the kingdom is in the middle of a political crisis of its own. You may be able to persuade King Darien to form an alliance with Kies Tor, but he is in no position to send military support."

Talin blinked. "How do you even know that?"

Red Wolf shrugged. "I overheard a few things at the inn yesterday."

"Very well, what about east?" Talin asked.

"East puts us in unmapped territory," Master Corvan said. "All we know is that the mountain range is steep and almost impassable. We'll find no aid there."

"And west lies the Draconian Empire," Talin said. "This doesn't give us many options."

"I can tell you now that you'll have better chances with the Drakels than the Fae," Red Wolf said. "There is a reason their conquest of the west has been so successful."

"The lizard-folk are vicious, unwelcoming beasts," Wormwood said, echoing her thoughts. "They'll not enter into a treaty with us. If anything, they'll seize the opportunity to conquer Kies Tor and add it to their ever-expanding empire."

"It appears that my lord has met these Drakels in person and must therefore be our most qualified expert on them," Red Wolf said icily. "By all means, Lord Felix, enlighten us on what vicious practices you witnessed during your time in the empire."

"*Red Wolf.*" Talin silenced him with a glare. "I will not have you speak like that to my Master of Coin. If you think to disrespect *any* of the people gathered here again, I will personally have you thrown out of all future council meetings."

"Apologies, my queen." Red Wolf bowed his head. "My lord. I spoke out of turn."

"Our priority right now must be to prepare the city for a siege, in case the good general fails to hold Vill's Crossing," Wormwood said. "Much as I would love to send a delegation past our borders, the threat to the capital is too great right now."

Red Wolf huffed through his nostrils. "With all due respect, my lord, if we do not seek allies and the Hellhounds do make it to Belanore, we are all dead. Diverting resources to a diplomatic party is the only choice we have."

"We'll send a letter to these Drakels," Talin said. "In it, we'll explain our situation and request their aid. If they are open to negotiation, we will organise a delegation to send west."

"They'll have to travel through enemy territory to reach the Drakels—" Wormwood began.

"That's enough, my lord," Talin interrupted. "We'll discuss the details should they become relevant. I will write the letter after this meeting. For now, we must ensure our northern lines hold. Can we divert any more resources from the Western Forts, General?"

"I'm afraid not," Virion said. "Our forces are stretched thin enough as they stand. Concentrating our forces at Vill's Crossing would leave the western front exposed."

"There must be something more we can do," Talin said.

"The way I see it, we're as good as dead either way." Virion shook his head. "We're losing this war, Your Majesty. The Hellhounds have proven themselves a superior force. Even if we could somehow hold the north front, it'll only be a matter of time before they sweep through the kingdom and take the capital. Perhaps...if I may be so bold...*surrender* is another option if all else fails."

"We cannot surrender," Talin said. "Not after all the sacrifices that have been made."

Virion pursed his lips. "Your Majesty, the Hellhounds will kill everyone if—"

Red Wolf cut him off, thankfully, before he could irritate Talin further. "I have reason to believe we may be able to squeeze something from the western front. With your permission, my queen."

"Go ahead."

Red Wolf approached the table and settled his hand on the Western Forts. "We know this position is our strongest defence. It has withstood every attack the Hellhounds have launched against it, while other forts have fallen. We also know this river separates us from the western horde." He pointed at the Calegate River cutting through the south. "The only way across is via the drawbridges at set crossing points along the Forts. The Hellhounds have no way across it. I'm sure you could safely reassign at least a quarter of the western garrison to Vill's Crossing."

Talin considered it. It was true; much of their success so far had been due to the Hellhounds' lack of siege weapons, which were necessary to breach the fortifications in the Highlands. But the Hellhounds were nothing if not patient—they were masters at wearing down their enemies.

This last-ditch attempt to save the Crossing could work.

"Send a bird to the Western Forts," she said. "Have them select a quarter of their garrison to depart for Vill's Crossing immediately."

"Your Majesty, are you sure this is a wise move?" Lord Wormwood demurred. "If the Hellhounds breach the Western Forts, they will be able to continue unimpeded to Belanore. The city would fall."

"Red Wolf," Talin said. "You're certain that pulling resources from the western front will work?"

"Nothing is certain, my queen," Red Wolf said. "But if I know the Hellhounds, they will focus on Vill's Crossing, the weakest link in our fortifications. I know they will not breach our lines to the west."

"Make it happen, General" she told Virion. "Have them rendezvous with you and the Fort Voraine troops at Vill."

"Consider it done," the general said.

"If there's nothing else, this council is dismissed," Talin said. "See to your duties."

Her advisors dispersed, save for Lord Wormwood and Red Wolf. The latter remained hovering to her left as he always did. He pretended to ignore the Master of Coin as the man went around the table to approach her.

"I'm sure that whatever decisions you have made will be the right ones," Wormwood said, offering her a reassuring smile. "I only offer objections so that I might provide another perspective on the matter. I hope you understand. Your father would be proud of you."

Talin swallowed. "Thank you."

She didn't miss Red Wolf's glare as Wormwood left the small hall.

"You shouldn't trust that patronising, slimy..." her bodyguard began, pulling himself up when he saw the glint in Talin's eyes. "Surely you see that he's quick to judge and unwilling to accept outside help."

"Red Wolf." Talin sighed. "He used to fight beside my father. He fought beside *you* whenever you accompanied my father to the front. Patronising or not, I know he can be trusted."

"*Tch*." Red Wolf crossed his arms. "I may have apologised for my intemperate words during the meeting, but I stand by what I said. We should not pass judgement against the Drakels so readily."

"No, you do have a point there," Talin admitted. "We do not know much about these Drakels, only that they have conquered most of the west in their name. Perhaps it would be wiser to reserve judgement until we have met them in person."

"Ah, so you do intend to send someone," Red Wolf said. "I cannot say I object, though I highly recommend running it by your council first."

"No, not yet," Talin said. "Ettrias is my priority at the moment. Once he has been detained, we can look to the Drakels."

"You must understand that your brother wants you *dead*," Red Wolf said. "He will not stop until the throne is his. The less opportunity you provide him to target you, the better. Actively going after him only gives him more chances to kill you."

"Which is why I must find him," Talin said. "He's still my brother."

"You think to reason with him?" Red Wolf asked. "He will not listen to reason, not from anyone. In his eyes, he has been wronged, and only by becoming king will things be made right."

"He will listen to me," Talin said. *Maybe he'll listen from a cell. But he will listen.*

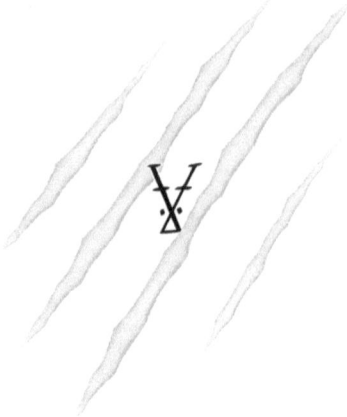

R   ed Wolf decided that it was far too wet to be training outdoors.

He and Ashera had snatched an hour's worth of blade practice in the morning drizzle before the storms picked up, washing out the entire training yard and turning the dry earth into a miniature mud lake. Already he could picture flowing gutters along the sides of the main road leading up to the palace, dumping water into the moat just ahead. He knew overflow drains along the inside of the moat walls would ensure it wouldn't flood, but even so, he would stare at it anxiously whenever he chanced to look out the windows.

"I wish we could go outside," Ashera remarked wistfully as she polished his armour. "Archery is much more fun than this."

Red Wolf shrugged. "When I trained to be a royal guard, there wasn't much difference between archery and armour polishing. My arms would be tired enough by the end that it didn't matter which I did." He picked up his helm and examined it, staring into the rings of molten gold that coloured his eyes. Ettrias was right; he was an outsider. He had never belonged here.

He looked up again, taking in the rest of the armoury. Two guards were lounging in the back corner, sharpening their steel, while Brakis, the Weapons Master, picked out a selection of old swords to send off to the smithy, so they might be melted down and reforged stronger.

"Will you tell me a story about you and King Arnas?" Ashera asked without looking up from her polishing.

Red Wolf picked up his dagger to oil it and drew his hand back immediately with a hiss of pain as the edge slashed open his thumb. He wiped the blood off on his dark pants before it could drip everywhere and rubbed the spot where the cut should have been. Nothing, not even the faintest trace of a scar to mark where the blade had bitten into skin. *I'm not worthy enough to tell you those stories, Ashera. Arnas was not worthy enough to warrant a story either.*

"What sort of story would you like?" he asked.

"I don't know. Something happy or exciting. Polishing your armour is growing awfully boring," Ashera said. "Oh, I know! How about the Siege of Castle Blackrun?"

Red Wolf couldn't help but crack a smile. "Castle Blackrun? I've told you that one many times before."

"I want to hear it again," Ashera said. "Please?"

"Alright." Red Wolf seated himself beside her. "As you know, I was knighted the year of my seventeenth birthday, in the middle of one of the worst storm seasons Kies Tor had ever seen. I'd squired for King Arnas for four years and served in the Royal Guard for a year. It just so happened that my predecessor had just retired, so I was appointed as the new lord commander immediately. My first task was to accompany

King Arnas to the front and help him drive the Hellhounds out of Castle Blackrun."

"And you were able to outsmart the Hellhounds, right?"

"That we were," Red Wolf said. "The Hellhounds are difficult to kill in combat due to their ability to heal instantly from almost any injury, so facing them in open battle was not an option. But I knew they had no siege weapons of any sort. They relied on their superior numbers and endless patience to outlast us in a siege. But Castle Blackrun was well-equipped and well-provisioned. Instead of fighting them head-on when we arrived, I suggested we take out their hunting parties. Without food, they were easy pickings."

"Why didn't you go with the king to Wycrest then?" Ashera asked. "If your job was to protect the king, and he'd asked you to help on the front as well..."

"The King wished me to remain behind to guard the princess," Red Wolf said. "I suspect he knew he was riding towards certain death and wanted to ensure his heir's safety." He glanced at the armour. "You missed a spot."

"Where?" Ashera squinted. "Are you trying to mess with me? That's just a scratch, not a dull spot."

Red Wolf laughed. "Perceptive of you."

"You're not even funny."

Red Wolf grinned. "You wound me, Ashera. I could be the court jester." He stood while she rolled her eyes at him. "Either way, that'll do. We can use the sparring rooms for a little more swordplay before lunch."

"But my arms are aching." Ashera pouted.

"You are, of course, welcome to continue polishing my armour," Red Wolf said. "Though I'm not sure how much shinier you can get it."

Ashera let go of the polishing cloth and stuck out her tongue. He turned away, still grinning.

"I do hope you're coming. It's not easy to spar alone," he called over his shoulder. Footsteps sounded as Ashera fell into step beside him.

"It must have been interesting to squire for the *king*, of all people," the girl said. "What was it like? Did you get special privileges?"

"It wasn't that different from squiring for any other knight or noble, you know," Red Wolf said. "My duties remained the same. Ensure the king's arms and armour were ready for battle. The only difference was that I was trained by Brakis instead of King Arnas."

They rounded a corner, bringing them past the soldiers' barracks and into the training quarters. The thick, red carpet gave way to simple wood, and he could hear his boots making light thuds on the floorboards as he walked. Ashera had a far lighter tread; she barely came up past his elbows, and she weighed far less besides.

"Do try to make more of an effort to hit me this time," he said as they stepped into one of the empty training rooms. He helped Ashera with the padded armour, and she took a weighted wooden sword from the weapons rack.

"I'll whack you over the head with this if you're not careful," she said, grinning.

"You'll have to catch me first." Red Wolf pulled on his own set of training armour, snatched another sword off the rack, and took up a defensive stance opposite her. He knew she was fast, and if she managed to get close enough, his size and reach could become more of a handicap than an advantage. He would have to keep his distance.

"Remember what I taught you," he said. "Get in quick, go for the kill, do not get hit."

"You say that every time," Ashera muttered.

"And have you remembered?" Red Wolf changed his stance in an instant and lunged. Ashera stepped away neatly and knocked his blade aside, forcing him back again as she tried to close the distance between them. He responded with another attack. She parried it with a grunt.

"Too far up the blade," he said. "Remember to parry near the cross-guard."

Ashera stumbled as he freed his sword, but quickly regained her balance. Red Wolf used her moment of distraction to press forward, forcing her further and further back until she was trapped against the wall. There she finally yielded, after receiving two heavy blows to the shoulder.

"Ow!"

"Do not let me drive you back like that," he said, as the girl nursed her injured arm. "Take the initiative. Control the fight. Again!"

He gave Ashera just enough time to process what he'd said before renewing the attack. She ducked under his arm and slipped around him, swinging her sword. He spun neatly and parried the strike.

"Better," he said. "Do not drop your guard."

Ashera raised her sword quickly, and he gave her a small nod of approval before aiming a low strike at her ribs. She was forced back again, and he seized the opportunity to press her to the wall. Unexpectedly, she stepped in, closing the distance between them in a heartbeat. Red Wolf parried her next strike and gave her a shove with his free hand, sending her stumbling into the wall again. He lifted his blade to her throat.

"Better," he said, "but you grew overconfident. Always stay alert. It only takes a moment for the odds to change. Again!"

"Red Wolf, wait."

Red Wolf turned to face the doors and discovered Talin standing there, clad in a white and green silk dress. She wore her hair loose this morning, kept back from her face by a few well-placed pins. A silver band adorned her head instead of a crown, elegantly forged into a pair of twisting vines, meeting together in the centre to form a peak that rested just above her eyes.

"My queen." Red Wolf dropped to one knee. He heard Ashera do the same behind him.

"Rise. You're needed in the western tower," Talin said.

Red Wolf nodded and placed his sword back on the weapons rack. "Ashera, you have the morning to yourself. I do hope you'll make some use of the time."

"Don't worry. I'll be here, still working on my genius plan to beat you at swordplay next time!" Ashera called as he joined Talin at the door.

"I take it you found Ettrias," he said, once they were in the hallway and well out of earshot of any passing soldiers.

"I was hoping to make it a surprise," Talin said.

"You should have sent a messenger, then." Red Wolf shrugged. "Though I suppose you would rather keep this matter between us for now."

"I'd expected him to be more difficult to catch, given the effort he'd gone into covering his tracks," Talin said. "But it's only been...what? Two weeks since we put the Owls on alert? I don't like it. He's going to tell me what he's planning."

"Has he said anything yet?" Red Wolf asked, feeling a sudden surge of panic at remembering his conversation with Ettrias at the inn.

"Nothing," Talin said, and he breathed an inward sigh of relief. "But we have him locked in the western tower. If he won't talk, a few days in solitude should loosen his tongue."

"You would do this to your own brother?" Red Wolf asked. "You were close once."

Talin scoffed. "That was before he murdered two people."

He never committed those crimes, Talin. By the gods, I would give anything to set things right. But at what cost to you?

"And if he had never been accused?" he asked instead.

"Then things would be very different between us now," Talin said. "As it stands, however, that was not what happened. We cannot change the past."

"Very true." Red Wolf found himself staring at the floor.

"You seem troubled."

"It's nothing, my queen."

"If you say so." Talin didn't sound convinced.

They stopped at the armoury briefly, where she ordered him to don his gear, and they continued on a few minutes later with him clad from head to heel in his usual armour. Ashera had polished it well, he reflected. Red Wolf lowered his visor, partly to dampen his keen senses, but mostly so that he might pass through the palace without someone staring at his eyes. While it wasn't uncommon for Weavers to have oddly coloured eyes, it still attracted attention, for magic was shunned in Kies Tor, and Weavers were seen as outcasts. He knew that people whispered of his powers in the hallways. They feared him; that much was evident. He passed for a Highlander with his rounded ears, but the palace gossip had always been about his magic and his height. Some speculated that he was descended from the half-giant clans in the far north.

They could be right, he mused. He recalled little of his childhood, before...

Red Wolf banished the thought and glanced at Talin instead.

She was lucky.

Born with electric-blue eyes that almost seemed *too* blue, nobody questioned whether she could be a Weaver. But being attuned to magic as he was, he could sense her powers, brimming within her, ready to be unleashed.

Does she know?

He had told Arnas the moment he sensed her magic manifesting. Whether the late king had passed on that information to his daughter was another matter.

"You're unusually silent today," Talin said.

Red Wolf glanced at her. "Would you prefer I spoke to you?"

"Only if you feel so inclined," Talin said, eyes glinting with amusement.

"So I have a choice?"

"Less of a choice and more of an obligation, but yes. Something is troubling you."

"Then it would not do for me to trouble you too, my queen."

"My father always said that it was a ruler's duty to tend to their subjects' wellbeing," Talin said. "You are more than welcome to share your troubles, if you wished."

Red Wolf sighed. "My burden is my own to bear. There are some secrets I'm sure you would rather not know."

Talin didn't press him further, and they spent the rest of the walk in silence. He knew he couldn't reveal anything, and certainly not where prying ears might hear him, but the secrets he kept were becoming harder to bear. Sooner or later, Talin would know the truth. There was no telling what Ettrias might reveal.

The stairs leading up to the western tower were steeper than he recalled, and with the additional weight of his armour, he found his progress slow. Talin's light dress was far more suited to the humid heat of the storm season. He tugged off his helm with a growl and muttered, "it's far too hot for armour, my queen."

"Oh, stop complaining." Talin smiled. "Besides, your armour is more intimidating."

Red Wolf responded with a grunt.

They bumped into Lord Wormwood as they neared the top of the steps, the Master of Coin muttering a quick apology and moving to step past them. Red Wolf held out an arm to bar his way.

"Care to explain what business you had with Ettrias, my lord?"

"Not Ettrias, Lord Commander. I have no business with a murderer," Wormwood said. "I was only talking to Captain Golmin about matters of palace security."

Red Wolf felt Talin's glare on the back of his neck and didn't push it further. The Master of Coin flashed them both a smile before continuing down the stairs.

"What was that about?" Talin asked.

"Nothing, my queen," Red Wolf said. "My apologies. I was being overly suspicious."

Golmin was indeed standing guard outside Ettrias' tower when they made it to the top, and Red Wolf felt a brief pang of guilt about openly questioning Wormwood again in front of Talin. The guard captain bowed to them both before opening the door. Red Wolf stepped inside first, in case Ettrias had plans to attack the queen.

He had always regarded these towers as well-furbished jail cells—compared to the dungeons for detaining common criminals. The cell was small, with a bed and bookshelf for crammed against the left wall, a rickety desk and chair occupying one corner, and a tiny window facing west but providing some light. Ettrias lounged on the narrow bed with an open book in hand as though he didn't have a care in the world.

Red Wolf halted in front of the bed. "I have to say, I'm disappointed. I was expecting you to be harder to catch."

"It's hard to run when the queen and half of Belanore wants you locked up," Ettrias said.

"Why did you return?" Talin demanded.

"Not even a greeting, dear sister?" Ettrias asked. "I'm fine, thank you for asking. How are you doing on your stolen throne? Is the crown a nice fit?"

"A word from me, and Red Wolf will gladly cut out your tongue. Don't give me a reason to do it," Talin said.

"Well, I'd rather not get blood all over my armour, but if my queen commands it..." Red Wolf said.

"Oh, you haven't changed one bit." Ettrias closed the book and swung his legs off the bed. "Tell me something: was it your idea to frame me for those crimes or Father's?"

"You still deny the truth after all this time," Talin said with a scoff. "It's a wonder I haven't sent you to the dungeons yet."

"I know what you did! You and him both! Stop pretending you don't know!" Ettrias snarled, starting forward. Red Wolf grabbed a fistful of his shirt and forced him back again.

"Answer my question, Ettrias," Talin said.

"I had my chance after Father's funeral. I wasn't going to miss it. I want what should be rightfully mine."

"The Crown is no longer yours. You'd do well to give up this pointless contest."

Ettrias went to the window and rested his arms on the sill. "Maybe I'm tired of being the outcast. The unwanted child."

"Ettrias, that's not true," Talin said. "You weren't unwanted."

"You were always the favourite. We both know that," Ettrias said. "I was a disappointment to everyone." He paused. "It must have been so easy to frame me, huh?"

"Frame you?" Talin shook her head. "For the love of the gods, Ettrias, how long will it take you to admit the truth to yourself? We're done here." She beckoned to Red Wolf, threw open the door, and strode out without another word. Her bodyguard followed close behind, feeling more uncomfortable by the second. He could almost feel Ettrias' eyes boring into the back of his neck.

"A word, Red Wolf," Golmin called from the door. Red Wolf stopped. Talin paused and turned a few steps down.

"If my queen does not require my immediate presence..."

"By all means," Talin said. "Meet me in the library when you're done." She continued down the stairs and vanished from sight.

Red Wolf let out a long breath. "You talked to Ettrias."

"Of course." Golmin crossed his arms. "He told me everything. His father and sister framed him for the murders *you* committed, and then you lied to the court to cover it all up."

"Ettrias...doesn't know the full story," Red Wolf said carefully. "Arnas orchestrated the coup, yes, but my queen is innocent. She remains unaware of her father's ploy to this day."

"And you?" Golmin asked.

"I was...shall we say...deceived into aiding Arnas initially. A matter of 'state security', is how he put it." Red Wolf couldn't keep the bitterness from his voice. "Talked it up like it was a national emergency and sent me to kill two fleeing villains. Imagine my horror when I learned, after bringing back the bodies, that he'd *used* me for his own ends. I spent four years squiring for this man and even longer as his lord commander, and he treated me like a weapon to be wielded."

Golmin's brow creased. "Then why not reveal everything at the trial? Why *lie to me* for all these years?"

"Arnas threatened to reveal what I am to the entire kingdom," Red Wolf said softly. "Maybe I was selfish. But I couldn't let him."

What am I, exactly?

He wasn't sure he even knew.

"Arnas knew about...?"

"He must have found out somehow." Red Wolf let out a long breath. "It makes no difference. The king is dead, and I trust those who remain." His gaze flickered towards the tower door. "Well, except one."

"*Ettrias* knows?" Golmin exclaimed.

"Accidentally. He did stab me in the chest," Red Wolf said.

"Ah." Golmin scratched his beard. "And the queen? Is she to be the only one entirely unaware of her family's secrets?"

"She cannot know," Red Wolf said.

"She needs to know! To absolve Ettrias of his crimes, at least. And you..."

"No need to remind me. I take responsibility for what I did, and you are free to deal with me as you see fit, provided my queen never finds out about any of this."

Golmin hissed through his teeth. "You..." He ran his hands through his hair. "I could arrest you here, free the man I love. I know you'd let me. The court will sentence you to death and I will lose my closest friend and partner. But if I let you go...Ettrias dies. What am I supposed to do with you?"

Red Wolf looked away. "Whatever you do, I'd rather you didn't tell my queen."

"You can go. For now." Golmin closed his eyes momentarily. "I pray to the gods that you come to your damn senses and do what's right."

"I'm sorry about all of this," Red Wolf said quietly.

"*Don't.* Just go," Golmin hissed.

"It's a full moon tonight," Red Wolf said.

Golmin cursed and worked his jaw. "Fine. *Fine.* I'll take the cellar shift and meet you there before dusk."

"Thank you."

"Don't thank me. I'm doing this for the safety of everyone else in the palace."

"I'll see you again tonight, then," Red Wolf said.

"You have to tell her the truth, Red Wolf," Golmin called, as he turned to leave. "For all our sakes. If you don't do it, I will."

U nder any other circumstances, Talin might have taken Red Wolf with her to visit her brother.

But she had woken early that morning with an odd sense of dread in the pit of her stomach and the nagging feeling that Ettrias was innocent all along, and she knew that she had to get to the bottom of things *alone*.

The rain had let up just before dawn, and Talin could see water droplets still clinging to the tower windows as she passed, but she knew that Torrian weather wasn't at all forgiving. The chances were, they would get another downpour before the day was over.

"Your Majesty." The guard at Ettrias' door gave a short bow when she approached.

"I need to see the prisoner," Talin said.

"I've been instructed not to let you in without an escort, Your Majesty—" the guard began.

Red Wolf's doing, no doubt.

"I'll talk to the lord commander," Talin said, cutting him off. "In the meantime, I'd like to see my brother."

The guard made no further protest and unlocked the door for her.

Inside, it appeared that Ettrias was already up, having his breakfast at the little round table with his back to the door. She glimpsed what appeared to be sausages on his plate as he cut into them with a blunted butter knife. Seeing no other choice, she drew up a spare chair and sat opposite him while she waited for him to finish.

"I'm surprised you trusted me with a knife of any sort," he said as he chewed his food. "Are you aware of just how easy it would be for me to put this through your eye?"

"Painfully so," Talin said. "First things first—I have a proposal for you, and then we must talk."

"I take it I won't like this 'proposal' you've thought up." Ettrias finished his sausages and wiped his mouth.

"No," Talin said. "But it's an infinitely better option than what the High Court would otherwise grant you, so perhaps you should listen after all."

"Tell me, then."

"You know the penalty for returning against the law is death. The court could order you hanged or beheaded without trial, and it would be done. Not even the Crown's authority will save you."

Ettrias leaned back in his seat. "What's the alternative?"

"I let you escape," Talin said. "The court will never find out, and you get to live. In return, you'll give up this foolish contest for the Crown and never return to Kies Tor again."

"The Crown should be mine," Ettrias hissed. "You have *no right* to it after what you all did."

"Did what? Exile you?" Talin asked. "That was a mercy on Father's part."

"And I am eternally grateful." Ettrias scoffed. "What about the things I was accused of? Things that I never did, that have marked me forever as a common criminal. Things that you helped frame me for."

"I wanted to ask, actually," Talin said, "why do you protest your innocence so strongly? Red Wolf caught you trying to dispose of the bodies. Nobody who testified could give an alibi for you. You murdered a girl out of jealousy and rage and killed her brother to keep him quiet. Why deny it when the evidence is clear?"

"Because I didn't kill them!" Ettrias straightened violently, sending his chair toppling backwards. "You know that as well as Father did—as well as Red Wolf does. Tell me, was it your idea to send him to kill the Harrisons or Father's?"

Talin fell silent. *What does Red Wolf have to do with this?*

"You didn't kill them?" she heard herself ask.

Ettrias stared at her.

"Ettrias?"

"You didn't know?"

"Know what?"

"By the gods, I thought..." Ettrias went to the window and pressed his forehead against it. "This whole time, I thought you'd been part of the plan, that you wanted the throne. But it was all our father's doing."

"What are you talking about?" Talin said.

"I didn't kill anyone. You have to believe me," Ettrias said, turning back to face her. "Father wanted you to succeed him. He needed me out of the way, and what better way to get rid of me than to frame me as a criminal?"

Oh, gods.

"You *are* innocent...?" Talin said quietly. "You...you mentioned Red Wolf. What does Red Wolf have to do with it? He *caught you*–"

No. That's not what happened.

"Red Wolf was part of the plan!" Ettrias snapped, and she felt her stomach drop. "He killed the Harrisons on Father's orders and Father used the bodies as proof. Father knew that he needed evidence to exile me, and what better way to acquire it than to take out his political opponents and dress them up as my victims?"

"No. That...that can't be right. *Ettrias*. Please." Talin blinked back tears. "Red Wolf would never agree to something like that."

"He tells me that he never agreed to the plan. That he was tricked and coerced into cooperating," Ettrias said. "It makes no difference. He's no less guilty for allowing my exile. Feel free to ask him if you don't believe me. I know he can't keep his secrets for much longer."

"Red Wolf *wouldn't do this*," Talin said. "He...wouldn't...keep these kinds of secrets."

The corner of Ettrias' mouth twitched. "You have no idea." He sat back down on the bed heavily. "In any case, Father...how shall I put it...bought his silence. You and I both know how effective that is, especially in the royal court."

"Father wouldn't do this to you," Talin said. Her voice sounded distant to her own ears. "He cared about you."

"He was always more fond of you. In his eyes, you were the perfect heir to the throne—unlike me."

"He was a good man. He couldn't have done this."

"Good people do terrible things too," Ettrias said softly.

"I...we have to...I don't know, we have to fix this somehow," Talin stammered. "By your account, Red Wolf has committed murder—"

"No. Do not incriminate Red Wolf." Ettrias shook his head. "I see now why he let me go at the inn. He wanted you to continue to think of Father as the perfect role model. A hero who fell in battle."

Red Wolf did what—

"Red Wolf needs to stand trial," Talin said. "To tell the world that you were innocent."

"I've already told you not to incriminate him," Ettrias said. "For his sake and yours. He was as much a victim of Father as I was—I understand that now."

"Then what would you have me do? I could overrule the court and pardon you—"

"That resolves nothing. Kies Tor will still see me as an outsider, only pardoned by the Crown's compassion."

Talin hissed through her teeth. "Then, *tell me*, how do I fix things?"

"You're about ten years too late for that." Ettrias offered her a humourless smile. "Either way, it's now clear to me that you were innocent in this whole affair and Father was the real villain all along. If we have nothing else to discuss, I'll take you up on that offer. Take me to the border tomorrow. I'll leave."

"Let me...try...to make things right," Talin said. "At least let me talk to Red Wolf first."

Ettrias shrugged. "If you wish. I wouldn't get my hopes up about fixing the situation."

Talin stood and made for the door.

"Tell him I already told you everything," her brother said. "He'll confirm everything I said."

She paused with her hand on the doorknob. "I owe you an apology. For all of this."

"It wasn't your fault."

Then why do I feel guilty?

"If Red Wolf confesses to murdering the Harrisons," she said, "you walk free. Until then, short of arresting him against your wishes, there's nothing I can do. I'm sorry."

I t was almost noon when Red Wolf arrived at her study. Talin had sent for him close to five hours ago, immediately after her conversation with Ettrias, and Golmin had been quick to tell her that the lord commander was feeling unwell. She had elected to deal with paperwork in her study while she waited for Corvan to brew a potion that would alleviate Red Wolf's symptoms.

When he did eventually appear, he was dressed only in a tight-fitting tunic, trousers, and his usual pair of soldiers' boots. It was unusual, to say the least; he rarely presented himself for service without being clad in steel. Underneath the dark tunic, she could see his chiselled form, muscles honed from years of constant training. He looked smaller, too, without armour to add to his bulk.

"Sit," Talin said, gesturing to the spare seat opposite her desk. Red Wolf remained unmoving at the door.

"Something is bothering you," he said.

Talin sighed. *No point in dragging this out.* "I talked to Ettrias."

"I heard. The guard told me," Red Wolf said. His eyes swept across the room and landed on a painting hanging to her left. "You had a productive chat, I take it?"

"He told me the truth," Talin said.

Something subtle flickered across Red Wolf's face, there one moment, gone the next. He didn't look at her. "You believe him?"

"He said that it was you who killed the Harrisons. That he was framed for the murders and it was all my father's doing, that I should ask you if I didn't believe him, and...damn it, Red Wolf, look at me!" she hissed. Red Wolf turned his gaze away from the painting and met hers. "So, I'm asking you now. Is it true?"

Red Wolf's expression faltered for a fraction of a second, long enough for her to catch a hint of sadness and guilt in his eyes. Her breath hitched.

"It is. Every word."

"No." Talin shook her head. "My father wouldn't have."

"He was a good king, but he didn't always do good deeds," Red Wolf said. "There was a reason behind what he did. There is a reason you are on the throne now."

"He framed Ettrias to ensure my seat as heir?" Talin asked. Her voice came out as a half-squeak.

"Yes." Red Wolf's mask was back; she could no longer see behind his stony face.

"Did you kill the Harrisons?"

"Yes."

Oh, gods, please let this be a dream.

"Why?" Talin asked.

"Your father sent me to kill them. He had me believe they were villains bent on harming the Crown," Red Wolf said. "I'd never seen their faces before; they looked like any Highlanders I might pass on the street in Belanore. But you already know this from Ettrias."

Talin turned away and ran her hands down her face, taking a few shaky breaths before facing him again. "You know the court could have you beheaded for this confession."

"Yes. Do what you must." Red Wolf stepped aside to unblock the door. "Rufus is waiting outside your door. You need only give the order."

Talin closed her eyes briefly. "Captain Golmin."

The door clicked, and Golmin stepped inside a moment later, exchanging a brief look with Red Wolf. "Your Majesty."

"Lord Commander Red Wolf, you're relieved of your duties henceforth. You are under arrest for the murders of Anna and James Harrison, perjury, falsifying court evidence, and conspiracy against the Crown. Golmin, by the gods, get him out of my sight."

"As Your Majesty commands." Golmin took Red Wolf by the arm and led him from the room. Talin watched them disappear with a growing sense of regret. *I can't do this to him. But Ettrias is innocent, and Red Wolf is the only one who can prove it.*

She knew she had to confront him again sooner or later, down in the dungeons. Not doing so would seem weak in his eyes, and she had to be strong. Not for him; she didn't need his approval. No, she had to do this for herself. She was the queen now, and as much as she hoped it would never happen, she had always known there would come a day when an ally might betray her. She had to be ready to do what was right.

Is it right to lock him up?

Whatever the case, she couldn't change her mind now.

Noon brought a drizzle of rain that came and went and came back again when Talin was finishing her lunch in her study. She craved company; Red Wolf would normally eat with her, though he rarely talked. But now he was sitting in a cell on her orders, and she was left to sup alone.

You knew it would come down to this, didn't you, Red Wolf?

Not that she should be surprised; he knew too much and too little. He knew she was different somehow but never suspected that she might be a Weaver too, and he knew she'd received weapons training but had no clue how incompetent with a sword she really was. And perhaps he couldn't recall where he had been born, but his angled jaw and rounded ears marked him as a Highlander. Few now believed that the mountain clans in the far north still existed, but there was no doubting that he had at least a trace of the giants' bloodline. His eyes, on the other hand...

Molten gold. Wolf's eyes.

Talin stood, leaving the rest of her meal untouched. She would have to find Red Wolf's squire and have someone look after her for the time being. The girl was only twelve and a long way from her home in the north. She would be lost on her own.

Twelve years old. Still too young.

At twelve, Talin had been dozing off during weapons lessons, chasing Ettrias through the courtyard and teasing William, who had been Red Wolf's squire then and would die beside her father on that fated day in the Glass Forest. Innocent as she was back then, she had lived under the sheltered roof of the palace and knew so little about the outside world. She certainly hadn't been rescued from a raided village in the Highlands and thrust into a strange place to squire for a mysterious man who bore no name.

She sent a servant off with orders to fetch Ashera and allowed one of her handmaids to clear away the food. The servant returned a few minutes later with the girl in tow, and Talin dismissed the man with a wave of her hand.

"Take a seat," she said, gesturing to the spare seat on the opposite side of her desk. Ashera did as she was bid. "Would you like a drink?"

"Y-yes p-please, Your Majesty, if it won't be too much trouble," the girl said hastily.

Talin smiled. "Not at all. Margaret?"

One of her handmaids stepped towards the queen. "Your Majesty?"

"Bring up some spiced wine—and a cup of mead for the girl."

Margaret bowed her head and hurried out.

"I trust Red Wolf treats you well?" Talin inquired.

"Of course, Your Majesty," Ashera said. "We train together whenever he has time. He's been teaching me how to aim properly with a crossbow."

"I'm glad." Talin forced another smile and pushed back a pang of guilt. "You enjoy squiring for him?"

Ashera nodded. "He says I'll make a good knight and that he'll train me as well as he possibly can, so I can join the Royal Guard."

Margaret soon returned with the drinks, and Talin used the opportunity to give herself more time to think. It was clear the girl looked up to Red Wolf; to break the news to her now could shatter her faith in him.

But if I don't tell her, who will? And what would she think of me once she inevitably finds out? It's better if the news comes from me.

"Ashera, this might be hard to believe, but..." Talin took a sip of wine and tried to come up with the right words. "Red Wolf was arrested this morning for crimes against the Crown."

Ashera swallowed. "You mean...crimes against you?"

"In a way, yes," Talin said. "Ten years ago, when my father Arnas was still the king, Red Wolf helped frame my own brother, the Crown Prince, for murder. He confessed to everything this morning when we spoke."

"Well...maybe...he's covering for someone else!" Ashera stammered. "He can't have done anything wrong, he—"

"I'm sorry, Ashera," Talin interrupted gently. "His confession to the head of state is enough to incriminate him."

"Oh." Ashera stared at her drink. "What will happen to me?"

"You'll need someone to look after you," Talin said. "Belanore is not what you would call a welcoming city. You can stay in the palace for the time being, until something can be arranged."

"Does that mean I won't be able to squire anymore?" Ashera asked. She looked on the brink of tears. "I can't...I can't go back home, there's...nothing there for me..."

"I know," Talin said, pushing back another wave of guilt. "I'm sure there will be someone else willing to take you on so that you can finish your training."

"But what if there's *not*?" Ashera wiped her eyes angrily. "Please, Your Majesty, I don't have anyone else. Red Wolf is the only family I have, I can't lose him too, I'll be alone again..."

Gods, I can't do this.

"I will personally see to it that you find another knight to train you," Talin said. "I promise."

Ashera sniffed and wiped her eyes again with her sleeve. Talin offered her a handkerchief. "Do...do you really mean that, Your Majesty?"

Talin smiled reassuringly. "Of course. I'll do whatever I can."

"Th-thank you." Ashera wiped her eyes and blew her nose hard before handing back the handkerchief.

"Keep it," Talin said. "Tirael, why don't you escort Ashera back to the barracks? You can stop by the kitchens for a biscuit or candy if you like."

Ashera stood quietly and followed the woman out of the room. Talin hesitated a few more moments before dismissing the rest of her servants too.

She wasn't sure how long she spent sitting in her chair in the study, but she did remember that it had been a soothing period of clear skies and no rain, allowing her to open the window for once and let in some fresh air. The light was fading when she heard an urgent knock on her door and a messenger appeared with a note.

"From the Draconian lands," he said, and then he was gone. Talin broke the seal on the parchment to read its contents.

> *To Her Majesty, Queen Talin Zylvaris, the second of her name:*
>
> *I am not the original recipient of your diplomatic letter, but I have heard the news of Kies Tor's plea through my network of spies. The current situation in the empire means that you will receive no aid from the Draconian nobility; we are currently oppressed under the rule of the insurgents who won our civil war years ago.*
>
> *I am, however, in a position to negotiate with you. For safety's sake, I cannot disclose much, but know that I am*

the leader of a rebel group seeking to reclaim the empire
under our rightful ruler, Emperor Fillius the fourth.
Send a delegation to the border between our lands, along
the Calegate Road. We may come to an arrangement
there.

- K

Talin tucked the letter away and summoned her council, her thoughts spinning. Assuming this 'K' person was telling the truth, they had a predicament. Sending a delegation to negotiate with these rebels could spark hostility between Kies Tor and the Draconian nobility currently ruling the empire, given that they would essentially be aiding their neighbour's enemies. But if they sent a delegation directly to the capital and were denied aid, they would have wasted precious time and resources.

I cannot believe I thought the matter simple three weeks ago.

Talin took her seat at the head of the meeting table and produced the letter.

"My lords, thank you for gathering on such short notice," she said. "I have here a reply, of sorts, from the Drakels." She slid the parchment to Lord Wormwood. "My lord, if you would be so kind as to read the contents of this message to the council at large."

Wormwood unfolded the note and did as he was bid. Talin saw Lord Cassius' brow crease as he read on. Corvan stroked his chin, looking deep in thought.

"This is not the news we had hoped for," Cassius said once Wormwood had finished. "The Drakels are in no position to help us if they are still recovering from the political instability caused by their civil war."

"We cannot risk sending out a delegation if we have no guarantee of the Drakels' aid," Wormwood said. "With the Hellhounds on the march, we must fortify the city. Begin our siege preparations."

"Surely we can spare some resources to send a delegation," Talin said. "If the Hellhounds break through our northern lines, we have *nothing* left. We need allies."

"I'm...inclined to agree with Lord Wormwood, Your Majesty," Lord Karl said. "Belanore is well-equipped for an extended siege and easily fortified. If we concentrate our resources on locking down the city, we may be able to repel the Hellhounds. They cannot penetrate our walls without siege weapons."

"Lord Cassius?" Talin asked.

"I'm no expert on warfare, Your Majesty," Cassius said. "But I know that Lord Wormwood has experience aplenty in that field. I see no reason not to trust his judgement."

"Master Corvan?"

"Sending a delegation will be risky, Your Majesty," Corvan said. "They will need to pass through the Western Forts, past Hellhound-occupied territory. Much as I agree that we need allies, I am afraid that Lord Wormwood is right. We do not have the resources to spare."

Talin let out a long breath. "Very well, it appears that I am outvoted. Lord Wormwood, talk to Brakis and Commander Hesar. Ensure they have the appropriate funds and resources to begin preparing the city for a siege. Lord Karl, inform the city that Belanore will be put under emergency protocol if the Hellhounds break through at Vill's Crossing. This council is dismissed."

Her advisors bowed to her before making their exits, though she noticed that Wormwood lingered behind again, staring at the map on the table. Talin followed his gaze to the pin that marked Vill's Crossing to the northwest.

"Something on your mind, my lord?" she asked.

"On the record, I suggested we prepare for a siege, to be safe," Wormwood said. "I know many people consider you inexperienced, given that you're barely of ruling age. We must show them that that you are just as capable as your father was, if not more."

Talin could see where this was going. "And...off the record?"

"Off the record, as your father's friend and your advisor, I would agree with you," Wormwood said. "Protecting the city will mean nothing if the Hellhounds sweep through the kingdom anyway."

"What do you propose?"

"Ride out yourself. See if you can negotiate a treaty with the Drakels in person."

Talin slid into an empty seat and rubbed her eyes. *By the gods, he must be mad.* But Wormwood's suggestion, as absurd as it sounded, did have some merit. Travelling to the Draconian Empire herself would save the time needed to put together an entire delegation, and if she truly could succeed here, then...

Then what? You'll be hailed a hero?

The thought was, much as she was loath to admit it, tempting.

"You propose I ride past the Western Forts *personally* to strike a treaty with these Drakels?" she said.

"Yes," Wormwood said. "Think about it. Putting together a delegation will take up the time we need to prepare for a siege. You need only select an escort from among the ranks of your Royal Guard. If you succeed, you will have proven to your people how capable you are, and they will have seen your bravery in riding past the western front."

"I…" Talin began. *This is not what rulership means. A good ruler does not seek fame.*

And yet…

"I truly believe this to be the best course of action," Wormwood said. "And I truly believe that you are Kies Tor's final hope. Your father would agree."

"Very well." Talin let out a long breath. "I'll…think on it, my lord. Thank you."

"Of course, Your Majesty, any time."

She studied the maps for a little while longer before making her way back to her study, a plan already beginning to form in her mind. If she were to ride west to negotiate with the Drakels, she would have to bypass her council entirely, and she knew that Master Corvan was the only one who would understand such a decision. Despite Wormwood's words of reassurance, she was sure her father would scold her for it if he were here.

Father isn't here.

Perhaps she knew deep down that she needed her parents' guidance; Queen Elora had passed when she and Ettrias were only toddlers, and her father had been left to rule alone. She wondered what might be different if her mother were here to help her rule.

Under normal circumstances, she could simply convene the Royal Council again come morning and explain her decision to overrule them. But there was a slight complication in Ettrias and Red Wolf both being in custody; without her in Belanore, Wormwood might decide to hold their trials, and the court might sentence one or both of them to death. A well-meaning gesture on his part, no doubt, but she couldn't take that risk. Even if she gave explicit orders to wait for her return, he might not understand the delicacy of the situation.

Master Corvan was already waiting for her by the time she reached her study, having been let in by one of the palace staff. Talin dismissed the guard outside, as well as her handmaids, and closed the door behind her. Out of the corner of her eye, she saw the old healer lift his brow.

"I suppose you did not call me here for a friendly chat, Your Majesty," he said.

"No." Talin went to the nearby cabinet and poured two cups of wine. "Lord Wormwood was kind enough to make some suggestions after our meeting. I have a plan to gain some allies, but I'll need your help. I only ask that you hear me out."

"I'm listening," Corvan said.

"I need to ride west to negotiate with the Drakels without the knowledge of the rest of the Royal Council," she explained, choosing her words carefully.

Corvan visibly paled but thankfully remained silent.

"You and Lord Wormwood will tell them I planned a visit to Fort Saria after the council meeting to see what further reinforcements we can reassign to Vill's Crossing," Talin continued. "Meanwhile, I need to sneak out of the city under cover of darkness and take the road through Stormwood. I know Captain Golmin will help—because my plan involves freeing Red Wolf and Ettrias."

"You cannot be serious," the old healer said softly.

"I am. I cannot risk Red Wolf's and Ettrias' trials going ahead without me. We both know that one or both of them will be sentenced to death," Talin said. "Master Corvan, you've always been opposed to the death penalty in Kies Tor. Help me here. I could overrule the High Court when I return."

Corvan sighed. "I suppose there is no changing your mind."

"My mind is made up," Talin said. "I need you to remain here and keep my council in check."

"Why do this? Against your council's advice, no less?"

"We need allies, Corvan. You and I both know there is no other way to win this war."

"Then send a delegation, Your Majesty," Corvan said, leaning in. "There are alternatives. Do not put yourself in harm's way so recklessly. Kies Tor does not need to lose another ruler."

"I have to do this," Talin said. "Corvan, please. You've served the royal family since my grandfather's time. I only ask this one favour."

Do you have to do this? Or are you doing it because you want recognition?

She pushed the thoughts from her mind.

"Very well." Corvan rubbed his chin. "I...suppose...you'll want me to do something."

"Write back to the Drakel rebel and tell them to expect our arrival," Talin said. "Otherwise, you must make yourself seem uninvolved in anything I'm planning. Preoccupy yourself somehow. Perhaps some light reading in the library or research on the Hellhounds, I don't know. Either way, make yourself seen."

"Of course," Corvan said, nodding his understanding. "I still cannot say I approve of this plan, Your Majesty."

"I know. It's a lot to ask. Just trust me."

Corvan finished his wine and rose. "Good luck, Your Majesty. I'll be in the library, as always, doing some...light reading, was it?" His eyes twinkled with amusement as he reached the door and glanced back.

Talin smiled. "My brother used to think that you did nothing else."

"Hah! Perhaps he's right." The door closed behind him. Talin let out a long breath. She would have to find Golmin now to explain her plan to him and bid him to arrange some way to sneak Ettrias out of the palace.

After that...

she would have to face Red Wolf.

VIII

The dungeons were silent. Talin could hear the occasional prisoner moving behind iron bars and the soft ringing of her footsteps down the corridor, but other than that, she heard nothing. With a torch in her right hand and a key in her left, she forced herself onwards, through the endless rows of cells and dark passageways. She knew where to go; Golmin's instructions had been clear enough. It was the thought of facing Red Wolf that sent her stomach plummeting.

Ettrias was innocent all along, and it was Red Wolf's fault that nobody knew.

Talin pushed the thought out of her head and rounded a corner. Golmin had snuck the key to Red Wolf's cell out of the prison warden's office earlier and later drew his attention to it by questioning him about losing the same key that she now held. A clever tactic, she had to admit, if risky. Golmin had to rely on his status as Captain of the Royal Guard.

She stopped in front of Red Wolf's cell and slipped her torch into a nearby bracket.

"An odd time for a visit." In the darkness of the space beyond, a giant's outline stirred from a narrow bench. "Unless you're not here for a visit."

Talin stepped closer as Red Wolf stood. "No. I'm here for something else."

"Not an official confession, though. You wouldn't have come alone for that." Her bodyguard looked at her, golden eyes burning into her. In the dark, they almost seemed to glow.

"We received word from the Drakels earlier today," Talin said.

Red Wolf lifted his brow. "You came down here just to tell me this?"

"I came here for your help," Talin said. "I'm riding west. Tonight. And I'm taking you and Ettrias with me. My council doesn't know. Corvan is to tell them that I'm visiting Fort Saria, and that he and Wormwood will lead the council in my absence. But I cannot risk you and Ettrias' trials going ahead without me, not when one or both of you could be executed."

There was a beat.

"...Red Wolf?"

"Are you *out of your mind?* Gods above, I could call you naïve, but this is suicidal!" Red Wolf snapped. "You go against your own council's advice. You plan to free two suspected criminals just so the court won't execute either of us in your absence. And you plan to ride through *enemy territory* with no escort of any kind! All for what? So you can play the hero? You are responsible for the lives of *thousands* in this city *alone*. Have you learned nothing of rulership from your father?"

Talin hadn't anticipated he would be this stubborn; here she was with an offer of freedom, and he was lecturing her on responsibility.

"My mind's made up, Red Wolf," she hissed through her teeth. "I'm offering you a way out of this cell, and maybe even the opportunity to walk free entirely. Just take it, please, for both our sakes."

"I..." Red Wolf looked away. "If...my queen...commands it."

"You know I won't make you do this," Talin said. "I only ask for your help. As a friend."

Red Wolf met her gaze again. "I will help you on one condition. Ashera leaves Belanore with us. And if she doesn't wish to stay on this journey, we find someone willing to look after her until our return."

"I can work with that." Talin turned the key in his cell and let the door swing open. "Captain Golmin has gone to free Ettrias. He'll meet you at the tapestry on the ground floor while I fetch the horses. We'll have to detour to the barracks for your squire beforehand."

"I understand," Red Wolf said, taking the torch from her.

"Let's go, then—" Talin began. Her bodyguard silenced her with a finger to her lips as he cocked his head and lifted an ear.

"The guard's coming this way. Lock the door back up." He moved to step back into his cell, thrusting the torch into her hands again.

We can't play that out, the warden 'lost' the key.

"No, that won't work, and in any case, I can't be seen with you tonight—" Talin was cut off when the torchlight from the guard rounded a corner, followed soon by the man himself.

Red Wolf let out a long breath. "*Orrlat.*"

He lunged out of the cell in the blink of an eye and barrelled into the guard, knocking him down. The torch and crossbow flew from his grasp and skidded across the floor. Red Wolf reached for the weapon, but the guard was faster, snatching it up as the two of them struggled.

Talin felt as if time had slowed. The guard aimed his crossbow. Red Wolf straightened.

Golden energy flickered around her bodyguard a split second before the crossbow bolt slammed into an invisible barrier an inch from his face...and splintered.

He's a Weaver. That's why his eyes are the colour of gold, I knew that...

It was true; some part of her had always known her bodyguard possessed magic and wasn't surprised by this revelation. She watched on in silence instead as he slipped behind the guard and wrapped his arm around the man's neck in a tight chokehold. The guard went limp a few seconds later.

"Apologies, you'll be sore when you wake," she heard him mutter under his breath.

"I— are you alright?" Talin asked.

"Fine. You saw the shield." Red Wolf reloaded the guard's crossbow and set it down by the man's side, then snatched up the bolt that had splintered against his shield. "With any luck, Rufus will be able to convince him that he hallucinated this whole event and passed out from dehydration."

"You're a Weaver."

"Yes. I can channel protection magic. Quite fitting for the royal bodyguard, I know," he said. "But this is not new information to you. Most of the palace suspects I possess some form of magic. Unlike you."

"You know that...I'm a Weaver too?" Talin asked.

"Yes."

"What— how? My father said that nobody was to know—"

Red Wolf took the torch from her hands and led the way back out of the dungeons. "And who do you think told King Arnas that his daughter was a Weaver? We can sense each other's magic."

"I can't sense..." Talin's voice trailed off. She *could* feel an odd sort of aura that always followed Red Wolf around if she let herself focus. She'd dismissed it before as her imagination, but now, looking at him...

"In any case, this is not the time or place for such a discussion," Red Wolf said. "If you plan to ride west, we will need supplies and weapons for a month's travel, given the storm season. And there's still the matter of fetching Ashera."

"I have supply packs ready in the cellar," Talin said. "One of us could pick them up while the other finds your squire."

"Very well. I can take the supplies if you find Ashera and our weapons," Red Wolf said. "Take the south staircase from the ground level and count the steps until you reach twenty. Pull on the torch bracket to your left and take the secret passageway to the barracks there. We'll meet at the butcher's shop on Thieves Lane." He snuffed out the torch. "Light attracts too much attention. Rely on your other senses."

"Alright. Good luck," Talin said.

"You too, my queen."

They parted ways there, him taking a left turn, her taking a right. She did as he bid her, taking the southern staircase upwards. It was hard work in the dark, but she kept track of how many steps she'd taken and stopped on the stairwell at twenty. The torch and bracket were there, as he'd said, though she had to feel around for a while. She gave it a sharp tug upwards. It responded with a quiet click, and the wall beside it parted to reveal a narrow corridor leading into complete darkness. Talin hesitated there for a moment before stepping inside. *Red Wolf had better be right about this.*

She emerged again sometime later in the familiar hallway to the barracks. From there, it was easy to locate Ashera and convince her to put on some travelling clothes. They collected two spare swords, two daggers, and Red Wolf's belongings before departing. The girl didn't ask questions, thankfully, though her unease was evident enough. Talin gave her the quick version of events as they made their way to the stables.

"Why are we being so secretive? You're the queen. You can do whatever you like," Ashera said.

"That would be wonderful, but it's not possible, not in this day and age. I have to be careful whom I trust," Talin said. *That and freeing Red Wolf and Ettrias is highly illegal.*

"You...trust me?" Ashera asked.

Not particularly.

"You're Red Wolf's squire," Talin responded, carefully dodging the question. It seemed to be enough to satisfy the girl, in any case, and she kept her mouth shut.

Golmin had mentioned that a secret passageway out of the palace was hidden behind the tapestry adorning one of the hallways on the ground floor, and that the exit led to a butcher's shop on Thieves Lane. How he and Red Wolf were so well-versed in the palace's secret passageways, she was unsure, but it mattered little right now. As long as they could all make it out of Belanore without arousing suspicion, she was willing to overlook whatever secrets they might know about the palace architecture. Talin peeked around the corner to the stables before ushering Ashera inside.

The stablemaster had retired by now, as expected, so she saddled four horses herself and led them from the stables into another secret passageway marked by Golmin. It put her some distance from the exit on Thieves Lane, but he had mentioned that it was the only one wide enough and tall enough to smuggle the horses through, so she had relented and allowed him to point it out on the palace map. She emerged five minutes later in an alleyway behind an alchemist's shop.

From there, it was easy enough to navigate their way through the dimly lit streets to their meeting spot.

"I trust you didn't run into trouble?" Red Wolf whispered as they approached. Ettrias stood beside him, hastily dressed and barely awake.

Talin shook her head. "None, thankfully."

"I never thought you the secretive type, dear sister," her brother said. "What's the occasion?"

"Just be glad you're not facing execution, Ettrias." Talin thrust a set of reins into his hand. "I'll explain once we're out of the city."

"Friendly," Ettrias muttered but didn't argue.

"I still cannot say I approve of this plan in the slightest, but then, I've never been able to refuse you," Red Wolf said as he strapped on his weapons and tied down his saddlebags. "Let's go. The sooner we're out of the city, the better I'll feel about the whole situation."

"Ettrias," Talin said. "You know the city. You've been sneaking around here for the last few months. What's the fastest way out?"

"Oh, now you ask." Ettrias scowled.

Talin shot him a glare. "I'm not in the mood. Hurry up."

Ettrias swung his mount lazily and took off at a light trot, Talin close behind. They rode through the streets in complete darkness for fear of being spotted, spurred on by a sense of urgency and the need to be well away by sunrise. Red Wolf brought up the rear, occasionally checking to ensure that they weren't followed. Talin flipped up the hood of her travelling cloak as they neared the wall.

At the northern gate, they were forced to a stop by the two guards on duty there, one of them brandishing a tall halberd while the other held a torch up high. Talin motioned for Ettrias to stay put and dismounted to meet them.

"I wasn't aware there was a curfew in place, gentlemen," she said, keeping her head down so that her hood concealed her features in the dim torchlight.

"The city's still under lockdown and will remain so until the queen issues new orders," the first guard said.

As I'd expected, then.

With Ettrias' capture not yet made public, she had ordered the lockdown to continue, with plans to lift it once she was ready to announce his arrest. A necessary move yesterday, but now...

Talin reached into her coat and produced a piece of folded parchment. "I have documents. Express permission for me and my companions to leave the city. Please, it's urgent." She showed them the royal seal stamped in the corner.

The two guards looked at each other, and then the one with the torch came forward to squint at the document.

"Well, I suppose, if it bears the queen's seal..." He shrugged. "Let them pass."

The gates swung open. Talin breathed an inward sigh of relief as they rode through. Red Wolf took the lead from there, and they spurred the mounts into a quick trot, heading for the forest beyond. It was difficult to appreciate anything in the dark, but as her bodyguard slowed the column for their horses to navigate the rough terrain and she heard wild wolves howl, Talin felt almost drawn to the forest. It made her curious and uneasy at the same time.

"I heard stories, growing up," she said. "Folks say a beast dwells in these forests. Hunters fear it. Wolves know to stay away. It kills for sport, without mercy, and if you see it, it will be the last thing you see."

"They're only stories, my queen. Magic is a dying power. It's impossible for such a creature to exist now," Red Wolf said. "Once, perhaps, but not anymore."

He was right, of course. Giants had been the first to vanish from Kies Tor, after her great-great-grandfather, King Braenern, outlawed the use of magic. The mountain clans had retreated further north soon after, and the last dragons flew east five hundred years ago. Weavers were growing rarer too. With the power in their land fading, fewer people dared practice their craft, and over hundreds of years, their magic had faded too.

That was part of why so many people feared Red Wolf, she supposed. He was too different. Those golden-yellow eyes, his unnatural height...they marked him as an outsider. And as much as he might like to pretend that he wasn't bothered by any of it, she could see how he felt, being so different.

Who are you, Red Wolf? Where did you come from?

"Remember when Father took us out hunting in these forests?" Ettrias asked. "You took down a deer with a single arrow to the throat. Father praised you for it all night."

Talin could see where this was going. "It was a long time ago. Besides, you were always better with a sword in hand."

"But did he ever recognise that?" Ettrias hissed. "Did anyone ever recognise that? No, because it was always about you. I wasn't good *enough* for him."

"Ettrias." Red Wolf's voice rang out from the front. A single warning.

"You knew, even then!" Ettrias continued, ignoring him entirely. "Yet you chose not to act. You chose not to defend me during the trial.

I was innocent, Talin! He was the real murderer!" He jabbed a finger at Red Wolf. Her bodyguard remained silent.

"How was I to know the truth?" Talin asked.

Ettrias looked almost hurt. "I'm your brother."

"Ettrias." Red Wolf stopped and turned in his saddle. "Not in front of the girl."

Talin glanced back at Ashera, who hadn't said a word since they left the city but looked uneasy. That was hardly surprising; their conversation wasn't exactly making things any easier for her. Ettrias looked back, too, and fell silent.

"We should find a place to set up camp once we're far enough out," Talin said after a while. "Much as I would love to close the distance between ourselves and the border quickly, neither we nor the horses can hope to ride through the night."

"I agree," Red Wolf said.

"So, tell me," Ettrias said, riding up alongside her. "Red Wolf mentioned the Drakels. Could it be that you're finally admitting that Kies Tor needs their help?"

"When Father sat on the throne, there were civil wars throughout the Draconian Empire," Talin said. "We couldn't have gone to them then."

"And it only occurred to you to ride west *now*, after you've been on the throne for...nearly a year?"

"By all means, if you think you're likely to do a better job..."

Ettrias scoffed. "Maybe I should take charge for a few months and find out."

"There's a clearing past these trees." Red Wolf indicated the bushes to their left. "It's as good a place as any to stop for the night."

Talin shook her head. "We're still too close to the city. I'd rather not risk being recognised in the morning."

"Any further on and the likelihood of us running into outlaws increases drastically," Ettrias pointed out. "I don't know about you, but having my throat slit open in my sleep isn't a great way to go. I'd rather show myself to the execution block."

"We can take turns on watch," Talin said.

"Unless you want the girl to join us, none of us will get much sleep."

"I don't mind taking watch," Ashera said quietly.

Talin sighed. "Red Wolf?"

"I agree with Ettrias." Her bodyguard turned in his saddle. "Outlaws like to frequent these forests, particularly at a safe distance from the city. Better to be recognised than killed. Besides, we won't be close to the road. No-one is likely to wander into our camp."

Talin gave a defeated wave of her hand, gesturing for him to lead the way, and they quickly turned off the road.

It wasn't long before Red Wolf halted again in the clearing, motioning for her to stay where she was while he made sure the area was clear. He beckoned them forwards a few minutes later, and they set up a crude camp with what supplies they had available.

"We can make do with what we have, but if the floods delay us for more than a few days, we might find ourselves short on food," Red Wolf said. "You brought some yarii at least?"

"Plenty, don't worry." Talin patted her coin pouch. "It'll be three days before we reach any sort of settlement in Stormwood, though."

"I wouldn't worry so much about a delay this close to Belanore," Red Wolf said. "We're fortunate to be sitting on elevated terrain. Most floods happen between Stormwood and Charrac Forest, where the land slopes downwards into a valley." He looked at his squire. "We're heading past the Western Forts, Ashera. If you don't wish to join us, we can find somewhere you can stay until our return."

"I want to stay," Ashera said quietly. "Please. I don't want to be alone."

Red Wolf's jaw tightened ever so slightly, but he dipped his head.

"I will take the first watch, then," he said. "The rest of you should sleep. We move on at dawn."

G olmin could hear the commotion before he even stepped through the palace's front doors.

Gods help us, this is going to be a long day.

He continued through the front courtyard and past the gates to meet Hesar. Wormwood had alerted the City Watch as soon as he'd seen the angry crowd gathered outside, and for good reason, too; the Chained Owls had the necessary equipment to manage a riot without causing significant injury. The Royal Guard was only suited for defending the palace and the royal family, not...whatever the seven hells was going on outside the palace gates.

"Commander. Thank you for coming," he said. "My guards aren't exactly suited to crowd control. Your response time is always commendable."

"Just doing my job, Captain," Hesar said. Golmin followed his gaze to the gathered townsfolk as they pushed once more against the City Watch's shield wall.

"Any idea who started this riot?"

"Not a clue."

"I don't suppose you could make out anything they've been shouting since you arrived?" Golmin asked.

Hesar shrugged. "Half of them have been screaming about the queen having fled west and abandoned her people. The other half is saying that Prince Ettrias has been detained after returning to Kies Tor illegally but was innocent of his crimes ten years ago. Meanwhile, there's also talk about the lord commander having also been arrested and escaping custody two days ago. I know better than to ask you whether any of that is true."

Golmin didn't like the sound of it. "Who started these rumours?"

"Who knows? Though, if you ask me, it doesn't matter so much now," Hesar said. "The whole thing has gotten completely out of control. People believe whatever nonsense they're fed."

"Can we convince them to disperse?" Golmin asked.

"Send out one of your squads armed with, I don't know, spears or pikes. Anything long and pointy. If they keep pushing against the shield wall, they'll impale themselves."

"That seems a little extreme."

"Captain, my men have been out here for twenty minutes now, and the crowd is as energetic as ever." Hesar shook his head. "If you want them to leave, you'll have to do *something*."

Golmin pinched the bridge of his nose. Much as he hated to admit it, Hesar was right; the crowd was determined to storm the palace today and would eventually succeed if they did nothing. He beckoned one of his lieutenants over and sent the man off with orders to form a spear team.

"I know I said I wouldn't ask, but..." Hesar began.

"I cannot tell you much about the rumours," Golmin said. "Your Chained Owls arrested Ettrias, so you know he's in the Crown's custody. There's no use pretending the queen is still in Belanore, but all I can say is that she is running an urgent errand. The lord commander is with her, obviously. That's all you'll get from me."

The gates swung open again a few minutes later to reveal the spears he'd sent for, clad in light helms and standing at attention. Golmin moved to direct them while Hesar climbed onto a wooden crate.

"Disperse!" the City Watch Commander shouted. "There is nothing to be gained by staying here!"

The spear formation moved forwards on Golmin's command and stopped with their weapons inches from the shield wall.

"This is your final warning!" Hesar continued. "Disperse now or these spears will be ordered to advance!"

The crowd seemed to hesitate, falling silent. Golmin ordered his spears forward two more steps. Several civilians hissed as the spear tips dug into their skin and drew blood. They backed up immediately, forcing the people behind them to follow. The spears pushed forward another step.

The majority of the crowd finally seemed to get the message and began to disperse.

"Spears, at ease!" Golmin ordered.

Hesar jumped down from his crate. "We were lucky that time. The crowd hasn't gotten so fanatical yet. But if these rumours continue to spread and escalate..."

"I understand," Golmin said. "The Royal Council will want a report as soon as possible. I'll relay what you said. Thank you again for the aid."

Hesar turned away to debrief his men, and Golmin grabbed the lieutenant from earlier, leaving him in charge at the gate while he returned inside to await his summons by the council.

How can these rumours have started and gotten out of hand so quickly?

From what he knew, the council believed that the queen was visiting Fort Saria and should be mere days from Belanore; Corvan's lie had seen to that. And as far as Ettrias was concerned, the public didn't know he'd been arrested at all. The queen had planned to keep the city under lockdown until his arrest was announced.

But most suspicious of all, perhaps, was the matter of Ettrias' innocence and Red Wolf's arrest. *Nobody* should have known about the former and only her council should be aware of the latter.

Who is getting hold of all of this information? And why release it as a rumour with a lie that the queen has abandoned her people?

His train of thought was interrupted by a messenger requesting his immediate presence in the small hall. Golmin thanked the man and made his way down the maze of corridors to the council meeting.

You should tell them that Ettrias is innocent.

Golmin cursed himself for thinking it. Even now, he was so quick to jump to Ettrias' defence, determined to prove his innocence. But revealing the truth would condemn Red Wolf to certain death. He wasn't sure he could make that decision.

They need to know.

He banished the thought and opened the doors to the small hall.

"Captain Golmin, thank you for joining us," Corvan said as he approached.

Golmin bowed to the council. "My lords."

"The situation at the palace gates has been taken care of?" Corvan asked.

"Aye, it has," Golmin said. "Commander Hesar and I were able to convince the crowd to disperse. The commander tells me that they rioted following several rumours that spiralled out of hand."

"Rumours?" Lord Wormwood raised his eyebrows. "Let's hear it, then."

Golmin recounted what Hesar had told him, phrasing his words as close as he could remember to what the City Watch Commander had said. He saw Corvan's frown deepen as he went on and Lord Cassius looking contemplative, though Wormwood appeared entirely unbothered.

"*Tch*. Baseless gossip." The Master of Coin scoffed. "Though I agree with Commander Hesar's sentiment. These riots are likely to get worse if we do not put a stop to the rumours."

"I'm worried about how fast the rumours have spread and who has spread them," Corvan said, echoing Golmin's thoughts. "The public should not have any knowledge of Ettrias' arrest, nor Red Wolf's, and it has only been two days since the queen set out for Fort Saria. Who could have gained knowledge of these events so quickly?"

"You believe there's a spy in the palace?" Lord Cassius asked.

"It's a possibility," Corvan said. "Though not one I would like to entertain."

"I'll have my own spies investigate," Lord Cassius said.

"Then I will speak with the city nobility and find out where the rumours came from," Lord Wormwood said.

"Excellent, thank you," Corvan said. "Captain Golmin, you're dismissed. See to whatever duties you have."

The rumours are true, my lords, Ettrias is innocent—

Golmin bowed to the council again and strode from the hall.

They were three days out in the dead middle of Stormwood when the outlaws fell upon them. Ettrias had been the one on watch, but it was Red Wolf who first heard them in the early hours slipping past trees and bushes, only giving themselves away by the gentle rustle of their clothes and the soft crunching of their boots on dead leaves. He rose silently and drew his sword, and Ettrias turned, quickly catching on. Dark Draconian steel and gold Elven alloy glinted together as dawn broke. Ettrias stepped back to the centre of the camp, standing over the remains of their fire. Red Wolf pressed himself against the trunk of a tree and remained unmoving. In front of him, Ashera and Talin slept on. He gave a nod to the prince. Ettrias bent down and shook the girl awake first, then Talin. Red Wolf silenced them both with a shake of his head. At a gesture, both of them moved behind Ettrias, who visibly tightened his grip on his sword.

Four scents. Four sets of footsteps. Red Wolf held up four fingers, and the prince nodded his understanding.

The first outlaw to venture into their camp received a longsword to the neck as Red Wolf stepped out from behind the tree. His opponent let out a surprised yelp and managed to duck under the swing as two more outlaws rushed at them from the other side of the clearing. Red Wolf left Ettrias to deal with them and dodged a strike from the outlaw's knife. Another one grabbed him from behind. He twisted to get free of his opponent's grasp as the first outlaw swung the knife again. Unable to move in time, he was forced to take the brunt of the blow with his shoulder, a grunt of pain escaping his lips as the blade drove into flesh. Ashera jumped up behind the man and plunged a dagger into his neck with a yell. He crumpled soundlessly. Red Wolf finished the other with a swing to the neck. Ettrias' opponents scarpered once they saw that they were outmatched.

"Good fight, both of you," he said, wiping his blade down and ripping the knife from his shoulder. "Ashera, make sure you clean your weapon, keep the blade from..."

He looked up. The girl had backed away from the dead man with her dagger still in hand, eyes wide. A splash of blood was visible on her sleeve.

"Did I...is he...dead?" she whispered.

"Yes," Red Wolf said.

"He was...going to hurt you. He would have killed you." Ashera's back hit a tree trunk. She looked as if she might cry.

Not exactly, Red Wolf almost said.

"You did what you had to do," he said instead. "Sometimes, to protect what we love, we must be prepared to fight and kill. This is what it means to be a royal guard."

Ashera swallowed. "I didn't...I don't know what I was thinking. I didn't *want* to kill him. It was so *easy*."

"I know." Red Wolf pulled her into an embrace. "It's hard the first time." His gaze landed on Talin. "We cannot linger here. More outlaws may have heard the commotion, or worse, an organised gang. We'll be far outmatched."

"Your shoulder—" Talin began.

Ah.

Red Wolf glanced at the patch of crimson where the knife had dug into his shoulder. The wound itself had already healed, had closed on its own the moment he removed the blade, but the blood staining his ripped tunic concealed that fact.

"Nothing serious," he said, pulling away from Ashera to wrap his shoulder with a roll of bandages. Behind Talin, he saw Ettrias lift a quizzical eyebrow. He shot the prince a warning look.

"There's a town not far from here. We ought to find you a healer," Talin said.

"That won't be necessary. Barely even hurts. I've seen soldiers take arrows to the chest and continue fighting on the front."

"If it festers—"

"That...would be...unlikely."

"He's right—we don't have time to find a healer," Ettrias cut in. "It's a month's travel to the border. We cannot afford any luxuries."

"If you're certain..." Talin looked at Red Wolf.

"Yes. I'll be fine," he said.

"Alright. We'll purchase some extra supplies for the road and then move on," Talin said.

They packed in silence. Talin seemed somewhat distracted as she mounted her horse, and Red Wolf paused briefly, wondering if he should say something. Then he turned away to feed his speckled mare a handful of oats.

Give her a few more days on the road. She will adjust.

Ashera appeared to be faring better, though, despite the shock of stabbing the outlaw. Part of him was glad she'd stepped in before the man could inflict a more serious injury; hiding a healed stab wound to the chest would have been a lot harder.

"I suppose I have to thank you, my prince," he said, as Ettrias swung himself into his saddle.

"Call it a returned favour for finally confessing the truth," the prince said. "Not that it's changed much."

"I suppose there's not much use in apologising."

Ettrias scoffed. "No. You're about ten years too late. Why did you do it, though? I know that Father tricked you into helping him, but you knew I was innocent the whole time. You could have revealed *something* in that courtroom. If the court had gotten wind of what Father had done—well, not even he would have got away with that."

"Your father knew my secret," Red Wolf said in a low voice. "I never told him. He must have found out somehow."

"Ah, blackmail, of course." Ettrias gave a bitter laugh. "Sounds just like him."

"In any case, even if I had spoken and was *believed*—don't forget, it would have been my word against the king's—and even *if* the council had stripped Arnas' powers, the people would have questioned your sister's claim to the throne," Red Wolf continued. "Arnas had already named her as his successor, and the rumours would have started that they had been working together, undermining her credibility as queen."

"Is that so different to the situation now?"

"Yes. You're alone in your doubts. Her people have no reason to distrust her, as far as I know. They believe in her. If you had been at the coronation, you would know that."

"That's not an excuse," Ettrias said.

"No. But it is what I believe. It's what your father believed." Red Wolf frowned. "Whether I'm right remains to be seen. She has a long way to go still."

"And what about me? Am I to remain forever as the disappointment of my family?" Ettrias asked.

"Talin doesn't seem to think you're a disappointment. Apart from your recent attempts to kill her... I imagine that was disappointing," Red Wolf replied with a wry smile.

"*Tch*. My father did."

"Then he was wrong."

"I don't need you to tell me that." Ettrias scowled. "I always knew that my father played favourites. I was never good enough for him. That's just how it was."

"Well, it bears repeating. You're not a disappointment." Red Wolf met his gaze. "And for what little it's worth, I truly am sorry about what I did." He rode on before the prince could respond.

They found themselves in the town before midday. It was much larger than Red Wolf expected, which he saw as both good and bad. Purchasing supplies should pose no problem, but the chances of recognition were greater. They'd need to be cautious about drawing attention to themselves. After acquiring directions to the various shops in town from a passing local, he sent everyone off to purchase their supplies, assuring Talin he would buy some bandages for himself.

Extra bandages couldn't hurt, he reasoned, even if he had no use for them, given his healing ability. Red Wolf kept his head down to avoid eye contact with anyone and made for the town square.

He bought a hand-carved southern recurve bow and a quiver of arrows from a fletcher's stall, as well as the additional medical supplies he'd promised to purchase. He then gained directions to the blacksmith at the edge of the village from a farmer, who hurried off soon after, clearly frightened by the bodyguard's height & yellow eyes. He resolved to keep his hood turned up after that.

As it turned out, Ettrias had the same idea. He walked into the blacksmith's shop to find the prince already there, examining a set of travelling armour. It seemed to be a good size for him, the quality of the leather and mail a bonus.

"Here for armour, good sirs?" the blacksmith asked.

"A weapon, actually." Ettrias straightened before Red Wolf could open his mouth. "I was just rather taken by this armour design. Quite impressive, I must say."

"You flatter me, sir," the blacksmith said. "What kind of weapon are you after? I supply the Royal Army Garrison at Fort Saria whenever Belanore's smiths are too busy."

"Something small and light. A southern arming sword, perhaps," Ettrias said. "Not the standard stuff they issue to the army. I want top-quality steel."

The blacksmith nodded. "I may have something for you out the back. Let me find it." He disappeared through a door.

"You already have a sword," Red Wolf pointed out.

"I would look so much more menacing with two swords, wouldn't you agree?" Ettrias said, his voice perfectly level. "But no. I'm getting a sword for my sister."

"She asked you to get her a sword?" Red Wolf blinked. "I...was not aware that she had any interest in weapons."

"Me neither. I asked why not confide in you instead, given that weapons is your area of expertise," Ettrias said. "She told me you were injured."

"I don't see how that prevents me from buying a weapon."

"She wanted me to train her. I convinced her to ask you instead. Once your...injury...is 'healed'."

Red Wolf's eyebrows drew together. "An odd time to be asking. I seem to recall her as a child sneaking out of weapons training with Brakis to read history books and whatnot."

They were interrupted by the shopkeeper returning with the weapon he had gone to collect. Red Wolf gestured to it, and the blacksmith handed it over for inspection. The handle construction was exquisite, truly something he might expect from a master craftsman, brass-plated metal and leather glinting in the light. He unsheathed a few inches of the blade and took note of the sharpened edges and engraved Old Torrian script. An ancient charm of some kind, he guessed, from what exposed lettering he could see.

"I must say, I like this."

Ettrias quirked an eyebrow. "Well, if my companion approves, we'll take it. How much?"

"Five hundred yarii."

"We'll take it for three hundred." Ettrias reached into his pocket.

"Four hundred if you want it so bad. I gotta feed my family, stranger," the blacksmith said.

Ettrias withdrew his hand again. "Three fifty."

The blacksmith seemed to hesitate. "Three seventy—"

They were interrupted by the back door creaking open to reveal a small boy, probably no older than six, holding a broken toy soldier figurine in his hands.

"Papa, my toy broke..." he said.

A faint memory tugged at the back of Red Wolf's mind, indistinguishable. It was quickly drowned out by a wave of anger and pain.

"That's your stuffed bear? What's its name?"

The shop was too stifling all of a sudden. He felt as if he couldn't breathe. He barely heard the blacksmith telling his son to wait a few moments.

"We'll pay the full five hundred." Red Wolf dug five gold coins from his pocket. His gaze managed to land on a table near the door lined with daggers. "How much for one of those daggers?"

"Fifty yarii apiece," the blacksmith said, taking his gold quickly before the bodyguard changed his mind.

Red Wolf dug out another five silver pieces and grabbed a dagger on his way out.

"Wha—?" Ettrias cursed, then thanked the smith for the weapons and jogged up to him, clutching the new sword. "What in the seven hells was that about?"

"Nothing." Red Wolf tossed the dagger at him. Ettrias fumbled with it for a moment but managed to catch it before it fell.

You were the boy's age before—

He stumbled into a wall and slid down against it, struggling to breathe. He would not entertain these thoughts, not here, not when he knew that trying to remember would only cause him more frustration and anger.

Phantom screams echoed through the empty alleyway. He smelled metal and rust and medicinal herbs...and blood. So much blood. He couldn't breathe. A rush of anger cut through the haze, and he struggled to push it back down.

"Red Wolf? By the gods, what's the matter with you?" Ettrias crouched down in front of him. "Talk to me."

"*Nothing.* Red Wolf staggered to his feet again, still breathing hard. "I'm *fine.*" He brushed Ettrias' hand off his arm. "Let's just get back and meet with the others."

"Well, forgive me for being concerned." The prince scoffed. "Why do I even bother..."

They met up with Talin and Ashera in the town square sometime later after they'd swung by the grocers for extra food. Taking the most direct route west would mean passing through one of the least populated areas of Kies Tor, and there was no telling when they might next find a village or town. Their supplies would need to last them half a month, if not more.

"We're ready to leave, I hope," Talin said as they approached. "I would rather not be recognised."

Red Wolf gave a brisk nod. "Ettrias has your sword. We'll take stock of our supplies once we're clear of the village."

Talin glanced at her brother but said nothing.

They rode on through Stormwood in silence, following the road where they dared and keeping to streams and creeks wherever possible so they would have a constant supply of water. Talin removed her cloak once they were far enough out, halting them eventually at dusk. There they organised their supplies and money and tethered the horses near the creek they'd been following.

"Ashera was able to secure two tents for us," Talin said. "I visited the brewer and bought the water-purifying potions you requested. You and Ettrias were able to find your respective supplies, I trust?"

"We were," Red Wolf said. "I have the bandages. Ettrias has food. We spent more money than I'd hoped, but that cannot be helped, I suppose." He flattened his bedroll on the ground.

"I have a favour to ask," Talin said.

Red Wolf looked up. "By all means, I'm at your service."

Talin drew her sword. "This. I want you to teach me how to use it. Not now, of course. When you're healed."

Red Wolf straightened and unsheathed his own sword. He lazily turned it in his hand before swinging it in a wide arc at Talin. She jumped back in alarm and knocked his blade aside. He stepped back again with a nod.

"I see you already know how to use a sword," he said. "Parry closer to the crossguard. Do not grip the weapon so tight. Stronger stance. Legs shoulder-width apart. Bend your knees a little more." Talin did as he instructed, and he raised his sword. "Now attack."

Elven metal glinted in the fading light as Talin swung her blade. Red Wolf parried easily.

"You have to *mean it*," he said. "If you are to swing at someone, your only desire is to best them in combat or kill them. Again."

Talin stepped in with another swing, and Red Wolf ducked underneath it, giving her a light shove with his free hand that sent her stumbling backwards.

"Your opponent won't fight fair in battle. Be prepared."

Talin raised her sword again. "I always figured you'd be a more encouraging teacher."

"I'm not." Red Wolf came at her again, forcing her back further and further as she tried to fend off his attacks. He backed her up as he always did with Ashera, until her back was pressed against a tree, and she could retreat no more. There he finally stopped his barrage of attacks and rested his sword lightly against her neck.

"I will teach you how to stay alive. Don't let your opponent control the fight. Don't follow them. Don't hesitate. If you are to kill someone, do it. Never pause to think," he said. "A moment is all it takes for the odds to change. Again."

Talin ducked under his arm and swung at his side, and he dodged out of the way easily. Her strikes weren't as strong as he would have liked, either; where he might have expected strong resistance on a parry, he found hardly any.

"More force, my queen. The weapon is sharp, but a scratch won't kill your opponent," he said. "They will not stop until you are dead. Show them the same courtesy."

They danced back and forth at the edge of the stream, blades catching the light as the sun dipped below the trees. Talin finally yielded under his blows with her back once again at a tree trunk.

"Your endurance is better than expected. That's good." Red Wolf sheathed his sword. "If you can exhaust your opponents without sustaining a serious injury, victory is yours."

"You shouldn't have sparred with me. Your shoulder must be hurting..." Talin's voice trailed off as she came forward, and he stepped back neatly.

"It's fine," he said.

"Of course." Talin cleared her throat and looked down. "I'll...I'll see how Ettrias is going with the fire."

Red Wolf left her to it.

The four of them had their supper eventually by the fire that Ettrias built, huddled under the shelter of a huge tree while storms raged around them, and the skies showered them with endless rain. Red Wolf opted to take the last watch; knowing how the weather was, he doubted he would be getting much sleep. Ashera woke him in the early hours for his shift, and he donned his gear in silence, watching from his spot at the edge of the camp as rays of sun struggled through the storm clouds. Talin joined him not long after; the others were still sound asleep.

"I'm not used to sleeping under the stars," she confessed. "I don't think I've ever had to sleep like this. Without a roof of some sort over my head."

"You'll get used to it," Red Wolf said, still watching the feeble sunrise. "You've lived a sheltered life, my queen. No different from any of the rich city folk. But you must remember to lead by example. The rich man sees all from his perch atop the world, but he only sees the forest and not its trees nor the individuals that dwell within it."

"What do you mean?" Talin asked.

"You may think you see everything from the top of the world, but the only way to see your people is by stepping down from that perch and moving among them. Your people do not live behind white, marble walls, nor do they dress in silks and fine cloth. Their lives are like this—eating what little they have to eat, sleeping where the storms do not reach."

"Sometimes, it does feel like I live in a totally different world from them," Talin confessed. She shook her head. "How far to the Western Forts?"

"At least three weeks if we're lucky. The Forts are the only thing left standing between the Hellhound horde and Belanore, but I suspect even they will not last." Red Wolf sighed. Truth be told, he was more worried about getting past the Western Forts in time to avoid the full moon. The Hellhounds drew their power from the moon, and as it waxed and waned, so too did their strength. If Talin and the others were caught between the border and the Forts under a full moon, he would be helpless to protect them.

"I'm not sure what to do if the Drakels do not agree to help us," Talin admitted. "If we make our plea to them and they refuse to send us aid, I will have left the kingdom for nothing."

"You'll think of something." Red Wolf shrugged. "You always were resourceful like that."

"And if we truly are on our own in this war?"

"Like it or not, you're the Queen of Kies Tor. If anyone can lead the people, you can. It is your destiny and your duty. Never forget that."

XI

G olmin had never fancied the night shifts at the palace.

    Back when he'd been a fresh-faced guard appointed to the royal family by Lord Blackrun, his commander had sent him on no shortage of night shifts to get him used to his duties as part of the Royal Guard. Red Wolf had often joined him on his patrols, though his helm was always on, preventing Golmin from seeing his face. It wasn't until they became friends, and he caught the royal bodyguard slipping out of the palace at dusk one evening, that he finally saw Red Wolf's face, and the golden-yellow eyes that marked him as an outsider. Now they confided in each other about many things. Golmin trusted the queen to find a way to stop the Hellhounds, and he trusted Red Wolf to protect her.

But without the queen's leadership in Belanore and the mounting rumours surrounding her supposed disappearance, things were steadily falling to pieces despite the Royal Council's best efforts. It was only a matter of time before they lost control of the townsfolk.

Golmin wandered past the meeting hall on his patrol. At this hour, the hall was locked and unoccupied, making it as good a place as any for assassins to hide.

Or for conducting secret meetings, he thought, turning his key in the lock to take a peek inside. All was well. He locked the door again and continued on his way.

A flight of stairs at the end of the corridor led up to the next floor of the palace. Golmin followed it and began his patrol of that floor. Two guards were posted at the balcony just ahead. He gave them a nod as he passed and turned a corner.

"Captain Golmin, sir," one of the guards called.

Golmin stopped and turned back. "What is it?"

"Master Corvan was looking for you earlier, sir," the guard said. "He said it was urgent."

Golmin didn't like the sound of that. "Where is he?"

"Headed back to his tower, sir," the guard said.

"My thanks." Golmin made a brief detour right at the next corridor and went straight to the old healer's tower. Corvan had been the first to learn Red Wolf's secret, and as far as Golmin was concerned, he and the old healer were the only ones that Red Wolf had actively told, if only to help him hide his secret. Golmin and Corvan had spent countless hours helping him search for a way to fix his condition, a task which they abandoned after Ettrias' exile. Perhaps the old man had decided to take up the challenge once more...no. Red Wolf had told him to stop wasting his time. This was something else. Golmin knocked on the door to the healer's living quarters.

"Go away, I'm busy," came the brusque reply.

"I was told you wanted to see me, Master," Golmin said.

"Captain Rufus." There was a shuffling sound before the door swung open to reveal Corvan. "Come in, take a seat. We have matters to discuss."

Golmin sat on a stool by the window while the old healer drew up a chair with a back to support his spine. "Matters concerning Red Wolf?"

"No, nothing of the sort," Corvan said, pouring some tea. Golmin politely declined a cup. He'd never much liked Corvan's herbal teas. "I'm sure you're aware of the emergency meeting held today?"

"Aye," the captain said, remembering that word had been going around in the barracks. "Still no news from the northern front?"

"None yet, not since the queen set out," Corvan said. "That is what concerns me. General Virion should have sent an update of some sort by now. We do not know if they've held Vill's Crossing or if they've been completely wiped out, which means we do not know how far the Hellhounds are from Belanore. We must send word to the queen somehow."

"Why not send a bird out?" Golmin asked. "It would only take a few days to reach the western front."

"It's not as simple as that. The queen plans to visit the Drakels," Corvan said. "We'll not reach her there."

"The Drakels!" Golmin glared. "She did not mention the Drakels. She told me she was going west to the Forts against her council's advice and was taking Red Wolf and Ettrias with her for protection, and to ensure they weren't executed in her absence."

"No doubt she had her reasons for not telling you everything," Corvan said. "But no matter now. You know Red Wolf better than most, and I'm sure he would have told you, given the chance."

"I wonder," Golmin scoffed, remembering the secret Red Wolf had kept about Ettrias. "A discussion for another time. How are we to reach her? What good would contacting her even do?"

"I...am still working on that," Corvan confessed. "But I do know that we cannot risk telling the rest of her council. Wormwood has been acting nothing like himself since the queen left—or perhaps exactly like himself. He is openly disagreeing with her methods and pointing out flaws in her administration. Lord Karl sucks up to him and goes with whatever he decides, so that he might provide more funding for the civil affairs department. Lord Cassius is our resident head of intelligence and has a spy network all over the city, perhaps even within the palace. And General Virion has sent no word for close to a month, breaking protocol almost as soon as he set out on such a crucial campaign. We cannot trust any of them. At least not at the moment."

"Very well. Still, I fail to see how contacting her would prove useful," Golmin said.

"She needs to be warned about these rumours and the riots so she and her escort can prepare for their return trip," Corvan said. "I doubt they will spend long with the Drakels, given the circumstances."

Golmin nodded. The healer was right; time was of the essence, and the sooner the queen knew about the situation in Belanore, the better. "Anything else from me?"

"Keep an eye on the rest of the Royal Council. None of them looked particularly fazed when I explained that the queen was heading to Fort Saria. I suspect they all wanted her out of Belanore."

Golmin stood and made a move for the door. "I hope you won't mind me getting back to my patrol, then."

"Of course, of course," Corvan said. "Don't let an old man like me get in the way of your duties, Captain."

Golmin headed back down the tower to finish his shift. It was uneventful, though his route did send him past the guards on one of the top floor balconies. He finished his lap of the floor and circled down to check the vault and cellars on his way back to the barracks. There was never really much need to check the vault; in all his years of serving the royal family, Golmin had never seen it breached. It was a secure, underground room layered with Elven steel and solid stone, with a door so heavy it took half a dozen guards and two pack horses to open. He barely glanced at the door on his way past.

The wine cellar was what he was worried about. There was a secret entrance into the palace hidden behind the wine shelves, a small trapdoor that Red Wolf used to sneak into Stormwood once in a while. The other side of the tunnel led out past the city walls, emerging in an overgrown magical site once used by Weavers to regain their strength. It hadn't been touched since King Braenern outlawed magic, and Golmin was certain that nobody even knew it existed anymore, but one could never be sure. He passed by the secret entrance to check nothing was amiss and paused when he heard hushed voices from behind a stack of wine barrels. Peering around briefly, he caught sight of Felix Wormwood and one of the Highett brothers. From the back, in the dim light, it was hard to tell whether this was Lord Karl or Lord Cassius; the brothers looked alike and even sounded alike. Golmin decided to assume both Highetts were involved somehow and slunk back a little to eavesdrop without being noticed.

"...out of Belanore, this plan can finally be put into motion," Wormwood was saying. "Why are you still waiting?"

"We've had no word from General Virion yet," Highett said. "I don't like the silence. He should have reported in as soon as he met up with the Fort Voraine troops, yet there has been no message of any sort. Part of me wonders if he's simply turned on Kies Tor entirely and thrown in with those Hellhounds."

Wormwood scoffed. "You truly believe that Virion would turn on all of us? The man swore his allegiance to our cause long before he set out."

"I only mean that we should be careful," Highett said. "Virion hasn't been the same since that battle in the Glass Forest. If he has thrown in with the Hellhounds..."

"If he has, we proceed with our backup plan," Wormwood said. "Prepare the city for siege. When we do repel the Hellhounds at Belanore, we'll be hailed as heroes. The public will denounce Queen Talin as a coward who fled at the first sign of danger."

"Fine. We'll discuss things further tomorrow, after the war meeting," Highett said.

Wormwood gave a nod. "Naturally. This same spot."

"Aye," Highett said, and grabbed a bottle of fine wine on his way out. Golmin saw him coming and quickly resumed his patrolling, but Highett turned down the opposite corridor and vanished from sight before he could catch a glimpse of the man's face. Wormwood came out a few minutes later with another bottle of wine, passing Golmin.

"Evening, Captain," he said cheerfully. "Still on patrol?"

"I'm returning to the barracks now," Golmin said. He noted the bottle in Wormwood's hand. "I take it you're out of wine, m'lord?"

"Ah, yes, unfortunately so." Wormwood frowned at his bottle. "There appears to be no stock left of my favourite Highlander wines, so I have to settle with this local brew. A pity, really."

"I hear the war makes it difficult to import goods from the Highlands," Golmin said carefully, trying to steer the conversation so he could get more information out of Wormwood, but the Master of Coin wasn't easily swayed.

"Ah, but trade has been the same for years," he said. "You know, there is an excellent winery just north of Belanore. The stuff they make is splendid, but still nothing compared to Highlander reds."

This talk of wine was incredibly dull to Golmin, who lived off good ale like all the royal guards. Determined to shake Wormwood, he quickened his pace, but the thin man had long legs and easily matched him.

"What brings you down to the cellars, anyway?" Wormwood asked abruptly.

Golmin didn't like this sudden change of topic. "Routine patrol, m'lord. There are...certain precautions that must be taken to keep the palace safe, including checking the cellars."

"Ah, I see," Wormwood said slowly. "Say, you didn't happen to see Lord Cassius down here, did you?"

Lord Cassius? Was he the one Wormwood was talking to?

"No, I haven't seen anyone else, m'lord," Golmin said.

"Hmm, never mind, then," Wormwood said. They parted ways at the top of the stairs, and Golmin headed back to the barracks with far more questions than answers.

It was obvious now that Wormwood was the one who coordinated this setup, whatever it was. Corvan was right; he was acting out of character. From what little Red Wolf was able to reveal about the Royal Council's meetings, Wormwood usually sucked up to the queen. That he would begin to work against her as soon as she left the city was odd, to say the least. But overthrowing her entirely...?

No, he must have something else to gain from all this. Perhaps Ettrias revealed the truth and Wormwood now believes the queen was involved.

Golmin met with Master Corvan again the next day, just before the healer gathered the Royal Council for the war meeting. They retreated to a private room to talk for fear of being overheard, and Golmin shared what he had overheard the night before. Corvan listened in silence, only giving the occasional 'hmm' or stroking his chin.

"So Wormwood and possibly both Highetts will carry out this plan," he said, once Golmin had finished. "That's the majority of the council."

"Precisely," Golmin said. "And General Virion is too far away to be of any help, even if we knew for certain that his loyalties still lie with the queen."

"I received Virion's bird early this morning," Corvan said. "Highlander cavalry and mounted archers have reinforced the White River fort. They're expected to hold position just south of the river for a while longer. Perhaps I should...delay the reveal of this information."

Golmin nodded. "Aye, perhaps that would be best. It will buy us the time we need to warn the queen of this plot—I hope."

"And try to find out if Ettrias was involved," Corvan added.

"That's what I'm worried about," Golmin confessed. "If Ettrias is involved in all this, the queen is in grave danger."

"Red Wolf would protect her with his life—we both know that."

"It has been almost a month. What happens when he cannot be there to protect her?"

Corvan sighed. "Then we must hope and pray that he finds a way."

XII

"**D**amned storm season," Red Wolf muttered as they rode through another relentless storm with their hoods turned up against the deluge. "We can barely go a day without getting soaked."

From the head of their column, Talin said nothing, her nose buried in their map as she tried to figure out where the nearest village was. Having been born and raised in the south, she was used to the constant rain in the storm season, whereas Red Wolf had only arrived in Belanore after presumably spending most of his childhood in the north.

"Storm's picking up," Ettrias said. "Much as I enjoy wandering through Stormwood, soaked to the skin, we'll all get ill if we continue in this weather. Might I suggest finding shelter somewhere?"

"We shouldn't be far from a village, but I can't find it on the map..." Talin said.

"Some of the smaller settlements out here can escape cartographers' notice," Red Wolf remarked. "They only show up on local maps." He beckoned for the map, and Talin passed it over silently. "We should be nearing the edge of Stormwood, given our current pace. The next marked town along our route looks to be...another week's ride?"

"That sounds right," Ettrias said. "I took this route with Father once before when we visited the Western Forts. We passed through a small village a week before arriving at the next major town."

"We're coming up on another stream. Most settlements tend to spring up near sources of water." Red Wolf hummed and handed the map back. "I believe we'll come across this village you speak of before sunset if we keep following the road."

Much as she wanted confirmation that they were on the right path, Talin knew that her bodyguard was right. Without any marker to indicate the settlement's location on the map, they were forced to rely on landmarks and guesswork. She sincerely hoped that they would come across the village today. Sleeping on the road in a storm this bad would only get them all sick.

True to Red Wolf's prediction, they arrived at the village just as the sun was beginning to set, soaked to the bone. Talin led the way through the tiny settlement; it was smaller than she'd imagined, with its houses built on raised trellises by the creek to avoid flooding. The creek itself had already overflowed, covering most of the village in a layer of ankle-deep water, forcing them to remain on horseback while they navigated the streets.

"Doesn't look to be an inn anywhere in town, sister," Ettrias called.

Talin groaned. "We'll have to keep moving, then." *Hopefully we can find a thick canopy somewhere to stay dry.*

"In this weather? Are you mad?" Ettrias shouted back. "I don't know about you, but I would rather *not* fall ill on this lovely road trip of yours. It kills the mood."

Red Wolf glanced back at him. "And where exactly do you propose we go?"

"I don't know—out of this rain seems like a good start," Ettrias muttered.

"I can ask around. There must be an inn somewhere around here..." Talin's voice trailed off as she glanced around and saw a woman's face disappear from a window just ahead. She approached and knocked.

"Can I help you?" The door opened inwards a crack to reveal the woman again, squinting at them suspiciously.

"I'm sorry to bother you," Talin said. "My companions and I were looking for an inn. Is there one nearby?"

"No," the woman said. She looked them up and down, gaze landing on Ashera, huddled at the back. "But if you're looking for shelter, you can shelter here. Much better than camping in the wilderness, in any case. You can leave the horses out the back."

Talin hesitated, sparing a look at Red Wolf and Ettrias. Her bodyguard shrugged.

"Anywhere is better than out here. Ashera's going to freeze in this rain," he said.

They led their horses around to the back of the house, settling them in the open barn, before squeezing into the woman's house. Ettrias wasted no time stripping off his soaked travelling cloak. Talin kept her hood turned up, not wanting to be recognised, though she suspected they were far enough from the capital that most of the common folk had no clue what the queen looked like.

"Thank you for the hospitality," Talin said to the woman. "You say there's no inn here?"

The woman huffed a laugh. "There hasn't been an inn here for years. The only inn we had closed down a few years before King Arnas' death, and the owners moved elsewhere, looking for better business." She moved aside to let them further into the house. "Come in. It's really no trouble. Lay those cloaks out by the stove to dry. Jarett, boys, we have guests!"

She doesn't recognise us. What about her family?

Talin pulled her cloak off hesitantly and left it by the stove opposite the door. Beside her, Red Wolf was helping Ashera with her cloak and outer clothing, paying no heed to his own state.

"What's this, then?" A man's head appeared from around a corner. "Travellers?"

"Apologies for the intrusion, sir," Talin said. "We'll be out of here as soon as the storm passes."

"You'll be here for a while yet," the man said. "Storm like this will probably last all night. I'm Jarett."

"Raia," Talin said. "That's my brother..."

"Taj Vinters," Ettrias cut in. He nodded at Red Wolf. "That's my sister's fiancé, William, and his niece, Ashera."

What—

Talin didn't miss the smug grin that Ettrias flashed her before settling down with his back against a wall. She looked at Red Wolf, hoping to gauge his reaction, but he gave no indication that the lie bothered him at all. He pulled his cloak off in a fluid motion and laid it out by the stove before finding a seat on the floor. Talin remained standing.

"Sorry about the lack of furniture," the village woman said. "I'm Caeda. You've met my husband, Jarett. Our four sons are in the other room. It's been difficult trying to get by these last few years, especially with the war and all." She pulled up a wooden stool. "Here, we have a chair if the floor is too uncomfortable."

"Oh, I'm...I'll be fine. Please, you sit," Talin said. She took in the tiny cabin while Jarett sidled into the stool. It was smaller than it had looked from the outside, with the stove near the entrance and their four cloaks drying on the floor in front of it. A neat stack of straw and fabric was nestled in the far corner, suggesting that this was the couple's bed, while a bucket near Ettrias slowly filled with water dripping from a ceiling leak.

"You say the inn closed down?" Red Wolf asked.

"Yes," Caeda said. "Out here, we have nothing, no funding to keep ourselves afloat. The inn's business relied on travellers passing through this village. But with the war and all, folk are scared to travel. The inn had to close."

"I was here many years ago," Ettrias said. "Things didn't seem nearly as bad then."

Caeda shook her head. "This village has been slowly declining. Nobody comes through here now. We don't have much to trade...it was a resting point for travellers and adventurers, that was all. There's not much left for any of us here."

"I don't understand. Didn't the Crown allocate funding to the towns and villages affected by the war...?" Talin's voice trailed off.

"The bigger towns, sure," Jarett said. "But backwater villages that don't even show up on the maps? No. The Crown doesn't *exist* out here. It's just us."

Talin fell silent. *Red Wolf was right. I've been blind.*

"Well, we do have a new queen." Her bodyguard looked at her. "I'm sure she will do something about the situation here."

"I'm not getting my hopes up," Caeda said. "Rumour has it that she's fled the capital and abandoned everyone to the Hellhounds." She leaned over to check the soup bubbling on the stove, then excused herself to tend to it.

"*What?* That's—" Talin began. Red Wolf silenced her with a wave of his hand.

"That's troubling," he said. "We rode out from Belanore before these rumours started. It seems that word travels more quickly than we do."

It's suspicious, he meant. Talin understood.

"I do not think the queen would abandon her people so readily," her bodyguard continued. "Not after her father's sacrifice to keep the kingdom safe. For all we know, this may just be baseless gossip set about by her enemies."

"Whatever the case, I'm doubtful that things will change much, even under a new ruler," Jarett said. "It's always been like this. We're used to it."

There has to be something more I can do. These people are suffering while I live sheltered in the palace.

"It doesn't seem fair," Ashera said softly, speaking up for the first time since they entered the house.

"It's not," Talin said.

"Oh, don't worry about us. We get by." Caeda returned with two bowls of soup, which she passed to Talin and Ashera, before returning for more bowls. "Boys, supper is ready!"

"We can't take this soup; you need to feed yourselves too—" Talin began.

"It's no trouble," Caeda said with a smile. "I've got enough soup here to feed everyone. It's about the only thing we can cook around here, so I always make extra."

"At least let us share some of our rations with you, then," Talin said, reaching for her pack and pulling out a few days' worth of dried meat, fruit, and hard biscuits. Her brother hesitated a moment before doing the same. Red Wolf's eyebrows drew together, but at a pointed look from her, he handed over a similar amount of food from his own pack.

"Please, we can't take these from you..." Caeda began, but was interrupted by four young boys appearing from the other room and lining up before her to receive their meals. They stole furtive glances at Talin's party huddled on the floor and mumbled out quiet hellos.

"It's no trouble. We can always purchase more supplies," Talin said.

"What brings the four of you out here, anyway? You say you came from Belanore?" Jarett asked.

"Headed to the Western Forts," Red Wolf lied smoothly. "I received word recently that my sister made it through the Forts and has been staying at one of the nearby towns. I'm taking Ashera back to her mother."

"We only tagged along to keep him out of trouble," Ettrias added with a grin. "He's always getting into fights back home since he's got those funny-coloured eyes. You know how it is with superstitious folk."

Red Wolf pursed his lips and said nothing more.

"You know, I always said that Weavers can't be all bad." Caeda shook her head. "But folks tend to believe everything these days. You're welcome here, William. Just know that."

"Thank you," Red Wolf said quietly, though Talin noticed he didn't meet the woman's eyes.

"Are you a Weaver?" one of the boys asked.

"...yes," Red Wolf said.

"Can you do magic?" another boy asked. "Can we see?"

Caeda *tsked*. "Come on, you two, finish your supper. It's rude to pry."

"It's alright." Red Wolf's shoulders visibly relaxed a fraction. "I can channel protection magic. It's not something I can show unless I'm in physical danger."

"That sounds *amazing*," the first boy said. "So, if someone tries to beat you up, you can just use your magic and make it so that they can't hit you at all?"

"Something like that."

Talin met her bodyguard's gaze briefly and offered a smile. He seemed to relax a little more as he sipped his soup.

"We usually turn in for the night after supper," Jarett said. "It's no issue if you four stay up a little longer, though we'd be grateful if you kept the noise down."

"Of course. We'll probably get some sleep, too," Talin said. "It'll be nice not having to take shifts for once."

"Well, then, goodnight, all of you," Ettrias said. "I, for one, am exhausted." He unrolled his bedding and lay down.

"Goodnight." Jarett went to put his sons to bed while Caeda took their bowls to be washed.

"You should sleep too, Ashera," Red Wolf said. "Keep up your strength."

"Pfft, you sound like my dad." Ashera stuck out her tongue at him but settled down anyway. Talin laid out her own bedroll and frowned at it.

"Something on your mind?" Red Wolf asked, as Caeda joined her husband in bed and snuffed out their candle, plunging them into near darkness, illuminated only by the light of the waning crescent moon.

Talin went to the window and watched the pouring storm, wrestling with her thoughts. She hadn't thought much about how *good* she was as a ruler before now, but hearing about the decline of this village and seeing the dire state that some of her people were living in...

"You were right," she said softly, keeping her voice low to avoid being overheard. "I've spent my whole life looking at the world through a keyhole, and when I finally opened the door, I realised that none of it was anything close to what I had imagined. I was never ready to rule alone, but I'd deluded myself into thinking that I could do it anyway. I told myself that I could change the world. Believed it, even. And yet all these months later everything is still the same." She shook her head. "I've been blind. People have suffered for it."

Red Wolf joined her at the window. "You can't save everyone."

"I have to try."

"You're just one person."

"I am one person with power over an entire *kingdom*. I could make things better here. I know I could," Talin said. "I could make things better everywhere. It's not fair that we lounge on mountains of gold in the royal palace while people live in poverty elsewhere."

Red Wolf huffed a half-laugh. "I'm glad you see it that way. Truth be told, I was worried that you wouldn't understand these people's plight even after hearing their story, sheltered as you were in the palace. Maybe all that reading as a child has taught you more about fairness and compassion than your father ever did."

"You give me too much credit. For all my reading, I still don't know a damn thing about rulership." Talin sighed and turned away from the window. "But enough of my problems. How are you faring?"

There was a beat.

"...I don't understand," Red Wolf said.

"You've been on edge ever since we set foot in here," Talin said.

"Ah." Red Wolf averted his gaze. "Well, small talk has never been one of my strengths. I could talk for days about weapons or history, but...gossip? The war? You'll have to forgive me. I'd be hard-pressed to find something to talk about."

"That's not all," Talin said. "You don't trust these people."

"I don't trust their good intentions," Red Wolf confessed. "Your father was nothing but kind to me until I refused to give him my cooperation. Then his whole tune changed. I won't make that mistake again."

Talin winced. "I'm sorry."

"Don't be. You had no part in it, and I made my choices ten years ago." Red Wolf sighed. "Get some rest. I'll be up for a while yet. I need to think."

"I'm not tired," Talin said.

"*Tch*. Stubborn."

"What? Don't want my company?"

"On the contrary, I welcome it."

Talin pulled up the nearby stool and sat. "Can I ask you something, then?"

"Yes," Red Wolf said.

"Did you...know my mother?" Talin asked quietly. "Before she passed?"

"Not well." Red Wolf's brow creased. "She was already ill by the time I arrived in Belanore. I rarely saw her."

"Of course." Talin looked away. "Never mind, then—"

"I remember she was a musician, though," Red Wolf said, and her gaze snapped back up to him. "I'd hear her play the violin sometimes, on her better days. The flute, too—she was an incredible musician. I think she used to play for you and Ettrias..."

They set off early the next morning as soon as the storm had let up, leaving the village and its inhabitants behind. Caeda had insisted that they stay for breakfast, but Talin had refused, saying that she couldn't possibly take more food from their family. The four of them had instead taken their breakfast on the road.

They had heard more rumours of the queen fleeing Belanore, too; Red Wolf had confirmed the other villagers' gossip had been about them once they were clear of the settlement. It was troubling news, to say the least. Talin hoped that Wormwood, Corvan, and Golmin were doing something about the situation back home.

"We should turn back," her bodyguard said. "So many rumours, travelling so quickly...it's far too suspicious. Somebody wanted you out of Belanore." He cursed. "What in the seven hells got into your head to ride west in person?"

"We can't turn back now. We're almost halfway to the border," Talin said. "And if you must know, I only rode out under Lord Wormwood's advice, so you can keep your assumptions to yourself."

Red Wolf scoffed. "Wormwood, of course, I should have known."

Orrlat, not this again.

"I *trust Wormwood*," Talin hissed. "He fought beside my father for *years* before joining the Royal Court as Master of Coin, not to mention that Father specifically named him Lord Regent until I could take the throne. Why in the seven hells *you* have such a problem with him is none of my concern, but I will not have you question my judgement again when it comes to him."

"I fought beside your father, too," Red Wolf muttered, but seemed to drop the matter anyway. "Apologies, my queen. It wasn't my intention to question your judgement."

Talin said nothing. Red Wolf's words weighed on her mind.

Could he have a point? Could Wormwood have ulterior motives for sending me out of Belanore?

Whatever the case, they were now halfway to the border. She had to push on.

A nother week's travel finally put the four of them past Stormwood and one step closer to the Western Forts. After being
grounded at the forest edge for four days owing to flooding in the
plains between Stormwood and Charrac Forest, they found themselves
dangerously low on supplies yet again, despite having restocked at the
town of Deepwood a week before. Talin had to put aside another hundred yarii to spend on food and waterproof bedrolls—the storms were
heavy enough now to wake them in the middle of the night, drenched
from head to toe. They lit fires and tried to dry off their sopping gear
whenever the weather allowed.

Red Wolf also kept up her training, despite the conditions. Talin
felt the strength of his blows in her arms for days afterwards, and the
knowledge that he was holding back sent chills down her spine. Once,

he pressed her on until she was forced to drop her sword, arms aching, only to be told she had to outlast her opponent if she wanted to live.

"Your opponent will not stop to let you pick up your weapon," he snapped. "Keep a strong grip!"

"You keep telling me that." Talin wiped the sweat from her brow with a sleeve. "How am I to outlast my opponents when I can barely parry a strike from you?"

"That will come with practice. Not much I can help with, unfortunately." Red Wolf sheathed his sword. "Though I think we will stop here tonight. I need you still able to hold your weapon for training tomorrow."

"I'm looking forward to it already," Talin muttered. "The sooner these floodwaters recede enough to allow us through Charrac Forest, the better. Much as I love the extra time to train, I'd prefer to be at the Western Forts by now."

"I agree. We cannot afford any more delays," Red Wolf said. "How much training have you had with your magic?"

"I..." Talin hesitated. *None, to be sure.* Her father had wanted to keep her powers a secret in the hope that they would one day diminish, and knowing now that he wanted her to succeed to the throne, everything made sense. With magic outlawed, her people would have feared her powers. They would never have accepted her as their queen.

"No matter. I will teach you." Red Wolf stretched out a hand, and golden energy snaked down his arm towards it.

"I've...tried teaching myself—in secret. Besides making my hands glow, I never figured out much," Talin confessed.

"Weavers used to be able to bend the very fabric of reality to their will with magic," Red Wolf said. "Nowadays, with the magic in our lands diminished so far, we can only manipulate the barest fraction of the power they used to wield. I can channel protection magic, for example, but nothing else. My magic is only good for shielding myself and others."

"You can shield other people as well?"

"Yes. But my protection magic will only hold for a few seconds at most, and it takes time to cast. I must know an attack is coming to be able to shield myself from it, and I must be touching someone else to shield them too."

"Could I channel something like that?"

"Maybe." Red Wolf shrugged. "There's only one way to find out: focus on the wild magic around us. You'll feel it in your fingertips, just...*waiting*. Let it out." He took her hand in both of his and opened her palm gently, then let go.

Focus? That's it? Talin looked down at her hand. There had to be more to it; she'd never been able to channel her magic just by *focusing* before...

"I...can't," she said.

"Of course you can. You're a Weaver. It's in your blood."

Talin concentrated on her palm, shutting out the rest of the world. Almost instantly, she felt the familiar pull of magic. It tingled in the air and the very ground she stood on, beckoning her to draw from its power. Red Wolf stood silent before her. She tried to do what he had instructed, letting it spill through her fingertips. Tiny arcs of lightning danced across her palm, flickering at first but quickly brightening. Soon, her entire hand was crackling with energy, spilling over with raw magic, desperately wanting to be released.

And it felt *good*.

"Lightning, then..." she murmured. *Almost fitting for the storm season.*

"Talin." Red Wolf's voice broke her concentration, and her magic faded. "Magic can be a dangerous thing if not controlled. Be careful."

Talin knew what he meant. She could feel the raw power of magic around her, beckoning to be channelled, and knew that true mastery came from *control*.

"If you two are done showing off your magic tricks, we're almost out of food again," Ettrias called from the campfire. Red Wolf made it to him in a few large strides, leaving Talin to struggle through the thicket behind him.

"We'll have to conserve what we have left, then," her bodyguard said, examining their food pack. "Looks like we'll be hunting game tonight or rationing until we can make it to another village."

"I know how to trap rabbits," Ashera said. "We could have some rabbit for dinner."

"Not in the storm season," Red Wolf said. "Their burrows get flooded, so they have to seal off the entrances and dig deep to avoid getting drenched while they hibernate. We're better off hunting deer." He snatched up the bow and quiver of arrows he'd bought in Stormwood. "I'd offer to send you, Ettrias, but you couldn't hit a brick wall with an arrow if it were two feet in front of you."

"Hey, I'm not *that* incompetent with a bow." Ettrias snorted. "You wound me, Lord Commander."

"Apologies, I only meant—" Red Wolf began.

Ettrias waved him off. "I know what you meant. And you're right. Well, off you go then. Be quick. I'm starving."

"You'll have to join me, my queen," Red Wolf said. "I'm afraid I cannot trust Ettrias to refrain from killing you while I'm gone."

"Oh, come on, we've gone three weeks without an incident!" Ettrias protested.

"You did send two assassins after me," Talin said.

"...point taken."

Talin held out a hand for Red Wolf's bow. "Mind sharing?"

"By all means, be my guest." Red Wolf passed across the weapon. Talin took it with a nod of thanks and strapped the quiver to her belt as they made their way through the thicket.

They wandered nearby for an hour, maybe more, before turning back empty-handed. With another storm undoubtedly on its way, most of the animals had fled the open to find shelter.

"A shame. I was hoping to see your archery skills for myself," Red Wolf said as they walked. "I hear you were a good shot before you stopped training with weapons—a legend is how some described you."

Talin shrugged. "They always exaggerate when you're a royal. I was about as good as any other elf with a bow."

"All the same, you've given me an idea," Red Wolf said. "Some archery training, perhaps, on top of bladework and magic."

"Gods, Red Wolf, your training regime will be the death of me." Talin laughed and shook her head. "But very well. I'll admit that archery training would be more interesting." A water droplet landed on her face. She wiped it off with a sleeve and sighed. Another storm was upon them, then.

"Let's hurry back before we're completely soaked," Red Wolf said.

"No argument here." Talin followed him towards the camp as fat drops of rain began to pound on them. They flipped up the hoods of their cloaks in an attempt to keep themselves dry for a little longer.

"This storm couldn't wait until we were back at camp?" Red Wolf grumbled. "Damned weather. Give me the dry season anytime. At least you can travel a day without having your damp clothes soaked again."

Talin was about to tease him for complaining so much when a shout from their camp stopped her. They looked at each other for a second before Red Wolf drew his sword and took off at a sprint. Talin nocked an arrow and followed close behind.

"What's the—?" Red Wolf began, bursting into the clearing. Talin skidded to a stop next to him to discover Ettrias and Ashera already locked in battle with half a dozen raiders. The two of them were slowly being backed into a thick cluster of trees. Red Wolf lunged forwards in half a heartbeat, cutting two down before one raider spun and parried his blade. All thoughts fled from Talin's mind as another enemy broke off from his duel with Ettrias and closed in on Red Wolf from behind. There was no time to shout a warning and she had an arrow at the ready.

Talin drew back the bowstring instinctively and let it loose.

There was a soft *thunk* as her arrow found its mark in her target's back, dropping the man behind Red Wolf. Her bodyguard spun, alarmed, and blinked when he saw the arrow protruding from the dead man's back.

Oh, gods, I just killed him.

"Watch out!" Ettrias barrelled into her and tackled her aside, just in time. An arrow sailed out of the bushes ahead and embedded itself into his thigh with a muffled sound. Talin scrambled to her feet, readied another arrow, and took out the archer before he could have another shot at them. Her bodyguard took the head off another and slit the final man's throat before he could run.

"You're unhurt?" Red Wolf asked, wiping down his blade and sheathing it.

"I'm...I'm fine. Thanks to Ettrias," Talin said.

"Don't thank me, I'm seriously wondering if I should have let that archer shoot you," Ettrias groaned from his position on the ground. She barely heard him, her gaze still locked on the dead raider at Red Wolf's feet, a single arrow protruding from his back.

I killed two men.

Red Wolf crouched beside Ettrias to examine his injury. "Well, you're lucky. Nothing too serious, but still, you'll need a healer to remove the arrow properly," he said. "Honestly, you're the last person I expected to be saving my queen. Three weeks ago, you were trying to have her assassinated."

"I'm her brother," Ettrias scowled. "I am *quite* unfortunate that I have a sister who frequently needs saving."

Talin felt the bow slip from her hands and clatter to the ground.

She had seen death before. Arnas had taken her to see no shortage of public executions, and though she had never had a taste for them, they had never bothered her to this extent. This was...

"Talin."

She forced herself to focus on Red Wolf's voice.

"Are you alright?" he asked.

"I..." Talin tore her gaze from the dead man and looked at him. "I will be."

Red Wolf's eyes darted across her face for a moment before he gave a nod. "I'll tend to your brother, then." He helped Ettrias hobble towards a fallen log where he could sit, allowing the bodyguard to bandage around the arrow shaft.

"How far to the next town?" Ettrias asked.

"The next town won't be till the Western Forts, I'm afraid," Red Wolf said. "Three days' travel. I'd remove the arrow if it were in a less dangerous position, but I cannot risk potentially dislodging it from an artery. The most I can do is cut the shaft—if you think you can endure it."

Ettrias squeezed his eyes shut with a grimace. "Do what you think best."

"Very well. Hold still," Red Wolf said. "Ashera, I'll need you to grab the shaft as close to the wound as possible and keep it in place." He drew a dagger, and Ashera obliged.

"You won't cut my fingers off by accident, will you?" the girl asked.

"No. I promise." Red Wolf wrapped his free hand around the tail-end of the arrow, over the fletching, and sliced clean through the wood in one fluid motion. Ettrias hissed through his teeth.

"Well, let's hope an infection doesn't kill me," he muttered.

"Infection is treatable. You bleeding to death in the middle of Charrac Forest is not." Red Wolf tossed the arrow shaft away. "But you don't need me to tell you that. Try to get some sleep. We'll set off in the morning."

"No complaints here." Ettrias struggled to his feet again and limped into the tent.

"Ashera, do you mind taking the first watch?" Red Wolf asked. "I'd like to keep an eye on Ettrias, at least for a while. If his condition does not worsen immediately, there may be some hope for getting him to the Western Forts."

"Alright." The girl wiped her sword clean and climbed to a low branch on the nearest tree.

"If all is well, I'll retire too, then." Talin stripped off her drenched cloak and ducked into the tent to change into drier clothes.

"Toss what you're not wearing out here," Red Wolf called. "I'll hang everything over the fire. Hopefully, they'll be less wet by the time we wake up tomorrow."

"I doubt it will make much of a difference," Talin said, but passed him her soaked garments anyway. That done, she left room for Ashera and lay down stiffly, trying to sleep.

She was woken some hours later by Ashera and reluctantly left the shelter of the tent to move into the still-pouring rain for her shift. She knew Red Wolf usually took first or last shift—for reasons he didn't share. That meant she would have to wake him next; Ettrias was in no condition to be keeping watch. As it turned out, however, Red Wolf didn't need to be woken. He joined her just before dawn, as the storm was finally beginning to pass, and fed what little dry wood they had left to the fire.

"Not going to sleep?" he asked.

"Sleep eludes me most nights," Talin said.

"Still thinking about those raiders?"

She found herself staring at the spot where the dead man had lain. No doubt her bodyguard had already disposed of the bodies somewhere. "I...know...it was necessary. Raiders and outlaws do not stop until they have what valuables they came for. I just...need a distraction, if you'll be so kind."

"Hmm. Perhaps some more training, then." Red Wolf snatched up his bow and quiver and handed them to her, then set about scratching a target into a large tree trunk in the distance.

"I'm beginning to think that archery training is simply an excuse for you to see my so-called legendary skill for yourself," Talin said.

"The Royal Guard train with bows and crossbows daily. I've seen Rufus send an arrow into a moving target at five hundred paces, and he's by no means our best archer," Red Wolf said when he returned to her. "Just shoot as fast as you can and as accurately as you can. There's not much you can faze me with, I promise."

Seeing no choice, Talin nocked an arrow, pulled back the string and loosed her first shot. It sailed wide and struck a neighbouring tree with a dull *thunk*.

"What an awful shot! I guess those stories were an exaggeration," she said. "See, Red Wolf, this is why you shouldn't believe gossip. The truth is often disappointing."

"I doubt that. It took you two arrows to drop two raiders last night. Again."

Her second arrow landed just outside the central circle that Red Wolf had carved. Her final shot clipped the previous arrow close enough that she swore she heard the tips whisper against each other.

"Your grouping is excellent, barring that wide shot," Red Wolf said. "Archery comes naturally to you, from what I can tell." He yanked her arrows free. "Impressive aim, even for a royal guard. I'd have trouble matching it."

"I...I'm flattered," Talin said, feeling her cheeks burn. "Though I must admit I've never fancied injuring another person, let alone taking a life."

Red Wolf hummed. "I understand."

"You say we're three days from the Western Forts?" Talin asked.

"Yes. Past it, there will be Hellhounds," Red Wolf said. "They will not be so easy to kill as outlaws and raiders. When we do come across them, aim for the head."

"I'll keep it in mind." Talin had no doubt she could send an arrow into the eye of a giant, charging wolf, but she knew that the others would have a much harder time, given the Hellhounds' healing abilities.

"You fought the Hellhounds beside my father before," she said after a pause. "Do they usually stay in wolf form?"

Red Wolf scratched his head. "It depends on personal preference, I believe. Some look like your average Highlander; others prefer to stay as wolves. Either way, they're dangerous."

"Then I hope we don't run into too many."

"With any luck, we can avoid the main Hellhound company and reach the Drakels without incident."

"Easier said than done."

"Indeed."

After catching wind of Wormwood's plot in the cellar, Golmin heard nothing more from the man, not even a hint of their conspiracy to overthrow the queen. With Master Corvan continuing to keep General Virion's message a secret from the council and no more suspicious activity anywhere else in the palace, he had assumed, perhaps unwisely, that they had managed to foil Wormwood's plans.

Nevertheless, he kept an eye on the rest of the council as Corvan had bid him; he had served in the palace long enough to know that the situation was far from resolved. Without the queen in Belanore, there was little more they could do than wait and hope.

"The full moon is in two days," Golmin said when they met again in the healer's tower to relay whatever new information they had found. "Red Wolf shifts in *two days*. That's when the Hellhounds will be strongest, and he will be able to do nothing. If the queen has not made it across the border by then…"

Corvan sighed. "No need to remind me. But have some more faith in him, Captain. If he cannot protect her in any capacity, he would not continue to hide the truth from her."

"I don't know. He's been hiding plenty of secrets he deemed 'necessary' for her protection," Golmin muttered.

"He would not put her in needless danger."

"Too much can go wrong for them. I don't like it."

"I understand," Corvan said. "But we can do nothing for them from here. Have you learned anything more about what Wormwood and the Highetts are up to?"

"Nothing," Golmin said. "I believe you were right in keeping Virion's message from the council. It seems likely, at this point, that Wormwood's plan hinges on the safety of Vill's Crossing."

"All the same, we cannot let our guard down," Corvan said, pouring himself some tea. "Lord Wormwood is not one to give up easily."

"I know," Golmin said. "I've been keeping a close eye on him. He comes down to the cellars occasionally to check if they've taken in any stock of his favourite wines. If his routine changes, I will know."

The old healer nodded. "Continue tailing him when you can. This is far from over."

"Aye, consider it done."

He headed back down the tower for his night shift, thoughts spinning. Much as he agreed with Corvan's logic, a part of him still worried for Red Wolf's situation; he and the healer had been the only ones the bodyguard had *willingly* talked to about his powers. He would not reveal anything to the queen for fear of being shunned.

Golmin rounded a corner in time to glimpse Wormwood disappearing down the steps to the cellar.

I saw him in the cellar just yesterday. Something's wrong.

He silently descended the steps after the Master of Coin, keeping back to avoid being seen or heard. He could almost hear the old healer in his head now, reminding him that this was why they could not jump to any premature conclusions or let down their guard.

"Lord Karl," he heard Wormwood say.

"Lord Felix."

Golmin crept between the storage shelves and quickly located the two lords. He pressed his back against a stack of barrels to eavesdrop on their conversation.

"You've talked to your brother?" Wormwood asked.

"I have. He remains unaware of our meetings here. Curious for a spymaster to be so obtuse," Lord Karl said with a sneer. "Though I am not sure how long that will last. Cassius has spies all over the city. If we are to act, we must do it soon."

"Not to worry, the rumours about the queen are working well," Wormwood said. "All we need do is wait for Virion's message and recruit Cassius."

"Never mind my brother. Virion is the worry!" Lord Karl snapped. "I'm telling you—he's a turncoat. He's allied himself with the Hellhounds, or if he hasn't, we've already lost Vill's Crossing. We can't rely on him anymore."

"Forget Virion," Wormwood said. "Our plan does not hinge on his negotiation with the Hellhounds. Focus on Cassius. We need his spy network."

"He's loyal to the queen," Lord Karl said. "Disgustingly so. Though, from what I know, Captain Golmin was close to the prince before his exile ten years ago. We may be able to recruit him to our cause instead, with your permission. He has the Royal Guard under his command. They could prove useful."

Ettrias put them up to this...?

Things began to slot together. Wormwood and Lord Karl must be acting under Ettrias' orders and working against the queen now. They wanted to put him on the throne instead.

Golmin decided that he'd heard enough. He straightened and made to slip away.

"Captain Golmin? What a surprise, we weren't expecting to see you here."

He cursed under his breath and spun back around. Lord Wormwood had appeared from behind one of the storage shelves and now faced him, Lord Karl lingering over his shoulder silently. Neither of them looked particularly happy to see him.

"M'lords. Apologies for the interruption," Golmin said. "I was simply doing my rounds here and happened to stumble upon you both. Whatever private business you have down here is none of my concern, sirs. I caught no wind of any conversation you may have had."

"Hmm." Wormwood shot a sideways glance at Lord Karl. "Lord Cassius didn't send you down here, did he?"

"Lord Cassius? No, m'lord. As I said, only a routine patrol," Golmin said. "Is...anything wrong? If there's a security issue that you'd like me to investigate, I'd be happy to do so."

"Not at all, Captain." Wormwood offered him a stiff smile. "Please, carry on, don't let us keep you from your duties."

"Of course, m'lords, as you say." Golmin bowed and quickly left the cellar. As soon as his shift was over, he would find Corvan again to relay what he had overheard. Knowing now that Ettrias was involved meant it was even more urgent to warn Red Wolf and the queen and bid them to return to Belanore immediately to deal with Wormwood. *If it isn't already too late.* He shook the thought from his head.

But do I really want to move against Ettrias?

Golmin cursed himself for even questioning it. He was loyal to the Crown; of course he had to move against Ettrias. What the prince was doing now was high treason regardless of whether he'd been innocent ten years ago.

You chose not to defend him ten years ago, Rufus. Was it your duty to the Crown then that prevented you from doing so?

But he had no idea of the truth ten years ago. Had no idea that Arnas had planned it all and no idea of the secrets that Red Wolf was keeping from him.

If he moved against the Crown, he would move against Red Wolf, who had been his friend for so long. Yet even friendship could not describe their relationship, for what they had was unique. He remembered confessing his feelings to the man years ago, standing half-drunk on the castle ramparts, in the middle of a downpour that threatened to flood the moat below. Red Wolf had been flattered, to say the least, though he'd explained that he already harboured feelings for another.

And Golmin had been shocked. He had half-expected the lord commander to recoil in disgust or threaten to expose him, but none of that had happened. Red Wolf had understood.

He had not turned against Golmin back then. For the captain to turn on him now would be a betrayal.

This is the same man who lied to the court about Ettrias. Whose testimony helped send Ettrias into exile. He lied to you about the case. Kept secrets from you.

So absorbed was he in his thoughts that he only registered Lord Cassius coming towards him moments before they collided, the spymaster muttering a curse and brief apology. Golmin opened his mouth to take the blame for it, but the man had already vanished down the hallway, leaving him standing half-stunned by himself. He glanced at the spot where Lord Cassius had been moments ago, then frowned.

He slipped something into your pocket.

Golmin dug out the note.

Spies in palace. Your involvement known. Corvan called away to small hall, thief to steal general's message. Burn this note.

Golmin crumpled the paper in one hand and hurried back to the healer's tower to find Corvan.

By the time he arrived, Corvan's study had been trashed. Papers were scattered all over the desk and floor, and one glance at the broken lock on the top drawer told him all that he needed to know.

They had severely underestimated Wormwood and Highett, and now, nothing was left to stop them from carrying out their plan.

We must contact the queen somehow.

He turned, tossed Cassius' note into the still-burning fireplace, and took the stairs back down towards the hallways two at a time. If Corvan had been called away to the small hall, no traffic would be going through the area. Palace staff were forbidden from accessing it without approval. It was the perfect place to make a person disappear.

That old man had better not get himself killed before I show up.

Golmin skidded around a corner and took the steps down again to the palace's second level, then opened a secret shortcut to the ground level which put him right by the small hall. He burst through the doors with his sword drawn and visor down.

"Come in, Captain. You're expected." Wormwood's voice rang out from the far end. Golmin raised his weapon and scanned the room. A dozen guards surrounded him, with another pair on either side who circled behind him to block his escape. One more guard held Master Corvan, who stood beside the meeting table with his hands tied behind his back. Lord Wormwood sat at the head of the table, sipping from a gold cup, with Lord Karl Highett standing just behind him.

"You know, I had my suspicions when I first caught you patrolling the cellars," the Master of Coin continued. "You might have fooled me, had you not tried to redirect our conversation. Lord Karl didn't believe me until we caught you again tonight."

Golmin felt his heart plummet. They'd known all along, and now he and Corvan had played right into their trap. "Let the old man go."

"No, no, you do not make the demands here." Wormwood set down his cup and leaned forward, pressing his fingertips together. "This is what will happen. In a moment, I will call out for your arrest on the charge of treason. You and this old fool here..." he waved a hand at Master Corvan, "...will stand trial in front of all of Belanore's nobility, facing the High Court itself. They will find you guilty and sentence you both to death."

"The only act of treason here is yours," Golmin spat.

Wormwood held up a finger. "Ah, but I'm not done yet. I am, of course, willing to let you both go...*if* you swear allegiance to Ettrias and recognise him as your rightful king. We will forget any of this ever happened, and you can both go on your merry way."

"I'll do it!" Corvan squeaked. "I swear my allegiance to Prince Ettrias. Please, whatever you do, do not kill me."

Golmin scoffed. "Swear my allegiance to Ettrias? My allegiance is to the Crown. To Queen Talin, as it should be."

"The queen helped frame her brother for murder, yet you still defend her?" Wormwood asked.

"The queen had no part in any of that."

"Yet Ettrias must bear the consequences. You would really turn your back on him again? I thought you were close."

Golmin hesitated. Join Ettrias...and condemn Red Wolf. Commit treason. Hedge his bets on a coup that might fail. Was that something he really wanted?

The time has come to choose. I'm sorry, Ettrias.

"Whatever our relationship may be, whatever it may have been, I cannot condone his actions now," he said. "He hired assassins to kill his own sister and now plots treason against the Crown. I will play no part in it."

"Oh, I grow tired of this," Lord Karl said dismissively. "Arrest him, and let's go."

One of the guards took Golmin's sword while another slapped manacles around his wrists.

"Traitors, all of you," he growled.

Wormwood only smiled. "When all this is over, Captain, the only act of treason will have been yours."

Despite the length of the war and the effectiveness of Kies Tor's western front, Talin had never seen the Western Forts up close. Now, at the foot of the wall that marked the border of the safe zone she'd been living in all this time, she finally saw what it was that made the Forts legendary. The wall was made of massive stone slabs, towering at least fifty feet into the air and giving no purchase for climbing on either side. Stairs every few hundred metres led to the top of the wall, with watchtowers placed next to them to give a good view of the land beyond. Gateways were carved into the wall, too, blocked with heavy iron doors and laden with traps. Beyond the wall ran the Calegate River, which branched off the White River in the north and ran south past the border into Astaria. The only way across was through the drawbridge crossings built into the wall.

"No wonder this defence has lasted so long," Talin said as they led their horses through the village just before the Forts, keeping their heads down and hoods up to avoid being recognised by any off-duty soldiers lazing around. Ettrias posed as a wounded villager who had been ambushed by outlaws. Red Wolf took him to find the town healer while Talin and Ashera were left to sign in at the inn and look for a tavern to have their supper.

"Red Wolf always told me stories about the Forts," the girl said as they led their horses through the town square. "I never thought I'd get to see them up close. Are all the stories true?"

"Most of them, yes," Talin said. "My grandfather, King Gandar, assumed the Hellhounds would try to cut through the White River from the west, at the edge of the Draconian Empire, and take Belanore from there. He ordered this built to stop their advance if they ever got through. But they found that breaking our northern lines was easier."

"Oh," Ashera said. "Then we'll run into Hellhounds once we pass the Forts?"

"Yes, though I'm more worried about passing the Forts themselves," Talin said. "We can hardly say we're planning to take a stroll in Hell-hound territory."

"Red Wolf mentioned bribing the guards with money," Ashera said.

"I remember." Talin sighed. Much as she hated to admit it, her bodyguard had been right; if word got out about her travelling past the Forts, it would only serve to confirm the rumours of her fleeing Belanore and leaving her people behind. She would lose all support from her people.

"Either way," she continued, "we cannot delay here. The sooner we cross the border, the better."

They found their way to the tavern by following the sound of music and the smell of food and took a table for four in the corner of the establishment. Talin noted a sign outside on their way in advertising some kind of 'dance night'. Ettrias and Red Wolf joined them not long after, the former explaining that he was well enough to leave tomorrow as long as he remained on horseback.

"The rumours have spread even here," Red Wolf said as he nursed his mug of ale. "They're getting worse, too. Wilder. Some say you've turned on your people completely and struck some kind of bargain with the Hellhounds to save yourself. Others are saying you never intended to lead your people, that you've been plotting to abscond for months with all the kingdom's gold."

Talin hissed through her teeth. "How could these rumours have spread so quickly and so far? My council wouldn't have allowed information to leak out, especially not...Wormwood and Corvan..."

Do you really trust Wormwood?

She shook her head. "Anyway, we'll rest up here and leave tomorrow morning. It'll be nice to unwind after so long on the road."

"I don't suppose I could convince you to stay until the full moon is past?" Red Wolf said. "Move out once the Hellhounds' strength is past their peak?"

"You know we can't stay," Talin said.

Towards the centre of the tavern, folk had already left their seats to dance to the bard's music. Some of them had even jumped onto nearby tables to make room for more people to join.

"Seems like a regular tavern event here," Red Wolf said. Ashera looked to him hopefully, and he gave a nod, sending her into the throng of dancing townsfolk.

"Looks fun," Talin said.

"Perhaps you'd care to join them, my queen." Red Wolf stood and offered her a hand.

"Oh, I...don't think...this is for me..." she began, but he was already pulling her to her feet. "One dance. Just one."

The two of them shouldered their way into the throng of people and onto a table as the music started up again. The crowd burst into cheers. Talin recognised the tune, too; it was the classic Highlander song *Raven Mountain*. Red Wolf offered her a small smile as the tune picked up. Despite all the royal balls and parties she'd attended, this type of dancing wasn't something she was used to. The table was rickety at best and threatened to break or topple any second, but Red Wolf's firm grip on her hand helped her keep her balance. At one point, she thought she saw something flicker across his eyes—sadness, maybe—but it was gone in a flash and she decided that she'd imagined it. She was out of breath by the time the song ended, though the thrill was enough to make her agree to a second dance. Talin glanced over at Ettrias at one point and discovered that he was singing along too, cup of ale in hand.

"Well, that was fun," Red Wolf said once they'd taken their seats again. He ordered another flagon of ale and leaned back.

"Yes...I suppose it was." Talin smiled. For the first time in years, she felt free to do as she pleased, without having to consider council meetings or news of the war or palace etiquette. This life was so much simpler, so much more...free. She met Red Wolf's gaze and smiled again. He grinned back at her, but it didn't quite reach his eyes.

"Oh, wow, would you look at the time," Ettrias said with an exaggerated yawn. "I'm going to head off to the inn and get some sleep. Ashera, come on, let's go."

"I want to stay," Ashera said. "There's music here. And dancing."

Ettrias waved his hand absentmindedly. "Suit yourself. Red Wolf's in charge of you anyway. Goodnight, everyone. Don't go staying up too late." He stood and hobbled off while Ashera disappeared back into the crowd to dance.

"Not going back out there?" Talin asked.

"It's too...loud." Red Wolf offered nothing more.

"I understand. I think." Talin took a sip of ale. "Though I do wish there were parties like this in the palace. None of that etiquette and protocol everyone must follow. Just...good folk dancing on tables and singing songs."

"Perhaps I could convince you to stay a few extra nights to enjoy their company." Red Wolf nodded at the bard and the boisterous crowd.

"We cannot stay. You and I both know that," Talin said.

"Well, then, I think I'll need to take you to a good tavern once all this is over, my queen," Red Wolf said. "Palace etiquette be damned."

Talin laughed. "I look forward to it." She looked at the table and realised just how close their hands were, and quickly reached for her mug. Red Wolf, thankfully, didn't seem to notice.

"Do you have a plan for how to get past the Forts?" he asked.

"I think bribing a guard may be our only option," Talin said. "Even if we could somehow sneak past the wall without drawing attention, we still need to cross the river. We can hardly operate the drawbridge by ourselves."

"Very well, then," Red Wolf said. "I take it that means we'll be leaving early in the morning."

"Any later, and we will never make it across the border before the full moon," Talin said.

"Hmm." Red Wolf seemed lost in thought. "I think it's time we retired to bed too. We'll need to be well-rested for tomorrow."

"I suppose you're right." Talin finished her drink and stood. Red Wolf found Ashera in the midst of the crowd, and the three of them left the tavern and its partygoers behind, with plans to meet at the wall before dawn. Red Wolf took the room next to Talin's that night and sent Ashera to claim the spare bed in the queen's room.

The four of them rose early the next morning, well before the sun, and met at the gate where a lone guard stood on watch duty. In a hushed voice, Talin explained that they urgently needed passage across, forking over a hefty sum of yarii to ensure the man's cooperation. He let them through as soon as he pocketed the coin. They travelled as far as they could before stopping to make camp in an open field under a star-speckled sky, while the waxing moon stared down from above, watching them silently. Talin glanced at Red Wolf at one point and found him staring at it as if in a trance.

They saw the full extent of the Hellhounds' damage in the morning. Their path took them through what had once been a small village near the White River, though there was hardly anything left to distinguish the buildings from one another. Everywhere they walked, Talin could see charred remains and rubble, and what was left of the villagers was no longer recognisable. The Hellhounds had torn through this place with no mercy and razed it to the ground.

"Do they...?" Talin began, then thought better of it and stopped.

"Eat the bodies?" Red Wolf finished, almost as if reading her mind. "Yes."

"I was hoping you wouldn't answer that," Talin muttered. The storm season had turned the village into a flooded mess; it was difficult to move two feet in any direction without kicking something under the mud and water. She sorely hoped she wasn't disturbing the bones of the dead.

They let the horses rest here for a while; the creatures seemed glad of the clean puddles left behind after the last storm, giving them a chance to drink. Red Wolf sparred with Ashera to sharpen her sword skills while Talin practised her magic. Ettrias looked at the three of them forlornly, nursing his bandaged leg. The girl eventually yielded under Red Wolf's brutal offensive, and Talin found herself now on the receiving end of her bodyguard's training.

"Control the fight. Do not let your opponent lead you where they want you to go," he said between swings. Talin could only block and hope to recover quickly enough to block again. She was growing better at noticing gaps in Red Wolf's defence, and even wondered how easy it would be for a skilled attacker to find those gaps and exploit them, but the thought quickly fled her mind every time she was forced to parry one of Red Wolf's blows.

There would be no time for an attacker to find a gap, she thought. *Not when they're so busy parrying blows this powerful.*

Nevertheless, she ducked under one of his wide swings and drove her blade towards his chest. He overbalanced but recovered in an instant. Talin jumped back to avoid a counterattack. He followed her movements neatly and tripped her when she tried to feint.

"Not bad. But your feints are too obvious," he said, helping her back up. "I could see what you're doing from a mile away. Whatever you do in battle, you must commit to it."

"Has anyone ever actually beaten you?" Talin asked.

"Your brother. Once." Red Wolf nodded at Ettrias. "I was challenged to a duel in the dungeons after his trial. He was...understandably angry."

"But you didn't kill him," Talin said, looking at her brother.

Ettrias exchanged looks with Red Wolf. "No. I...I couldn't. I suppose I still saw him as a friend then."

"Times have changed." Red Wolf shook his head. "But it doesn't do any good to dwell on the past. We should get moving. The full moon is tonight. We must get across the border before it rises."

"Yes, let's move out," Talin said, mounting her horse. Red Wolf helped Ettrias up before getting his own horse.

"I'll scout out the area, if it's all the same to you, my queen," he said. "Clear the path ahead, so to speak. I will return in the morning."

"We should stick together," Talin protested. "I won't have you make the road safer only to get yourself killed."

"You needn't worry about me. I have my magic to defend myself," Red Wolf said. "I will return by morning. I promise."

"Red Wolf..." Talin began. "No, I am giving you an order. You will remain with us."

"My queen—"

"You should let him go," Ettrias cut in. "He can clear the way for us if there is a threat."

"I..." Talin sighed. Much as she hated to admit it, Ettrias knew Red Wolf better than she did, and if he was confident in her bodyguard's abilities, she knew she also had to have faith. "Very well. But I expect you back tomorrow, first thing."

Red Wolf dismounted. "Best not to risk the horse. The Hellhounds have a particular taste for horsemeat." His horse gave a panicked *whinny*. "Don't worry. You'll be safe with Ettrias." He handed the prince the reins and took off at a fast jog.

"How is he expecting to outpace us on foot?" Talin asked.

"Shortcut through the woods, no doubt," Ettrias said, a little too hastily. "Come nightfall, we should be safe, don't worry."

"It's Red Wolf I'm worried about," Talin confessed.

"He'll be fine. Have faith."

They set up camp that night by an ancient log just off the road and ate cold rations. With the full moon rising fast, Talin hadn't dared to light a fire, fearing the Hellhounds would smell it from miles away and track them down. Ettrias entertained them with stories of his time in exile, travelling the Fae lands in the south as far as the Silver Ocean. As always, Ashera had an endless stream of questions, and Ettrias tried his utmost to answer them. Talin kept watch.

"Did you really cross the mountains into the far north?" Ashera asked.

"Not far. The road through the Northern Range was long and treacherous, and the climate was far too cold for me." Ettrias grinned. "I'd like to go back someday, though. See all that snow again."

Talin caught a flash of movement in the trees and reached for her weapon. Seeing her move, Ettrias jumped to his feet and drew his own sword. Ashera did likewise, and the three of them faced the forest together.

"What was it?" Ettrias asked.

"I'm not sure," Talin said. "It looked like...something with fur."

"Hellhounds. They're circling us. We need to run." Ettrias grabbed her hand and half-led, half-dragged her to the horses. He helped Ashera on and hauled himself up with some effort, just as a chilling howl cut through the air, soon echoed by a dozen more. Talin felt a shiver go through her as she mounted her steed and followed her brother and Ashera at a gallop.

"If they're here, then Red Wolf—" she began.

"We can't worry about him right now!" Ettrias snapped. "Our priority is to stay alive!"

"I knew we shouldn't have split up," Talin said.

"Get mad at him all you want later. Right now, we need to— Woah!" Ettrias ducked just in time as an enormous, black shape leapt over him. It crashed into the bushes and shook itself off, and Talin caught her first glimpse of a Hellhound. It was a massive, wolf-like creature, at least the size of a bear, with savage eyes the colour of burning coals and a row of vicious teeth. Its claws looked razor-sharp as if sharpened for a kill. Talin spurred her horse on, but the creature bounded after them, pouncing again and landing a bite on the horse's flank. It cried out in pain and threw her. She had just enough time to break her fall to avoid landing on her neck. The Hellhound brought the horse down with no effort and began to tear into it.

Talin knew she had no hope of fighting the creature on her own.

She took the opportunity while it was distracted with the horse and sprinted. Ahead, she saw Ettrias slow, glance back and curse before wheeling around to grab her.

"Ashera, follow the road, don't stop!" he yelled. The girl continued on her own and disappeared soon enough. Ettrias was halfway to her now, and then Talin could pull herself onto the horse...

A second Hellhound sprang from the bushes on her left and tackled her to the ground, jaws clamping down over her shoulder. Blinding pain shot through her arm as its teeth dug in deep. The creature made a low growl in its throat.

Oh, gods, I'm going to die here.

Flat on her back, her shoulder burning, she stared down the Hellhound that had attacked her. Its jaws dripped with blood—her blood, maybe—as it jumped on top of her, ready to make the kill. Through the agony and confusion, Talin saw Ettrias' blade flash, cleaving off the head of the Hellhound. He was about to reach down and help her up when another Hellhound appeared, forcing his horse back as it advanced. Clutching her shoulder, Talin managed to roll over enough to free her dagger from underneath her and tugged it free of its sheath.

"Ettrias, *go*!" she hissed. Mustering what strength she could, she slashed the Hellhound in the leg. To her dismay, the wound healed almost immediately as the beast turned its attention to her. Ettrias slashed at his left and managed to stop a fourth Hellhound from devouring his horse. Too weak to conjure up another swing, Talin looked at the Hellhound advancing on her and resigned herself to her fate.

A blur of red fur and claws launched out of the bushes with a feral snarl and into the Hellhound, sending it crashing aside. Talin's vision swam as her mind grappled with what was happening. The newcomer—yet another Hellhound—tore out its brother's throat and pounced on top of her. She gazed up, into its eyes, and recognised them. That hypnotic molten gold couldn't belong to anyone else.

"Red Wolf...?" she croaked. The creature cocked its head a little at that.

It's him, he's one of them, he's...

The Hellhound attacking Ettrias dropped its advance and turned on the newcomer instead. The one feasting on Talin's horse stopped its meal to stalk towards its red-furred brethren. The newcomer responded by baring its teeth in a silent snarl and approaching the challengers. Ettrias used the moment to reach down and haul Talin onto his horse.

"Hang in there," her brother said. "You better not die on me before we get to the border!"

Talin wanted to respond, but every word seemed to require too much effort to vocalise, and she gave up. Looking back, she was just in time to witness the red-furred creature swipe at one of the black Hellhounds. It drew back with a whimper while another lunged to tackle its opponent. The two of them rolled off the road and into a bush in a blur of movement and fur.

Red Wolf... I see where you got your name...

"Talin? Talin, remember what I said—no dying on me," Ettrias' voice sounded distant to her ears. "Hold on!"

Can't...

Talin closed her eyes and let blissful nothingness swallow her up.

R ed Wolf was in her dreams.

In one, he was a Hellhound, staring down at her as he opened his jaws to tear out her throat. In another, he was himself again, but they were duelling to the death and her blows had no effect on him. His visor was lowered, too, revealing only the golden wolf eyes that marked him as an outsider.

"...she...alright?"

"It's too early to tell. I'll keep an eye on her condition..."

She eventually saw herself as a child, playing hide-and-seek with Ettrias in the palace. She peeked out from under her father's bed as her brother breezed right past the royal chambers, failing to notice the open door, and stifled a giggle. A pair of boots soon came to a halt in front of her, and her father bent down to look at her.

"Shh, I'm hiding from Ettrias," she whispered. Arnas smiled and left her to it.

"I'll find you, Talin!" her brother's voice rang out from the hallway. "I always find you. You can't hide forever!"

Talin retreated further under the bed. Ettrias soon doubled back to the royal chambers, and she watched as he searched the wardrobe, then behind the curtains. Sighing loudly, he turned to leave, and Talin had to stifle another giggle.

"Gotcha!" Ettrias appeared behind her, catching her by surprise, and she let out a high-pitched squeal. Her brother burst into a fit of laughter.

"That wasn't funny!" she protested, but soon joined him and started laughing too. "How do you always find me?"

I'm your brother.

Talin jolted awake with a start and a groan as searing pain shot through her wounded shoulder, sending agonising needles down her arm and back towards her neck. She flexed her fingers gingerly and, to her relief, discovered that she could still do so.

Being asleep was better. Everything hurts.

She turned her head to take in the room. A single window occupied the wall opposite her, with a potted plant on the windowsill. She was in a narrow bed, covered with a blanket, though she had no recollection of ever arriving at a village or inn. Her shoulder was heavily bandaged. Even so, she could see patches of crimson that marked where the Hellhound's teeth had sunk in. And sitting by her bed in a wooden chair...

"Red Wolf?"

He looked the same as ever, sporting tousled hair and days of stubble and dressed in his spare set of travelling clothes. He looked different enough with facial hair that Talin almost didn't believe it was him, but there was never any mistaking his golden eyes. He said nothing but merely grunted an affirmative.

"You..." Talin sat up with a groan and tried to scramble to her feet, only to be defeated by a rush of nausea. Red Wolf held up a hand, motioning for her to stop, as he averted his gaze.

"You're, uh, you're not dressed," he said, and dropped his hand. Talin looked down and realised that she had, indeed, been stripped down to her undergarments. She lay back down awkwardly and covered herself up.

"You're one of *them*," she hissed.

A flash of anger flickered across Red Wolf's eyes, gone so quickly she almost thought she'd imagined it.

"I am *not* one of those things," he said softly. "And I would be grateful if you made no further comments of the sort."

"Then *explain*. What are you?" Talin demanded. It dawned on her that she may have been captured. "Where is this? Some kind of Hellhound camp?"

Red Wolf winced. "Nothing of the sort. We made it across the border. You're in a Draconian stronghold, quite safe from Hellhounds." He sighed. "As for...what I am, well, truthfully, I don't even know."

"But you..." Talin grimaced as another wave of pain lanced through her shoulder. "You looked like them."

"I know." Red Wolf stood and handed her a small vial filled with clear liquid. "I was told to give you this when you woke. It should help with the pain."

Talin took the potion and downed it in one gulp. "At least...explain...why you looked like one of those things."

Red Wolf sat back down. There was a beat before he opened his mouth to explain. "When the Hellhounds first invaded Kies Tor, four years before you were born, they kidnapped Highlander children for their mages and alchemists to experiment on," he said. "Their goal was to create some kind of...half-breed—Hellhounds who could disguise themselves perfectly as an elf and infiltrate the kingdom from within. The problem was that children...are fragile. None of them survived. Except me."

"So, they...gave you their healing and shapeshifting powers?"

"Essentially, yes. They were almost successful. I can heal like them. I have heightened senses like them. As the moon waxes, I grow faster and stronger like them. The only thing they could not figure out was how to control my shapeshifting. I'm cursed to turn into a wolf every full moon with the Hellhounds' instincts and thirst for blood. When I shift back, I have no memory of what occurred the previous night, no notion of who I might have attacked or hurt."

"You escaped?" Talin asked.

Red Wolf looked uncomfortable. "Sort of. I was sent to Belanore under the guise of a young squire looking to secure a place in the Royal Guard. My mission was to assassinate the royal family and bring about an end to their reign."

"You're a Hellhound *assassin*?" Talin exclaimed.

"I was supposed to be," Red Wolf said. "Instead of working for the people who turned me into a monster, I turned my back on them entirely to serve the Crown. When I first rode north with Arnas as lord commander, the Hellhounds called me a traitor. I was told never to return to my pack, and if any of the hordes in Kies Tor saw me, they were to kill on sight."

Talin's mind spun. With the number of secrets her bodyguard had kept from her this past month, she wondered why she trusted him at all; he clearly didn't trust *her* enough to share anything he deemed important.

"First, you fail to tell me about your plans with that assassin. Then you lie to me about meeting Ettrias at the inn. Then I find out you lied to the *High Court* and kept the truth of my father's corruption from me. Now it turns out I never even knew who you *were* until today." Talin scoffed. "And you have the gall to tell *me* not to trust Wormwood. We are only here because I listened to your initial advice and sent word to the Drakels! Am I to believe that was a lie too?"

"I have never lied to you about anything else, or kept anything else from you," Red Wolf said. "On my word as lord commander and as a knight of Kies Tor."

"You're a disgrace to your bloody knighthood."

"Perhaps I am."

Talin let out a long breath. "Who else knows about your powers?"

"I...hardly think that's relevant—"

"Red Wolf."

"Master Corvan was the first to know, then Captain Golmin. And...Ettrias," Red Wolf said.

"Ettrias," Talin scoffed. "My own brother knows your little secrets but not me?"

"He was never meant to know. We duelled to the death after his trial. He tried to kill me," Red Wolf said.

Talin only responded with a glare.

Red Wolf was silent for a while. "You should dress and head downstairs if you feel well enough," he finally said. "The Drakels who saved you have a proposal for us and wish to speak to you."

"Very well, let them know I'll be down shortly," Talin said.

"As my queen commands." Red Wolf stood and backed out of the room, leaving her alone. She struggled out of bed and into the spare set of clothes left for her: simple trousers and a woollen tunic. Clutching her shoulder, she made her way out of the room and down the stairs. Ettrias was at the bottom to escort her.

"I'm glad you're alright," he said gruffly.

Talin followed him down a well-lit corridor decorated with paintings and sculptures. "Do I hear *relief* from the man who was trying to have me assassinated last month?" she teased.

"These Drakels who saved you claim to be the rebel group awaiting your delegation," Ettrias said, quickly changing the topic. "Their leader, Kadis, is the one who wrote to you, or so I'm told. When we crossed the border, we stumbled into a skirmish between his scouts and the insurgents who took over. They'd set up a small camp and had been waiting for us for days. The healers were able to stabilise your condition at the camp, and we rode back to their base of operations as soon as possible for proper treatment."

"Where's Ashera?" Talin asked.

Ettrias sighed. "None of the Drakels saw her before we showed up. They believe she may have been captured by the insurgents if she followed the same road as us."

"We must find her, then!" Talin said. "If she's been captured, they'll want information from her—"

Ettrias nodded. "That's...where the Drakels' proposal comes in. I suppose Kadis is a better candidate to tell you about it, though."

They stopped outside a set of double doors that swung inward to reveal a war room. A massive map of the Draconian Empire took up the table in the middle, covered with various pins and flags. Drakels surrounded the map, dressed in finely crafted armour and cloaks. At the head of the table was a tall Drakel with deep green scales and gold pauldrons on his armour, and an intricate helm that showed him to be in charge. Red Wolf stood to his left.

"Your Majesty, welcome. I must admit, we were not expecting the queen herself to arrive at our borders, much less so in such a dire condition." The Drakel leader dipped his dragon-like head respectfully, though there was a mischievous twinkle in his eye. Looking more closely, Talin could see that some of the Drakels had horns of various shapes and sizes, including their leader.

"I am told your people were the ones who saved me, sir," Talin said. "I owe you my life and my gratitude."

"Come. Join us." The Drakel leader nodded at the other end of the table, closest to Talin, and she took up a spot there with Ettrias beside her. "My name is Kadis Kilo Karrillius, the third of my name. My father is Emperor Fillius Kaeso Karrillius the fourth and the rightful ruler of the Draconian Empire. I will spare you the rest of the formalities, but what you do need to know is that he was overthrown by the insurgency at the end of our civil war twelve years ago. He is still missing. We do not know if he's alive or dead, and without any leads, it's impossible to scour the entire Draconian Empire to find him. I was driven into hiding here at the den, with the last of my allies and associates. We have been trying to strike back at these insurgents ever since." He paused before continuing. "Red Wolf has already explained your situation in detail. I can tell you now that the insurgents have no interest in treaties. They despise those who are not part of the Draconian Empire."

"I've been told you have a proposal for me," Talin said.

"I do." Kadis flattened his clawed hands on the table. "My father is a good man, and I know he will honour whatever agreement we come to. If my rebels can restore him to the throne, I will see to it that Kies Tor is provided with the finest legions our empire can offer."

Talin lifted an eyebrow. "Why do I sense more terms?"

"Naturally." Kadis dipped his head. "You elves are excellent archers, from what I know, and your brother is one of the best swordsmen I've seen. We could use your help in our final push against the insurgents."

"Our help for an entire army? It seems an incredibly small price to pay," Talin said.

"A member of your party has been captured by the insurgents," Kadis said. "As it happens, I am looking to free an informant held by these same people. With your help and your bodyguard's abilities, it should be easy. You need an army; I need specialists. It seems a fair deal to me."

Talin was still suspicious. "All the same, I'd like to discuss this with my companions before we reach an agreement."

"By all means," Kadis said. "Take what time you need."

Talin pulled Ettrias and Red Wolf aside, out of earshot of the Drakels. Her bodyguard crossed his arms and said nothing.

"I can't be the only one who thinks this is too easy," she said in a low voice.

"It does seem that way," Ettrias admitted. "Our cooperation for an army when Kadis restores his father to the throne? Besides, we don't even know when that's going to happen."

"But if they are telling the truth and we go to the insurgents alone, we may be captured and killed," Talin pointed out.

"These Drakels saved your life," Red Wolf said. "And they say they can help us find Ashera. We owe them our trust."

"Oh please, your opinion on trust is—" Talin hissed through her teeth and held back the rest of the sentence. "Regardless, you're right—I owe them for saving me, at least."

"I say we work with them, at least for now," Ettrias said. "They were willing to take you in and treat you despite not knowing who you were at first and when they could have easily turned us away."

Talin sighed. "Very well. We'll ally ourselves with these Drakels."

They returned to the war room and relayed their decision to Kadis. The Draconian prince gave a nod and pointed at the map table.

"My advisors and I have been discussing the way forward," he said. "But first, we'd like to familiarise you all with the area around the den, given that you'll be staying here for the foreseeable future. As for my spy and your squire, I have reason to believe they are being held in El'Vane, our capital, two days' ride from here." Kadis took a stick and jabbed it at the capital on the map. "Getting inside may be difficult, however. The insurgents have every gate guarded day and night. Their leader is a man named Ve'Tehll. My informants on the inside have told me that he has installed numerous defensive mechanisms in the gate and along the walls. A direct assault will be impossible."

"We'll have to infiltrate the capital covertly then," Talin said.

"I agree—it's the only way," Kadis said. "If Your Majesty is up to it, we have time today to show you the den and its surrounds. El'Vane will have to wait until you are recovered in case the insurgents put up a fight. For now, perhaps you'd like some breakfast."

Talin realised she was hungry. "Breakfast would be wonderful."

Kadis motioned for a servant. "Take the queen and her friends to the dining hall. Breakfast should still be on, but if not, tell the cooks to make whatever they wish to eat."

The servant nodded and hurried to Talin. "This way, Your Majesty."

They had breakfast in a large dining hall near the front of the den without Red Wolf, who remained in the war room to help Kadis plan. Talin couldn't help but feel Ashera's absence; she had grown fond of the girl over the past month. And despite her youth, she had proven herself more than capable.

Red Wolf, on the other hand...

"My queen."

Gods, not now.

Talin looked up to find her bodyguard standing by the edge of the table, towering over her despite keeping a respectable distance.

"I wished to apologise for deceiving you—" he began.

"For both our sakes, we will not speak of this right now," Talin said. "In the meantime, I think it best if you stayed out of my way."

Red Wolf said nothing but bowed and left the hall. Talin stared at her food for a few moments before pouring herself more coffee.

"Much as I hate to admit it, Red Wolf isn't our enemy," Ettrias said in between mouthfuls of sausage and bread. "Trust me. He hates those Hellhounds almost as much as they all hate us."

Talin scoffed. "I find it ironic that he tells me not to trust Wormwood, yet he keeps more secrets from me than the rest of my council combined."

"He was worried about you," Ettrias said. "For all the...unwise decisions he's made...well...saying he's not a terrible person is a bit of a stretch for me. But I will admit that he'd never willingly do anything to hurt you. He cares about you too much."

"He..." Talin's voice trailed off. "Don't be ridiculous."

Ettrias shrugged and went back to his meal.

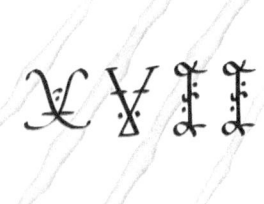

How long has it been? One day? Three?

Golmin had lost count.

They had thrown him into solitary confinement in the lower level of the dungeon, where the cells were underground and no light penetrated the cold, stone walls. He guessed it was past the full moon by now. If Red Wolf and the queen were still alive, they should be out of danger.

For now.

With no way out of his cell and no way to warn them of Wormwood's takeover, he could only pray to the gods and hope. He paced the cell once more and contemplated his options. No doubt Wormwood and Highett would visit eventually and convince him to pledge his loyalty to Ettrias, and he could simply do as they wished. But he knew that Red Wolf would never do such a thing. Out of respect for the man,

Golmin decided to do the same. At least he'd be executed with some sense of honour left in him.

I could pretend to join their cause. Do as Corvan had done.

He was not Corvan. To him, an empty pledge made him no better than Wormwood. Pledging his loyalty to Ettrias only to betray him a second time.

What about working with Ettrias? Absolve him of his crimes, put him on the throne.

Golmin felt like he was going in circles. Ettrias or Red Wolf. The man he loved or his closest friend. He cursed Red Wolf for putting them all in this situation and Ettrias for plotting something like this.

Some hours later, after he'd been given his usual serve of prison slop, Wormwood visited him, escorted by half a dozen royal guards. Golmin contemplated making a break for it—the guards, his own men, might support him. Then again, they might have been corrupted by the scheming coin-master. He decided it wasn't worth the risk.

"Don't even think about it," Wormwood said. "These men will cut you down without hesitation. Money talks, you see." He set his torch into a socket in the wall and considered Golmin. "Seeing you brought so low...well, I could almost rejoice. Changed your mind yet?"

"I hope the seven hells takes you, *abijo*."

Wormwood huffed a humourless laugh. "I thought you might be stubborn. But think about it, Captain. You can help fix things here. Put Ettrias on the throne, as he deserves. Where he should be."

"Not like this," Golmin said, and offered nothing more.

"Excellent. Your trial will be held in the morning, your execution probably later that day. Enjoy your final moments while you can," Wormwood said, retrieving his torch from the bracket. "I believe we're done here."

"Someone will stop you," Golmin said. "Talin has always been the rightful queen, and there will always be someone who recognises that."

"I look forward to killing them too," Wormwood said, and spun on his heel. Golmin watched his torchlight fade down the hallway.

He must have fallen asleep at some point, because it was cold when he woke and water was dripping into his cell from a crack in the ceiling. He sat up and scooted away from it. A sliver of light curved around the corner at the end of the corridor and grew, moving closer and closer. Golmin got to his feet groggily. Was it time? Had Wormwood's guards come to take him to his rigged trial? He had some time to prepare, and silently prayed to whatever gods were watching before readying himself to tackle the guards as soon as they opened the door.

He realised he was mistaken, however. The man carrying the torch was none other than Master Corvan, followed by a certain Lord Cassius Highett, who had only shown his face briefly to warn them about the thief.

"Master. M'lord." He approached the bars.

"We have a plan," Lord Cassius said.

"Oh? Let's hear it, then," Golmin said.

"Since your arrest, Corvan and I have been discussing how best to contact the queen," Lord Cassius said. "Sending a bird is impossible without knowing her location. However, I believe with someone skilled enough in tracking, we might be able to follow her trail and deliver a message in person."

"And I suppose that's where I come in," Golmin said.

"You once served Lord Whitehall as a scout and light infantryman. You are the best tracker we know," Corvan said.

"I'm the only tracker you know. How do you plan to get me out?"

"Everything has been arranged." Lord Cassius turned a key in the lock and let the door swing open. "I take it you know your way around the secret passageways in the palace?"

"Aye, I do," Golmin said. He stepped out of his cell, and Lord Cassius quickly passed him a bundle of weapons and travel clothing.

"Once you are out of the city, you must ride for the Western Forts," the spymaster said as they walked. "I have a contact at each crossing who can get you past them and into the Hellhounds' territory beyond; only tell the soldiers that I sent you. Find Queen Talin in the Draconian lands and tell her what has happened here. Warn her and Red Wolf. We will try to delay Wormwood's plans here, but she must know that half her council intends to overthrow her."

"It takes weeks to get to the Draconian lands," Golmin said. "The queen and her escort left on horseback. How can I possibly catch up to them?"

"I've arranged for a horse to be left outside the northern gate, right by the entrance to the secret passageway," Cassius explained. "You'll have no trouble finding it."

At the top of the stairs, they spied half a dozen on-duty royal guards, playing a game of Tavern Cards in the corner out of the way. Corvan passed what appeared to be an empty vial to Lord Cassius, who threw it against the wall closest to the guards. They scrambled to their feet, drawing their weapons, and Golmin reached for his sword.

There was a beat.

The six guards crumpled soundlessly.

"Black Byur flower," Corvan said softly. "They'll be unconscious for a few hours."

"As long as you haven't killed them." Golmin didn't like moving against his own men, but desperate times called for desperate measures.

The three of them stopped in front of a plain section of wall in the hallway, and Corvan pulled on an empty torch bracket to reveal a sliding door built into the stonework.

"Go, now, Captain," the old healer said. "And may the gods favour you on your journey."

Golmin ducked into the tunnel without hesitation. "I will find the queen. You have my word that I'll not fail you."

"Our future depends on it." Corvan released the torch bracket, and the door slammed shut again.

Right. No pressure, Rufus. No pressure at all.

Golmin took a deep breath and descended further into the passageway.

XVIII

"I must thank you for this past week, Master Celio," Talin said, as one of Kadis' healers finished cutting her stitches free and wrapped fresh bandages around her shoulder. "Were it not for your care, I'm not sure I would be here today."

"You were fortunate to receive medical attention when you did," Celio said. "Any later and your injuries may very well have been lethal."

"All the same, thank you," Talin said.

Celio smiled. "Only doing my job, Majesty. And don't strain your shoulder too much. If you must train, I would recommend only light sparring."

They parted ways there, with the Drakel healer moving off to tend to whatever other patients required his attention. Talin headed outside for some fresh air.

Red Wolf was in the middle of the training yard to her left when she made her way down the path leading to the front doors, sparring with a Drakel almost as tall as himself. She watched as the two of them danced back and forth across the yard, training blades ringing sharply against each other whenever they made contact. Ettrias sat on a bench not far off and looked to be enjoying the show. Downhill, at the edge of the forest, a team of archers honed their sharpshooting skills at the range. Talin's fingers itched to pick up a bow and join them, but she knew she'd only hurt her shoulder.

She brought her attention back to the yard just as Red Wolf tripped his opponent neatly and sent him crashing to the ground. His sword was at the Drakel's throat a moment later.

"Who's next?" He grinned at the rest of the gathered swordsmen. Talin made her way to the bench and sat down beside her brother.

"Here to watch the show?" Ettrias asked. "Or are you here for Red Wolf?"

"Both, I suppose." Talin sighed. "Part of me simply wants to forgive him and be done with it all. The other part is still upset that he's kept all these secrets."

"I suppose he hasn't yet told you *why* he went along with Father's plan," Ettrias said.

"No," Talin said.

"The way he tells it, Father found out about his powers," her brother said. "Kept it all a secret, even from him, until that ill-fated day he brought the Harrisons' bodies back to the palace. Father told him that framing me was absolutely necessary to ensure your safety when you became queen. When he protested, Father threatened to reveal his powers to *everyone* if he didn't comply."

"Father changed his tune awfully quickly when Red Wolf didn't cooperate," Talin said bitterly.

They were interrupted by a roar of approval from the Drakel soldiers when Kadis stepped into the duelling ring to face Red Wolf, who had now ditched his padded armour and tunic. From Talin's position, she could see a maze of scars across her bodyguard's torso and arms, far too neat to belong to any sword cut or battle wound.

"Are you sure you don't want the armour, sir?" Kadis asked with a grin. "Wouldn't want to beat you black and blue."

"That's only if you can get a hit in, sir," Red Wolf said.

Kadis laughed. "Don't come complaining to me afterwards!"

"Anyway," Ettrias continued, "the fact is, Kies Tor has never been welcoming to outsiders. Most would consider him the enemy if they knew what he was."

Talin looked towards her bodyguard again. "But if he told Corvan and Golmin..."

"He told them because they can cover for him," Ettrias said. "Besides, he tells Rufus everything."

Talin rubbed her eyes. "So, what? He kept it all a secret because...?"

Because he's different. Like Father kept my magic a secret from the rest of the world.

"I think that unlike you, dear sister, your bodyguard knows Kies Tor will never accept someone like him as an ordinary member of society," Ettrias said. "You've seen it too. Weavers on the street beaten and left for dead. The Crown's justice has never cared for outsiders like him, nor will it ever, unless the laws change."

"It doesn't justify *lying* to me," Talin said.

"Maybe not." Ettrias shrugged. "Either way, please at least talk to him. We've been here a week, and this awkward silence between you two is getting on my nerves."

Talin watched Red Wolf and Kadis dance across the ring for a few more minutes before the Drakel, out of breath and with a blunted sword at his throat, finally admitted defeat. He and Red Wolf shook hands before he stepped out of the ring.

"Your endurance is impressive, sir," he said with a breathless laugh. "All that back and forth, and you're not even breathing hard."

"I get that a lot," Red Wolf said. "Alright, who's next?" He scanned the gathered soldiers before his gaze landed on Talin.

"Good morning, my queen," he said.

Talin stood. "Spar with me," she said on impulse.

Red Wolf blinked.

"Come on. You've never been one to pass up an opportunity for training."

"I'm...not sure that's wise." His brow furrowed. "Not with your injury—"

"I have a perfectly functional right arm, and last I checked, an arming sword can be wielded in one hand," Talin said. She unsheathed her blade and approached. "Well?"

"Even so, I don't think—"

"Raise your sword, Lord Commander, and face me. Or are you too much of a chicken?" Talin grinned.

Red Wolf let out a long sigh. "As my queen commands." He waited until she'd taken her position opposite him before coming forward with his first swing. Talin parried it easily, expecting to meet strong resistance and instead finding very little. He'd clearly decided to go easy on her today. Thinking she would teach him not to make the mistake again, she pressed him, forcing him on the defensive as he knocked aside her strikes with his own blade. Finally, near the edge of the ring, she managed to slip under his lightning-fast parries and brought her sword around in an upward swing, intending to break his block.

She realised too late that she'd overestimated how much force to use. Her blade kept travelling, scoring a deep cut across Red Wolf's face. He stumbled away with a loud curse.

"*Orrlat*! I didn't mean to do that, I'm so sorry..." Talin began, all other thoughts fleeing from her mind.

Red Wolf straightened and met her gaze, and she saw, to her surprise and relief, the cut she'd inflicted was already closing. Soon it had vanished completely, leaving no trace.

Of course, he heals like the Hellhounds.

"That *tickled*." Her bodyguard swung at her again, and this time his brutal strikes were back. She managed to parry a handful before one of her parries met empty air instead. The cold bite of steel appeared against her neck from the other side as Red Wolf straightened his sword arm.

"Don't let your opponent lull you into a pattern," he said. "You won't be able to predict the fatal strike."

"I'll keep it in mind." Talin sheathed her blade. "Walk with me. And...put some clothes on."

Red Wolf snatched up his tunic from the edge of the arena and struggled into it as she moved off. "I was under the impression that you were avoiding me."

Talin let out a long breath. "I talked to Ettrias. He made some good points. I can't keep avoiding you like this."

Red Wolf grunted but said nothing.

"I think I understand why you kept your secrets," Talin continued. "Kies Tor has never been fond of outsiders, especially not...someone like you. I felt the same way about my magic. As if I didn't...belong as the queen...because I'm a Weaver. I know it's nothing like what you have to deal with, and I'm sorry that my father used the people's prejudice against you."

Red Wolf still didn't respond.

"I don't think you kept those things from me for any ill intent," Talin said. "But I want to be clear, Red Wolf. I don't want any more secrets between us. If you have anything else to tell me, do it now."

"No more secrets, my queen," Red Wolf said. "I promise."

They stopped at the cliff to the east of the den, which dropped into a valley below, stretching for miles into the distance. Talin was certain she would see the border of their two kingdoms if such a thing were visible.

"Can I ask you something?" she said.

"Certainly." Red Wolf dipped his head.

"The Hellhounds must have given you your name, yes? Red Wolf. What was your name before then?" Talin asked.

"They did." Red Wolf's brow creased. "If I had a name before I was Red Wolf, I do not remember it. My earliest memories are of the Hellhounds' experiments. I remember nothing of my childhood before then."

"I'm sorry."

"Why? You had no part in this."

"Oh, I don't know, I—" Talin began.

"You have no need to apologise. It's alright." Red Wolf averted his gaze and became intensely interested in admiring the scenery. Talin felt herself growing increasingly flustered in his presence, but leaving now, in the middle of a conversation, seemed rude.

"I'm not apologising, I'm only—oh, never mind. Why did you decide to remain in Belanore all these years instead of trying to find out where you came from?" she asked, desperately trying to change the topic. "You could have turned down the position of lord commander and travelled the Highlands."

"I've no notion of where to even start," Red Wolf said. "As I said, I remember nothing of my childhood before the Hellhounds. *Nothing*, my queen. Not even a fragment of a name. Beyond the walls of Belanore, I have nothing."

They were interrupted by the sound of approaching footsteps. Talin spun around to find one of Kadis' lieutenants hurrying towards them.

"Apologies for the interruption, Your Majesty," he said. "We have a situation. Kadis asks you to attend his meeting immediately."

Talin looked at Red Wolf, who simply shrugged. "Well, we wouldn't want to keep him waiting. Lead on," she said.

The lieutenant led them back across the fields and into the den. At the doors to the war room, he stopped, dipped his head and hurried off, and the two Drakels standing guard opened the doors for them. Talin took her spot opposite Kadis, Ettrias hovering by her shoulder, while Red Wolf slid into position on her left.

"We've received news of the insurgents' movements in El'Vane," Kadis said. "I believe we now know where they are keeping my spy, as well as your squire. It is time we launched our operation to free them."

"You have a plan?" Talin asked.

"Yes." Kadis waved a hand, and two Drakels stepped up to unroll a map of El'Vane on the table. "Our attacks on the trade caravans have been a nuisance for the insurgents for months now. They plan to double their guard on the north-eastern gate into the city, here." He pointed to a spot on the map. "That will leave the other gates less guarded. We can slip in through the south without too much difficulty."

"And you want our help?" Red Wolf lifted his brow.

"Indeed. We will use another caravan raid as a diversion while a small group sneaks into the city," Kadis said. "With the resources required to conduct such a raid and make it look convincing, I'm forced to send out most of my garrison here. I'd like you and your companions to help free our targets."

"What of the danger?" Red Wolf asked, looking at Talin. She stared back, lost in his gold eyes.

"If you'd prefer your queen to remain at the den, I would have that discussion with her, not me," Kadis said coolly. Red Wolf blinked, and Talin suddenly remembered where she was.

"I'd like to help—if it's all the same," she said.

"My queen, this seems to be a dangerous assignment–" Red Wolf began.

"And I will not have you fight all my battles for me," Talin finished for him. "If this is the price I must pay for an alliance, then I will pay it. I cannot sit behind stone walls and locked gates forever if I want to win the war."

Red Wolf's jaw tightened, but she knew he wouldn't question her authority here, not in front of all these people. She had won this round. Whatever argument he would make about her safety later, he'd so do in private, and as a friend rather than an advisor. But that was a conversation for another time, and Talin was more interested in learning what sort of plan Kadis had concocted.

"Our caravan raid will go ahead as it normally does," the Draconian prince explained. "The only difference is that our covert team will arrive early under the guise of merchants looking to gain access into the city to sell our wares. When the attack begins, the guards will be forced to usher all civilians inside the walls for safety. That will be our chance to slip away into the crowd."

Red Wolf crossed his arms, showing his muscled form under that tight-fitting tunic of his, the result of years upon years of swordplay and training. "That's risky. If they discover the ruse before you can slip away, you won't get a second chance."

"This whole operation is risky," Kadis said. "Bo'Galesh will lead the raid. I will be posing as the head merchant. Bo'Kata, we will need your archers to follow the attack force from behind and provide reinforcements should the situation call for it."

"Consider it done." A red-scaled Drakel without horns dipped her head.

Kadis turned to Talin. "Your Majesty, if you intend to join us, I must ask that you and your companions hide your faces when we queue up for entry approval. Elves will raise far too many questions among these Elitists."

"I understand," Talin said. "Perhaps I can bring up the rear with Bo'Kata's archers instead while Red Wolf and Ettrias go with you into the city?" She shot a look at her bodyguard that amounted to: *We can discuss the details later*.

"Actually, with your injury, you will be better suited to joining us instead of the archers," Red Wolf said. "But, of course, I leave the decisions to Prince Kadis."

Kadis shrugged. "No opposition either way. We set out tomorrow. Bo'Galesh, organise your men and choose who you want to take with us. We will need two more to pose as security escorts. This war council is dismissed."

Talin watched as Kadis' officers filed out of the room. The prince was the last to leave, and Talin found herself walking beside him as they made for the main doors of the hideout.

"I confess I'm surprised you decided to join this operation yourself," he said. "My father often said that leaders should keep themselves out of harm's way wherever possible."

"As you do?" Talin said with a smile.

"Ah, you have me there." He grinned.

"Truth be told, I'm tired of sitting back and letting others fight my battles for me," Talin said. "I'm tired of not being able to help."

Kadis shrugged. "Perhaps. But there is a difference between leading by example and charging recklessly onto the battlefield." He offered her an awkward smile. "I don't mean to lecture you, of course. My apologies if I came across that way."

"No, I understand," Talin said. "It's food for thought. Though I am more interested in learning about this civil war of yours."

"Ah. I shall give you the quick version," Kadis said. "The Elitists are led by a Drakel named Ve'Tehll. He was the face of the insurgency during both civil wars and has been running things in the empire ever since I was driven into hiding."

"Why did they rebel?"

"Disagreements over my father's administration," Kadis said. "It's always the same. Instead of diplomacy and reason, they resort to violence and bloodshed." He shook his head. "We pushed them back the first time when I was still a child, but we suffered severe losses—my mother among them. We never thought that Ve'Tehll would come back so much stronger."

"I'm sorry."

"It's all in the past now," Kadis said. "We can only pick up the pieces and try to push back."

"My queen..." Red Wolf called from somewhere behind them.

Gods, I don't want to deal with him now.

"I'll leave you two be." Kadis dipped his head and continued to the training grounds before Talin could open her mouth.

"We have nothing to discuss, Red Wolf." She reluctantly faced him. "I'm going."

"I cannot let you put yourself in danger like this," Red Wolf said. "Remember why you are here."

"I came here to seek help from the Drakels. Kadis has asked me to help him in return, and that is what I will do," Talin said. "I'm grateful for your commitment to protecting me and your counsel as a friend, but I cannot rely on you and others to fight my battles for me."

"My queen..." Red Wolf ran a hand over his chin.

"Why are you so insistent on protecting me?" Talin asked. "You were not like this when you served my father."

Red Wolf cleared his throat. "I don't understand."

"Do you think I can't handle myself? Is that it?" Talin asked.

"No, that's not..." Red Wolf's voice trailed off, and she knew she had him there. "I...my only wish is to keep you safe. You almost *died* at the border because I failed. I cannot let that happen again."

"You are not at fault for what happened at the border," Talin said.

"I know, I..." Red Wolf cleared his throat again. "I should...pack. For tomorrow."

"Of course." Talin gave a nod. "I'll...be at the archery range."

They parted ways quickly, and Talin made her way to the range. She recognised the red-scaled Drakel named Bo'Kata from the war meeting and a few other officers training their troops.

"Your Majesty." Bo'Kata dipped her head. Her lack of horns made her seem smaller than most of the other Drakels from the war room, though Talin wasn't sure it mattered, given that some were almost the same height as Red Wolf.

"Bo...Bo'Kata, yes?" Talin asked.

"Kata is fine," the Drakel said. "In my culture, 'Bo' denotes a military general's rank. We only use it for formal occasions and as a sign of respect if the Drakel is not present."

Talin took a light bow from a nearby rack and found a full quiver. "Kadis doesn't have a title?"

"Bo'Galesh and I hail from the Draconian deserts," Bo'Kata explained. "As evidenced by our scales. We have a more traditional way with names than others in the empire." She nodded at Talin's bow. "You've shot before?"

"A few times." Talin undid her sling and tested the draw on the spare bow before readying an arrow. The tug against her wound was a little uncomfortable but not unbearable, and she sent her first shot into the edge of the bullseye with ease.

"An excellent shot," Bo'Kata said. "I suppose the stories are true about Elven archers."

"Well, not entirely." Talin sent another arrow into the target next to the first. "Southern elves have a natural aptitude for shooting, but not all of us are as good a shot as the stories would have it. Put my brother in the archery range, and he might be able to hit a bullseye once out of ten shots if he's lucky."

Bo'Kata chuckled. "Perhaps we could improve on that with some training."

"He was always fonder of swordplay," Talin said. She fired off two more arrows in rapid succession, landing them both close enough to each other that the tips almost touched. Her fifth shot split the shaft of her previous arrow clean in two.

"Impressive." Bo'Kata nodded in approval. "Very impressive." She made a low rumbling sound in her throat. "I seem to recall you showed interest in joining my archers for the attack. We would be most honoured to have you."

"Thank you," Talin said. "Though truth be told, I'm not sure I'd be able to wield a heavier bow with my injury."

Bo'Kata only smiled. "Rest and recovery are important. You do not want to worsen your injury before it's healed. When you are recovered, I would be more than happy to have you join one of our operations if you wish it."

Talin gave a nod of thanks.

That night, after one of Kadis' servants had dropped off some warmer clothing for the Draconian winter and Talin began packing, she noticed that a familiar-looking Elven bow had been left on her bed, along with its equally beautiful quiver of arrows. Assuming that Red Wolf had left it lying around somewhere and someone had mistaken it for hers, she picked up the bow and quiver, intending to return them. A carefully folded note slid off the quiver and landed unceremoniously on the bed. Curiosity quickly set in, and Talin set everything down to unfold and read it. It was scrawled in an elegant flourish that could only have come from Red Wolf or Ettrias, and she had her suspicions even before she started reading.

> *I cannot stop you from joining Kadis's operation, and it is not my place to question your decisions. Consider this gift an apology. I suspect you will make much better use*

of it than I ever could.
–RW

Talin blinked. She hadn't expected an apology from him at all, much less something so...personal.

Who are we to each other, then? Friends, or...

She dismissed the thought.

It is a sweet apology, though.

Talin propped the bow and quiver against the wall with a faint smile and continued folding her clothes.

Talin had thought the cold nights in Kies Tor were the worst sort of weather. How wrong she was.

By morning on the second day of their journey, she had discovered just how cold the Draconian lands could be. Frost covered everything when they woke and didn't dissipate until midday. Even Red Wolf, who was only ever bothered by the storm season, had huddled himself in a thick tunic and cloak. Talin was forced to put on a pair of gloves to keep her fingers from freezing as they walked.

"I didn't think it was possible for the temperature to get this cold," she muttered, when they settled down again that night and lit a fire in front of their tent.

"If you think this is cold, give it a few more days," Ettrias said, limping up and taking the seat beside her. His leg was healed enough now that he could walk but not run, and he had insisted on joining them in the city.

"I remember riding with the king to Castle Blackrun," Red Wolf said. "It was the dead of winter. You could feel the cold as soon as we crossed the White River. We were gods-damned lucky it didn't snow."

"We set off at the usual time tomorrow in our positions," Kadis said, on his way past them. Red Wolf gave him a nod of acknowledgement.

"I don't suppose you have any more stories to share before bed?" Talin asked, looking at her brother.

"Truth be told, I didn't do very much." Ettrias picked up a stick and poked the fire. "My first few years were spent roaming the Draconian border villages, getting drunk and wallowing in self-pity. The rest I spent on a wasted effort to bring you down. Have you thought about what you're going to do about me after all this is over?"

"Seems obvious to me," Red Wolf said. "I confess to my crime and prove your innocence in front of the court. I'll probably be sentenced to death or branded a criminal for the rest of my life; you go free."

"I can't tell if you're joking," Ettrias said icily.

"I'm not."

Ettrias didn't respond.

"I can't sentence you to death, Red Wolf," Talin said.

"You must do what is right," Red Wolf said. "I've lived with my guilt for ten years. This is the only way to fix things."

"We can discuss this when we return to Belanore," Talin said. "Whenever that will be."

"As you wish, my queen." Red Wolf dipped his head. "Whatever happens tomorrow, promise me you will not do something irrational. My place is at your side, but I cannot guarantee anything, especially if it comes to a fight."

Talin sighed. "I've told you, Red Wolf, stop overthinking this. I will be perfectly safe with you and Kadis."

"You'd better be, I'm not interested in taking another arrow to the leg for you," Ettrias muttered. "Why were you so insistent on joining us, anyway? Nobody would have thought any less of you if you chose to remain at the den."

"I..." Talin wrestled with her thoughts for a moment, trying to decide how best to explain. "I guess I've lived a sheltered life until now, even compared to you, Ettrias. Father expected me to lead my people, but I knew so little of the outside world that I couldn't possibly understand what was truly best for them. I'm starting to realise that being queen involves far more than sitting on a throne, solving domestic disputes, and dividing our resources in the battle against the Hellhounds."

"Wise words," Red Wolf said. "You're learning well."

"I...appreciate that," Talin said with a slight smile. The two of them quickly focused on the fire instead.

"Gods, if I didn't know better, I'd think you two were courting." Ettrias snorted. "I'm going to bed, lovebirds. Don't stay up too late."

What—

Talin practically felt her mind grinding to a halt.

"What in the seven hells—" she began, but her brother had already disappeared into the tent. She went back to staring at the fire instead.

"We, ah, we should retire, too." Red Wolf cleared his throat and climbed to his feet. "Not coming, my queen?"

"I..." Talin tore her gaze from the flickering flames to look at him. "Are we..." She frowned. "Who am I to you?"

Red Wolf blinked. "You're my queen. The ruler of Kies Tor. The woman I've dedicated my life to protect."

She felt...*something*...flicker in her chest at those words.

"That's who I am to the lord commander," Talin said, frown deepening. "Who am I to *you*?"

Red Wolf hesitated.

"A...friend, if you like," he finally said.

The flicker in her chest turned into a twisting knife.

"Of course." She offered him a strained smile and stood. "Thank you."

"If I may be so bold, my queen, who am I to you?" Red Wolf asked, when she reached the tent flap. He hadn't moved from his spot by the fire.

"A friend, if you like."

The words tasted bitter on her tongue.

They woke the next morning to another layer of frost covering the normally green grass around the camp, turning the ground silver as the ice particles reflected the light. Talin changed into her merchant's disguise and met Kadis at the edge of the camp, along with the soldiers selected to pose as their security detail.

"We're ready?" the Draconian prince asked.

"We are," Red Wolf said.

"Good. Remember to keep your faces hidden."

The six of them moved off ahead of Bo'Kata's and Bo'Galesh's troops, following the road while their diversion kept to the trees, completely hidden from sight. Talin had sorely wanted to bring the bow and arrows that Red Wolf had gifted her, in case their cover was blown, but shooting a heavy recurve bow like that with her wounded shoulder was impossible. She'd settled on her sword and a dagger instead.

Slowly, excruciatingly so, the tall city walls of El'Vane loomed into view. Talin saw Red Wolf's sword hand tense and touch the hilt of his blade briefly. He stole a glance at her.

"Be careful," he said softly. Talin nodded.

"Halt!"

The Draconian guards at the gate motioned for them to stop. Talin thought she saw a flash of movement in the trees bordering the road, there one moment, gone the next.

"What is your business here?" They spoke in an unfamiliar dialect of Kier Dekkel, but Talin had been taught the language as part of her tutoring and could still piece together what was said.

"We're simple merchants, good sir," Kadis replied. "We have been trapping rabbits and other animals to sell their meat and skins in El'Vane, as well as some trinkets we have traded from the border villages. The roads have been dangerous, what with all the...rebel attacks we've heard about. My companions and I were lucky to make it here without incident."

"We'll have to search the caravan," the guard said, signalling for his men to move in.

A single arrow sailed out of the trees and punched clean through the guard's throat.

No backing out now.

Talin drew her sword, as did the rest of their group, and the remaining guards quickly raised their shields to protect themselves from further shots. Red Wolf stepped back neatly to place himself between her and the City Watch guards.

"Into the city, now!" the guard captain snapped. "We'll deal with your paperwork and permits later!"

They were ushered past the guards and through the city gates along with the first caravan in the column. Talin stole a glance back just in time to see Bo'Galesh's infantry rush out to swarm the second caravan as reinforcements came to meet them.

"Keep your hoods up and wait until we have their full attention," Kadis said in a low voice.

Archers were running up to man the walls now. A lone guard made it to the gate mechanisms and stood ready to lock the city down. On the street, a small crowd had gathered to watch the commotion.

"There, that's our chance," Ettrias said.

The six of them slipped into the crowd silently and left the southern gate behind. Finding an empty alleyway, they tethered the pack horses and caravan, and Kadis left two of his Drakels to guard them while the rest of their team continued towards the heart of the city on foot.

"Look up, above the buildings—that's the keep, Ked'Vane." Kadis pointed to the fortified castle towering over the rest of the city. "Our targets are held in the dungeons beneath them. There's a delivery gate to the southwest that should be unguarded. We can enter through there."

"By all means, lead the way," Talin said.

Their path took them through the winding main roads and side alleys to a bustling market square; Talin glimpsed traders selling foods she had never seen before, as well as expensive-looking rugs made from animal skins. Nobody noticed them in the middle of the crowd. Kadis continued at a brisk pace, long legs making it difficult for her and Ettrias to keep up, particularly with her brother still limping slightly.

"The guards will surely sound the alarm when they realise we've vanished," she said.

"Unfortunately so," Kadis admitted. "But it is my hope that Bo'Galesh and Bo'Kata will keep them preoccupied for a while yet.

With most of the City Watch positioned at the other gates, they will have to funnel their reinforcements from elsewhere."

They left the crowd behind and found themselves in an open space just before the keep. Tall walls loomed before them, the dark stone foreboding. Kadis quickly crossed to a small door set into the wall and gave it an experimental tug.

"This area is off-limits, citizen. State your business here."

Kadis cursed under his breath as two guards approached.

"Deepest apologies—we're new to the city." Talin stepped in front of him neatly. "My companions and I are merchants from Kies Tor to the east and have only just arrived in the city on official trade business with Ve'Tehll. My good friend Celio is a servant at the keep and only wished to show us around a little. We were under the impression that this delivery route would be left open for us."

Kadis opened his mouth as if to say something, then closed it again.

"We only wish to acquaint ourselves with the keep a little," Talin said. "If there are security concerns, I'm afraid you'll have to bring it to Ve'Tehll directly. This delivery gate should have been unlocked."

"Yes, that's right." Kadis cleared his throat. "I distinctly remember having someone unlock this gate before showing the Torrian delegate around the city. I'm sure we would all be grateful if you could let us through now."

"We would...have to clear it with Ve'Tehll." One of the guards scratched his head. "I'm sure you understand. Standard protocol and all. It shouldn't take too long."

Kadis and Red Wolf exchanged glances. Talin motioned for her bodyguard to stay his hand.

"Ve'Tehll already knows who we are and why we're here," she said. "Or should I report you to him for failing to comply with simple directives?"

"N-no, not at all!" the guard stammered. "My apologies, honoured guests. I didn't mean to be rude. Please, don't let us get in the way."

The two Drakels stood aside to let them pass. Talin saw Red Wolf's hand still tensed near his sword and prayed to the gods that it wasn't obvious. She put a hand over his wrist. He relaxed a fraction at the contact.

"Good thinking back there," Kadis said, once they were out of earshot of the guards. "But I'm afraid it's only a temporary solution. Those guards will get suspicious eventually."

"How long before we're discovered?" Talin asked.

Kadis hissed through his teeth. "Impossible to know. We must work quickly."

This is not going to end well. Talin let out a long breath. "Lead on."

Golmin's route through Stormwood had led him off the main path and into the depths of the forest where few travellers had ever tread. Part of him was glad of it; in the wilderness, it was easier to track which way the queen's party had gone. The soft ground here made deep impressions of horse hooves and footprints, and the thick canopy made it difficult for the rain to wash out the tracks. He had passed one of their camps yesterday and found little more to track them with. Red Wolf had taken care not to leave anything that might indicate where they were headed.

There were things he could use, however, like the way they were moving southwest instead of directly west to the border. It meant that Red Wolf had sensed a heavy storm close to their position and adjusted their route to avoid it and the floods that it had no doubt brought.

Golmin wondered again if they had made it across the border before the full moon. If not...

He pushed those thoughts aside. Red Wolf knew how dangerous the Hellhounds were and how dangerous the wolf could be. He would have made sure the queen didn't come to any harm.

But he doesn't know about Wormwood's betrayal, nor of Ettrias' potential involvement.

Golmin picked up the pace.

He found another one of their camps at dusk, though this one was accompanied by two bodies. Judging from the remains of the fire, they had been ambushed early in the morning—no doubt the first of many bandit attacks they would have faced on the road. He brushed aside some of the fallen leaves and picked up a bloodstained dagger.

Red Wolf was injured, then, he concluded. The outlaws who lay dead had clean blades otherwise and no man in their right mind would remove a protruding blade, lest they bleed to death. But Red Wolf had his healing and the queen's naivety to his advantage.

"Unless he told her?" Golmin mused to himself, then shook his head. That was unlikely. Red Wolf had been adamant that his abilities remain secret. Golmin had suspected that bandits and outlaws might come after them, but this deep in Stormwood?

People are getting desperate.

Dragging the bodies out of the camp, he settled down by the remains of the fire and lit it again, feeding it some more fuel to keep it going. It was getting dark, and he didn't particularly fancy travelling after sundown.

Golmin set out again at dawn as the first rays of light struggled through the canopy above. The sunrise brought with it another storm, and he soon found himself soaked to the bone despite his thick travelling cloak. He could see why Red Wolf hated the storm season; Highlanders were used to dry summers and the occasional snow in winter, and Red Wolf's Hellhound blood was more suited to the frozen far north. Golmin remembered adjusting to the weather in the south when he first joined the Royal Guard. He'd served in Lord Whitehall's army in the Highlands before Red Wolf recruited him and hadn't ever been south of the White River. Nobody had warned him about the storm season. His first year at the palace had been an interesting one, to be sure.

Checking his map, Golmin realised he was close to a town, but the tracks left by the queen and her escort were quickly fading. He briefly wondered if he should stop for supplies and shelter from this rain but decided not to risk losing the trail completely.

If Red Wolf feigned an injury, they would have passed through the town for supplies and healing.

Golmin turned north and headed for the town. With luck, the locals could tell him which direction they had gone and save him some trouble.

He arrived in the early hours of the morning, as market stalls were opening up and the townsfolk were beginning their work. A quick exchange with a vendor told him where to find the nearest tavern, and he headed there first to listen to the gossip. He doubted that the queen would have stayed here; the camp was far too close for them to waste an entire day's travel to sleep under a roof. But the locals always gossiped, and he knew that tales of a giant with golden eyes and a woman in fine travelling clothes would find their way through town. Golmin took a seat at the bar and ordered a drink.

"I'm looking for a tall man with golden eyes," he told the barkeep. "Around seven foot. He's travelling with a young girl and two southerners."

"Aye, I heard someone fitting that description passed through," the barkeep said, making his coin disappear and producing an ale. "Word is that he's one of the giants, returned from their slumber in the mountains. All nonsense if you ask me. Giants went extinct a thousand years ago."

"Do you know where they went?" Golmin asked. "Or which way they were headed?"

"Not a clue," the barkeep said. "I can tell you where they won't be headed, though. Further north. The storms have flooded the roads."

"Right." Golmin took a swig of ale. "What about west? To the Forts? Which crossing would be closest?"

"Crossing?" The barkeep looked dumbfounded. "Are you mad, pal? Nobody who goes past the Western Forts has ever returned."

"Which crossing?" Golmin repeated.

The barkeep scoffed. "Morvale if you head directly west, but the roads are flooded. More likely they went to Aldurin, directly south of it."

Golmin produced his map. "Where exactly?"

"Here's Morvale. Aldurin to the south." The barkeep pointed, and Golmin scribbled it in with a charcoal pen.

"My thanks."

"The Hellhounds have completely taken over in the west," the barkeep warned. "If your friends have gone to the Forts and passed them, they're as good as dead. You'd be wise to turn back now instead of trying to find their remains."

"Hmm." Golmin stuffed his map into his pack and finished his drink. "I'll take my chances."

He stopped by the market briefly to purchase food for the road before setting off. The shopkeeper who served him told him that he'd sold some supplies to a man with dark hair and blue eyes, who had been travelling with a giant. They'd followed the unflooded road southwest. That gave him some more information to work with. He decided to follow their route out of the village and consulted his map as his horse continued at an easy trot. The road he followed led through another village before branching out towards two crossings at the Forts. The northern fork led directly to Morvale.

Assuming they did follow the road all the way, he thought to himself with a sigh. They had left almost a month before him, and although he could track them through which villages they had stopped at, Red Wolf had taken care to cover up the trail. Most of the villages they could have passed had a single road leading out of them which only branched out much further down, making it impossible to determine which path he'd taken—if he'd taken the road at all. Their trek through the wilderness before had showed Golmin that their movements were irregular and evasive. The queen and her lord commander had not wanted anyone to follow in case her council figured out where she was going.

This isn't good. Golmin stopped his horse and frowned at his map. If Red Wolf had decided to lead them back into Stormwood, they could have gone to any of the crossings south of Morvale. Assuming they did make it through the Hellhound-infested west, they could be anywhere in the Draconian Empire by now. They could even be on their way back home. If he looked for them in the capital and they weren't there...

Golmin felt like he was following an endless trail of bread-crumbs—only the breadcrumbs might not even be there. He only knew that he had to find the queen and tell her of the plot to take her throne.

The full moon. What if I'm already too late? What if Ettrias got to her while Red Wolf wasn't there?

He pushed the thoughts out of his head. There was no time to be thinking like this, not now. He resolved instead to work with what he knew to be true. Red Wolf and the others couldn't have gone much further north due to the floods, and he doubted they would have any business going north anyway. If they had followed the road and en-countered no difficulty, Morvale was closer and smaller than the other crossing on the fork. They were more likely to have gone there. If they'd vanished back into the forest and continued their journey there, Red Wolf would try to take the quickest route through Stormwood, cutting directly west. The other crossing would be a more likely place to look in that case.

Think, Rufus! You know Red Wolf. Would he follow the road?

No, of course not. The road was far too open, too easy for a tracker to follow. They would have gone south, vanishing into the forest, and...

And then he would have circled northwest again to Aldurin once he was sure he'd made their trail disappear.

Golmin changed course and headed for the southern crossing.

By the gods, I'm never forgiving him for leading me on this wild goose chase, he thought. If only the man would take a reasonable path like normal people, make it easier for him to track...

He understood the secrecy, though, especially in light of the treach-ery he and Master Corvan had uncovered. Wormwood's rumours had already turned most of the kingdom against the queen. By the time she returned, he would have everyone convinced that she had fled Kies

Tor and left her people to die at the hands of the Hellhounds. Her reputation would be destroyed, and Ettrias would become king.

Golmin wasn't going to let that happen.

He would find them in the Draconian lands, explain the situation, and implore them to return. Wormwood and Highett would never expect it. They would be unprepared. Their plans would be dashed to bits.

Golmin put away his map and headed deeper into the forest.

T he six of them had managed to make it across the rear courtyard and all the way to the steps leading down into the dungeons before two more guards stopped them. Kadis had been quick to spin the story they'd made up earlier to dismiss their suspicions, but it soon became apparent that these guards would not be so easily fooled. None of them had keys specifically for the dungeons, and Kadis' master key for the keep would have raised far too much suspicion; only Ve'Tehll and the other insurgent leaders were thought to have copies after the end of the civil war.

"Say again. You have express permission to visit the dungeons for...what, exactly?" The first guard scratched his head. He was a short Drakel with scales the colour of sand and long horns.

"Just showing our guests around," Kadis said.

"Our 'honoured guests' wanted to see the dungeons, of all places?" the guard lifted a scaled brow. His eyes narrowed.

Beside Talin, Ettrias' hand inched closer to his sword hilt.

"Don't," she said in a low voice.

"They're not buying this story," Ettrias muttered.

"I'm sure we can call Ve'Tehll down here right now and have him confirm things, wouldn't you agree?" the guard said.

"That won't be necessary," Kadis said. "Surely there's no need to trouble our supreme leader for a matter so trivial..."

"I know you." The guard made a low growl in his throat. "You're the outlaw prince. Kadis."

"I was really hoping we could ignore that part." Kadis' lightning-fast hook punch knocked the guard out cold. Red Wolf threw a jab at the other guard's face before sending him to the ground with a kick to the liver. A choke from behind put him to sleep completely.

"Get them out of sight," Kadis hissed, and his two infantrymen dragged the bodies behind a thick bush.

"Well, that could've gone better," Ettrias remarked.

"No matter." Kadis produced his master key. "Better that we encounter these two guards now, when we're almost at our objective. Less time for someone to notice their disappearance before we're all out of here."

"Get that gate open, then," Red Wolf said, jerking his head towards the barred door that guarded the dungeon entrance. He drew his sword and took up a position at the top of the steps beside Ettrias. Talin unsheathed her own weapon and joined him.

"No, absolutely not," her bodyguard said. "Go with Kadis. You've had, what? A *month* of formal weapons training after twenty years without it?"

"Oh, please, I don't even know the dungeon layout," Talin said. "I could do more here."

Two crossbowmen rounded a corner and saw them. One shouted an alarm and pointed his weapon forward.

Oh, gods.

Red Wolf shoved her behind him neatly as two crossbow bolts embedded themselves deep into his gut with a soft *thunk*. He let out a snarl and bared his teeth at the crossbowmen. They stared at him, wide-eyed, as he strode forward, but then one of them seemed to shake free from his stupor and drew his sword. Red Wolf knocked the weapon away without breaking stride and slammed his pommel into the side of the man's head. The guard went down soundlessly. The other one stepped forward with a swing. Red Wolf took the cut to his arm and similarly knocked his opponent out cold.

"*Go!*" Red Wolf snapped. "Find Ashera. You'll only get in the way up here."

"Red Wolf—" Talin began, as he ripped the bolts out of his torso with a curse and tossed them aside.

"I have my healing. I'll be fine." Red Wolf backed up towards the staircase. "Quickly!"

Seeing no other choice, Talin hurried down the steps to join Kadis, taking a spare torch from the wall and bringing it close to her free hand.

If a lightning strike in the storm season can start a forest fire, lighting a torch shouldn't be hard, she thought.

It took a few tries, but the sparks of lightning from her magic eventually caught on the torch, setting it alight. Kadis brought a second torch close to the flame to light it as well, and they descended further into the dungeon together. He ducked into the prison warden's office at the bottom of the steps to steal the master key.

"Take the right side. I'll take the left," the Draconian prince said when they reached a fork. "My spy is one of the desert folk and has a broken horn. The girl?"

"Short, brown hair, low ponytail, rounded ears," Talin said. "Though I imagine she'd be the only elf down here."

"Well, you never know. El'Vane was a trading hub before Ve'Tehll took over. Let me know if you find either of them. I'll come around with the master key."

Talin made her way down the corridor slowly, stopping by each cell to check who was inside. Most seemed entirely uninterested in her. A few banged on the door and demanded to be released. She found herself oddly reminded of the lower level of the palace dungeon in Belanore, which was reserved for prisoners locked away in solitary confinement. She had been adamant about stripping that floor entirely and filling it in, expanding and refurbishing the upper level to give the prisoners better accommodations, but with the war stretching their resources thin, they had neither the coin nor the time for such a task.

Steel rang together faintly above her. A fading scream echoed down towards the dungeons.

Near the end of the corridor, she finally spotted a young girl huddled on the stone bench in the cell with her knees drawn up to her chest. Talin pressed her face against the door's barred window.

"Ashera?"

The girl looked up. Her eyes widened.

"Kadis, I've found the girl!" Talin called down the corridor. The prince was at her side a few moments later, supporting a limping, sand-coloured Drakel with a broken right horn.

"Take Vohlan's weight for a moment, Your Majesty, if you'll be so kind," he said. Talin allowed him to transfer the Drakel's weight to her uninjured shoulder briefly so he could unlock the cell door. Ashera jumped down from the bench and approached cautiously.

"Your Majesty?" she whispered.

"It's me." Talin smiled. "Are you hurt?"

Ashera shook her head. "I thought you were Ve'Tehll. He said he would come back and make me answer more questions but I don't know anything."

"Let's get you out of here," Talin said.

Kadis led the way back out of the dungeon, supporting the spy, Vohlan, while Talin accompanied Ashera. They emerged from the dark corridors to find Red Wolf, Ettrias, and the two Drakel escorts still standing guard by the staircase, all now splattered with blood and surrounded by a dozen dead Drakels. Kadis cursed under his breath.

"Apologies for the carnage," the bodyguard said. "There were too many of them. We held them off the best we could before resorting to killing."

"No matter," Kadis said. "I knew it might come to this. Let's go."

"You found Ashera?" Red Wolf asked.

The girl peeked out from behind Talin. "Red Wolf?"

Red Wolf's shoulders visibly relaxed. He closed the distance between them in two strides and wrapped her in an embrace.

"You're unhurt?" he asked when they separated.

"I'm alright," Ashera said with a sniffle. "I missed you."

Red Wolf let out a half-laugh. "I missed you too." He straightened and wiped his sword down on his sleeve before sheathing it. "But we'll have to catch up once we're out of the city. There's no telling how many more guards are coming."

They were met with more resistance back at the delivery gate when half a dozen guards rushed to investigate the disturbance in the keep.

Red Wolf cut two down while Ettrias dealt with another. Kadis' two infantrymen took out a guard each, and Kadis dealt with the final man.

"The southern gate will be under lockdown by now," the Draconian prince said as they wound their way back through the streets and disappeared into the crowded alleys and market squares. "We'll fetch our cart and horses and get out through the north-eastern gate instead."

"You have a plan?" Talin asked.

"Of course." Kadis flashed her a grin.

Their caravan had been left untouched, thankfully, with the two guards still sitting nearby, playing cards on an empty crate. They both stood to attention when they saw Kadis approach.

"Get the caravan ready. We're leaving through the north-eastern gate," the Drakel prince said. They scrambled to work and packed the cards before loading the empty crate back onto the caravan. Ettrias untethered the horses.

"How much of this plan of yours were you planning on sharing?" Red Wolf asked, as he helped Talin into the back of the caravan and climbed up after her. Ettrias quickly joined them.

"We'll pose as merchants again, transporting perishable goods," Kadis said. "There are exceptions under lockdown for the transportation of such goods. The three of you will have to stay in the back. Elven traders leaving from El'Vane are almost unheard of." Talin gave a nod, and he closed the caravan doors, plunging them into complete darkness. The wagon began to move a few moments later.

"Cramped in here," Red Wolf muttered. His voice sounded strained.

"It won't be for long," Talin said. "You're alright?"

"Fine." Red Wolf let out a long breath. "Just...don't particularly enjoy being trapped in small spaces in the dark."

Of course, the Hellhounds probably kept him in similar conditions.

"I understand," Talin said.

The caravan rolled to a stop a few minutes later, and she heard Kadis hop down from the driver's seat to explain the situation to the guards. She felt Red Wolf tense beside her.

"Permit?" a guard said.

"We haven't had the opportunity to acquire a permit," Kadis said loudly. "Let me get one of the crates—you can see for yourself."

Red Wolf pulled her and Ettrias down behind the tallest stack of crates just in time. The doors swung open, and Kadis pried open one of the crates to show the guard. Whatever was in it appeared to satisfy the Drakel, because he grunted an affirmative and ordered the doors shut again. They continued through the gates without incident.

Kadis stopped the caravan after some time and threw open the doors. "We're safe, you can come out."

Red Wolf clambered out gratefully before extending a hand to Talin, and she allowed him to help her from the wagon. Taking in her surroundings, she saw they had stopped a safe distance from the city gates in the middle of a small clearing in the forest, hidden from the road. She glanced back as Ettrias limped out of the caravan too.

"What was in that crate you showed the guard?" Talin asked. "I was under the impression that we were transporting empty boxes."

Kadis rumbled a laugh. "Surely you didn't think we would plan such an operation without backups in mind? I had some soft cheese and butter loaded into the crates before we set off. They'd last long enough on the road for us to use them to pass inspection if we were searched."

"I'll give it to you—you thought of everything," Red Wolf said.

"Ah, you give me too much credit," Kadis said. "It was Bo'Galesh's idea. And speaking of him, we will need to meet up with his men, as well as Bo'Kata's rangers. The rendezvous is a few hours from here."

"Lead on, then," Red Wolf said.

Bo'Kata and Bo'Galesh had already set up camp at their agreed rendezvous when they arrived after a few hours' hike from the capital. By the time Talin saw the site, the tents had been fully pitched, the trenches for water drainage fully dug. Kadis sent Vohlan off to a healer and debriefed his soldiers before joining them at the communal fire.

"No sign of your father?" Bo'Kata asked, as some of the archers skewered their day's hunt onto sticks to roast them. Talin soon caught the scent of cooking rabbit and duck.

"Unfortunately not." Kadis sighed. "But my spy, Vohlan, has found a lead on where he might be, if he is indeed alive. Perhaps it's a foolish hope, but I hold onto it regardless. I had imagined that he might be held in El'Vane. However, it is as Kata had told me. El'Vane is far too obvious a location."

"You think they might try to leverage him if this rebellion of yours continues to pose bigger problems for Ve'Tehll?" Talin asked.

"Yes. It would be a reason to keep him alive." Kadis' tail twitched. "But now is not the time to be discussing such topics. Supper is almost ready, and I am more interested in learning about your home."

They took their meal at the communal campfire, exchanging stories and legends of their lands. Talin wasn't sure why her people had believed that these Drakels were vicious, unwelcoming beasts; gods, she'd even believed it herself. But Kadis had shown her a different side. He explained that his father was generous and believed all Draconian children should be allowed an education, not just boys and nobility. However, his steady dismantling of the old social hierarchy had made him many enemies, and eventually, the Draconian warlords banded together to overthrow him.

"He told me the support of the people was the most important thing if I wanted to keep my throne," Kadis said. "But he also believed in ruling with kindness, not an iron fist governing all. And sometimes your people will not agree with you. But you must do what you believe is right, what is just and fair."

"What's fair." Talin looked at Red Wolf.

Once all this is over, what will happen to him? What must I do?

She couldn't sentence him to death, not when they'd known each other for so long and been through so much. But if she let him go after what he'd done...

"I do not think you are a bad ruler, Your Majesty," Kadis said. "You were willing to risk everything to come here and seek our help. But you must remember what is important to you and to your people. If you wish to win the war, you must unite them. Whether or not you lead them on the battlefield, you must make them believe in something, some*one*."

"I'm not sure I could do that," Talin said. It felt odd to admit. "I barely even know how to lead my people as queen, let alone my armies on the battlefield."

"Hmm." Kadis leaned back and crossed his arms. "I understand. My father's advisors did not believe in my ability to lead at first. But he did. He believed that anyone could if they were willing to learn. To listen."

Ettrias' brow creased. "I'd be an awful ruler, in that case. Guess Father was right to choose you after all."

"What do you mean?"

"Come on, Talin. I'm not cut out to be a king. All I cared about as a child was swordplay and impressing Red Wolf with my skills. I didn't know any more than you about how to rule a kingdom, but at least *you cared*. You still do. It was always 'How can I make things better?'

with you. When you have the power to change the world, why wouldn't you?"

"Learn with me. When we return home..." Talin's voice trailed off. "When we return home, and your name is cleared, I want you to stay. As my brother and as one of my advisors."

"If I stay, he dies." Ettrias nodded at Red Wolf.

Talin winced. "I'll...work something out."

"I'm sure you will," Ettrias said with a scoff.

"Ettrias."

"What? It's not like he's going to object."

Red Wolf shot a glance at the two of them but made no comment.

They were interrupted, thankfully, by another round of roast rabbits being passed along, with wine to wash them down. Red Wolf took his portion and began tearing into it, still pretending to be oblivious to the conversation.

"What do you think I should do with you?" she asked him.

Red Wolf stopped chewing and swallowed carefully. "That is not up to me. If you wish to discuss my fate, you will need to confide in a different advisor."

"Like Master Corvan?" Talin lifted her eyebrows.

"Perhaps." Red Wolf shrugged. "A good queen listens to all her advisors, not just the ones who will give answers she likes. And if I recall correctly, Master Corvan has expressed his disapproval over the death sentence since before I was knighted."

Talin opened her mouth to protest, failed to think of anything to say in retaliation, and simply stared at him instead. Then she managed a chuckle. Red Wolf cracked a faint smile.

"Gods, you're the worst advisor anyone could ask for," she said.

Red Wolf's smile didn't waver. "Truly, it's a mystery to me why you would confide in Master Corvan. He'd be the one helping you justify why I shouldn't be executed."

Talin couldn't help but laugh at that. Red Wolf turned back to his food with a chuckle.

"Oh, before we part ways for the night," Kadis said, chewing on his own rabbit, "I've heard that you elves measure age differently to us Drakels. How do you age?"

"We physically grow at the same rate as you lot for the first seventeen years, but our minds mature much slower. And since we live far longer than Drakels, we measure age by maturity, rather than years lived," Ettrias said. "Red Wolf might be older than us physically, but we're a similar age. Talin and I only turned twenty-one a few months ago."

"You're telling me you've only *just* come of ruling age?" Kadis looked incredulous.

Bo'Kata laughed and clapped him on the shoulder. "He's used to being the youngest here. The other generals and I are all his seniors."

"If it's any consolation, we've probably lived longer than you have," Ettrias said.

"It's not. But onto other matters." Kadis let out a long breath. "When we return, we must shift our focus onto our primary objective: taking back El'Vane. I have waited years to strike back at the source of Ve'Tehll's power, and now I almost have my banners rallied. What we need are resources."

"If it's all the same to you, I'd like to learn from your Draconian war councils. Provided you don't object," Talin said.

"Of course." Kadis gave a nod. "I welcome it. Your brother has taught me much of your Elven tactics, it seems only fair that I return the favour."

"It's settled, then."

They finished their supper at the main fire and retreated to their respective groups for the rest of the evening. Red Wolf took the time to catch Ashera up on what they had gotten up to in the past week before the two of them got up to spar. Ettrias chatted to one of the archers in Bo'Kata's company. Talin watched them all from the corner of her eye as she practised her magic.

"Watch your parry," Red Wolf snapped. "If my strike had been any stronger, you would be missing half your face, Ashera! Parry further down the blade."

Ashera resumed her stance, and they continued dancing back and forth at the fire.

"What if you're just not strong enough, even if you parry right where you're supposed to?" the girl asked after yielding again to his blows.

"You are strong enough, Ashera. If you parry properly, no blade in the world can break through it," Red Wolf said. "Never let anyone tell you that you're not strong enough."

The girl nodded. "I'll beat them all up if they tell me that!"

Red Wolf smiled. "I know you will." He lifted his blade again. "Once more, and then you should rest."

"Alright," the girl said. Talin left them to their training and tried to focus again on practising her magic. She could feel lightning in the air itself, tiny, minuscule arcs of energy waiting to strike. She could draw on the power if she wanted; it was so *easy*. But Red Wolf had told her to contain the magic. *True magic comes from controlling one's powers*, he'd said. He was right, in a way. It was easy to let her magic take over like it had when she'd first harnessed her lightning, but the amount of raw power she'd wielded had been terrifying. She knew that if she didn't control it, she would inevitably hurt someone around her, including herself.

"Still practising?" Red Wolf asked when she made a spark appear in her hand and vanish again. Talin looked up and found that he'd finished sparring with Ashera, possibly some time ago now. The girl was poking the fire with a stick.

"I've been...trying," Talin said.

Red Wolf nodded. "When you want something, you do whatever you can to make it happen. Much of the nobility in Kies Tor would rather wait for their servants to bring it to them. But you do not hide behind palace servants or royal guards. I suppose I've always admired that about you."

Talin smiled. "Thank you."

"Ettrias was right about why your father wished you to rule," Red Wolf continued. "Though I think you have more to offer your people than kindness, much more. You have the potential to become one of the greatest rulers in Torrian history so long as you stick to your beliefs. And I know that you still think you are not ready to be queen, but this is your duty. Embrace it, and you might find that things will become much easier."

"What would I ever do without you?" Talin ducked her head to hide her blush. Red Wolf didn't seem to notice, thankfully.

"Doing paperwork back home, probably," he said.

"Probably." Talin cracked another smile.

"It's getting late."

"You don't like stargazing?"

"When you put it that way..." Red Wolf looked up. Talin followed his gaze to the waning moon and all the stars speckled across the purple Draconian sky.

"I remember a time when Ettrias threw a tantrum during an astronomy lesson," she said. "We were, what, nine or ten? He was desperate to get out and practise swordplay with you. Corvan told him, 'Sure, as soon as you pass the quiz!'—but he just couldn't get the answers right."

"Ah, I recall Ettrias running to me with tears streaming down his face after the good master told him off." Red Wolf chuckled. "I had to let him win, naturally."

Talin couldn't help but laugh. "Gods, I'd give anything to be a child again. We just ran around the palace and didn't have to worry about the war, about any of this." She gestured around her.

"Once we win this war, you can do whatever you like. I do owe you a drink at a tavern, don't forget," Red Wolf said.

Talin was acutely aware that he'd shifted his hand closer to hers, and now his fingers were practically on top of hers. He appeared to be completely unaware, and she didn't want to embarrass him by moving her hand.

"Imagine the scandal! The Queen of Kies Tor, drinking at a common tavern!" She grinned.

"We'll have to go far into the Highlands, where nobody will recognise your face," Red Wolf said. "Of course, you'd have to lie to your council, but I imagine that won't be a problem for you."

"They'll believe anything." Talin took his hand almost instinctively and immediately realised what she'd done. They both inched away at the same time.

"What is it about the moon that enhances the Hellhounds' power?" she asked, trying desperately to pretend that nothing had happened.

"They..." Red Wolf cleared his throat. "Uh. The Hellhounds aren't even sure. It could be the moon is another source of magic that only the

Hellhounds can draw from." He stood. "Anyway. We should...retire. We start the march back to the den tomorrow."

"Of course, you're right." Talin allowed him to extinguish the fire and help her to her feet.

"After you, my queen," Red Wolf said, gesturing for her to enter the tent. She ducked through the flap but paused just inside.

"That was nice," she said. "Thank you for the company."

Red Wolf blinked.

"Likewise," he said. "I'm glad. I thought it was nice, too."

The weather seemed to grow ever colder over the next few days as they made their way back to the den. Ettrias grumbled every now and then, saying he much preferred the tropics back home and the *warmth, damn it,* as opposed to the freezing temperatures here. Talin couldn't help but agree. She often woke in the morning to find frost forming on the outside of her bedroll.

Kadis and Red Wolf, on the other hand, basked in the colder temperature; the former remaining relentless in his search for his father. Talin joined his war councils whenever she could, watching and listening while he laid out his plans and tactics to lay siege to El'Vane. Red Wolf and Ettrias made the occasional contribution to tell him about any potential weaknesses on his map. But the search continued, and they were no closer to news of the emperor than they were a week ago. Talin could tell the Draconian prince was getting desperate.

"What's the latest?" she asked, as another scouting party led by Bo'Kata returned.

"We know the emperor is nowhere in the west," the general said. "But that does not narrow our search down by much. The empire spans several kingdoms; it's impossible to search everywhere. Kadis has also been working on securing the support of those warlords who have not yet pledged their allegiance to Ve'Tehll."

Talin nodded. "Any luck?"

"We have more allies than we did a week ago," Bo'Kata said. "There are a number of warlords in the south who have agreed to rally their banners for Kadis. We have almost enough resources to go ahead with the siege."

"Almost enough?" Talin asked.

Bo'Kata sighed. "Yes, there is a catch. If we wish to take El'Vane, we need heavy weapons. Trebuchets, siege towers, battering rams. These will cost a hefty sum to purchase from mercenary factions and independent arms dealers."

Talin understood. Back home, the Hellhounds' main weakness up to this point had been their lack of siege weapons; they relied on sheer physical power and their great numbers to break through any heavily fortified defensive positions they held, such as the White River and the Western Forts. But the Hellhounds were also patient, and they had eventually worn down her kingdom's resources in the north, allowing the hordes to continue pushing towards Belanore. Kadis' rebellion would have no chance against the insurgents without any way to break through the fortified El' and Ked' strongholds.

"Do we have the resources to purchase these weapons?" she asked.

"Nowhere near enough," Bo'Kata admitted. "Short of plundering every village near the den, we have nothing."

"What about trade?"

Bo'Kata considered it for a moment. "I'll talk to Kadis."

Talin left the party and moved downhill to the training grounds. Red Wolf was there, as expected, sparring with some of Kadis' newer recruits. He wore no tunic but seemed entirely unbothered by the near-freezing temperatures.

"Not cold?" Talin called.

"Not at all!" He grinned back at her. "I don't know what you're talking about, this is perfect weather!"

"For you, maybe." Talin continued to the archery range. Her shoulder was feeling considerably better now, thanks to Kadis' healers, but she had to stretch it to ensure she didn't lose mobility in the joint. Archery practice was a good way to do it. She sent a few arrows into the various targets lined up down the range before resting her shoulder, and some of Bo'Kata's archers took over in the meantime to sharpen their skills.

"I never understood why you stopped formal weapons training. You're quite good at this," Ettrias said, appearing beside her with a short bow borrowed from Bo'Kata's armoury. "You make hitting those targets look easy."

"To be fair, you *have* improved," Talin said. Her brother shrugged.

They watched the archers for a little while longer, until the range finally cleared up enough that they could get a few shots in without bumping elbows. Talin offered to swap bows with Ettrias for a few rounds to see if that made any difference to his shooting. It didn't.

"Just admit you're good at this and stop embarrassing me," he grumbled.

"You're the one who came to practice," Talin said.

"My queen."

Talin turned to see Red Wolf approaching, fully clothed now, Ashera behind him.

"Kadis wants an audience," he said, boots drawing to a halt at the edge of the range. "I couldn't tell you why."

"Well, I'll admit, I'm curious," Talin said. "Where is he?"

"Waiting at the stables," Red Wolf said.

"I don't suppose he wants to take us riding," Ettrias muttered. "I'll stay, if it's all the same."

"Oh, how bad can it be?" Talin left her bow at the range and joined Red Wolf. "Besides, do you really want to keep embarrassing yourself in front of the archers here?"

Ettrias scowled. "Fine."

Kadis was waiting for them at the stables, as Red Wolf had said, with their three horses saddled and another half dozen being prepared. He dipped his head when he saw them.

"Thank you for coming so quickly. Bo'Kata told me of your idea," he said, "and I think I may have a solution."

"I'm glad to hear it," Talin said. She nodded at the horses. "Where are we going, then?"

"Over the past few days, I've been working to locate a secret storehouse in the forests north of the den, built by my father during the first civil war as an emergency supply cache. The resources there are untouched as far as I'm aware, and we could trade them or use them for our siege weapons," Kadis explained. "I am unsure exactly where this storehouse is, but Bo'Galesh tells me he can find it."

"How much stuff are we talking about?" Ettrias asked.

"Enough. More than enough."

Talin chose one of Kadis' horses to ride while the others took their own respective mounts, and Bo'Galesh soon arrived with half a dozen swordsmen. Kadis exchanged a few words with him in Kier Dekkel before the general vanished again, leaving the swordsmen.

"These scouts have been studying the maps," Kadis said. "They will lead the way."

It turned out that they didn't need to go far from the den; a ten-minute ride at a quick trot put them in the scouts' search zone. The sergeant produced a marked map of the surroundings and explained what they needed to do and which places to look first.

"This is a big area to cover," Red Wolf said. "Not to mention that we do not even know for certain that the supplies are here."

"Oh, cheer up." Talin nudged him in the ribs when he dismounted. "It's better than doing nothing. Besides, the search would go faster if we helped."

"If my queen commands it," Red Wolf muttered.

"Please, as if I've ever been able to make you do anything."

"I would never refuse an order from you, my queen."

"You—" Talin began. *Gods, he's infuriating.* She turned away to search her own area of the forest. Ashera and Ettrias had teamed up and were busy with their area. Red Wolf would sometimes pause to sniff the air or the soil, but other than that, his search seemed to be going about as poorly as her own.

"Why do you keep sniffing the soil, anyway?" Talin asked. They found themselves shoulder to shoulder on the ground again, searching yet another section of the forest floor.

"Trying to detect any scent of metal or rust in the ground," Red Wolf said. "The hatch we're looking for is probably made of metal, or it would have rotted away years ago to reveal the storehouse we're after."

"You can tell whether the soil has metal or rust in it from a sniff?"

"I have the Hellhounds' powers. That includes their sense of smell."

"Does it ever get...*too much*," Talin asked, "having to process the scents of everything around you? It sounds like torture."

Red Wolf worked his jaw and swallowed. "It is. It's...part of why I wear my helm everywhere in Belanore. Dampens my senses, at least a little. Imagine being able to hear and smell everything around you, *all the time*. It's always too much." He climbed to his feet. "There seems to be nothing more to uncover here. Perhaps we should meet back with Kadis and see if his team has found the storehouse."

"Good plan." Talin gave a nod, and they made their way through the bushes and thick trees to where the Draconian prince was searching.

"You've finished your search already?" he asked, seeing them approach. "Gods, you're faster than I anticipated. Come, help us. Perhaps the stash will be here somewhere."

Red Wolf glanced to his right, at a section of the ground that Kadis' men had already searched. He crouched and sniffed a handful of soil as he had done a dozen times before.

"It's here."

Kadis blinked. "We've searched that area three times, sir. If the storehouse entrance truly is there, we must have been blind."

"It's buried under years of soil and undergrowth. Right here." Red Wolf dug his hands into the ground and scraped aside a sizable chunk of soil, revealing a section of rusted metal. Kadis let out a stunned exhale.

"Well, I'll be damned, sir," he said. Red Wolf quickly located the hatch handle and gave it a sharp tug upwards. An ear-splitting screech echoed through the forest as rusted metal grated against itself, and the edge of the hatch shifted ever so slightly. Red Wolf stumbled away with a curse and covered his ears. Kadis grabbed the handle in the meantime to make a second attempt, but it seemed as if the hatch had decided not to free itself any further.

"Are you alright?" Talin asked Red Wolf.

Her bodyguard pinched the bridge of his nose. "I'll be fine. Not likely to receive permanent hearing damage, given my healing. It's hardly the worst kind of noise I've been subjected to."

"Perhaps we should return with some rope and a pack horse. We need more leverage, and stronger tools," Kadis said. "And perhaps some oil to loosen this rust."

"That could work," Red Wolf said. "Send two of your men back to fetch the rope and horse. We can continue trying to open this in the meantime."

Kadis nodded and beckoned to his sergeant. The Drakel hurried over, and the two of them exchanged some quiet words in Kier Dekkel before the sergeant hurried off again.

"In the meantime, I don't suppose you have any ideas?" the Draconian prince mused.

"Perhaps if we both tried..." Red Wolf scratched his chin. "But I can't imagine that we'd both be able to fit our hands around the handle."

They puzzled over it for a few more minutes before giving up and resigning themselves to waiting for the scouts to return. The rest of their party had gathered by now and were taking turns to try to open the hatch by hand.

"What if we can't get it open?" Ettrias asked.

"We'll need a blacksmith to remove the pins in the hinges." Talin tossed a stick at the hatch absentmindedly.

"That's going to take a while," Ettrias said.

"I know. I hope they can open it."

The two men Kadis had sent back eventually returned with a length of rope, a tall, muscular-looking pack horse, and some oil used for lubricating hinges and gears. They quickly dropped what they were doing and attached the rope to the hatch and horse while Kadis applied the oil. Talin heard another *screech* as soon as the horse started pulling.

"Get on the rope and help!" Kadis commanded. Grabbing a section of the rope, he tugged it as the horse continued to pull. Red Wolf did likewise, and two of the swordsmen joined them. The hatch inched upwards a little more. Red Wolf and Talin exchanged glances.

"On three!" Kadis yelled. "One...two...three!"

The hatch finally gave way with a loud *crack*, sending them staggering. Kadis dropped the rope and pushed it open completely.

"Get me a torch," he said. Red Wolf lit one for him and tossed it. "Now, let's see what we have here..."

They followed him down into the storehouse cautiously, careful not to trip over anything. Four of his swordsmen stayed at the top to guard the area.

"Here." Kadis lit the two other torches in the storehouse and set his down in an empty bracket. "Look around. We must take stock of our new inventory."

Red Wolf beckoned to Talin, and she followed him down one of the narrow aisles between the shelves. She could see each shelf was filled with crates and barrels, all nailed down. Her bodyguard pried one open with his bare hands and revealed a dozen high-quality swords.

"Oh, Kadis is going to be happy about this."

Talin helped him lever open a few more crates with a knife, all of them containing weapons. Another one revealed tiny vials of liquid, probably some type of poison or potion. One of the barrels was filled to the brim with steel ingots.

"I told you there would be more than enough." Kadis flashed them a grin from the other side of the storehouse.

"These weapons are incredible," Red Wolf said, examining one of the swords. "Folded Draconian steel, dark oak handle...perfectly balanced. Where did your father get them made?"

"Master blacksmiths in the far south," Kadis said. "I could not ask for better blades to arm my men with."

Red Wolf examined a few more blades before taking the crates out of the storehouse.

"I've arranged for transports to pick up these supplies," Kadis said. "We have finished much earlier than I expected. Perhaps you would care to return to the den with me?"

"I don't see why not," Red Wolf said.

"Excellent. By all means, lead the way." Kadis gestured for Red Wolf to lead and mounted his horse. Ettrias joined him too, leaving Talin to ride with Ashera and Kadis' two guards.

"So, what are your plans now that we have these supplies?" Red Wolf asked. "You could gain a hefty sum if you sold them, or you could arm your troops with the weapons and sell your old ones."

Kadis shrugged. "We will trade what we can afford to trade. Either way, we should have plenty of resources to build our siege weapons and take El'Vane."

"El'Vane will not be easy to siege," Red Wolf said. "Especially if you wish to do so with minimal civilian casualties. I doubt the insurgents will simply surrender the capital."

"I have more spies on the inside, ready to act on my order," Kadis explained. "Vohlan was able to gain access to some of the city blueprints and memorise them before his capture. We know roughly what to expect; it's only a matter of sabotaging the defences."

"An interesting tactic. I like it."

"I'm glad you do. We will discuss more at the next war council. For now, we must focus on transporting our supplies back to the den and trading them."

"I'll leave the battle strategies up to you, of course."

"Please, don't hesitate to provide input. I cannot hope to take the city on my own."

"What can you tell us about the insurgents?" Talin asked. "We've been here for almost a month now. Apart from understanding that they're cold-hearted Elitists who want nothing more than to rule the empire, we know nothing about them."

"Most are warlords and nobility who are dissatisfied with my father's rule, and Ve'Tehll is the one who rallied them together. They believe in keeping a strict social hierarchy which means the commoners stay poor while the nobility grows ever richer. Others are enemies of the state who share common purpose with the warlords in usurping my father. Either way, they got what they came for."

"You said many warlords still support your father," Talin said. "Why didn't they rally when the insurgents took over?"

"They were afraid. The insurgents at the time had the support of three different mercenary factions. There were perhaps over a million troops at their disposal. But since taking over, they've spread thin, and the largest faction has left Ve'Tehll's service. I've spent years finding and rallying those loyal to the true emperor. The insurgents' hold on the empire is loosening, and even without our help, it will crumble eventually. People are growing bolder. More dissatisfied."

"If I could make a suggestion—" Red Wolf cut himself off. Talin watched as his gaze swivelled to the bushes to their left.

Just in time to take an arrow to the chest.

His horse reared and threw him, forcing him into a roll to avoid breaking his neck on impact. He quickly scrambled to his feet and freed his weapon.

"Ambush!" Kadis growled, drawing his sword.

"Yep, we'd gathered." Ettrias unsheathed his own weapon, Elven steel glinting gold in the light. Talin quickly realised that she'd left her bow back at the range.

"Take this!" Red Wolf drew a dagger and passed it up to her. He spun in time to parry an attack from a charging insurgent and slit the Drakel's throat. The horses reared again at the scent of blood, and Talin found herself flying from the saddle, landing unceremoniously on the grass. She got back up without missing a beat and managed to parry a strike from an attacking Drakel before Kadis' sword flashed past and dropped the man dead.

"Flank around, find that archer," Kadis growled. His two guards steered their mounts into the bushes immediately. Talin turned as three more insurgents jumped out from their left. Ashera parried a strike and stabbed the man in the stomach, sending him toppling. Talin muttered a silent apology and drove her blade into the second Drakel's chest while he was distracted. Kadis rammed his shoulder into the third before taking off his opponent's head.

"Watch your right," Red Wolf growled. Another two arrows sailed out of the air towards them, almost too fast for Talin to see. He knocked them both aside with his sword. Talin saw more movement in the trees. They were outnumbered here, far outnumbered.

"Here." One of Kadis' swordsmen returned and passed her a bow and a handful of arrows. She gave him a nod of thanks as he took up a position beside his prince. Red Wolf had backed up beside her now, completely covering her from any attacks from the right, and Ashera was defending her left, giving her an easy position to shoot from. She sent two arrows flying without hesitation and dropped two charging insurgents. On her right, Red Wolf took a slash to the ribs, glared at the insurgent who'd cut him, and took the man's head off with his blade. He rolled his shoulders and scowled at his dead opponent as another insurgent watched on. The Drakel hesitated a second before turning and running. Talin let him go.

"Archer in the trees," Red Wolf hissed. Another arrow sailed out and buried itself in his gut. He took the hit with a grunt. Talin scanned the nearby branches, found two archers perched there, and shot them both. Ettrias backed his horse towards them too and tightened the circle they'd formed.

"I should've stayed at the den," he muttered.

"You can dream." Talin saw a Drakel charging beside him and sent an arrow under the soldier's helmet and into his eye. Another one came at her while she was distracted. Red Wolf stepped between them neatly and cut him down. Two more insurgents charged him at the same time. One Drakel managed to get through his defence and land a blow across his arm, but he took off the man's head in retaliation, while the other took the opportunity to stab him in the side. He cut that one down as well, and the remaining insurgents finally seemed to get the idea and fled.

"An unusually small attack force," Kadis said, dismounting to check the bodies. "Perhaps they hoped to catch me unprepared."

"I'm more worried about how close they are to the den," Red Wolf said. He tugged out the dagger in his side with a wince and dropped it. "If they've learned of your location, then you're no longer safe there."

"The insurgents could not have known about the den," Kadis said. "More likely their spies recognised me in the area and sent assassins to kill me. It's not the first time something like this has happened."

"Either way, I recommend we take precautions," Red Wolf said. He grabbed the arrow in his gut and was about to free it when Talin noticed that he was still bleeding.

"Red Wolf, *wait!*" she cried. His gaze snapped up to her.

"Something wrong?" he asked.

"Shouldn't you have healed by now...?" Talin's voice trailed off. Red Wolf stared at her for a few moments as if she'd gone mad before bringing his hand to the stab wound in his side. His fingers came away covered in blood.

"That's new." He fell to one knee heavily. "Very interesting."

Oh, by the gods.

"Red Wolf." Confusion quickly turned to alarm, and Talin ripped off her cloak to press it into his side.

"What's going on? Why aren't you healing?" Ettrias demanded.

"As I said, it's...new." Red Wolf hissed through his teeth. He let out a breathless chuckle. "Fascinating. Didn't think I...*could* bleed like this."

He slumped forwards, and Talin had to put an arm across his shoulders to stop him from falling face-first onto the grass.

"Get him back to the den, quickly," Kadis said, helping Ettrias carry the bodyguard and lift him onto his horse. Talin snatched up some of the insurgents' weapons before following, determined to find out if the blades had anything to do with it.

They managed to drag Red Wolf back to the den, where a few more of Kadis' men rushed to help carry him upstairs. There, the healers stripped his gear and cut his tunic free, fully revealing the extent of his injuries. Talin watched them remove the arrows still lodged in his torso and bind his wounds. Ettrias snatched her cloak off the floor and offered to wash it for her. She didn't complain.

"Bring those blades you took from the insurgents," Master Celio said. She handed over the weapons silently.

"Come, come, we must take these to my lab," the healer continued, rushing off without waiting for her. She glanced at Red Wolf before following.

"Will he...be alright?" she asked Celio.

"Time will tell." He didn't look back at her. "Your friend has informed me of his...shall we say...abilities. I may have some idea as to what is happening."

"I thought the Drakels didn't study magic anymore," Talin said.

"Not magic, science," Celio said. They rounded a corner and continued down another flight of stairs. "A great deal can be achieved with science nowadays if you're willing to learn it. Magic is overrated. Powerful, yes, but unpredictable. Science is reliable."

Talin wasn't entirely sure what Celio was talking about, but she decided that the old Drakel must know his stuff. She kept silent as he led her to his laboratory at the bottom of the stairs. She recognised the glass flasks and tubes of an alchemist's lab, as well as a number of odd contraptions and magnifying devices that she'd never seen before.

"You're an alchemist as well as a healer?" she asked. *Like Corvan back home.*

"Well, I suppose that is what you elves would call us." Celio flashed her a smile and turned to his equipment to tinker with the blades. "Interesting, very interesting." He left his workbench and moved to his shelves to look for a book, occasionally muttering to himself. He found the right book eventually and began thumbing through the pages. Kadis and Ettrias soon joined them in the lab, and the three of them watched in silence as the healer continued his research.

"I can tell you it's some kind of poison, but unless my records are wrong..." Celio scratched his head. "No, no, there's nothing else it could point to."

"What?" Kadis growled.

"*Torslek*," the healer said, looking grim.

Kadis visibly paled. Talin hadn't thought it was possible for a Drakel to go pale.

"What's that?" she asked.

"A very rare kind of venom artificially produced by our brewers. They say a few drops can kill a man within minutes," Kadis said. "We call it torslek. Deathbane."

Talin felt a chill going through her. "Red Wolf...he's..."

"Still alive, yes," Celio said. "His healing is extraordinary, but this venom must be powerful enough that it is stopping his wounds from closing."

"But he..." Talin wasn't sure what she had wanted to say.

"We will do what we can for him." Celio stepped away from his workbench. "Time will tell if he lives. I have seen this venom at work before, and I can tell you it acts fast. Any ordinary man would be long gone."

"Don't you have an antidote for it?" Talin asked.

"Torslek is expensive and the antidote even more so. We do not have the resources to make it or source it from elsewhere."

Her head spun. She felt like she couldn't breathe. "So...what? We just...hope that he'll recover?"

"He's dying, Your Majesty. There's no denying it." Celio sighed. "His healing may still take over, but I cannot be certain. I'm sorry."

Kadis hissed through his teeth. "Celio, gather the generals and tell them about the torslek. I want a war meeting." He turned and headed back upstairs.

Talin still couldn't breathe. She felt as if an invisible force had grabbed her throat and cut off her airways, crushing her slowly from the inside.

This was never meant to happen. Red Wolf was never meant to get hurt.

"I'll...go to the war meeting in your stead," Ettrias said. "You should stay with Red Wolf."

Talin gave him an absentminded nod and left the lab, quickly finding Red Wolf's room upstairs. She took a seat at the foot of the bed. He'd tell her that this was part of his job, most likely, that he would die for her if he had to, but it didn't make her feel any better. Here they were, so far from home, all because of her decision to go west. Red Wolf would be fine if she hadn't left Belanore.

He would be fine, and my people would be dying.

She had to stop denying it, she supposed. She had let Red Wolf get close to her in these last few weeks; too close, perhaps. Now she couldn't step away. Whatever happened now, she had to help Kadis take back the throne for his father and get the army she'd come here for.

If it's not already too late.

Talin looked to the window, at the forests beyond the den. Far beyond those trees was the border between their two lands. They had come such a long way from Belanore. She wasn't sure she believed it had been possible.

"I never thanked you for all your years of protecting me," she told Red Wolf. "Protecting my father. Being a good advisor. For being a friend." She hesitated. "Are we...friends?"

Talin was glad he couldn't answer. She wasn't sure she wanted to know what he would say, or which answer she preferred.

After some deliberation, she headed downstairs for the war council. There was nothing to be gained from her staying with Red Wolf; it wasn't as if she could do anything for him, not with her limited knowledge of healing. The guards at the door to the war room let her in without hesitation. Inside, Kadis' generals had already gathered, and Ettrias was busy studying the map table. He looked up when he noticed her.

"Joining after all?" he asked.

"There's nothing I can do upstairs. I can make more of a difference here."

Ettrias shuffled to make room for her. The room fell silent when Kadis entered.

"Thank you for convening at such short notice," he said. "As you may have already been informed, we are facing a new threat. The insurgents have a supply of torslek. We must find their stashes before they can strike again."

"If they have torslek, how are we to win now?" one of his generals demanded. "I have heard stories of that venom. A simple scratch with a poisoned blade can kill."

"From my understanding, it's expensive," Talin said. "They can't possibly have a large supply of it. Enough for a small team of trained assassins, perhaps, like the group we ran into. Not enough to poison every blade in their army."

"Her Majesty speaks the truth." Kadis nodded. "We are not looking for a large supply of torslek, only enough that they might give to assassins sent to kill me and my generals. All of you."

"A stash that small would be impossible to find," Bo'Kata said. "Even if my scouts were to search every inch of the empire..."

"But we can find the brewers who make them." Talin tapped the map table. "If it's so expensive to make, it cannot be a task for any inexperienced brewer apprentice. We are looking for masters of their craft, most likely."

"Again, very true," Kadis said. "I will contact my spies in El'Vane and find out if there are any brewers producing torslek there. In the meantime, we must send word to the warlords who have agreed to rally for me. Their spies can also collect information."

"You will need better armour in case you cannot find the torslek," Ettrias added. "No offence to your armourers—they produce excellent work—but your current armour leaves too many gaps for small blades to get through."

"I will talk to the armourers," Kadis said. "Bo'Galesh, send out the messages to the warlords. The rest of you will continue to search for my father. This council is dismissed."

The generals disbanded while Kadis remained behind to stare at the map table. Talin paused at the door to look back at him.

"The attack force that ambushed us was awfully close to the storehouse. I suspect they had a secondary objective." Kadis' brow furrowed. "I think it will be best if you and your brother accompany the transports tomorrow. Red Wolf's squire, too."

Talin understood. "Yes, a necessary precaution."

They set off early the next morning after breakfast, this time properly armed to defend against potential attacks, Ettrias and Ashera with their swords and daggers and Talin with her bow. She wished that Red Wolf was here too; he was still breathing when she checked on him after breakfast but hadn't shown any signs of improving. Celio had come in to change his bandages and she had been called away before he finished.

"Still thinking about Red Wolf?" Ettrias asked as they neared the storehouse.

"I…" Talin sighed. "Yes. I didn't mean for any of this to happen. We're so far from home and he might not even survive."

"I know." Ettrias rubbed his chin. "How do I put this? You have feelings for him."

Talin was about to protest when she stopped herself. "I don't know, I—"

The two of them stopped at the same time. Behind them, the rest of the transport escort also halted.

"Oh, no…" Talin whispered. The guards whom Kadis had assigned to the storehouse last night all lay dead in pools of blood. Some of the crates left outside had been smashed and others were missing. Ashera ducked down to check the inside of the storehouse while Kadis' soldiers rushed to secure the perimeter.

"Kadis is not going to be happy about this," she said. Talin quickly joined her at the entrance, feeling her stomach drop and her blood turn to ice.

The storehouse was empty.

XXIII

"What do you mean, completely empty?" Kadis growled. He stopped and glared at them before continuing to pace in front of the map table.

"They raided it in the middle of the night, killed all your guards, and took the supplies," Ettrias said. "Everything. They left a few swords behind but nothing else."

Kadis snarled and slammed his hand against a box of map pins, scattering them everywhere. "Find them! I want those supplies back!"

"Bo'Kata's rangers are already on it," Talin said. "We will head back in a moment to help find some tracks."

"*Go.* I want my supplies." Kadis turned away. Talin took it as a sign to leave.

"Red Wolf could help us track them down," Ettrias muttered, once they were outside. "How is he?"

"Still in no condition to be going anywhere," Talin said. "We have to do this ourselves."

"We should have known they were going to do this." Ettrias cursed. "Without those supplies..."

"Yes, no need to remind me." Talin knew what this meant. Without the supplies, Kadis couldn't hope to get the siege weapons he needed to take the capital, and she wouldn't get the troops she needed to save Kies Tor.

"They must have left something behind," Ettrias said. "Those boxes would have been heavy. They must have left wagon tracks from their transports."

The two of them met up with Ashera back at the storehouse. Bo'Kata's archers had left already, following a trail.

"I found the tracks," the girl told them proudly. "There. In the dirt, all these footprints. Plus, all these sticks were broken, and all the dried leaves stepped on."

"Well done," Ettrias said. "Which way?"

"That way, silly." Ashera pointed towards the nearest road. "Come on. If we're quick, we can still catch up to the rangers."

The girl rushed off without waiting for them, and Talin had to run to keep up. The tracks seemed to zigzag through the forest and towards the main road, but after following Ashera for several minutes, they came across Bo'Kata's rangers clustered at the side of the road.

"Oh, no." Talin felt her heart sink. "You lost the trail."

"Yes." One of the rangers turned away from the group to acknowledge their presence. "The tracks end here and just...vanish. We don't know where they went."

"That's not good." Talin looked around for anything they might've missed and came up with nothing.

"How do they leave a trail as clear as day and make it just disappear like that?" Ettrias asked.

"They...might have left it on purpose," Ashera suggested. "They must have known we would try to follow. This could be the work of some scouts or someone to throw us off."

"The girl has a point," the ranger said. "We should return to the storehouse and look for other clues."

They picked up their gear and followed the trail back to its source. Kadis himself had arrived by now and was busy examining the area.

"I take it you lost their trail," he said without looking up.

"Unfortunately." Ettrias shrugged. "No matter, though. Ashera believes it was a sort of red herring to throw us off track."

"Then they must have left some other clue as to where they went," Kadis said. "Conduct another search."

The rangers moved off immediately.

"Your Highness!"

Talin and Kadis looked up simultaneously to find Bo'Galesh hurrying towards them, red scales standing out in the greenery surrounding him. Two swordsmen followed behind, dragging a hooded elf after them.

"He claims he's looking for Queen Talin," Bo'Galesh said. His swordsmen pushed the man forwards and pulled off his hood. Underneath, he had a tuft of dark hair and a beard from days of travel, and he looked like he'd been caught in more than one Torrian storm, but there was no mistaking who it was. Captain Golmin.

"It's fine. I know him," Talin said. "He's a friend. Do him a favour and free his hands, please."

Bo'Galesh looked to Kadis, who gave a barely perceptible nod. The general drew a knife and sliced through the ropes binding Golmin's hands.

"Thank you," he said.

"What in the name of the gods are you doing here?" Talin demanded.

"My apologies for coming unannounced, but we had no idea how to reach you." He glanced past her shoulder, where Ettrias was hovering. "Could we, ah...discuss it in private? Where is Red Wolf?"

"It's a long story," Talin said. She pulled him aside, out of earshot of everyone else. "What's the matter?"

"Master Corvan and Lord Cassius sent me. We've uncovered treachery in your Royal Council," he said. "We know Lord Wormwood is plotting to overthrow you. He's working...uh..." He faltered there. "Apologies. Lord Karl is working with him, and Virion has been acting odd since he left Belanore. We suspect he is either working with Wormwood or has betrayed all of us and allied himself with the Hellhounds."

Talin stared at him, unsure if she'd heard right. She'd ridden west under Wormwood's advice, but if Golmin's report was true...

"You're certain?"

"Absolutely," Golmin said. "I know why you are here, but you must return home, Your Majesty. Stop Wormwood before it's too late."

There's something he's not telling me.

"That's not the full story, is it?" Talin asked.

"I...don't understand," Golmin said. His gaze flickered ever so briefly towards Ettrias.

"I need to know everything, Captain," Talin said. "If this is about Ettrias, you have my word that there will be no consequences for revealing the truth."

Golmin ran a hand over his beard and hissed through his teeth. "Ettrias...is the one who put Wormwood up to all of this. They want to put him on the throne."

"Thank you," Talin said. *My own brother working against me. I should have known.*

"Wormwood asked us to swear allegiance to your brother and recognise him as our rightful king," Golmin continued. "Corvan has pretended to do so, but I refused. What he's doing now, trying to destroy your legacy...I couldn't be a part of it."

"I understand." Talin let out a long breath. "I thought he might be better than this. But no, he'd been planning all this from the beginning."

"I could find out if he is still involved in this plot," Golmin said. "If you wished."

Talin shook her head. She had to do this herself. "I will talk to him."

"As you wish, Your Majesty," Golmin said. "But I've been tasked with seeing you home. Wormwood is trying to destroy the people's faith in you by spinning a lie about you fleeing west and abandoning everyone. You must return and prove them wrong."

"We cannot leave, Captain. Not now." Talin's face fell.

Golmin was quick to realise the cause. "Where is he?"

"Back at Kadis' hideout. I will explain everything, I promise, but we have another problem for now," Talin said. "Insurgents have taken all of Prince Kadis' supplies. We think they left a trail to throw us off, but that would mean there is a second trail somewhere nearby. Red Wolf has always praised your tracking skills. Perhaps you could find them."

"It would be my honour." Golmin followed her back to the storehouse where Ettrias and Ashera were still helping the Drakels search. They both straightened when they noticed him return.

"I missed you, Rufus!" The girl said, wrapping her arms around his waist. He gave her a slight smile and ruffled her hair.

"My prince," he said, looking up again.

"It's good to see you," Ettrias said. Talin was put off by how genuine he sounded. Perhaps he didn't have anything to do with the plan...?

"Likewise," Golmin said stiffly. "The queen tells me we are looking for a trail to follow."

"We haven't had much luck so far, I'll admit," Ettrias said.

"Hmm." Golmin crouched down to examine some of the smashed crates. "Was there much left?"

"A few crates of weapons, nothing else," Ettrias said.

"Swords, I assume? Or other weapons?"

"Yes, mostly swords. A few maces, one or two crates of axes," Kadis called from the other side of the clearing.

"It was too heavy for them to carry, most likely," Golmin said. "They left the cheapest crates behind and took off with the rest. They didn't know how many supplies to expect and weren't prepared." He looked at the prints and disturbed undergrowth that marked the false trail. "Sloppy. This starts right at the entrance. Check the opposite direction."

Talin turned her attention to the other side of the clearing. "I don't see anything."

"Easy to miss, not to worry. Especially when you've been bringing horses in all day." Golmin stood and crouched again some distance from the storehouse entrance and poked a pile of horse dung with a stick. "A horse stood here, waiting. Took a nice dump." He brushed aside some of the freshly fallen leaves to reveal faint hoofprints in the dirt, barely visible.

"Tracks here. They brought only one wagon," he continued, pointing at a spot closer to the storehouse, where two deep grooves had been made in the ground. "They loaded everything up but realised it was too heavy for both wagon and horse. They tossed the crates off the back and then paved a temporary path for the wagon to hide its tracks. That way." He pointed again, into the forest with his stick, before tossing it into a bush. "Follow it to the nearest road. You might find something there. I'll be happy to assist."

"Rufus, you're a genius." Ettrias clapped the captain on the back.

Golmin cracked a faint smile.

"Rangers, follow the trail but do not engage any insurgents," Kadis said. "If you come across the supplies, report their location."

The rangers darted off into the trees.

"You, Highlander." Kadis pointed at Golmin. "I'll have you escorted back to the den. My servants will draw you a bath and prepare a room."

"I suppose this isn't an offer," Golmin said.

Kadis shrugged. "I could always have you escorted to the dungeons instead if you don't want somewhere comfortable to sleep, or let you set up camp outside the den." He broke into a grin.

Golmin snorted. "Far be it for me to refuse your generosity, then."

"Good." Kadis waved two of his guards over to take Golmin to the den.

"If we're not needed here, I think we will retire too," Talin said. She glanced at Ettrias. "We have some catching up to do."

"Of course, feel free," Kadis gave another absentminded wave, dismissing them. "I will send for you if we have need of your assistance again."

The four of them made the trek back to the den together, led by the two guards. Golmin was taken down to the bathing areas to get himself cleaned and shaved, and Ettrias offered to spar with Ashera in Red Wolf's absence. Talin considered going to the archery range again for more practice, but decided she wasn't in the mood for it and went back to Red Wolf's room instead. He still lay there unconscious, immobile save for the rise and fall of his chest. She took the chair in the corner of the room and sat herself by his bed.

"I'm sorry," she said, even though she knew he'd tell her it was unnecessary. "If I'd never come here, this wouldn't be happening."

Silence.

"Maybe it doesn't matter who I am to you," Talin continued. "But I...I think..." she swallowed and shook her head. "Never mind. Just...please, *please* get better. I can't lose you. Not here, not like this."

She stayed by his bed for several more minutes, pondering all that could have happened instead. Perhaps, in the end, he was lucky that neither arrow had gone through his heart and killed him instantly.

Footsteps sounded behind her. She turned her head to see Golmin pull up a spare chair and slide into it, beard and hair now neatly trimmed.

"Kadis' men caught me up on what happened," he said.

"This was my doing," Talin said softly. "I brought everyone here. I should have kept him safe."

Golmin huffed a quiet laugh. "I think it's Red Wolf's job to keep *you* safe, Your Majesty, not the other way around."

"If we hadn't gone west..." Talin's voice trailed off. "Gods, we shouldn't even be here. I followed Wormwood's advice like a damn fool. I *trusted him*. Maybe if I'd listened to Red Wolf when he warned me about Wormwood, if I'd known how to fight, how to lead my people and *stayed in Belanore*..." She shook her head. "All of this is my fault."

"Gods, you *do* have feelings for him," Golmin said under his breath.

"What?" Talin looked at him.

"Nothing, Your Majesty," Golmin said. "You are not at fault for this. Red Wolf would tell you the same. Perhaps trusting Wormwood was a mistake. Perhaps riding here was a mistake. But it doesn't matter now. The *only thing* that matters...is doing what's right from this point onwards."

Talin let out a long breath. "Maybe. I just..."

She didn't dare admit her feelings to herself.

"I should talk to my brother," she said instead, rising to her feet. Golmin remained unmoving by Red Wolf's bed as she took her leave.

She found Ettrias still on the training grounds with Ashera, as expected, watching the girl go through her drills on a training dummy. He saw her coming and motioned for Ashera to continue practising.

"Ettrias, we need to talk," Talin said. Her brother looked up.

"Something tells me I'm not going to like this." He stood.

"No, you won't," Talin said. "You should know why Golmin came all the way out here to find us. To find *me*."

"And?"

"He says my council is conspiring against me. That *you* swayed them to your side in your efforts to take the throne."

"Ah." Ettrias scratched his head. "I'll admit, I had been...how shall we put it...working against you in Belanore. But you already know that. Hear me out, Talin. Things have changed. I promise. I've changed. After everything that's happened...after what Kadis said...well, I realise now that neither of us was prepared to rule a kingdom. But you're better suited to it than I ever will be. You wanted to make things better; I just...wanted to be in charge." He sighed. "I will leave Kies Tor after all this if that is your wish. For now, I only want to clear my name."

"And what about Wormwood? Are you to tell him nicely that you no longer want the throne and to drop whatever plans he's concocted?" Talin demanded. "I don't think you've quite thought this through, Ettrias!"

"I know it looks bad, but I promise I will fix this," Ettrias said. "I started this mess. I will clean it up."

"I hope you do." Talin turned away. "Yours and Red Wolf's lives are both at stake here."

She left without another word.

XXIV

"How is he?"

Golmin looked up to see Ettrias step through the doorway of Red Wolf's room, Ashera in tow. One look at his guilty expression told the captain that the queen had already talked to him, and the conversation had gone less than favourably. Golmin sighed and refrained from making any comment.

"I've never seen him bleed," he said instead. "We'd spar in private with sharpened blades. Every hit I landed, he would heal from instantly. This is...well, I don't know what to make of it."

"Funny how he's just an ordinary man without his powers," Ettrias said.

"But he'll...he'll get better, won't he?" Ashera asked. "I don't want him to die. I don't want to be alone..." Her bottom lip wobbled.

"You're not alone." Ettrias crouched and put his hands on her shoulders. "You've got me, you've got Rufus, my sister the queen of all people...we'll look after you. Promise."

Ashera burst into tears.

"Oh...Ashera... Shh." Ettrias pulled her into an awkward hug and looked to Golmin for help. The captain gave him an incredulous look.

Orrlat, why do I always end up doing this?

"Here, come with me." He stood and stretched out a hand to the girl. "We'll get you some hot cocoa from the kitchen. You'll feel better in no time. A warm drink always helps."

Ashera sniffled and looked up, lip still wobbling. Golmin offered his best reassuring smile and wriggled his fingers.

"Go on, it'll help," Ettrias said. "Really."

Ashera took Golmin's hand hesitantly and allowed him to lead her from the room. Together, they made their way down to the kitchen, where he awkwardly explained the situation to the cooks in Torrian and asked if they had any hot cocoa for the girl. One of the serving ladies who could understand the Elven language took pity on her and offered to let her help with making some honey cakes.

"Thank you," Golmin said to the Drakel woman.

"It's no trouble at all," she said. "It must be a difficult time for all of you, being so far from home."

"We're coping," Golmin said. "You'll be alright here, Ashera?"

The girl nodded. "It'll...be nice...to make some honey cakes."

"Alright. Behave yourself and stay out of trouble." Golmin ruffled her hair and returned to Ettrias alone.

"How is she?" the prince asked once he'd taken a seat again.

"A little better. I think," Golmin said.

He knew Red Wolf had always felt responsible for the girl since he returned with Arnas from the Battle of Fallbjorn with her in tow. The town was razed, its people scattered, and despite Red Wolf's protests, Arnas had refused to spend some of their strained resources to help the civilian survivors. The royal bodyguard had, however, insisted on satisfying one dying woman's plea to take her daughter to Belanore and keep her safe.

Was it worth it?

Red Wolf would probably tell him that it was.

"I'm...sorry if telling the queen about Wormwood has resulted in any unpleasantness between you two," Golmin said after a beat. "I had hoped to keep you out of trouble, but..."

"Better that she knows sooner than later," Ettrias said. "Besides, things have changed. Maybe it's a good thing that you came to warn her."

"Why did you ally yourself with Wormwood?" Golmin asked. "Why work to not only overthrow the queen, but destroy her reputation? *Why didn't you tell me anything?*"

"I knew you wouldn't approve." Ettrias looked away. "When I first came to Belanore, I had no idea that Talin was clueless about my father's plan. I thought she was part of it, the same as Red Wolf. I had to have revenge."

"Revenge." Golmin scoffed. "I considered joining you. Working with Wormwood and putting you back on the throne, like it was supposed to be. But going to all these lengths for *revenge*? This isn't like you."

"I was angry at the world for abandoning me. Angry enough that I wanted to get back at the people who wronged me," Ettrias said. "That's...changed. I thought I was angry at my sister, at Red Wolf.

That's faded now that I know she had no idea what our father did. If she had, she wouldn't have stood by and done nothing. And Red Wolf...well, I haven't forgiven him yet. But I now know why he did it."

Golmin didn't respond.

"I suppose I owe you an apology for going behind your back. Forcing you to choose between me and your duty to the Crown."

"I would probably have joined you if you'd asked."

Ettrias huffed a half-laugh. "It's a good thing you didn't. As it stands, it's not too late to undo the damage that Wormwood has caused. I hope."

"You're serious about this?" Golmin asked. "Fixing things, I mean."

"Yes," Ettrias said. "I want my name cleared. After that...maybe the two of us still have a chance to pick up where we left off ten years ago."

Golmin cracked a smile. "That would be good."

Ettrias glanced at Red Wolf. "I just wish...it wasn't him. Father could have sent someone else. Anyone. Hired some *abijo* assassin. But he used Red Wolf instead."

"It's all in the past now," Golmin said. "Red Wolf made his choice."

He had to admit, much as he still wanted to be upset at the man, that there had been little 'choice' in such a matter at all; Red Wolf would either condemn Ettrias or himself. And perhaps it was ultimately a selfish decision, but Golmin understood why he made it all the same. Refusing the *king* would never have gone well for someone like him.

Ettrias quirked an eyebrow. "Are you still mad at him? You're not the only one he's kept secrets from. Talin didn't talk to him for a week when she found out about his Hellhound abilities."

"I thought...we trusted each other." Golmin shook his head. "Turns out he's been lying to me for *ten years*."

And if he had told you, then what?

"I count it as a good thing you didn't know," Ettrias said. "Knowing how far my father went to pull off his plan…"

Golmin understood. If he had known, if Red Wolf had told him, and Arnas had found out, there was no way he would have escaped the king's wrath. Arnas would have made *certain* that he never told another soul.

There was a knock on the door. Ettrias stood and went to answer it, revealing a messenger.

"Kadis' search parties have returned," the Drakel said. "He asks that you attend his war meeting, Prince Ettrias."

"I'll be down in a moment," Ettrias said. He turned back to Golmin. "Well, duty calls, or whatever the seven hells you guards like to say. We'll have to catch up some other time."

"Of course," the captain said. "I'll see you later."

The door creaked, and then Ettrias was gone. Golmin turned his attention back to Red Wolf.

"Get better soon, you big oaf," he muttered. "I promise not to be too mad at you when you wake up."

I don't know what I'll do otherwise. He didn't voice the thought.

K adis' storehouse group returned at dusk with the rangers who had been following the insurgents' trail. They looked grim, and some of the rangers looked battered, as if they had been caught in a skirmish of some sort. The Draconian prince called an emergency war meeting without bothering to change out of his armour, dragging his generals from whatever downtime they had been enjoying.

"We found the supplies," he growled once they'd all convened. "But we're no closer to our goal than we were before. They saw us coming and fled before we could get close. Engaging them did nothing to slow them down."

"Did you get a glimpse of their numbers?" Talin asked.

"Yes. A small party, hardly likely to put up resistance, but moving back past the den on horseback. We can cut them off tomorrow if we set out early and take a shortcut through the forest." Kadis removed his helmet and set it down on the map table. "I hope we are not too late by then."

"I'll join you," Talin said. "I've been training to shoot on horseback. We would gain a huge advantage if we can cripple them."

"I agree." Kadis gave a nod. "If we can distract the insurgents for long enough, Bo'Galesh might be able to manoeuvre his cavalry past them and block the road." He pointed at the map. "They're moving down this road, heading southwest, circling the forest and the den directly to the west. We can catch them easily. I could have the engineers craft some explosive arrows with black powder. That would take out the wagon's wheels on impact. They would be forced to stop, which would buy us the time we need to surround them. Can I rely on you to fire them?" He looked at Talin.

"As long as they're similar enough to a regular arrow, I can send it wherever you want," she said.

"Good. Bo'Kata will provide a backup shot if you do miss." Kadis flattened his palms on the table. "Bo'Galesh, how many horses do you have?"

"Ten war steeds, twenty if you're willing to lend the other mounts too," Bo'Galesh replied.

"Ten will do." Kadis took a flag and set it down on the road. "They will have to stop for the night somewhere around here. If we ride directly west early in the morning, we can intercept them along the road before they get too far ahead. Once the convoy is brought to a halt, Bo'Galesh and his cavalry will seal the road ahead, here." He set down another flag. "We will box them in and take back our supplies. Once the wagon is secured, we will bring in our own transport and transfer everything back to the den. Any objections?"

There was a mutter of 'nays' around the table. Kadis straightened.

"Very well. I will talk to the engineers and have the arrows prepared for tomorrow. The rest of you know your duties. This council is dismissed."

The room dispersed. Talin went to find Golmin to inform him of the plan, and he offered to join the party. She told him to take it up with Kadis, though it was unlikely the Drakel would refuse an extra sword. He went to find the prince, and she decided to ask the engineers to craft a dummy explosive arrow so she could get used to the weight. They happily obliged. Talin took her practice arrow to the range as the sun dipped below the horizon. She made a few shots with it, going down to retrieve her arrow each time, before heading back to the den.

She wasn't sure what made her recall the day the news of her father's death reached Belanore, but the memory appeared just as she opened the door to go inside. A messenger on horseback had ridden through the gates to deliver the note, written in the king's own hand and splattered with blood. In it, he explained they had lost the battle in the Glass Forest with no survivors and that the Hellhounds would be pushing south to Belanore unless reinforcements arrived. The bells had rung that day as the city mourned. Talin could only remember the last time she'd seen him, riding out with his army, telling her he would return as soon as he secured the Glass Forest and pushed the Hellhounds out of Wycrest.

He'd never chastised her for her reluctance to finish her weapons training, though he often told her that a good ruler had to be ready to fight beside their troops if need be. Reflecting on it now, she realised that perhaps he had played favourites even then; Ettrias had always been the one on the receiving end of his criticism for his poor archery skills. She had lived her life wilfully ignorant of how her brother had been treated because it had been easier to pretend that nothing was wrong.

Perhaps you wanted his approval so much that you were willing to overlook everything else.

Talin cursed herself for not seeing it sooner. She had been so *blind*, failing to recognise how the people around her were suffering until she could no longer run from the truth.

And perhaps that was why she felt guilty about Ettrias now; if she had realised back then how their father had treated him, she could have prevented the coup, or done *something* at least. But now, proving his innocence in front of Kies Tor would condemn Red Wolf. Saving her brother at the cost of another man's life.

Could you do it?

It should not even be a question. Ettrias was her brother. Red Wolf was merely a bodyguard.

Yet she had allowed herself to get close to him over these past few weeks. He was no longer 'merely a bodyguard', but her friend, and...

Talin banished the thought.

They set off the next morning just before dawn, after Kadis' engineers had supplied her with the explosive arrows to blow the wagon wheels. She'd been warned that they were highly volatile and to be extremely careful with them so as not to set one off accidentally. She and Bo'Kata had been given three arrows each in case they missed a shot.

"Look, up ahead," Kadis said, pointing down the road. Talin glimpsed the wagon in the distance, barely a speck. It looked like they had only just started moving, exactly as the prince had predicted. Kadis whistled and his cavalry broke off to seal the road ahead of the wagon.

"Can you hit it from here?" he asked.

"I need to get closer. You can't even see the wheels from this distance," Talin said. "I think they hear us. They're picking up the pace."

"Then we shall match them." Kadis spurred his horse on, prompting the rest of them to do the same. Talin unslung her bow and nocked her first explosive.

"These explosives had better work," she muttered under her breath, and let the arrow fly.

She didn't see where it struck; the wagon was still too far away. But she did hear a sharp *crack* as the arrow exploded and saw a small cloud of dust kick up by the wheel. The wagon kept rolling.

"Aim for the axle!" Bo'Kata said. Talin nocked her second arrow and loosed. This time it struck the wheel dead-on. There was another *crack*, louder this time, as the wheel broke, sending the wagon skidding sideways and eventually coming to a stop. She readied her third arrow just in case, but there was no need. She swapped it for a regular arrow and sent it at the insurgent closest to them. Kadis and his riders overtook her and Bo'Kata to get into the melee. Ahead, she saw Bo'Galesh's cavalry circling, cutting off the road ahead. The only way out of this was into the forests on the right or towards the fields on the left. Talin helped pick off the insurgents trying to slash at Kadis, Golmin or Ettrias. Some of the Drakels had already fled; she could see them running for the trees after throwing down their weapons. She let them go. They were unlikely to be a threat.

Gradually, as the remaining insurgents were struck down or fled, the road grew eerily silent. The cavalry dismounted to finish off the injured insurgents.

"That was a good shot," Kadis said, nodding at the broken wagon wheel. Talin followed his gaze and saw that her arrow had struck it dead on the axle, ripping the wheel completely off. She looked at the dead insurgents sprawled across the road and winced. Some of these deaths had been at her hand; she saw the distinctive Elven fletching of her arrows sticking out from eye sockets and torsos. It was frightening how easy it was to kill a man.

"Get the transports in," Kadis said. "Let's get these supplies out of here."

Talin retrieved what arrows she could salvage and cleaned the tips. Red Wolf had made it look so easy to cut down attackers, but she knew she could never get used to it. All she could do was push the thoughts out of her mind. Worry about it afterwards.

"You're not used to violence. I can see that." Kadis stopped beside her.

"No." Talin didn't see any point in denying it. "I never liked weapons training. I didn't mind archery for hunting, but..."

"I was not used to it at first either. I was a child during the first civil war and understood so little. My father desperately wanted to protect me from the violence. When the insurgents took over, I was inexperienced and didn't know anything about combat. I had to learn everything from my advisors."

"Did it bother you? Relying on your advisors?" Talin asked, mounting her horse again. "On guards to protect you?"

"No. I knew they could not fight my battles for me. They could help; that was all," Kadis said. "You should stop worrying too. If you wish to spend time with your bodyguard, you must learn to fend for yourself. The people around you will not always be there."

"Red Wolf is..." Talin began.

"A friend? Of course." Kadis gave her a slight smile and moved on, leaving her behind. She considered yelling after him that he shouldn't make assumptions, then decided against it.

She knew he was right.

They spent most of the day transporting the supplies back to the den. With the insurgents' wagon out of commission, they had to move everything to their own wagons and ferry them back. Ettrias and Golmin helped guard the road while Talin provided protection for the column from the safety of the trees, and Ashera had joined the transports in the morning and decided to stay as an escort until they were done. Talin admired the girl, in an odd way; here she was, in a strange land, only twelve years old, but she did her part to help the Drakels.

Below, Ashera was happily chatting to one of the younger Draconian swordsmen in Torrian, occasionally pointing at objects around them. The Drakel would nod and repeat the word, then say something in Kier Dekkel. Talin figured she was trying to teach him Torrian and he was teaching her his language in return. She wasn't sure how they had come to their arrangement without understanding each other's language, but in any case, it was better communication than some of the disputes between kings. The wagons rolled on behind them.

A whistle sounded, signalling for the convoy to halt. Talin made her way to the front, keeping to the treetops, to see what was going on. Upon discovering that they were simply stopping the marching swordsmen for a rest, she sat herself down on a thick branch and lowered her bow. Ashera and the Drakel chatted on in their respective languages. Talin saw Bo'Kata watching the convoy from a tree on the other side of the little path they'd carved, and the two exchanged a brief, understanding look.

The whistle sounded again, and the swordsmen began to move. Talin pulled herself to the next branch and tried to keep up. Weeks of training had strengthened her muscles, but she knew she was in no fit state compared to Golmin or Ettrias, who often worked long hours after dark to sharpen their skills. All this climbing through the trees was going to make her sore in the morning. Red Wolf would probably laugh at her complaints and tell her he would go easy on her.

His version of 'easy' isn't very easy at all, Talin thought. She hoped he was recovering; the full moon was tonight, and he would shift, assuming the torslek didn't stop that too. He had told her that Corvan had tried a number of milder, Torrian poisons on him to control his shifting, but they had never worked.

But if the venom does stop him from shifting, does that mean his healing power is permanently gone too?

She preferred not to think about it. If his powers were gone, that would mean that he wasn't likely to survive. He had to survive. She couldn't lose him here.

This was the last convoy they had to escort; after this, all that was left was for the guards on the road to clean up and vanish without leaving any trace of where they'd been or where they had gone. Talin could soon see the outline of the den in the distance, the keep walls rising at the forest edge. They were safe now. She dropped down from the trees and accompanied the convoy on foot the rest of the way. Ashera continued chatting to the swordsman until they had to part ways at the gates, where the wagon was escorted to the warehouse for everything to be sorted and stored. The girl skipped off with a grin on her face, muttering the phrases she'd learned, and the swordsman seemed to be smiling too. Talin could never tell with the Drakels. She bathed and had her clothes sent off with the servants for washing, changing into more comfortable attire. Celio was busy changing Red Wolf's bandages when she entered his room.

"Has he improved at all?" she asked.

"A little," Celio said. "Tonight is the full moon. He tells me he draws his powers from the moon. He will improve further throughout the evening, I believe."

Talin swallowed and tried not to betray her relief. "Thank you."

"You care for him very much, I can tell," Celio said, tying off the new bandages and wiping his hands.

"We're friends," Talin said. Celio didn't respond.

"Let me know if his condition worsens," the healer said instead, shuffling out of the room with his supplies. Talin was about to pull up the chair and sit when Ettrias burst in, still clad in his armour.

"He's recovering?" he asked.

"Celio seems to think so," Talin said.

"Kadis is calling another meeting. His spies have found the torslek suppliers."

"That's excellent news!" Talin followed him back out of the room.

Kadis and his officers had already gathered by the time they entered. Bo'Kata shuffled to make room for them.

"My spies tell me the torslek is being made by private brewers hired by the Elitists and warlords," Kadis explained. "This makes it difficult to halt the supply. The good news is that all of the brewers are situated in one place to make the poison easier to transport in large quantities. Right here. Ked'Fald." He positioned one of his flags on top of a large, fortified castle, several miles south of the den.

"That's a castle," Talin said.

"I'm aware." Kadis sighed. "We have a dilemma, as you can see. With the supplies we have, we could either build our weapons to siege Ked'Fald, or we could ignore it and storm El'Vane. Either assault will be risky."

"The insurgents are less protected in El'Vane. The city is not de-signed to withstand an extended siege. If we can hammer at their walls for a few days, we could get through—or try to starve them out," Bo'Galesh continued. "Ked'Fald is well-fortified and well-supplied. We could be there for months. Of course, from this information, it might seem wiser to storm El'Vane. But if the Elitists have hired private brew-ers to make the torslek, they could more easily make large batches of the poison. Enough to...arm a city, perhaps."

"If we are to siege El'Vane, we would have to spread out and blockade every gate," Kadis said. "The insurgents cannot be allowed to smuggle their torslek into the city."

"And they would get wind of your efforts to siege the capital," Talin said. "Ked'Fald would start sending out as much torslek as possible, and to as many of their troops as possible."

"Exactly." Kadis made a low, rumbling sound in his throat. "We cannot allow the insurgents to distribute the venom."

"Ked'Fald would be a better target if we wanted to prevent them from distributing it," Talin said. "But I fear it will take too long to siege."

"I'm worried about that too," Kadis said. "The castle could survive for months in a siege, but we may not have the supplies to last that long. Besides, a few months is...perhaps too long for you and your companions."

"Unfortunately so," Talin confessed.

"Then we take El'Vane. My engineers will work on crafting better armour to withstand their blades, but if their alchemists find a way to make the poison potent in the air, we will not stand a chance," Kadis said. "We will discuss strategy in the morning. This council is dismissed."

Talin found herself by Red Wolf's bed again after supper, long after the sun had dipped below the horizon and the full moon had risen. Golmin had told her that he shifted at dusk each time. Perhaps he would not be shifting tonight. The temperatures were dropping rapidly, too; Celio had predicted snow. Talin wasn't sure what that looked like but had heard stories of blankets of white ash covering the Highlands in winter.

"My queen..."

Talin turned her head and almost jumped when she saw Red Wolf's golden eyes locked on her.

"You're awake," she breathed.

"Hmm. Wish I...wasn't. Why do you...visit so often?" he asked.

"I...don't know what you mean," she said. How could he know how often she'd visited? He had been unconscious for all of it.

"I hear it. The wolf smells it." Red Wolf grimaced and pressed a hand to his side. "What...what'd they do? How did...my healing...fail?"

"Artificially brewed venom, native to the Draconian Empire," Talin said. "But if you're awake, it must finally be wearing off, surely?"

"Feels like it." Red Wolf tried to struggle into a sitting position but soon gave up with a curse.

"Do you think..." Talin began. "If the venom stopped your healing to this extent, do you think it will work on the Hellhounds?"

"It seems likely," Red Wolf said. He dragged himself to the edge of the bed and half-rolled, half-stumbled off, almost falling face-first onto the floor. "Help me...help me outside. Full moon's...calling. I need to be out there."

"You should rest," Talin said. "The full moon came up hours ago, and if you still haven't shifted..."

"I need...to be outside." He staggered to his feet again and leaned on the windowsill, throwing open the curtains. Talin saw for the first time that flakes of white ash were falling from the sky, covering the ground below.

"What's...?" she began.

"Snow, my queen. No doubt you've never seen anything quite like this before," Red Wolf answered. "This is what a Highlander winter looks like when it gets cold enough in the mountains."

"It's beautiful," Talin said.

"Come, fetch a coat. I will show you." Red Wolf pushed himself away from the window again and somehow made it to the door without collapsing. He leaned on the doorframe heavily for a few moments before continuing.

"I don't think you should be up and about like this—" Talin began, but he was already out of sight. "Oh, for the love of the gods." She threw on a coat and caught up to him at the top of the stairs. He bent over and allowed her to duck under his arm to support some of his weight. Together, they made their way down and out of the den, stopping just before the archery range gave way to trees and shrubbery.

"You never did answer me," Red Wolf said. "Why did you keep visiting?"

"You're...well, you're a...friend," Talin said. "If anything happened to you, I'd feel responsible."

"A friend?" Red Wolf's expression faltered for the barest fraction of a second. "And here I thought we were supposed to have a...professional relationship." He flashed her a teasing smile and bent down to scoop up some of the snow that was forming, placing it into her hands.

"It's cold!" she exclaimed, dropping it.

"Yes, it is." A snowball struck her in the arm. She looked up to see Red Wolf readying another one. "Whoops."

"You know, I have a better aim than you." Talin scooped up a handful of snow and flung it at his head. He brushed it off with a grin. His second snowball landed square on her hip. She flung another handful of snow at his face and laughed as he was forced to wipe it out of his eyes.

"Much as I'd like to continue this, I believe it's time you returned to the den," he said, looking up at the moon. "He's dangerous. I doubt he'll recognise you. If he sees you and decides you're a threat, he will attack without hesitation."

Talin shook her head. "I'm not afraid of him. He saved me at the border."

Red Wolf began unwinding his bandages. "Perhaps, but I cannot take that risk. He is the one thing I cannot protect you from." He let the bandages fall, and she saw then that his wounds had completely healed, leaving no marks behind, save for the old scars across his torso and arms. She didn't dare ask about them.

"I won't just leave you here," she said.

"Please, I can't—" Red Wolf dropped to his hands and knees with a roar of pain as bones cracked and reformed. Talin took a few instinctive steps back. Skin turned into fur and muscles rippled as he transformed. His hands and feet soon became huge, clawed paws, digging into the thick snow. She watched on, unable to look away, until all she could see was a massive, bear-sized wolf with streaks of red running through its coat. Golden-yellow eyes locked onto her, and she could see him, or whatever was left of him, as the wolf's mind took over.

"Easy," she breathed. The wolf stared back, unmoving.

I will not be afraid.

"Red Wolf?"

The wolf cocked its head at that and padded towards her slowly, paws leaving tracks in the snow.

"I know you remember me," Talin said. "I know the world thinks you're a monster."

The wolf growled softly and continued stalking forward.

"You are not a monster." Talin stretched out a hand gingerly. Her heart slammed against her ribcage hard enough for her to hear her own heartbeat. Part of her told her this was suicide, that she should run back inside as fast as she could before it was too late, but she stood her ground.

I will not be afraid.

The wolf stopped with his snout inches from her fingers, close enough that she could feel his breath against her fingertips.

He nudged her hand.

Talin's fingers brushed against his head, and he seemed to allow it, waiting for her to pet him. She ran her hand down the side of his neck, through his fur, watching him in case he decided to attack. He never did. She lowered her hand again gingerly, and he let out another soft growl, stealing one last glance at her before stalking off into the forests beyond. Talin stood there for a while longer, unmoving, listening to her heart pounding against her ribs as the wolf disappeared through the trees.

Then she turned and headed back inside.

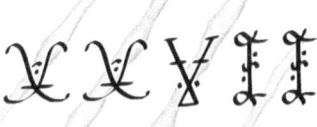

XXVII

Talin arrived in the war room the next morning to find Red Wolf already there, discussing strategy with Kadis. He looked up when she approached the table, and his ears turned bright red, as if he remembered what had happened the night before. Talin smiled and took the spot next to him.

"You were wrong; he was very friendly," she whispered.

"That's a first," he said, trying to sound surprised. She let him have the benefit of the doubt.

"Kadis has caught you up, I hope?" she asked.

"Yes. So has Rufus," Red Wolf said. "I was right about Wormwood, then."

Talin huffed a short exhale. "Fine. You can say it once."

"If Wormwood and Highett plan to move against you, we must ride back as soon as we're able," Red Wolf continued. "Wormwood is cunning. He will use every day you are gone to his advantage. You were right to go for El'Vane. Ked'Fald is far too well-fortified for us to siege."

"What's our plan?" Talin asked.

"We have a few ideas." Kadis let the last few stragglers file in before starting. "El'Vane has four main gates we need to seal. One in the south, where we last made our assault, two in the east, and one more in the northwest. We will need to attack every gate if we want to cut off supply and trade to the city."

"Any secret exits we know about?" Red Wolf asked.

"None," Kadis said. "My hope is to hit the insurgents hard enough to force a surrender. Make them believe they are hopelessly out-matched."

"If they don't? Are we to starve them out?" Bo'Kata demanded.

"Our siege weapons should get us through the walls if we hammer at them long enough. Ve'Darr has already rallied his banners and his generals, as has Lord Marius and most of the far south. The rest will meet us at the capital's gates," Kadis explained. "We have the numbers and the firepower. The insurgents will not last long."

"All the same, we cannot underestimate the city," Red Wolf said. "The insurgents will not give up easily. We must not alert them of our intentions. If they find out we plan to siege the city, they will send their torslek in, and we would see a very short defeat once we breached the walls."

Talin looked at the map of El'Vane that Kadis had rolled out. She pointed to a small marker by the southern gate. "What's that?"

"Sewage grate, too small for anyone to fit through," Kadis said. "We haven't thought of a use for it yet."

"The sewage line runs all the way under the wall?" Talin asked.

"Yes." Kadis crossed his arms. "You have an idea?"

"What's the most powerful explosive your engineers can craft?"

Kadis's mouth twitched. "I like the concept, but my engineers are not *that* good."

"Very well, we'll move on. I assume the insurgents will retreat into the keep once we break through the gates?"

"Of course," Kadis said.

"Your spies could sabotage the drawbridge and prevent them from raising it."

"I like it. I'll send out word."

"Any news of your father's whereabouts?" Red Wolf asked.

"None yet. But if we can take El'Vane, it will not matter where he is," Kadis said. "More warlords will rally to me. Ve'Tehll will lose the capital, the source of his power. They won't be able to hide him forever."

"I'm worried they will try to use him as a bargaining chip," Red Wolf said.

"A possibility, yes," Kadis confessed. "But he would never let them."

Red Wolf nodded. "Still, we must be careful."

The council debated the best way to approach El'Vane for a while longer before finally settling on an agreement; they would move in from the south while Ve'Darr moved in from the west. The southern lords would march with them until they were just out of sight from the city before splitting up and circling to cut off the northwest gate. Talin listened to most of it without giving input. She had little knowledge of how the Draconian warlords functioned or what kind of troops they had at their disposal. From what she could tell, though, Ve'Darr had command of a massive army, large enough to block off both eastern gates without much difficulty.

"When will the siege weapons be ready?" she asked.

"A few days at most. We've already begun producing them," Kadis said. "Never fear, Your Majesty, we will be at the city by the end of the week."

Talin stared at the map table. *We're running out of time. The Hellhounds march south, and Wormwood conspires against me.*

"I'm afraid we cannot stay much longer," she said. "We will help you take El'Vane, as part of our agreement, but we must ride home afterwards. I cannot leave my people to suffer any longer."

"I understand." Kadis dipped his head. "My rebels and I will escort you back to the Den for your belongings once the city is taken."

"Thank you."

"I will send reinforcements to you as soon as we are able. I made a promise and I intend to keep it." Kadis turned his attention back to the map. "Now, if there are no objections, I think we are done."

Later, once Talin had discussed her plans for returning with Golmin and Ettrias, she threw on a warm coat and headed out into the snow-covered fields surrounding the den. The main pathways to the training grounds and the main road had already been cleared, and she could see plenty of footprints where people had been taking shortcuts. For a moment, she considered taking her bow and doing some more training at the range, then decided that she needed a day off after all the climbing she'd been doing yesterday. Her muscles still ached, and her hands were still sore.

"You know, we didn't settle our snowball duel last night," Red Wolf said, appearing beside her. The two of them stood together at the top of the hill, looking down at the fields and forest below.

"I know." Talin crouched down, scooped up a handful of snow and packed it together in her hands. Red Wolf was busy watching the swordsmen training and didn't seem to notice, so she took a few cautious steps away from him and flung the snowball. He ducked, and it sailed over his head harmlessly.

"Trying to go for an ambush? Come, now, that was never going to work." Red Wolf scooped up another snowball and sent it straight into her shoulder. She flung a handful of snow at his face. He shook it off and was about to retaliate when a snowball hit him in the back. Talin leaned over to see who it was and noticed Ashera bending down for a second snowball. Red Wolf grinned and nailed a shot at the girl's head.

"That's not fair!" she exclaimed, straightening and throwing her second snowball at him. Talin aimed one at him too before he could recover.

"Ah, I see I am outnumbered and outmatched." He brushed himself down, still grinning, and raised his hands in surrender. "A good warrior knows when he's beaten. I must concede defeat."

Ashera stuck her tongue out at him. "Come to training?"

"Later, Ashera," Red Wolf said. "I have matters to discuss with my queen."

"Sure you do." Ashera ran off towards the training grounds.

"So, you wanted to discuss something?" Talin asked.

"No, that was a lie." Red Wolf shrugged.

"Oh? Could it be that the lord commander himself is slacking off on his duties?" Talin asked.

"You simply looked like you needed some company, my queen."

Talin smiled. "Well, thank you for providing it."

She looked to the training grounds and saw the tiny figure of Ashera stepping into the duelling ring with Golmin. Compared to everyone else training nearby, she looked so small, Talin was certain that one of the Drakels could pick her up and toss her in the air without much effort. But there was no denying that the girl had talent and spirit.

"You picked a good squire," she said.

Red Wolf watched Ashera and Golmin spar together for a few moments. "Perhaps. I wouldn't trust many people to take my place at your side, but the girl...maybe. In time."

"Coming from you, that has to be the highest of compliments." Talin laughed.

"I trust you to look after yourself. More than I had before," Red Wolf said. "I'm...honoured to have you as a friend."

Are we friends? Talin wanted to ask, but she kept her mouth shut. A twisting knot formed in her chest that refused to go away.

"You still don't believe in yourself." Red Wolf frowned. "Why is that?"

"I think these past few weeks have made me realise all the things I could have been doing for my people," Talin said. Gods, that wasn't what she had been confused about, but she supposed it was better they talked about this instead. "I thought I knew what was best for my people, but I don't. Or I didn't. Now I don't know if I can be good enough."

"You are good enough." Red Wolf met her gaze, golden eyes rooting her in place. "I know it."

"Thank you. For believing in me."

"I always will."

Talin realised that he'd taken her hand. She didn't pull away; he didn't seem to realise, and she wanted to avoid another awkward moment between them. Snow began to fall.

"The other night, by the campfire..." he said.

"After we infiltrated the capital?"

"Yes. You took my hand."

"That was..." Talin felt heat creep into her cheeks. What was he playing at now? "That was an accident."

"I see." Red Wolf turned his attention back to the training grounds. He didn't let go of her hand.

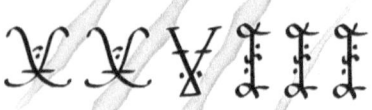

R ed Wolf had heard of winter sieges in the Highlands before, had read about them in the history books in the palace library. But he figured none of that knowledge was useful now.

Kadis' banners totalled over twenty thousand troops under an assortment of banners, all rallied in support of their rightful ruler. They had dragged their siege weapons all the way to El'Vane, after days of marching through the biting cold and snow, and now, at the gates of the capital, Red Wolf could see the city had been sent scrambling in a panic. Archers lined the tops of the walls, ready to shoot down at them, but the southern lords had supplied their army with legionaries—shield bearers—who could block out an entire volley of arrows once they were in formation. Kadis predicted the siege wouldn't last more than a day. Red Wolf had doubted him at first, but now, seeing their numbers against the hastily assembled defence at the wall, he could believe it.

They had kept their operations a complete secret until Kadis' allies began their march, taking the insurgents by surprise. In a last-minute turn of events, Kadis had decided to send half of his banners to Ked'Fald instead, stopping both the torslek production and sieging the capital at the same time. They had the numbers, after all. After so many years in the shadows, the insurgents had stopped seeing Kadis as a threat and never considered an attack on this scale. Red Wolf admired the Drakel's patience.

"When Kadis said we had the numbers, I wasn't quite expecting this many," Talin said, riding up beside him. Clad in mail and plate now, with her hair braided back, she looked magnificent.

"No, me neither," Red Wolf said. "Don't get me wrong, I'm not complaining. We'll have the city by tomorrow."

"I believe it." Talin rode on. With so many troops to coordinate, Kadis had placed her at the head of a company of archers—and quite fittingly so. Red Wolf didn't doubt her for a moment.

It was calm for now, he reflected. The archers on the wall were ready to fire, but the legionaries spanned the length of the wall, covering the field with their shields like tortoise shells, just out of range. But those arrows would start flying soon, and anyone not behind the legionaries' shields would have to take cover.

They had left Ashera back at the den, in the care of Kadis' servants and a few guards and healers who had stayed behind to ensure the staff's safety. The girl had been understandably upset, but given the danger involved in such a siege, Red Wolf hadn't wanted to take any chances. He hoped she wasn't causing any trouble with the servants.

"What in the world are they waiting for?" Golmin asked, stopping his horse on the bodyguard's left.

"A break in our formation," Red Wolf said. He glanced at Talin, who had stopped behind the archers to ready them. "Or for us to attack first."

Golmin followed his gaze. "Are we going to attack first?"

"If our archers do, so do we."

They both fell silent for a moment. Talin appeared to be waiting too.

"You should tell her how you feel," Golmin said.

"I can't." Red Wolf turned his attention to the city again. "Not ever."

"Why, you're afraid of what would happen if she doesn't feel the same way?"

"I'm afraid of what would happen if she does."

"Loose!"

But it wasn't the archers on the wall that moved. Talin had given the order. They watched as the volley sailed over their heads and at the wall.

"What are they doing? They're going to fall short," Golmin said.

"I don't think they were aiming at the archers."

The volley exploded mid-air in a cloud of smoke that obscured the ramparts beyond. Red Wolf watched as the legionaries opened their formation and moved aside for the line of trebuchets.

"I didn't know they could do that," Golmin muttered.

"You have to admit Kadis' engineers are resourceful," Red Wolf said. Truth be told, Talin had let him in on her plan to supply the archers with batches of explosive arrows that would release a thick smoke on detonation, completely obscuring the defenders' view of their army. Kadis had ordered the legionaries to form up as usual so the archers on the wall wouldn't suspect a thing. Red Wolf had been worried about the archers' aiming initially but figured that Talin knew what she was doing.

And the arrows had worked perfectly. Their trebuchets could get a few free hits at the wall before the smoke cleared and the ballistae on the wall could start targeting the crew at their siege weapons. He heard Kadis shouting orders up ahead as the trebuchets swung, one after the other, pummelling the wall with heavy stones. Arrows sailed out blindly from the wall as the archers tried to shoot at them but fell short, piercing the snow harmlessly.

"The sooner the wall comes down, the happier I'll be," Golmin said. "Not exactly much to do while we wait."

"Savour the taste of victory, Rufus. It's a rare thing for us since we're always stuck at the palace guarding the royal family." Red Wolf clapped him on the shoulder.

"See, now I'm considering quitting the Royal Guard and going back to the army," Golmin said with a grin.

Red Wolf snickered. "And leave me by myself in Belanore? You wouldn't."

The smoke was clearing now, and the ballista teams could see what targets to hit. The legionaries fell back as bolts began to fly.

"Loose!"

The second wave of smoke arrows exploded mid-air, again obscuring the ramparts. Red Wolf knew they had only one more volley left. Crafting enough of those for every archer in Talin's company had taken a fair amount of time and resources.

"We need to bring down those ballistae," he said. "In the meantime, perhaps we should move a bit further back."

The two of them retreated well beyond the defenders' range and watched as the trebuchets were readied and launched again. Parts of the wall were weakening now but still held. Red Wolf briefly wondered how the sieges at the other gates were going. The plan was to simply hold the other gates until they broke through in the south and took the keep, but the other gates didn't have the smoke arrows that Talin had requested. If they couldn't put enough pressure on the other gates, the insurgents would be able to retreat and slip away once they broke through. They would still take the city, of course, but Kadis needed to capture Ve'Tehll in El'Vane so he couldn't disappear again and set up his operation elsewhere.

The smoke cleared once again, and the archers were more prepared this time. Arrows began to rain down on them. Two ballista bolts shot out and took out two trebuchets.

"Oh, we're in trouble now..." Red Wolf muttered under his breath. If those ballistae took out their remaining siege weapons, they would have no way to breach the walls, and they would have to rely on their siege towers and ladders to make it into El'Vane.

"Loose!"

The final smoke volley shot over their heads and exploded, followed by a barrage of ordinary arrows. Red Wolf saw most of them fall short save for a few that took out the archers at the very edge of the wall.

Of course, we're out of range.

It made sense, he knew; if they moved their archers within shooting range, the defenders on the wall could aim at them too. Still, it didn't make him feel any better. He turned his horse and galloped to the back of the formation to find Talin.

"I need a spare bow and arrows," he said as he neared her.

"I know what you're thinking." She had a second bow and spare waist quiver already in her hand and tossed them to him. "And I'm coming."

Red Wolf caught the spare gear with one hand and strapped the quiver to his belt. "I cannot let you ride up there. We need to be well within range of the archers on the wall if we want to fire on those ballistae."

"I'm aware." Talin turned her attention to the wall. "Unfortunately for you, I'm an excellent shot." She galloped off before he could protest. Red Wolf cursed and urged his horse on after her.

"If something happens to you—" he began.

"Don't worry. I have a plan!" Talin called back.

"Why do I bother," Red Wolf muttered. The two of them broke free of the front line of legionaries and turned, riding parallel to the wall, directly underneath the cloud of slowly clearing smoke that obscured the defenders' view. He glanced up and took one hand off the reins, ready to shield them both if need be. Talin nocked an arrow as they neared the first ballista. He was quick enough to glimpse a thin metal chain attached to the shaft before she let it fly.

"What's the plan?" he yelled.

A flash of lightning jolted down the chain and set the ballista alight. *That will work.*

Red Wolf glanced up again. The smoke was dissipating steadily; the sky above was almost visible now from where they rode. His hand hovered near Talin's arm, just in case.

"We won't be able to take out all the ballistae along this wall!" he said. "There's not enough time—"

"Trust me." Talin loosed a second arrow and chain. The second ballista met the same fate as the first when her fingers touched the metal.

"We *have to go*," Red Wolf hissed, glancing up again. The smoke had cleared enough by now that he could make out the clouds in the sky. He turned his head to see the wall. They hadn't been spotted yet.

He knew it wasn't going to last.

"I can take out one more," Talin said.

She's mad. Red Wolf kept pace and prayed to whatever gods were watching. They were almost in range now, a little further and she'd be able to shoot...

The ballista swivelled, changing targets unexpectedly. Too late, Red Wolf realised it was aiming straight at them, and he couldn't possibly shield them from an attack that powerful.

"*Talin...!*"

"I know. I can make it!" She let the third arrow fly and sent a flash of lightning down the chain after it. The ballista stared back at them, projectile ready to rip them to bits. Red Wolf tackled her out of the way.

The bolt struck the ground in front of their horses, sending the poor animals flying and kicking up a cloud of dust and snow. A blinding flash seared his eyes moments later as Talin's arrow struck, and the ballista went up in flames.

"We're not safe yet!" Red Wolf reached out and managed to touch her back as arrows sailed down from the wall, splintering inches from their heads. Talin nocked two smoke arrows and sent them upwards in rapid succession. He saw her fingers brush against the tips to light them with a spark.

"*Touvir,*" he muttered under his breath, grabbing her arm and pulling her away from the wall as arrows sailed down at them blindly. Some splintered against his shield; others lodged into the ground harmlessly. He looked up briefly to notice a small group of legionaries advancing towards their position, shields locked together in a tortoiseshell formation.

"That's our way out of here," he said. "Get down."

"What are you—" Talin began, but he had already pulled her to the ground, using himself as a shield against the arrow barrage. Most glanced off his plate armour. Some found gaps and punched clean through the chainmail underneath. He didn't dare budge until the legionaries swarmed them, shield formation completely blocking out the rain of arrows from above. One of the Drakels helped Talin to her feet while he remained crouched to stay inside the formation. Slowly, painfully slowly, they retreated out of the defenders' range, keeping behind the legionaries' shields for cover.

"Gods damn it, you could have died," he growled, finally straightening and tugging free what arrows he could reach. Talin helped him with the rest.

"In my defence, I...thought we had enough time," she admitted with a wince. "I wasn't expecting the wind to clear the smoke so fast. Thank you for shielding me."

Red Wolf sighed. "Just doing my job."

"Congratulations, you two just took out three entire ballistae by yourselves," Kadis said, approaching them with two new horses. "I must admit, I'm impressed."

"The praise should go to Talin," Red Wolf said. "I never would have thought of destroying the ballistae like that."

"Well, I would never have made it out of there without your help," Talin replied. Red Wolf felt his ears turn red and cleared his throat.

"We, uh, we should pull the rest of the trebuchets further back," he said. "They may be more accurate up close, but if they counter with their own siege weapons behind the wall, it's only a matter of time before we lose the rest."

"I don't want the projectiles to fly over the wall," Kadis said. "There are civilians within the city, and I would rather not injure them."

"We should focus on getting our infantry over the walls then." Talin slung her bow over her shoulder. "Forget bringing it down. We're only making dents. Bring in the ladders and siege towers. We'll engage them in combat."

"We'll never get close with those arrows sailing down on us," Kadis said. "Unless you're willing to risk moving your company closer to take them out."

"I'm afraid we'd only be trading blows," Talin said, glancing at the wall. "If we can keep their focus on the trebuchets, the legionaries can help bring in that battering ram. We'll break down the gate while they're distracted."

Kadis nodded. "That may work. I don't suppose you have any more smoke arrows?"

"None left," Talin said.

"Bring your archers closer to the wall and keep them busy."

Talin rode off to give the order. Red Wolf followed Kadis along the back of their ranks to where most of his generals were gathered.

"We're sending in the ram. Lord Marius, I take it you have legionaries to spare?" the Draconian prince said.

"As many as you require, Your Highness," one of the generals said. His scales were deep green, tinged with gold, and his long horns showed him to be quite old. On his armour was the crest of a honey badger.

"Good. Send two for every man needed to carry that ram." Kadis rode on. "Lord Commander, I wish you to lead the cavalry charge once we break through the gates. I will call for the trebuchets to stop once the archers are in position. Manoeuvre my cavalry behind the ram then."

"Consider it done," Red Wolf said, breaking off to find the horse riders. He saw that Golmin was already in position there amid of all the Draconian warriors. He took up his position at their head.

"Listen up! We will be the first through the gates!" he yelled. "Be ready for anything, and do not hesitate!"

He could soon see the ram rolling forward, flanked on both sides by legionaries with their shields up in their tortoise-like formation. Talin's archers had moved forward, too, and begun trading arrow-fire with the archers on the wall. Kadis was shouting orders at the front again, telling the trebuchets to retreat. Red Wolf moved his troops onto the road, ready to charge once they broke through.

"I've been told you're the ones leading the charge," Ettrias said, riding up beside him. "Naturally, I would feel terrible if I missed out."

"Your sister will probably kill me if you die," Red Wolf muttered.

"Then it would be in your best interests to keep me alive."

"Right now, it's more tempting to let the insurgents kill you first."

"You would never."

Red Wolf shrugged. "As insufferable as you are, you're not bad company."

"A real shame, I'm sure." Ettrias grinned. Up ahead, the battering ram made its first blow against the gates. Arrows rained down at it but were blocked by the legionaries' shields.

"Surely this can't be the only defence they mounted..." Ettrias began, but quickly clamped his mouth shut. The archers were retreating now, and they could see slits in the wall opening up one by one. Red Wolf recognised them immediately.

They had similar defensive measures in the palace walls in Belanore.

There was no time for him to act; the wall was so far, and it happened so quickly. Hot oil poured out of the slits in the wall, raining down on the troops below as they worked the battering ram. Shields couldn't protect them from this; Red Wolf saw it splash over the formation and between the gaps and heard screams as it burned the legionaries alive.

"I guess we know what they were doing this whole time," he muttered. Kadis was shouting orders again, organising more men to the ram to continue battering down the door.

"Kadis, no!" Red Wolf motioned for Ettrias and the rest of the cavalry to stay and spurred his horse on. This was exactly what they wanted; taking out the legionaries at the ram was just bait.

"Hold positions!" he roared. "Hold!"

Kadis looked at him as if he were mad. Red Wolf opened his mouth to explain when a single fire arrow sailed over the wall and arced down towards the ground.

The oil caught instantly, setting the heavy, wooden gates ablaze, as well as the ram and anyone else unlucky enough to be caught in the area. He heard Kadis curse in Kier Dekkel.

"How did you know?" the prince asked.

"We have a similar setup back home." Red Wolf watched as the fire burned on. "You said they had nothing of the sort."

"The insurgents must have installed these in secret without my spy's knowledge," Kadis said with a hiss. "Damn the bastards. I should have known."

"They knew we would give up with the trebuchets eventually. It seems the city is better prepared than we anticipated."

"Well, on the bright side, they did set their own gates on fire."

"That will burn out long before it creates a large enough opening for our cavalry," Red Wolf said. "We need another way in."

XXIX

The battlefield was silent now. It had been a few hours since sundown, and Kadis had halted the trebuchets' barrage against the wall. The insurgents on the wall had retreated, too; Talin could see a few guards and sentries posted along the battlements to watch for any potential night-time attacks. The wall itself had partially crumbled under the heavy barrage, but most of it still held strong, and it was still far too difficult to climb without any kind of siege ladder or tower. Kadis, meanwhile, had spent most of the evening with his generals, discussing plans, but the southern lords were wary of elves, and so Talin and Red Wolf hadn't been invited.

"Those southern lords are about as welcoming of outsiders as most of Kies Tor," her bodyguard muttered. Their troops had fallen back now, and most were gathered around campfires, waiting. "What was it that one of them called you and Ettrias? Pointy-eared freaks?" He made a low growling noise in his throat. "I swear to the gods, I should have done far worse than knock out one of his teeth…"

"Much as I appreciate the move, if I felt that my honour was slighted every time someone threw an insult, you'd be fighting half the kingdom," Talin said with a smile. "Let it go. There's nothing you can do to change their minds."

Red Wolf huffed. "I know."

"If we can surprise the insurgents in the middle of the night, we might be able to get over the wall before they have time to react," Talin continued. "There has to be a way in."

"I hope so too," Red Wolf said. "But anything we do must be under cover of darkness, or the guards will notice. You and the others can barely see anything out here without tripping over something. Manoeuvring this many troops would be near impossible." He hissed through his teeth. "If they would just let us join the meeting…"

"I don't know—from what I've heard, it's been mostly arguing," Talin said. "Not many of these warlords get along, and they only rallied their banners for Kadis. He has no other allies. I'm afraid we'll have to put up with the warlords' attitudes for a little while longer."

Red Wolf scowled but made no further comment. Talin poked the fire with a stick.

"Any news from the generals?" Ettrias asked, joining them by the fire. Golmin wasn't far behind. They both still wore their armour, probably in anticipation of a night-time siege. Red Wolf had stripped his at the first hint of sunset and refused to put it back on. Talin had teased him about his hatred of wearing plate and mail all the time in Belanore, but clad in armour herself now, she understood why. It wasn't what she would call comfortable, and she imagined he saw no point in wearing it when he could take a sword to the chest and live.

"They're still arguing," Red Wolf said. "Nothing new."

"So much for assuming we'd have the city within the day," Golmin said.

Red Wolf glanced towards the city. "Those walls were built for a siege. No doubt the insurgents made some modifications in the years that Kadis was gone."

"We could attack if we can take out the guards on the wall," Talin said. "If we knew how many guards there were."

"Tell it to the generals," Red Wolf muttered. "Oh, wait."

"You seem more irritated than usual," Talin remarked.

"I'm worried about what's happening back home. We need to return before Wormwood makes a total mess out of everything."

"He's worried about you, Your Majesty," Golmin said. Red Wolf shot him a glare.

"You told me you trusted me to look after myself," Talin said. "And I *can* look after myself. Far better than before. What's the concern?"

"Captain Golmin was jesting, weren't you, Rufus?" Red Wolf said icily.

"You know, you can sort this out between yourselves; we're taking a stroll." Ettrias flashed them a smile and looped an arm around Golmin's shoulders, steering him away. Red Wolf watched them leave, his golden eyes glowing in the dim firelight. Talin turned her attention on him.

"Well?"

"Back at the wall, when we took out the ballistae..." he began.

"I know, I miscalculated, and I can't thank you enough for protecting me," Talin said. "It won't happen again."

"I meant...before. When that last ballista turned its aim on us." Red Wolf frowned. "I thought there was nothing I could do to stop that thing from smashing us to bits. If I hadn't been fast enough, I..."

"But we made it," Talin said. "That's all that matters."

"I've been thinking. About something that Rufus said." Red Wolf dropped his gaze, then appeared to decide it was a bad idea and looked at her again. Talin hadn't seen him do that before.

"And...what did he say?" she asked, not sure if she liked where this was going.

"Some life advice, nothing much," Red Wolf said. "But, you know, he had a point. There's something I need to tell you."

Talin definitely wasn't going to like where this was going. "Go ahead...?"

"Talin, I—"

Red Wolf was cut off by a Draconian messenger running up to their campfire.

"Kadis requests to see you both," the Drakel said. "Urgently."

"Very well, lead the way." Red Wolf picked up his sword belt and buckled it on. Talin reached for her bow and arrows. The messenger darted off ahead, and they ran to keep up, weaving between scores of Draconian soldiers gathered around their respective fires.

Kadis was alone by the time they arrived, standing in an open tent illuminated by lanterns and pondering over the map on the table in front of him. A few chairs sitting askew around the tent indicated that his generals had left recently.

"Your Majesty. Sir." Kadis nodded at both of them. "Thank you for coming on such short notice. We have reached an agreement."

"I'm glad to hear it," Talin said. "What do you have planned?"

"We would very much like to launch an attack during the night, as you are aware," Kadis said. "But the guards on the wall pose a significant problem. We believe we know their numbers now, thanks to a little note slipped through that sewage grate by one of my spies. We need the army's top ten archers to sneak up to the wall and shoot each guard at the same time."

"I'm flattered, but that will be difficult to coordinate," Talin said.

"We are working on a solution," Kadis said. "Bo'Kata will be joining you, of course, but what about our new Highlander friend? How is his shooting?"

"Captain Golmin received the same training as me," Red Wolf said. "He can send an arrow into a man's eye at five hundred paces."

"Good. Then he makes four." Kadis sent another messenger off to find the big man. "I will have Bo'Kata select the rest. You will find her at the road just past the camp once she is ready."

Talin nodded. "I take it she will give us further instructions?"

"Of course."

"Then we'll take our leave."

"Allow me to extend an apology on behalf of those warlords," Kadis called when they reached the door. "I loathe being allied with them, truth be told. Rest assured they will be removed from office once my father retakes his throne."

"It's alright. You have no need to apologise for their prejudice," Talin said. "They're the ones who owe us an apology."

They left Kadis and made a quick stop at the armoury to fetch a spare bow for Red Wolf before heading to their meeting spot. Talin was glad to have avoided the warlords; they reminded her of the petty court gossip and palace etiquette back in Belanore. She knew she would have to return to it all eventually, but this was a nice change.

"You wanted to tell me something earlier?" she asked.

"Uh..." Red Wolf cleared his throat. "I suspect it's a conversation better suited for after we carry out this plan."

"If you say so." Talin didn't press him further. She wasn't entirely sure she wanted to know what he had been about to tell her.

They were soon joined by Golmin, who seemed rather cheerful about finally getting a job to do. He stole a glance at both of them and pretended to mind his own business. Bo'Kata arrived not long after with the rest of the archers.

"Good, we're all here," she said. "There is a guard on the wall for each of us. They will be spaced out, but we can see all ten of them from the road. Kadis believes the most accurate of us should aim for the furthest guards. Naturally, Your Majesty, you'll be taking the guard furthest to the left."

"I'm flattered," Talin said.

"Your lord commander will aim for the guard next to yours. Captain Golmin will aim for the next closest," Bo'Kata continued. "The rest of you know your positions. Do not forget them. I have a hooded lantern. As soon as you see a flash of light from it, you will know to shoot. Watch your step—we are operating under total darkness."

Talin glanced back and saw that the troops had begun snuffing out their campfires, no doubt on Kadis's orders to make it seem like they were getting ready for bed. She could hear hushed commands being relayed across the camp and shuffling as everyone readied for attack. The sheer size of their army meant that they would draw attention with the sound of their marching, but nevertheless, taking out the guards would delay the insurgents' attempts to mount a defence in the middle of the night.

The ten of them stopped a short distance from the wall, just close enough to shoot the guards but not close enough for them to notice the movement in the moonlight.

"Ready," Bo'Kata whispered. Talin nocked an arrow and drew back her bow. Beside her, she heard the soft click of wood against wood as eight other bows were drawn. Bo'Kata set down the lantern and opened it, then grabbed her bow and loosed an arrow. Talin let her own arrow fly and watched it sail over the wall. It struck her target clean in the throat, dropping him silently. Nine other guards also dropped along the wall. Bo'Kata lifted the lantern again and turned it back towards the camp. The signal to attack.

"Time for us to go," she said. Their little group dispersed and spread out with their backs against the wall, waiting for the ladders to be placed and the siege towers to roll forwards. Talin could soon see several teams of swordsmen running up with the wooden contraptions, along with pack horses pulling the towers just behind them. The first few soldiers had already reached the wall and were busy trying to raise the ladders with a sort of turning winch. She watched as the gears in the contraption turned and slowly cranked the ladders upright. The one nearest to her was already up. Red Wolf grabbed it and began to climb. She followed right behind.

The warning bells in the city started tolling when they were about halfway up, but she knew it was too late by then. Some of their troops were already on the wall and were busy trying to secure the ramparts for themselves. Once that was done, all they would have to do was open the gates. Talin could hear shouts and combat at the top and climbed faster. Red Wolf was way ahead of her, his height making it easier for him to scale the ladder. He was almost at the top now, close enough to swing at an insurgent soldier who had peered over the edge to stab down at the climbers. The Drakel tumbled over the wall with a gash in his neck, and Red Wolf vaulted onto the ramparts, disappearing from sight. He reappeared a few moments later to help her up too.

"We need to get that gate open," Talin said. "Go! I'll clear you a path."

Red Wolf hesitated.

"I'll be safe up here. Trust me."

"I always have." Red Wolf took off at a sprint, making for the stairs as more soldiers came up to meet them. One scored a slash to his neck but he didn't seem too fazed. Talin took the man out with an arrow to his chest, and Red Wolf rolled his shoulders as his wound healed. The next insurgent saw him healing and his eyes widened. Red Wolf cut him down too and kicked the body down the stairs, sending it crashing into the Drakels below. Talin made a mental note to have the engineers in Belanore design wider staircases for their walls.

A group of insurgents had come up a different staircase now, however. She shot two and had her third arrow ready when one of them surprised her from behind. She reacted instinctively and dodged his axe swing, stabbing him in the stomach with her arrow instead. He didn't appear to notice the wound, driven on by battle frenzy, and swung at her again. She rolled aside and drew her sword to knock his third strike out of the way. Her counterattack landed between his ribs and dropped him for good this time. Talin left her blade there and readied another arrow, searching for Red Wolf. He was almost at the bottom now. She saw three more insurgents blocking the way and shot them all. He jumped over the corpses and continued without breaking stride.

"Watch your left!" a Drakel shouted. Talin spun just in time to see another insurgent coming up the stairs. She freed her sword from her last opponent and parried his swing as he got to the top. A slash to the legs crippled him and sent him tumbling back down the stairs. She saw the Drakel who'd shouted the warning and gave him a nod of thanks. Nearby, Golmin had made it to the top, too, and was backing towards her. She wondered where Ettrias was and whether he had made it up yet.

"Your Majesty," the captain said when he reached her. "Where's Red Wolf?"

"Gone to open the gates," she said. The words were barely out of her mouth when she heard gears turning and wood creaking. The huge wooden gates slowly swung inward for their waiting troops.

It was over, or rather, the odds were so overwhelmingly stacked against the insurgents that it might as well be. Talin looked at the axe-wielding insurgent she'd killed, lying in a pool of his own blood, and winced. She needed a good cup of wine after all this was over.

"We should find your brother," Golmin said. Talin nodded; she had to make sure Ettrias hadn't gotten himself killed during all this. They descended the stairs together and headed for the gates, cutting down any insurgents still left in the area. Red Wolf was there, as expected, and she saw that he had found Ettrias. The two of them stood just off the road while Drakel rebels poured into the city by the dozen.

"You're both alright?" she asked.

"No, I missed out on all the fun," Ettrias said. "I was one of the last to climb the ladders, but then Red Wolf got the gates open, so I thought I'd go through those instead. Turns out the fighting's already finished at the wall."

"Well, I'm glad you're unhurt," Talin said.

"Likewise, Talin," Ettrias said.

"The last of the insurgents should be holed up in the keep by now," Red Wolf said. "As much as I'd like to rest and catch up, we have more work to do. Time for us to press on."

"Aye, that would be best," Golmin said. "Perhaps we should stay together from now on. I'd hate to get separated and find out hours later that you had all died."

"Aww, I'm flattered that you care so much," Ettrias said.

Golmin snorted. Talin led the way down the streets, following the wave of infantry still pouring through the gates behind them. She tried to push the thought of killing those insurgents out of her mind but couldn't stop thinking about it.

"Doesn't it bother any of you?" she asked. "All this killing?"

"You learn not to think about it after a while," Golmin said. "I fought in the Highlands before Red Wolf recruited me to the Royal Guard. We painted the grasslands red with blood. When you see your comrades fall every single day to those Hellhounds, you just...don't care anymore."

"The Hellhounds taught us not to care." Red Wolf frowned. "But then, as far as I can remember, I've always been a murderer."

Ettrias didn't speak for a while. Red Wolf looked away and kept walking.

"I don't like it either. But I've fought beside Father against the Hellhounds," her brother finally said. "You can see the rage in their eyes. There's nothing but rage and hate. I think you'd have to truly hate what's in front of you to want to kill it. And when you're in the midst of a battle...sometimes there's nothing else for you to do."

"When all this is over, nobody else had better start any wars," Talin said. "I have no interest in fighting anyone else."

"That's for the best, perhaps," Red Wolf said. "Too many rulers are too quick to declare war. The world needs someone like you."

The keep had already been stormed by the time they arrived; guards and soldiers lay dead everywhere, and Kadis' infantrymen were busy herding the castle staff out of the main gates. Talin saw Bo'Galesh standing at the drawbridge and hurried over.

"Is Kadis inside?" she asked.

"He's having a little chat with the insurgents who took charge of the city, yes," Bo'Galesh said. "You'll probably find him in the throne room."

"Thank you." Talin made a move to continue into the keep.

"Kadis asked me to give you credit for your idea to sabotage the drawbridge," Bo'Galesh called. "His spies were able to do it. The insurgents tried to raise it when they saw us approach, but it didn't exactly work as expected."

"I'm glad," Talin said. The four of them crossed the drawbridge together and wound their way through the clusters of rebels gathered in the front courtyard.

"I don't suppose Kadis is having a nice, civil conversation," Red Wolf muttered.

"I don't suppose so either," Talin said.

The soldiers guarding the inner gates opened them when they saw her approach. Past the guards, Bo'Kata was briefing some of her rangers.

"Straight through the front doors!" she called. Talin gave her a nod of thanks and headed up the steps to the castle itself. The doors opened into a tall, pillared antechamber with torches lining the walls. Insurgent banners were being stripped down as the soldiers worked. A second set of double doors at the far end stood open; beyond them, she could see the throne room. Kadis sat on the throne, legs crossed and playing with his sword. Three Drakels knelt on the floor at the foot of the throne, tied up and badly beaten.

"Ah, Queen Talin! I'm glad you could join us!" Kadis called, and turned his attention back to the prisoners. "See, the thing is, Her

Majesty here came to us for *our* help. She wanted to save her people. Had you been more welcoming of outsiders and *not* tried to kill them all as soon as they crossed the border a month ago, we would not be in this situation. I certainly wouldn't have control of the capital again." He uncrossed his legs and leaned forward. "I won't ask again. Where is my father?"

"You want to know so badly?" the Drakel on the right spat.

"I know Ve'Tehll would never let you run things here, would you, Ve'Tehll?" Kadis looked at the Drakel in the middle. "No, didn't think so. Shoot him."

"Kadis, don't," Talin said. "This isn't the way to do things."

Kadis's nostrils flared. "And what would you have me do to these traitors?"

"You, Ve'Tehll, is it?" Talin nodded at the sand-coloured Drakel in the middle. "You're in charge?"

Kadis sighed. "He is their leader, yes."

"Tell him where his father is."

"And why would I do that?" Ve'Tehll asked.

"Because Kadis will sentence you to death either way, and I suspect you will want a quick death as opposed to something slow and torturous," Talin said. "Or, as the judges say back in Belanore, a swift execution to please the masses or a lifetime rotting in jail."

Ve'Tehll didn't speak, so Talin continued.

"You've already lost. Kadis has Ked'Fald under siege, stopping your torslek from ever going anywhere. We have the city. Even if you've killed the emperor, Kadis would take the throne. Tell us where he is now and save everyone some time and trouble."

Ve'Tehll only responded with a glare.

"Take him to the dungeons to rot." Kadis waved two of his guards forward. "I have no more use for this traitor."

"Wait!" Ve'Tehll's eyes widened. Kadis lifted a scaled brow.

"He's being held at Ked'Kivanh," the insurgent leader said. "It's where the majority of my mercenary armies are garrisoned. I...will tell them to stand down, along with Ked'Fald. They are outnumbered against your banners. There's no need for more bloodshed."

Kadis hissed through his teeth. "Get them out of my sight."

His soldiers grabbed the insurgent leaders and dragged them away. Talin watched them disappear through the main doors.

"I suppose I owe you some thanks," Kadis said. "He wasn't nearly so forthcoming when I threatened him with death earlier."

"You said that your father told you once to do what's right," Talin said. "I think he would have liked to keep these insurgents alive, to put them on trial."

Kadis nodded. "You're right. Thank you for stopping me." He stood and made his way off the dais, waving one of his rebels over. "You're free to use any of the rooms in the keep for the night. Your companions, too. We will return to the den in the morning, and from there, I must free my father."

"He's survived this long—I'm sure he's safe," Talin said. "Goodnight, Kadis."

"Likewise, Your Majesty."

The four of them made their way through the dimly lit passageways and upstairs together, led by the Drakel rebel, where Red Wolf allowed Talin to have the first clean bedchamber they found and steered Golmin off to find somewhere else to sleep.

"You can have this one if you're tired—" she began, but he'd already vanished down the hallway. Talin shook her head and opened the door.

"Talin," her brother called.

Talin paused with her hand on the doorknob.

"You and Red Wolf..." Ettrias began.

"We're friends," Talin said, perhaps a little too quickly.

"Talin, please, I'm not stupid," Ettrias said.

"Ettrias."

"You should tell him how you feel."

"*Ettrias.*"

"I'm just saying." Ettrias shrugged. "Don't wait until it's too late. But what do I know? It isn't like I'm speaking from experience or anything."

"You know why I can't."

"*Tch.* Excuses. You're the Queen of Kies Tor. Who's going to stop you from being with whomever you want? Goodnight, Talin." He disappeared down the hallway after Red Wolf and Golmin, leaving Talin to ponder his words.

It's not so simple, she wanted to say, but he wouldn't understand. It was only a matter of time before her council started pressuring her to choose a suitor from the Torrian nobility, and in their eyes, Red Wolf was neither Torrian nor nobility. But if he could gain the people's gratitude for saving the kingdom...

Maybe her first step should be to stop denying her feelings.

Red Wolf is a friend. We're not—

Talin shut out the voice in her head and closed the door.

The weather seemed to grow a little warmer each day of their march back to the den, melting most of the snow and allowing them to take off their heavy cloaks for a change. Ettrias still complained that it was too cold, which was understandable, Talin supposed. Golmin and Red Wolf, on the other hand, enjoyed the weather, the former waxing lyrical about how the far northern stretches of the Highlands were always the first to see snow and the last to see the start of spring. Talin was just glad they were finally heading home. She was beginning to miss Belanore, if only a little. They arrived at the den a day later than planned, owing to the short days providing precious few hours of light for travel, but Talin didn't mind so much. So long as they got home safe.

"Perhaps I can tempt you to stay one more night?" Kadis proposed as they climbed the hill to the front doors. "All this effort calls for a celebration, don't you think?"

"I'd love to, but we have no time," Talin said. "The Hellhounds could already be at Belanore for all we know. Wormwood plans to overthrow me. I've been gone far longer than I anticipated."

Kadis nodded. "I understand."

"One more night couldn't hurt, surely," Ettrias said. "We deserve a break before setting off for the road again. *You* deserve a break, dear sister."

The doors swung open, and Ashera ran out to greet them. She wrapped her arms around Red Wolf's legs before he could react, pinning him in place.

"I missed you all!" she said. "You're *late*. I thought something must have happened!"

Red Wolf smiled and extracted himself from her tight embrace. "We're all fine, Ashera. Thanks for worrying."

"Are we staying another night?" the girl asked. "The servants said we might, so we can all set off in the morning rested and everything."

Red Wolf glanced at Talin and raised his eyebrows.

"We..." She sighed. "Alright, we can stay one more night."

"Excellent! I'll gather my generals," Kadis said with a grin. "It would be a shame for you to leave without experiencing a formal Draconian celebration."

"As long as there's some good wine to go around," Talin said.

"Count on it, Your Majesty." Kadis crossed the last few feet to the door and disappeared inside.

"I don't know about the rest of you, but I could do with a long bath and some fresh clothes," Talin said, following him through the doors. "And I'm not having any of you turn up to dinner in travelling clothes."

"Aye, I second that," Golmin said. "Shall we meet outside the dining hall?"

Ettrias shrugged. "Sounds fine to me."

They stopped at the staircase and split up. Red Wolf escorted Talin upstairs; their rooms were close to each other, after all. They parted ways at his door.

"My queen..."

She stopped and turned. Red Wolf had his hand on the doorknob but didn't move.

"Seeing as this is a formal dinner, perhaps you'd allow me the honour of escorting you there?" he said.

"Of course," Talin said. "I'd like that."

"Thank you, my queen." Red Wolf disappeared into his room. Talin continued down the hall and towards her own room. Inside, a bath had already been drawn for her, and a set of clean clothes had been left folded on her bed. She stripped off her equipment and dirty clothes and hopped into the hot water. Undoing her braids, she let her hair fall, and washed it before scrubbing herself clean. She glanced down at her shoulder at one point to notice the healed bite scars there and felt a phantom jolt of pain. Red Wolf had saved her from those Hellhounds at the border, consciously or not. Did some part of him remember who she was when he shifted? Talin hoped he did.

She got out of the bath to dry herself and change into the fresh clothes left for her. It was nothing out of the ordinary—just a spare tunic and trousers. She rummaged through the wardrobe for a few minutes in the hope that it might contain something more suitable but came up with nothing.

There was a knock at her door. Talin answered it and found a servant standing just outside with a folded bundle of clothing.

"Formal clothes for dinner, Your Majesty," she said. "Prince Kadis was able to find these for you to choose from. I'm told they're part of an old shipment of trade goods from Kies Tor."

"Thank you." Talin took the bundle. "And give the prince my thanks too."

Later, once the servants had cleared away her bath and taken her dirty clothes to be washed, Talin unfolded the dresses and tried them on in front of the full-length mirror. Kadis had certainly taken his time to find these; they were similar to what she wore in Belanore and some had a hint of Elven design to them. It was a shame that the two she had liked the most were both too big for her. She eventually settled for a white dress with blue highlights and sleeves that fit snugly around her arms, and had just braided her hair again when another knock came at the door.

"Come in," she called. Red Wolf opened the door and stood just inside the room, waiting silently. Talin finished pinning any loose hair in place and turned to face him.

"You look incredible, my queen," he said.

Talin smiled. "Thank you. You look stunning, yourself." It was true; dressed in silk doublet and formal trousers, she had never seen him look so good. His hair was as immaculate as ever and he'd shaved the last few days' stubble off his chin.

"Shall we?" he asked, and she looped her arm through his. They made their way down the stairs and to the dining hall entrance.

"Well, don't you two look amazing!" Ettrias greeted.

"I'm flattered, brother," Talin said, unsure whether he was teasing.

"What? I mean it," Ettrias said. "Come on. We don't want them to start without us."

Golmin pushed open the double doors and gestured for Talin and Red Wolf to enter first. They stepped past him together and made their way down the centre aisle between the tables. A large table at the end of the hall had been set up, undoubtedly for Kadis and his generals and anyone else he deemed important enough to join him. The Draconian prince himself sat in the middle of it with two empty seats to his right. He beckoned for Talin and Red Wolf to sit beside him. Ever the gentleman, Red Wolf helped the queen to her spot before taking his own. Ashera was given a seat at the head table, too, on Red Wolf's right. Golmin and Ettrias sat on Kadis' left.

"I hope you don't mind if things get a little...loud, down there," Kadis said, nodding towards the soldiers' tables. "My men haven't had a celebration like this in a long while."

"They're not the only ones." Talin poured herself some wine. Red Wolf helped himself to a cup as well, and Ashera was given cider instead.

"Is there going to be dancing?" the girl asked. "I love dancing."

"Of course," Kadis said with a grin. "It wouldn't be a proper Draconian party without dancing."

They were served an assortment of dishes with salad, washed down with wine. Talin tried not to drink much at first, conscious of their need to set off early the next morning, but Red Wolf was already on his fourth cup and didn't seem to be slowing down. She decided that a few extra drinks couldn't hurt. Besides, it was good Draconian red, something she'd rarely had the pleasure of tasting back in Kies Tor. The soldiers' tables were getting rowdier by the minute. Two soldiers had already challenged each other to a duel with butter knives while the rest cheered them on. She allowed herself a brief smile at the sight of two grown Draconian warriors, almost too drunk to stand, fighting each other with blunt cutlery.

"That cannot be a good idea," Kadis remarked, watching them duel.

"Just be glad they're not steak knives." Red Wolf shot them a glance before going back to cutting his chicken. Clearly, he'd seen worse behaviour by the royal guards when they were drunk.

"If you're about to tell me that Belanore's royal guards are like this when they've had a few drinks, I'd rather not know," Talin said.

"A wise decision," Red Wolf said. "Still, you can't ask for better guards."

Talin finished off whatever was left on her plate and poured more wine. Her bodyguard was busy downing another cup. "Easy on the wine, Lord Commander. Don't you ever get drunk?"

"Look at me. I'm a foot taller than most people here. It takes a lot to get me drunk," Red Wolf said. "Not to mention my healing neutralises most toxins and potions."

Talin allowed herself a chuckle. "You're drinking like this is your last meal."

Red Wolf shrugged. "I usually live off ale like the rest of the royal guards. This is a nice change."

Dessert was a fruit pie topped with fine sugar and served with cream. Talin had no doubt Red Wolf, Golmin, and Ashera had never had anything of the sort.

"Do you get to eat this all the time?" Golmin asked between mouthfuls. "Because I'll be honest, this is incredible. You've got to serve this to the royal guards."

"If I did that every night, the kingdom would run out of coin very quickly." Talin smiled. "But I could make an exception for special occasions."

Dessert soon finished, and the soldiers' tables were pushed aside, making room for a dance floor and musicians. The hall was soon filled with dancers. Ashera jumped into the midst of it all without hesitation.

Be it the wine or the boisterous mood in the dining hall, Talin wasn't sure, but she plucked up the courage to climb to her feet and offer Red Wolf her hand. "Not going to ask me to dance this time?"

"I..." Red Wolf's ears turned scarlet, "...don't know how. Not..." He gestured to the hall. "Not like that."

"Nothing could be simpler. I'll show you. Come on." Talin grabbed him by the hand, and he stared at her for a moment before standing.

"You're drunk," he said.

"I'm in the mood for a dance," Talin said.

The two of them stepped onto the dance floor as the next song started. Talin went over the basics as they came up, trusting Red Wolf to follow where he could and guiding his footwork where he couldn't. He was a quick learner, she soon discovered; by the second song, she hardly had to give him any instruction and simply went with his movements. She wondered if he might have made her dance lessons as a child any less dull.

Probably not. There's no saving how bad those lessons were. Talin thanked him for the dance once it was over and headed to bed.

She dreamed of the Hellhounds again that night, of burning red eyes locking onto her as one of them sank its teeth into her shoulder. Red Wolf had saved her then, but she had seen the hate etched in the wolf's eyes when he looked at his brethren. She remembered what Ettrias had said about having to truly hate whatever was in front of you to enjoy killing it. The wolf had shown no mercy in killing one of his own. But she refused to believe he was just a monster.

Dawn hadn't yet broken when Talin woke, feeling no more rested than the previous night and nursing the inevitable headache she'd acquired from drinking two cups too many. Carefully, so as not to make too much noise and wake anyone, she tip-toed out of her room and down the hall. At Red Wolf's door, she paused, listening for any sign that he might already be awake, but it appeared that the Draconian red had been enough to knock him out too. She continued past his room and downstairs out of the den. It was much colder outside than she'd anticipated, and for a moment she considered going back in, but the cold cleared her head, and she wasn't willing to bet her chances on sneaking back past Red Wolf's chambers undetected. Instead, she headed towards the cliff behind the den, watching as the first traces of light broke across the horizon.

Footsteps sounded behind her, almost silent. Only Red Wolf could be so quiet. Maybe she hadn't been so successful at sneaking past him.

"The wolf sees this sunrise in the morning and knows his time to hunt is over. The night gives way to creatures of the light, to those who fear the darkness," he said. "But it is still early, and yet you are here."

"I don't seem to be getting much sleep these days," Talin confessed. "But that's not for you to worry about. Your job is to 'make sure I don't die', as you so elegantly put it once."

"I still stand by that," Red Wolf grumbled.

"Gods, you're impossible to tease," Talin said with a smile. "Ettrias and I had a competition to try to tease you when we were children."

"I remember." His brow creased.

"Something's on your mind."

"The wolf saved you once, and the other night, when I shifted, he didn't attack you. He may be fond of you, but I wouldn't want you to get the wrong idea about him. He will attack if provoked."

"I don't think he's dangerous," Talin said. "You said it yourself. He'll only attack if he's provoked. I don't believe he's a threat to anyone otherwise."

"Perhaps. But that's not a risk I advise you to ever take." Red Wolf turned to face the sunrise. "Have you ever seen the Glass Forest at dawn?"

"No," Talin said. Red Wolf pointed, and she followed his finger, settling her eyes on the transparent leaves half a kingdom away. Together, they watched as the sun climbed above the horizon, scattering the first rays of light across the world below. It hit the Glass Forest and broke, the transparent leaves splitting light into a thousand pieces, reflecting off the forest like fire.

"Gods, it's beautiful," she breathed.

"You ought to see the forest from directly below the canopy," Red Wolf said. "The dawn light makes the sky look like it's burning."

"Well, then, you'll have to show me when all this is over."

"If you wish, my queen."

"Can I ask you something?"

"Anything."

"Is there a limit to what you can heal from? Apart from...well, the torslek."

"You already know that Hellhounds cannot heal from anything that is instantly fatal," Red Wolf said. "I could take an arrow to the heart and live if it were removed quickly enough, but an arrow through the brain would kill me. I also cannot regenerate entire body parts."

"And the Hellhounds heal the same way?"

"Yes," Red Wolf said. "Through their experiments, I acquired most of their powers, for whatever that's worth. I only wish I could have inherited their control over shapeshifting, too, and save the damn trouble of having to ensure the wolf doesn't kill everyone close to me when I shift."

"They didn't continue experimenting after they failed with you?" Talin asked.

"If they did, I was never made aware of it." Red Wolf let out a long breath. "But perhaps it's for the best that I remain the only monster in Kies Tor."

"You are not a monster," Talin said sharply. She cupped his face in her hands, and he leaned into the touch, her blue eyes meeting his golden ones. "He let me touch him that night. You said he would be dangerous, yet he was anything but. He was gentle. If you truly are a monster, then the wolf would have ripped me to shreds the moment he lay eyes on me back at the border."

"My queen…" Red Wolf's voice trailed off.

"I'm not afraid of you," she said. "I'm not afraid of the wolf or what he can do. He doesn't define who you are."

Red Wolf's gaze softened a little as she took a step forward, her eyes still locked on his. And as the sun bathed the clifftop in a gentle, golden light, she finally found the courage to kiss him. It only lasted a moment before he jerked back in surprise, staring at her with a mixture of shock and confusion. Her heart pounding hard enough that she was certain he could hear, she made to step away, thinking she'd made a mistake. Red Wolf wrapped an arm around her to pull her towards him and kissed her back. He said nothing still when he straightened, but simply sat down at the edge of the cliff and drew her down beside him. She took his hand in hers as they watched the sunrise.

"All of that is yours," he said, gesturing to the land in the far distance beyond the border. "But it belongs to your people. Do not forget it."

"This journey has taken much longer than I thought," Talin confessed. "Kadis must free his father first, and by then it may be too late to stop the Hellhounds."

"You are still alive. You can still give your people hope. Let them believe in you. Let them have something worth fighting for *in you*. That is how you will win this war. And I will stay by your side for as long as it takes, for as long as I can. That I can promise."

"I appreciate it," Talin said. She turned her attention to the clouds slowly gathering on the horizon.

More rain.

In the distance, thunder roared.

XXXI

Their journey through the Draconian lands took them north of the White River, avoiding the storms and floods, to a ghost town near the border, where the waters were shallow enough to cross. It was the only crossing they could find anywhere near their position, and knowing that the Hellhounds were trying to push east towards the capital, they'd decided to risk it. The town itself had been abandoned only recently; there were still tracks in the roads, and the houses were still standing upright. Conscious of any Hellhound stragglers left behind, the five of them split up and began searching through each building. Talin saw possessions left behind and valuables abandoned in the villagers' rush to leave. A few bodies lay outside, the flesh torn from their bones, evidence that not everyone had made it out before the Hellhounds' rampage.

"Do you think they escaped?" she asked as they combed through an empty house.

"Maybe." Red Wolf picked up a child's stuffed doll, dusted it off and set it back down. Talin could tell he was just trying to get her hopes up.

"I'll check the town centre," she said, ducking out of the house. Red Wolf looked deep in thought as he stared at the doll.

There was a well in the centre of the town, with the road curving around it to allow travellers to fill up their flasks. Talin peered into it and found there was no bucket.

So much for getting some water, she thought, and turned away to search the houses nearby. A shuffling sound from within the well made her spin back with her sword drawn. Red Wolf quickly joined her; evidently he'd heard her draw her weapon from wherever he'd been.

A young girl about Ashera's age scrambled out of the well and stared at them. She wore no shoes, and her feet were filthy, as was her dress. Her arms were so thin they looked like they could break at any moment.

"Just a child." Red Wolf sheathed his sword. Talin did the same.

"What's your name?" she asked.

The girl didn't speak.

Red Wolf crossed his arms. "How long ago did the Hellhounds pass through?"

"Red Wolf." Talin motioned for him to be quiet. She took out some dried beef and offered it to the girl, who snatched it up immediately and began to chew on it.

"A few days ago. I'm Mara."

"Are you the only one left?" Talin asked.

The girl nodded.

"Have you been hiding in the well this whole time?"

Another nod.

"We could take her to the Western Forts. She'll be safe there," Talin said, turning to Red Wolf.

Her bodyguard winced. "Much...as I wish to agree...we are pressed for time. The girl would slow us down."

"If there are any Hellhounds left here, she'll die," Talin pointed out.

"Unlikely," Red Wolf said. "Hellhounds rarely leave stragglers behind. If there are Hellhounds in the area, they'd be roaming in pairs or threes—hunters trying to find food. She's too small to interest them."

There was a soft growl from behind them. They spun at the same time to find a huge wolf stalking towards them.

"You were saying?"

"Just get your bow." Red Wolf drew his sword. "I'll distract it."

The Hellhound lunged forward too fast for Talin to react. Red Wolf met its swipe with his blade, slashing its leg. The cut healed almost instantly. Talin sent an arrow at the Hellhound's eye and it went high when the creature ducked. Red Wolf swung his weapon at its neck, but the blade didn't cut all the way through, allowing the creature to heal. The Hellhound pounced again, jaws opening wide and dripping saliva. Red Wolf brought his sword up to counter it but was too slow. The creature's jaws clamped around his arm and latched on tight. He grabbed a fistful of its fur, trying to keep it steady, and Talin loosed a second arrow. This one struck the Hellhound's neck as the two struggled.

Golmin and Ashera came sprinting out of an alley to Talin's right, followed by her brother. She shifted her aim as she saw a second Hellhound charging towards them. This one was in the perfect position for her to aim at. Her arrow struck dead centre in the creature's eye, and it crashed forward, skidding along the ground before coming to a stop.

"Is there a third?" she demanded.

"Behind it!" Ettrias turned to face the alley. "That one walks on two legs."

The third Hellhound came to a stop in front of his fallen brethren. Apart from the glowing red eyes and wolf-like nose, Talin might have mistaken him for a Highlander, but the way he bared his teeth in a silent snarl reminded her that he and his brethren were here to kill. She glanced at Red Wolf, still struggling with the first beast. The Hellhound's eyes flickered to the two of them, and he uttered something in a guttural tongue she didn't understand. Red Wolf responded with a similar growl and stuck his dagger into the first Hellhound's skull. Talin saw a flash of rage in his eyes that she had only ever glimpsed in the Hellhounds at the border. He dropped the dagger and the dead creature and turned to face their remaining foe.

"Red Wolf—" Talin began.

"I'll handle this." His arm had already healed. "Just stay back."

The Hellhound's face twisted into a sneer as he dropped his weapons and shifted, clothing ripping as he turned into a huge black wolf, red eyes burning like hot coals. Mocking Red Wolf for his inability to control his shifting, no doubt.

"So be it." Her bodyguard dropped his sword belt. "I'll kill you with my bare hands."

The two of them collided in a blur of claws and fur. Red Wolf grabbed the Hellhound by the neck, but the creature had bitten into his shoulder and held fast. Talin readied an arrow just in case.

"Don't!" Red Wolf flipped the Hellhound over him and drove a fist into its jaw, forcing it to release its hold on his shoulder. Talin had always known that he was stronger than the average elf, but seeing him move now, she realised that his supernatural strength came from the Hellhounds. He wrapped his arms around the Hellhound's neck as she watched and squeezed hard. It struggled in his grip for a while, clawing at him as they wrestled on the ground, but he never let go. The Hellhound got a good swipe at his exposed neck at one point but never managed to get him to loosen his grip. It eventually stopped struggling and fell limp. Red Wolf held on for a few more seconds before finally letting go. Talin kept her arrow trained on its body as her bodyguard scrambled to his feet and buckled his sword belt on. Drawing his spare dagger, he crouched in front of the Hellhound and drove the blade up under its jaw, piercing through its brain.

"Can't be too careful." He wiped the weapon clean and sheathed it.

"What did he call you?" Talin asked. "I've never seen you react like that."

Red Wolf sighed. "A conversation for another time. We need to move. When these Hellhounds fail to return, they will send a search party. Where's that girl?"

Talin looked around and found the girl peeking out from inside one of the abandoned houses. "Come out, Mara, it's safe now. They're dead."

The girl shook her head and pointed at Red Wolf. "He healed like the rest of 'em. He's like those monsters too."

Red Wolf made a soft growling sound and turned away.

"He's not like them, Mara," Talin said. "Red Wolf is different."

"Well, I'm not coming!" Mara said. "He'll gobble me up when nobody's looking. That's what Gran would have said."

"Red Wolf isn't like them. He's...a Highlander. You can tell from his ears," Talin said.

"That's cos they're shapeshifters, Gran said. They'll disguise themselves to look like anyone, and then *bam*! They eat you up!"

"They only shift into wolves, but that's fine. I didn't want to take you along anyway," Red Wolf muttered. "Let's go. The longer we stay, the more danger we're in."

"Red Wolf, she's a *child*," Talin said. "Come with us, Mara, you'll be safer at the Western Forts."

"No! Anywhere is safer than with *him*!" Mara shrank away when she tried to approach.

Red Wolf scoffed and turned away. Talin was quick enough to glimpse the regret and resignation in his eyes.

"Red Wolf is right, Your Majesty," Golmin said. "We need to leave this place before our numbers attract more Hellhound hunters. The girl is safer without us, and if she wishes to stay, there's nothing we can do."

"I suppose you're right." Talin retrieved her arrows, and the five of them fetched their horses, leaving Mara and the ghost town behind.

They settled for the night in a small glade in the forest just south of the White River, surrounded by white lilies that only bloomed near the river's edge. Red Wolf took the first watch, as usual, and promised to wake whoever was next. Ettrias called an early night and took the final watch before anyone could argue. Talin figured that he was probably trying to get out of taking the full shift on account of her waking early. She took the shift after Red Wolf dejectedly. Golmin taught Ashera how to play Tavern Cards before turning in for the night too.

Red Wolf fed the fire some more fuel.

"Back in that town," Talin said, "the Hellhound said something to you. I've never seen you look so...angry. What did he say?"

Red Wolf's brow creased. "He called me 'brother'. Said I betrayed my pack, betrayed the horde. I told him I was never one of them, but...what the girl said...that's what everyone else sees."

"You're *nothing* like them," Talin said. "Those things feel nothing but hatred for the world around them. You're different."

"What difference does it make?" Red Wolf scoffed. "I look like them when I shift. I heal like them. I have their powers. As far as the world is concerned, I am one of them. You should sleep before your watch."

"Why? Don't want my company?" Talin gave him a teasing smile. He tried to keep a straight face and look unamused but eventually cracked.

"Fine, I admit to enjoying your company." He looked at her. "But we need to talk about what happened yesterday."

"Yesterday...?" Talin feigned innocence, but she could feel her heart begin to pound harder against her ribs.

"Please, I can hear how fast your heart is beating," Red Wolf said. "You kissed me. On top of that cliff."

Talin had no idea what she was supposed to say to that. Admit it? Try to brush it off as an act of impulse? "I...guess I did." She had to retaliate with *something*. "You kissed me back."

"I guess I did." Red Wolf smiled. "It was nice."

Talin felt her cheeks burn. "I..."

"I know."

"You—"

By the gods, he's infuriating.

"Rufus wanted me to tell you how I felt. He was very insistent," Red Wolf said. "I was going to, back at El'Vane, but then the opportunity passed, and I wasn't sure I'd ever get it again. I, uh..." He hesitated. "To tell you the truth, I've had feelings for you for years. I know you said there should be no more secrets between us, so I suppose...this is me confessing my last secret to you now."

Talin felt her mind grind to a screeching halt.

"...can I kiss you? Properly this time?" she managed to say.

Red Wolf blinked.

"Yes."

Talin reached up to cup his face in her hands, pulling him in towards her. She pressed her lips against his and felt him practically melt into the touch, hand snaking around her waist, pulling her closer as he deepened the kiss. When she broke away, breathless and half-dazed, he lifted his free hand and laid his palm against her cheek.

"If you would have me, my queen, I am yours," he whispered against her lips. "As I have always been...and always will be."

Perhaps it was unwise to have let him get so close; Ettrias' fate still rested on his confession to murder and conspiracy against the Crown. But here, right now, she realised that she didn't care in the slightest.

Enjoy these moments while they last.

"Damn the palace protocol, then," Talin said, and kissed him again.

N ow back in the warm forests of Kies Tor, they made much better time. The land was familiar, and they were all much more accustomed to the southern weather, making navigation much easier compared to the cold north or the Draconian lands. They would be at the Western Forts before nightfall if they made good time across the flooded farms.

For now, though, they were moving at a snail's pace; a recent storm had brought the water level back up to knee height, and they were forced to lead their horses through the treacherous terrain on foot. One wrong step on horseback could break their mounts' legs.

"I'm going to need new boots by the end of all this," Golmin muttered.

"If we make it through all this and survive the Hellhounds, I'll buy you a pair myself," Talin said. "You deserve it after braving the storm season for a month just to warn me about Wormwood."

"I'd be honoured, Your Majesty," Golmin said.

"What, I don't get new boots?" Red Wolf asked.

"The Crown supplies you with new equipment all the time, unlike your poor captain." Talin shrugged. "Any more pairs of boots and I'd be out of coin."

"So, that's a 'yes'?" Red Wolf lifted his eyebrows.

"I'll think about it."

"Anyway..." Ettrias cleared his throat. "How are we planning on getting that drawbridge down once we arrive at the Forts? It's not like you can just ride up and announce that you're the queen, returning from a little trip to the Draconian Empire. Certainly not with those rumours still going around."

"I'm working on it," Talin said.

"We could make up some story about being refugees," Ashera said. "I doubt the guards will look too closely at a group travelling with a little girl."

"That could work," Red Wolf said. "Rufus, what's the nearest town to the crossing?"

Golmin slowed briefly to examine his map. "Tarnel. Unoccupied by Hellhounds when I passed through the crossing."

"Good. We will say we're from a small village north of it, fleeing from the Hellhounds," Red Wolf said. "Not the best story I've come up with, but it will do. With our straggly appearances, we should pass for poor villager refugees."

They were almost out of the flooded zone now; the water was only up to their shins. Another five minutes put them on dry land.

It felt strange to be walking on solid ground again and not trudging through mud and debris, Talin reflected, as the group stopped awhile to rest and dry their clothes. She stripped off her boots and tipped rainwater out of them. "That's the last time I'm taking a shortcut through a flooded zone," she said.

Red Wolf wrung the water from his trouser legs. "At least it hasn't rained."

A low rumble of thunder split the air above them.

"You had to say it," Golmin grumbled.

They donned their cloaks and mounted their horses again, determined to make it to the road before the storm set in and turned the ground to mud once more. The horses were tired, too, and reluctant to keep going after their trek through the floodwaters. They stopped a little while longer to give the mounts some more rest.

"We'll never make it to the Forts at this rate," Ettrias muttered.

He wasn't wrong. The storm was already well underway by the time they reached the road, blocking out the sun entirely. Red Wolf managed to keep them going in the right direction by sensing the position of the moon below the horizon, but it quickly became abundantly clear that they were not going to make it to the Western Forts before dark. The sky was turning blacker by the hour and the storm showed no sign of letting up.

"We could find a spot just off the road for the night and pass through in the morning," Talin said.

"We can make it," Red Wolf said.

"Red Wolf, we can barely see anything," Talin said. "Just because you can see in the dark—"

"Light a lantern. We'll move slow." Red Wolf glanced back. Ashera poured some oil into the lantern and lit it with a match. He took it from her and led the way onwards.

They stumbled in the rain and near darkness for an hour longer before finally giving up. Finding a small clearing just off the road, they lit a fire, tried to dry off their boots and assigned their shifts. Red Wolf took the first watch, as usual, and Talin stayed up for a little while to keep him company.

The five of them set off early the next morning while the skies were still clear. Talin took the lead this time. She knew Red Wolf meant well, but his enhanced eyesight in the darkness made him a terrible judge of when it was too dark to keep travelling. Now on the road again, Golmin examined the tracks that were half washed away by the storm.

"Pawprints, boot prints, a few horses," he said. "Old tracks, too, made before the ground dried up. Else there'd be nothing left for us to find."

"Hellhounds, then," Red Wolf said. "They'd be long gone by now if these tracks are as old as you say. We should be safe."

"Hellhounds this close to the Forts worries me." Talin's brow creased. "There have never been Hellhounds this close to the Forts. Not this many."

"I agree. Something's wrong," Red Wolf said. "I suggest we proceed carefully. We'll find out more once we get to the crossing."

Another hour's worth of travelling put them at the edge of the crossing. Talin could see signs of a battle as they neared, from arrows left in the ground to the occasional Hellhound lying dead. It seemed the Hellhounds had sent another attack force against the Western Forts.

Were they successful?

The crossing itself stood ahead, drawbridge raised, completely silent. Talin scanned the ramparts for guards and saw nothing.

"Shouldn't there be guards up there?" she asked.

"Yes." Red Wolf dismounted and went to the edge of the river. "Hellhound corpses don't decompose as quickly as Elven corpses. There's no way of determining how long ago this fight happened. The crossing could be overrun for all we know."

"Regardless, we need to get across," Talin said. "And I'd rather not jump in and try to swim it."

Red Wolf scratched his chin. "Wait here. I could swim across and check."

"No, I won't have you swimming across that," Talin said. "If we could just get the drawbridge down..."

Red Wolf looked up at it. "There's no way we're getting that down."

"Do you have any better ideas?" Talin asked.

"Send an arrow over the wall. They'll retaliate if they're still around." Red Wolf stepped away from the moat and mounted his horse. "Go ahead, we'll wait."

Talin aimed high, trying to guess a good angle for the arrow to go over the wall. Her first shot sailed over the ramparts, just barely clipping the wall on its way back down. She heard a shout, followed soon by a dozen crossbowmen appearing at the top of the wall, ready to shoot. The drawbridge was lowered, and she saw a man in a captain's uniform standing at the open gates. He was flanked by two swordsmen in light mail.

"I recognise the Elven fletching," he called. "So, before you get any closer, I'd like to ask a few questions."

"We're just simple refugees, sir, running from the Hellhounds," Red Wolf said.

"That's funny. The last of the Hellhound horde broke through here five days ago," the captain said.

"Broke through? How are you all here, then?" Talin asked. "The Hellhounds leave no survivors."

Red Wolf's hand rested on his sword casually.

"They overran us. We thought it was over, but they didn't stay to finish us off. They're headed for Belanore, most likely," the captain said as he approached. "And now that I see you clearly, I recognise you, Your Majesty."

Talin let out a long breath.

"Is there anyone in the Torrian Royal Army who *doesn't* recognise you?" Ettrias muttered.

"I won't ask what business you had past the Forts, but you should know that Lord Wormwood has issued a warrant to the entire kingdom for your arrest, should you ever try to return," the captain said.

"He has no authority to order anyone arrested." Talin stole a sideways glance at Red Wolf.

"That may have been true when you left, Your Majesty, but he has taken control of Belanore," the captain said. "In light of the new accusations against you, the High Court has ruled that he will assume temporary regency of the kingdom until you and your bodyguard are tried."

Red Wolf moved to unsheathe his sword but froze when one of the crossbowmen loosed a bolt at his feet. Talin nocked an arrow in half a heartbeat and aimed it up at the ramparts.

"Easy, Your Majesty. Lord Commander. I'm not here to arrest you," the captain said. "Lord Cassius sends his regards. He said to warn you that you may find yourselves powerless upon your return to Belanore."

Talin lowered her bow. "How are things in Belanore?" she asked.

"I'm not entirely certain," the captain said. "My men and I have been stationed here since before you left. From what Lord Cassius tells me, however, I can only say it does not sound good. He has tried to stall Lord Wormwood as much as he can, but he could do nothing against the court once those rumours spread far enough."

Talin sighed. It was as she had feared, then; Wormwood had convinced most of the population that she had abandoned her people and had branded her a traitor, along with Red Wolf. She cursed herself again for trusting Wormwood.

"Thank you," she said.

The captain bowed and stepped aside to let them pass.

"Interesting encounter," Red Wolf muttered once they'd left the Forts behind. "But if what that captain says is true, we must hurry if we want to beat the Hellhounds to Belanore."

"I know a few shortcuts through Stormwood," Golmin said. "Am I right in assuming that these Hellhounds will wait for the northern hordes before marching on Belanore?"

"Yes, if the northern hordes still haven't crossed the White River," Red Wolf said. "If they have, they will wait for the western hordes. We must act on the assumption of the latter and pray the former is true."

"We stayed too long in the Draconian lands, against my better judgement," Talin said. "Now Wormwood has seized control, and the Hellhounds are on the march."

Red Wolf scratched his chin. "We need to be careful. If the Hellhounds haven't yet overrun the White River, something is wrong."

Talin looked north, where the banks of the White River sat in the distance, obscured by miles of forest. Part of her wished that the White River hadn't been taken yet, but she also knew that Red Wolf was right. If General Virion's forces hadn't been overrun, it was either a miracle, or something was terribly wrong. She desperately hoped that they weren't too late.

XXXIII

By following Golmin's shortcuts and setting off at dawn each morning, they made good time through Stormwood. Talin knew that every shortcut they took put them closer to the marching Hellhounds and hoped against all odds that they were in time to stop the invading hordes. Red Wolf had said that the hordes would be moving slowly; with so many troops to coordinate, it would be difficult to navigate the dense forests of the south, and Hellhounds only moved as fast as the slowest members of their pack. Getting back to Belanore before the horde was no problem, according to him. Setting up a defence in time, on the other hand...

Talin tried not to dwell on it. They were halfway to the city now. Halfway home. She stared up at the full moon as she lay on her bedroll that night, watching the stars while Ettrias guarded the camp. Red Wolf had split up from them at midday so he could shift far away without fear of hurting any of them and promised to be back in the morning. She wondered what the wolf was doing now. Hunting a deer, perhaps; Red Wolf had said he believed the wolf liked a good hunt.

"Can't sleep?" Ettrias asked.

"Trying to," Talin said.

"I'm...sorry for causing all this," Ettrias said. "Truly. Wormwood has done so much more damage than I imagined. He's good at spreading rumours and making them believable. Too good."

"What's done is done," Talin said. "We can only pick up the pieces and hope it isn't too late."

Ettrias didn't speak, the silence only broken by the crackle of the campfire and the occasional hoot of an owl.

"It'll be dawn soon," her brother finally said. "You're sure you don't want to get a few more hours of sleep?"

"I doubt I will, at this rate," Talin said.

"Alright, then tell me something," Ettrias said. "You and Red Wolf. What's going on with you two?"

"What does that mean?" Talin blinked at him. "We're friends."

"He's my friend, and he's never looked at me how he looks at you," Ettrias said.

"I...don't understand." Talin linked her hands behind her head and pretended not to know what he was talking about.

"Talin, I'm not blind," Ettrias said. He frowned. "Did he kiss you?"

Talin had no suitable response to that.

Ettrias shrugged. "Your silence indicates that he did."

"I kissed him first, if you're so curious." Talin wished she had taken him up on his offer to let her sleep.

"Wow, that's...not entirely unexpected, I guess; Red Wolf would never have the guts to initiate," Ettrias said.

"How long have you known?" Talin asked. "And why do you care so much about my personal life?"

"I'm only interested because it's my solemn duty as your brother to tease you about your personal life," Ettrias said with a grin. "And I know Red Wolf has had his eyes on you for years, but he was too much of a coward to make a move. Said something about you having to marry some noble or another. Excuses, really. There's no *law* that states that."

"His confession to murder sets you free," Talin said.

"I'm not going to let him confess."

Talin propped herself up on her elbows and stared at him. "Ettrias, they'll sentence you to death. The law doesn't allow exile a second time—you know that."

"I know." Ettrias stole a glance at her before looking into the fire. "The alternative is for Red Wolf to confess and let them execute him instead. He'll either survive and show the whole kingdom what he is, or he'll die."

"I'll figure something out," Talin said.

"And if you don't?"

"I..." Talin hissed through her teeth. "What's your plan, then?"

"I fix things with Wormwood, then disappear. Leave Kies Tor in secret. You tell the court that I escaped."

"Why?" Talin asked. "You're always saying you want your name cleared. Why do this now?"

"Because I know what it's like...having to say goodbye to everything you've ever known, everyone you've ever loved," Ettrias said. "Being told you're no longer welcome in your own home, in the place you thought you belonged..." He let out a long breath. "That's what awaits Red Wolf if he survives whatever execution the court plans for him. I wouldn't wish it on anyone."

"And Golmin? Am I to believe he's agreed to lose you a second time?" Talin asked.

"Yes and no. He's agreed to the plan but won't be losing me," Ettrias said. "He'll be leaving with me. While Red Wolf gets to stay in Belanore, we'll settle down someplace quiet and start a farm. Seems like a mutually beneficial arrangement to me."

"I'm not going to *lie* to the court, Ettrias," Talin said.

Ettrias raised an eyebrow. "You'll do it to save Red Wolf. You won't chance losing him if you don't 'figure something out'."

"I *will*," Talin said. "It's what I do. I think of solutions."

Ettrias sighed. "At least promise you'll go through with my plan if you don't find a solution."

Sentence Ettrias again to save Red Wolf? Could I really do it?

"I...alright," Talin said. "But only as a last resort. It doesn't mean I like it."

He gave a twisted smile. "Talin, I knew the risks in coming back here. I deserve *some* kind of punishment for plotting to overthrow you and kill you twice, don't you think?"

Deserve? Does he deserve this? Talin thought, but didn't voice it out loud. There would be time to argue over who should take the executioner's axe after they saved the city and stripped Wormwood of his power. For now, they had to outpace the Hellhounds to Belanore.

Red Wolf joined them again as promised a few hours after sunrise, having tracked their path through the forest. Talin was glad to see him again; the camp had felt a little lonely without his company last night.

"I passed through a village not far from here," he said. "Naturally, I had to find out the local gossip. The Hellhounds have been passing through villages and leaving them untouched for the most part. Hunting groups would sometimes drag off villagers, but other than that, they're not attacking. This is highly unusual behaviour for Hell-hounds."

"If they're marching on Belanore, it makes sense not to waste their resources plundering villages," Talin suggested.

"No, this is different," Red Wolf said. "It's like...it's like they know you're not in the city."

"But that's impossible," Talin said.

"I don't know. I've no idea if some of those Hellhounds you en-countered at the border survived their meeting with the wolf," Red Wolf said. "If they did, they would have relayed your whereabouts to command."

"We need to hurry, then," Talin said. "If they catch us unawares outside the city..."

"I know." Red Wolf sighed. "Rufus, how long before we're home?"

"Two weeks, give or take," Golmin said. "At our current rate, maybe one and a half, but I wouldn't push it."

"Good. That gives us two weeks before I shift again. Enough time to mount a defence and drive them back, hopefully."

"Those Hellhounds at the border were afraid of the wolf," Talin said.

Red Wolf nodded. "That was a small team of hunters. The wolf is much stronger than a regular Hellhound due to my size. But against a horde, they'll outnumber him easily. He won't be of much use, even if I could guarantee that he won't turn on the city."

Talin sighed. There wasn't much they could do against the marching horde, it seemed, other than pray and hope. This was an enemy they had barely kept at bay for countless years now, and her people were exhausted. She was exhausted.

If Kadis' armies can make it to Belanore in time, we might stand a chance.

But that wasn't going to happen, and she knew it. Kadis' armies had to march through the same dreary weather they'd had to endure, and the Drakels weren't accustomed to travelling through the tropical south. With an entire legion to coordinate, their chances of reaching Belanore in time to provide reinforcements were slim.

The next few days were relatively uneventful. They set off at dawn each morning and stopped for the night just before dark, giving them a precious hour of daylight to settle down before supper. Talin sparred with Red Wolf whenever Ashera wasn't bugging him for training; sparring gave them an excuse to be alone without seeming too suspicious. She suspected Golmin had caught on to what was happening just as Ettrias had but decided to act as if he hadn't all the same. It gave Red Wolf the illusion of privacy, anyway.

Stopping by a village near Belanore to stock up on supplies before continuing home, they decided to spread out to pick up the local gossip. Talin found herself with Red Wolf again as they listened in on conversations in the tavern. It was a shame they couldn't stay so he could buy her a drink as promised, but she figured they would have the opportunity eventually. She kept her hood up and her head down. Red Wolf hunched his shoulders a little to make himself seem smaller than he was, but he still towered over everyone else.

"I saw the horde camped just a few days away, I swear it," a traveller was saying to the barkeep. Red Wolf tilted his head ever so slightly, but he kept his eyes on the table.

"Don't be daft. They're barely a week from Belanore. They would be marching on the city by now," the barkeep said.

"That's the thing. They're not. It's like they're waiting for somethin'."

Red Wolf turned. "You there, you say there are Hellhounds camped nearby?"

"Aye, that's right," the traveller said.

"How many?"

"Hundreds, thousands even. Like I says, there's a whole horde of 'em."

Red Wolf stood and strode from the tavern. Talin sighed and ran to catch up. They returned to the village well to meet up with the others.

"Alright, what's the bad news?" she asked.

"I have never heard of Hellhounds stopping on their march, and certainly not so close to their target," Red Wolf said. His voice shook ever so slightly. "But we can also assume the White River horde hasn't made it yet. I'm not sure what to make of that."

"General Virion could have held the Crossing better than we thought," Talin said. "The Hellhounds have no siege weapons, and you saw how easy it was for us to take El'Vane with those trebuchets and ladders."

"Not to dash your hopes, Talin, but I doubt that's the case," Red Wolf said. "I know the Hellhounds. With all of this unusual activity...I suspect that General Virion has made some sort of deal, as Rufus and Corvan feared."

Talin didn't argue; she knew he was right. "I'll send a bird to Virion as soon as we return. I hope he can explain the situation or that Cassius or Corvan at least have some news."

The others soon returned with similar news of the Hellhound encampment, and they all agreed to pick up their pace. The sooner they returned to Belanore, the sooner Talin could act on the Hellhound situation and deal with Wormwood. She saw a village woman nearby whispering to two guards and watching them out of the corner of her eye. The woman pointed at them. Talin glanced at Red Wolf; it seemed her bodyguard had noticed too.

"We should leave *now*," he said in a low voice. Talin spurred her horse on before the guards could stop them, leading the way out of the village.

"You think they recognised you?" Ettrias asked once they were a safe distance away.

"Possibly," Talin said. "But we'll be back before any gossip can reach Belanore. How far from home are we?"

"Another week's travel," Golmin said.

"Then let's hope the Hellhounds' movements don't change."

The five of them reached the northern gates of Belanore as expected six days later, just after the new moon had passed. Talin looked up at the walls of the city she called home and felt only relief. She had been away for too long. It felt good to be back at last.

But first, they had to get past the guards.

"Halt! Show me your permits," one of the guards shouted. One of Hesar's City Watch, judging by the black cloak of his uniform.

"I wasn't aware we needed a permit to enter," Talin said.

"New decree by Lord Regent Wormwood," the guard said. "Until the fugitive Red Wolf and the False Queen are captured, nobody is to enter or leave the city without a permit."

Talin stole a sideways glance at Red Wolf, warning him to stay quiet. "And how exactly would we get a permit?"

"Application to Commander Hesar of the Chained Owls," the guard drawled. "I'll be happy to pass on the application if you'd like to make one, but don't expect it to get approved anytime soon. The commander is a busy man."

"We're a little short on time, too, I'm afraid," Talin said.

"Then bugger off and find someplace else to be," the guard said.

Talin pulled her companions away from the gate. "This makes things more difficult. Neither Red Wolf nor I can reveal who we are without being arrested. Even if we could get back into the city, there's no way we'd make it to the palace without being recognised."

"There is a secret passageway that leads into the palace cellar," Red Wolf said. "I use it sometimes to slip into Stormwood to shift and slip back in unnoticed in the morning. Perhaps we could get into the palace that way. We'd have to leave the horses, though. There's a ladder at the other end."

"It's a possibility, but we would still need to deal with the fact that the entire palace will recognise me on sight," Talin said.

"I could sneak in," Ashera said. "Nobody will recognise me, and I can get a message to either Master Corvan or Lord Cassius."

"That could work." Red Wolf looked at Talin. She nodded.

They were interrupted by a grating sound as the gates swung open and two dozen City Watch guards filed out. Most held a crossbow while the rest wielded a sword and shield. Commander Hesar stood at the front in plate and mail, blade drawn.

"Queen Talin, you and your companions are under arrest for conspiring to murder Anna and James Harrison," he said. "Surrender your weapons and turn yourselves in, or we will use force."

Red Wolf reached for his sword, but Talin saw the movement and caught his wrist. They were outnumbered here, even with his healing ability, and she didn't want to hurt these guards.

"We'll come with you," she said, unbuckling her sword and quiver and dropping them on the ground with her bow. Red Wolf, who looked on the verge of running his blade through Hesar's chest, also dropped his weapons. Golmin and Ettrias immediately followed. Talin looked around for Ashera and found that the girl had disappeared; her small size must have made it easy to slip away. She looked to Red Wolf for confirmation. Her bodyguard's glance towards the tree line was all she needed.

"I think there's been a tiny misunderstanding, I'm the one convicted of those murders," Ettrias said.

"Prince Ettrias, the Lord Regent has ordered you to stand trial for returning to Kies Tor against the terms of your exile," Hesar declared.

Talin felt a weight drop into her gut. Wormwood had never intended to work with Ettrias; the man had simply wanted to take the kingdom for himself. And with the Hellhounds on their doorstep...

There was nothing she could do here. Feeling resigned, she followed the guards through the gates and towards the palace.

XXXIV

Talin hadn't imagined returning to Belanore with more than a dozen crossbows aimed at her.

Then again, returning at all was an accomplishment for them; she had half expected that they would never make it home with Wormwood's rumours running rampant across the kingdom. The Master of Coin had been plotting from the start, and she had never caught on. Now they would all suffer for it.

"Say the word, and I could wipe the street with these guards," Red Wolf said in a low voice. "Please."

"No, I won't hurt these guards," Talin said. "I'll think of something. Trust me."

"I always have."

They were marched into the palace as royal guards—troops once loyal to her, to their captain and the Lord Commander—looked on, none of them lifting a hand to stop it. Wormwood had taken over completely.

"Talin, just say the word," Red Wolf said.

"There is a time for action, and there is a time for patience," Talin said. "We will get our opportunity."

They were taken into the throne room first, where Wormwood lounged on his stolen seat at the end of the hall, flanked by two guards. Talin thought the silver-gilded metal of the throne looked different with him on it.

"Ah, I'm glad you could join us, *Your Majesty*," he said with a smirk. "The kingdom believes you have fled. I see you've returned, but where is the army you rode west to find?"

"On its way," Talin said. "You think you've won?"

"I know I have." Wormwood plucked an apple from the nearby fruit tray and took a bite. "You and Red Wolf will be sentenced to death by the court," he said between chews. "Captain Golmin will be executed for treason, and your brother will be executed for returning against his exile. There's...not very much else left for me to do."

"How are you planning to deal with the Hellhound horde camped a week's ride from here?" Talin asked.

Wormwood smiled. "Oh, you think I don't know about that? Let's just say our dear friend General Virion has that front sorted."

Red Wolf was right, then. Virion has made a deal with the Hell-hounds.

"You really think to reason with the Hellhounds? If such a thing were possible, we would have come to an agreement with them long ago," Talin said. "As it stands, you'll rule for what? A few days? They will march on Belanore eventually and wipe out *everything* in their path."

Wormwood shrugged. "If the army you found is really on its way, the Hellhounds shouldn't pose much of a problem. I'd take this opportunity to explain my grand scheme to you, but that seems like a waste of time. Take them to the dungeons to await trial."

Talin glanced around. None of the guards here had crossbows. The two flanking Wormwood didn't even have their weapons drawn. The dozen or so guards coming to escort them all wielded spears and weren't likely to be of much use up close.

"Now!"

Red Wolf headbutted the nearest guard wearing a full-face helm and sent the man staggering. He shook his head a little before ramming his shoulder into another guard and stealing the dagger from his belt. His hands were free a moment later. Golmin and Ettrias both tackled the two guards nearest to them. Talin went for Wormwood.

The first guard swung a punch at her head, but she ducked and tripped him without much difficulty, sending him tumbling. She dodged around the second guard as Red Wolf grabbed the man from behind, flipped him and drove an elbow into his face. She heard a sharp *crack* as his nose broke. Talin ripped a dagger free from the guard's belt and held it against Wormwood's throat.

"Interesting turn of events," she said.

"Hmm." Wormwood didn't move. More guards were streaming into the throne room now, some wielding crossbows.

"I *trusted you*," Talin hissed. "Were you ever my father's friend?"

"Arnas grew soft after your brother's exile," Wormwood said. "Wanted to shape you into the 'perfect' ruler so that you might be a better person than him. He sought personal redemption in *you* over what's good for the kingdom. We were friends—once. Our disagreements set us on different paths. I only want the kingdom restored to its former glory."

Talin scoffed. "Yet you've plunged Kies Tor into chaos and fear. Tell your guards to stand down." She pushed the dagger tighter against his throat.

"See, the difference between you and me is that I'm perfectly willing to wound you and your companions to get what I want," Wormwood said. "But I think...no, I *know* you won't injure these guards." He looked at the dagger at his throat. "And that means no weapons. You wouldn't harm anyone in this room, let alone kill an unarmed man."

He's right. I can't kill him. Talin knew she needed a bluff.

"Want to test that theory?" She pressed the dagger closer, drawing blood.

"By all means, kill me," Wormwood said. "But the High Court no longer recognises your power in Belanore. They will treat you like a common criminal."

At the edge of her vision, Talin saw Red Wolf backing up towards her. Guards surrounded them on all sides. He didn't look happy.

"Now, here's the deal. I will order my guards to shoot Red Wolf if you do not let me go. If what Ettrias has told me is true, he will live," Wormwood continued. "If he dies, then I suppose we will have no evidence that he framed Ettrias for those murders, and we shall just...have to try you and your brother the old-fashioned way. But *if* he lives, and I presume this is the more likely outcome, you will both be executed in the city square without trial. Or, if you would prefer *not* to gamble with fate, you could let me go, and you will both stand trial."

Orrlát.

"Alright! Don't shoot him." Talin moved the dagger away from his throat.

Wormwood nodded at the weapon. "Drop it."

Talin let go of the dagger, and it clattered to the floor.

"Good." Wormwood waved one of his crossbowmen forward. Two more guards approached to restrain Ettrias and Golmin.

Talin realised what was happening too late.

A crossbow bolt struck Red Wolf clean in the chest with a soft *thunk*, sending him to one knee with a grunt. He hissed through his teeth, grabbed the shaft, and ripped it free again, letting the bloodied bolt clatter to the ground. The guards around him took a few steps back.

"You said—" Talin began.

"Ah, so the rumours are true," Wormwood mused, ignoring her entirely. "Off you go now to the dungeons. You are now all enemies of the state and will be executed without trial."

"Traitors, all of you," Red Wolf growled.

"No, in the eyes of the people, I have dealt justice." Wormwood turned away as guards chained their hands to prevent another scuffle.

"I'll be back for you, Wormwood!" Red Wolf yelled, as they were dragged out of the throne room. "You cannot hold us forever!"

The doors slammed behind them.

Down in the dungeons, they were split up despite Talin's protests; Red Wolf was marched to solitary confinement in the lower levels while she was locked up with Ettrias and Golmin.

Knowing Wormwood, he would have extra security on Red Wolf's cell to ensure that her bodyguard didn't escape, given his knowledge of the dungeons. She hoped he would at least be allowed to move around his cell.

Ettrias scowled. "Yes, let's try to break out in the middle of the most heavily guarded room in the palace—that was always going to work."

"I saw an opportunity. It was worth a try..." Talin said.

"Forget about that. We need to focus on what to do now," Golmin said. "Ashera should have warned Master Corvan by now—unless she's still hiding in the palace somewhere. In the meantime, we should look for a way to escape."

"You know these cells better than Ettrias and I," Talin said. "Any ideas?"

"The bars are far too sturdy, but we may be able to lever the door off its hinges if we had the right amount of force." Golmin examined the cell door. "Can't say I've ever seen it done before, though. We could try to bribe the guards, but I'm willing to bet that Wormwood has them convinced that we're all criminals who deserve to hang."

"Red Wolf would know..." Talin sat on the wooden bench. It wasn't particularly comfortable.

"If I know him at all, he's already planning something," Golmin said.

"I hope so."

The cell was much colder than she'd expected; even in the humid heat of the storm season, she found herself shivering at times. She didn't get much sleep that night.

"I know you're worried about him," Ettrias said when he caught her staring into the darkness of the corridor beyond. Talin glanced over at him and saw that Golmin was fast asleep, head in her brother's lap, snoring gently.

"If you're going to tell me he's fine, I know," she said. "I just...I can't help it."

"He's probably losing his mind over not knowing how you are." Ettrias snickered. "He thinks he's subtle. That's the funniest part."

"You've known how he felt about me since *before* your exile and you never deigned to inform me? What kind of brother are you?" Talin looked at him incredulously.

"He was always going on about how you're supposed to marry some nobleman's son or another," Ettrias said. "I mean, think about it. Nobody even knows who he is. He had no reason to believe it would ever work out between the two of you."

He had her there. Their father had often told her that it was her duty to marry well, but after his death, the war effort had occupied most of her time. Most of the kingdom expected her to choose a choose a suitor from among the nobility, not a nameless bodyguard who couldn't remember his own past.

Damn the palace protocol, she had told him, but could they throw it all aside without suffering the consequences?

"I wouldn't worry so much—a scandal like that is the *least* problematic thing you have to deal with at the moment, Your Majesty," Golmin murmured, cracking open an eye.

"Well, *your* knowing it isn't as much of a surprise. Red Wolf tells you everything," Talin said.

"Naturally. Ettrias and I spent the better part of a year trying to get your idiot lord commander to confess, but he was too much of a chicken." Golmin shrugged. "Rumours had gone around the palace for a while. Obviously, nobody spoke about it openly while King Arnas was alive for fear of finding their heads removed if he overheard."

"And...after his death?"

"You...never focused on finding a suitor, but saying you were focused on the war was the perfect excuse. Red Wolf and I went around dispelling the rumours for good."

"Understandable," Talin said.

"People fear him because he's an outsider," Golmin said. "But you saw what happened with the girl in that village and then with Worm-wood. They didn't believe he had the Hellhounds' abilities until they saw him heal. It might not be too late to convince the kingdom that he's just an ordinary man."

"If we can get out." Talin lay back on the cold floor and stared at the ceiling. She supposed she could lure a guard to their cell and stun him with her magic, but there was no guarantee that she could hit him with a non-lethal lightning bolt. In any case, High Court was practically wrapped around Wormwood's little finger; they would be hunted like common criminals even if they escaped. She had to take away his power, and for that, she needed allies.

There was a shuffling sound in the corridor, and Talin glimpsed a familiar-looking silhouette. A little girl, perhaps, no older than twelve.

"Ashera?" she whispered.

"Can't stay. Regards from a friend, slip it back after." A scrap of parchment slid under the door. Talin grabbed it and unfolded it.

> *Nobles cannot move against Wormwood. Drakels on the march and only a few weeks away. No word from the White River. Hold out until the full moon, I will delay the executions.*

"The full moon?" Talin mused. "What's Corvan planning?"

She slid the parchment back under the door. The silhouette disappeared a moment later.

"The Drakels will never arrive in time," Golmin said.

"It seems like we have some of the nobility on our side," Ettrias said. "That has to count for something."

"But they can do nothing from the outside," Golmin pointed out. "Not with Wormwood controlling who goes in and out of the city. We have to do this alone."

"It would seem so." Talin lay down again. "I hope you know what you're doing, old man."

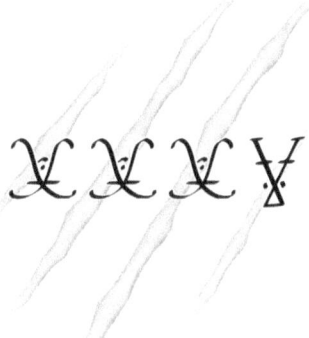

R ed Wolf could hear movement in the corridor. It had to be
Ashera; nobody else would be sneaking around down here
without a torch. He sorely wished he could move closer, but they had
chained him tightly to the wall. He had some room to wiggle his arms
and legs and take a piss on the floor if he wanted, but that was all.

He could soon hear footsteps down the corridor, likely too faint for
the girl to pick up. Guards were coming.

"Later, go hide," he hissed, and Ashera scrambled away. Torchlight
crept under his cell door a moment before it swung open. He squinted
in the sudden wash of light.

"Not too uncomfortable there, I hope?" Wormwood's voice. Red
Wolf blinked a few times until his vision adjusted.

"Come closer and I'll show you," he growled.

"No, I don't think so." Wormwood stepped back. "The High Court wants your confession to the two murders you committed, and your admission that the queen was involved."

"My queen wasn't involved in this. She had no idea until Ettrias told her the truth," Red Wolf said.

"Interesting," Wormwood said. "Of course, that's not what I'll be telling the court."

"Why are you even here? You could tell them anything."

"Oh, I just wanted to see the lord commander, the royal family's personal bodyguard, reduced to this." Wormwood looked him up and down. "Can you even take a piss without getting it all over your boots?"

"Don't tempt me into trying it. You are standing awfully close," Red Wolf said. "Wouldn't want to ruin those clothes."

"You think you're so funny, don't you?" Wormwood drew a small dagger from his belt. "If I stabbed you right now, you wouldn't even be able to remove the blade. That *would* hurt, wouldn't it?"

"I don't care what you do to me, but if you've harmed my queen in any way, rest assured, I will have your head."

"Awfully protective of her, even now." Wormwood smiled, but there was no warmth to it. "But what can you do to protect her from a cell?"

Red Wolf scowled. "I don't know—strangling you right here seems like a good start."

"Oh, I'm sure you'd like to." The Master of Coin spun on his heel and left. A guard locked the cell door behind him.

Red Wolf heard Ashera creeping back a few minutes later and strained to hear any sign of guards approaching again. Nothing. They were alone now.

"You've gone to my queen?" he asked.

"Yep. She's fine. They're all fine," the girl said. "I passed on a message from Master Corvan."

"Good. That's good." Red Wolf felt some part of him relax a little. "What news from the old man?"

"Not much, we're on our own for now, but the Drakels are coming," Ashera said. "They'll be here in a few weeks at the most. Corvan says to hold out until the full moon."

"Two weeks till the full moon," Red Wolf mused. Either Kadis and his legions will have arrived to provide reinforcements and vouch for Talin's innocence, or a public execution will have been prepared, and they could break out while they were being moved.

"I think the queen wants to know how you are," Ashera said. "What should I say?"

"Tell her I'm fine." Red Wolf looked at his chains. "And...don't come sneaking down here again, Ashera. It's too risky. I won't have you getting discovered."

"But—" Ashera began.

"Please. You're..." Red Wolf hesitated. "Well. You're family, Ashera. I can't let them take you too."

"But I—"

"I know. You want to help. And you can help master Corvan and Lord Cassius. So long as you keep yourself *safe*. You can do nothing from a prison cell."

Ashera was silent for a moment. "Alright. But that doesn't mean I like it."

Red Wolf huffed. "Go on, now. Before more guards come around."

The girl's footsteps faded down the corridor. Red Wolf looked around the cell for anything he could use to escape and came up blank. There was nothing in here, not even a bucket to piss into. They were probably planning on spoon-feeding him prison slop in the morning, for all he knew.

He received more visitors a few hours later, just as his lack of movement was becoming unbearable. He braced himself for more of Wormwood's gloating.

The lock clicked, and he found himself face-to-face with Lord Cassius instead. The man held a key in one hand and was flanked by four guards.

"My lord," Red Wolf said.

"Spare me the formalities." Cassius came forward and unlocked his chains one by one, allowing him to stretch and move his limbs. One of his guards set down a bucket in the corner.

"Not to say I don't appreciate the freedom, but isn't this risky?" Red Wolf asked.

"I talked to my brother about your prison conditions. He was able to convince Wormwood to get rid of the chains," Cassius said. "I tried to have you moved out of solitary confinement and upstairs with the others, but he wouldn't hear of it. Our new Lord Regent is...paranoid, to say the least. Believes that you four might plot an escape if you were placed in a cell together."

"That's not paranoid," Red Wolf muttered.

Cassius glanced at his guards, then waved them out of the cell. Red Wolf took the opportunity to stretch his back and shoulders.

"I take it you have more news."

"I do." Lord Cassius glanced at the door before dropping his voice. "The city is at breaking point. There was another riot at the palace gates earlier. Wormwood overruling the court to order your executions without trial was...not received well."

Red Wolf understood. Despite having the power to overrule the High Court, such a move from the Crown was generally considered bad form, implying that the Crown didn't trust the court to carry out the sentencing. Wormwood must truly fear their escape to bypass the court entirely.

"I take it that it's backfired on him," he said.

"Yes. Good news for you, no doubt," Lord Cassius said. "Half the city protests your innocence. In their eyes, Wormwood's move to bypass the court raises more questions than answers. He has no evidence, and they know it."

"Good. That counts for something, at least," Red Wolf said. "You and Corvan have a plan?"

"Not yet. We're still working on it."

"Keep yourselves safe," Red Wolf said. "And...my queen..."

"Corvan and I will do everything in our power to keep her safe, that I can promise," Cassius said. "My loyalties lie with her and always will."

"Thank you."

"I'll see about getting you better food, too," Cassius continued. "Though I wouldn't get my hopes up. Wormwood isn't keen on spending any more coin than necessary on your accommodation."

He spun and left the cell. Red Wolf watched as the torchlight faded from under the door once more, plunging him into complete darkness.

Two weeks until the full moon. Can I last that long?

Red Wolf slid down to sit on the cold floor with his back against the wall. Much as he hated social gatherings, he shared the Hellhounds' blood, and the Hellhounds were naturally social at their core. Trapped alone like this, without the freedom to move...he couldn't last forever.

But he could do nothing here. Without a way to escape, without any resources, he had to rely on Cassius and Corvan. All he could do was wait.

And hope.

XXXVI

The days were beginning to blur together.

Red Wolf had spent the first few days concentrating on keeping track, feeling his powers grow slightly stronger each night with the waxing of the moon. But it wasn't long before he gave up; being locked up inside, under several feet of solid stone, metal, and wood, where he couldn't fully draw on the moon's magic...it was a concentrated effort to even reach out and make a connection. He had instead resorted to keeping count of how many meals he'd been given.

Wormwood truly is treating me like a dangerous monster.

Not that he should have been surprised; he'd seen worse conditions before. The Hellhounds had kept the stolen children in cells much smaller than the one he was in now, treating them as nothing more than animals to be experimented on. He didn't remember much of what they'd done before they turned him into a monster, but maybe that was for the best. He wasn't sure he wanted to remember. His earliest memories had been of the laboratories of the Hellhound alchemists ,and none of it was pleasant.

There was a boy, though, perhaps the same age as he had been then. They never knew each other's names, and he was whisked away by the alchemists not long after they met, but he had been the only child Red Wolf had talked to. Neither of them could speak Torrian well; they must have been so young when the Hellhounds took them. He wasn't sure why he remembered the boy when he couldn't even recall his own name.

Velnora. Was that where he came from? He seemed to remember hearing the name as a child and being unsure of where it was. Why was he remembering it now?

"Useless pup. I would have you thrown from your pack if you weren't the sole crowning achievement of our alchemists."

General Kehlvor had told him that. He remembered the man all too well.

He took everything from me.

Red Wolf opened his eyes slowly and stared at his cell door. Perhaps he was starting to lose his mind down here, remembering his time with the Hellhounds despite having locked away those memories so well.

His cell door opened eventually, revealing a dozen guards, one of them carrying his food. He allowed himself a brief smile at the unusually large detail that always accompanied his meals.

"Not so tough down here, are you?" a guard snickered as he left. Another swapped his bucket with an empty one on his way out. Red Wolf watched them leave, contemplating tackling the nearest while he still could, and decided against it. They could easily decide to chain him back up.

How many days has it been? How many more days must I endure?

Ashera hadn't visited since he was first locked in here, indicating that she had either followed his instructions or been captured herself.

No. Corvan or Cassius would have told him if she'd been captured. He had to assume she was safe, hiding somewhere with their help.

Footsteps rang out down the corridor, not belonging to any of the guards. Red Wolf swallowed his bite of stale bread and scrambled to his feet. The door swung open to reveal Master Corvan and Lord Highett.

Finally.

"What's the occasion?" he asked. "Is it time to enact our escape plan?"

"We have a situation," Cassius said.

Red Wolf squinted through the torchlight. "What situation?"

"We had thought your executions would have been scheduled already," Cassius said. "But they want to wait until after you shift."

"Why?"

"Wormwood wants to execute the queen first, tomorrow evening, as the full moon rises, to make sure you cannot escape and come to her aid. He's...gotten increasingly agitated, as of late. I suspect he believes something will go wrong at the last second."

"Then get her out!" Red Wolf hissed. "I don't care *how*, just—*please*."

"We don't know where she is. She was taken to a private cell a few days ago, and Wormwood hasn't informed us where," Corvan said. "He may be onto what we're planning."

"So free me and the others, and we can find her," Red Wolf said. "*Corvan.*"

Corvan looked incredulous. "And go where? There are a dozen guards just outside the dungeon. We wouldn't make it five feet before an alarm was raised."

"*Orrlát*, old man, I don't know! The full moon is tomorrow. They will execute her *tomorrow*. You cannot have come all the way down here after *two weeks* only to tell me you still have no plan."

"We will find her, I promise."

Red Wolf hissed through his teeth. "That's not good enough."

Corvan and Highett exchanged a look. He knew that look in the old healer's eyes.

"You understand it will be very risky to free you," Cassius said.

"I know."

"Very well." Corvan nodded at Lord Cassius, who backed out of the cell to guard it in case anyone came. "Later tonight, Ashera will steal the master key for the dungeons and slip it to Lord Highett. He will visit again, taking two guards from their post at the dungeon stairs as an escort, drawing them away from the main group. Once you are free, you must take them both out. The two of you will then free Prince Ettrias and Captain Golmin from their cell."

"The four of us won't be enough to take out the ten remaining guards," Red Wolf said.

"Ah, but that's where I'll come in." Corvan smiled. "I can brew a potion using the petals from the Black Byur flower. Not lethal, but it will release a strong sedative when exposed to the air. It should be enough to knock out all the guards there."

"And what about Talin?" Red Wolf asked.

"We will crash the execution tomorrow. You don't have to worry about a thing."

"I'd have to stay out of the city to shift. Not to say I don't trust you, Corvan, but I need to be there."

"I know you care for her a great deal, but this is not worth risking your secret for," Corvan said. "We can handle it."

Red Wolf sighed. "Fine. Just...keep her safe."

"No matter what power Wormwood holds over the city, she is the true Queen of Kies Tor. We will protect her with our lives."

The old healer exited the cell with Highett, leaving Red Wolf alone in the dark once again. A few more hours and he would finally be free of this cell. He looked forward to it.

His mind drifted back to Talin, sitting alone in a cell somewhere. He hoped the guards hadn't harmed her in any way. If any of them even tried...

No.

She hadn't wanted to hurt the guards that captured them. Even with a dozen crossbows pointed at her, she still thought of them as her people, and maybe believed they were simply following orders. He doubted he would ever understand why she held back against all those traitors.

Lord Cassius returned with the guards and master key as promised a few hours later. They waited outside, as expected, and the spymaster entered alone.

It's time.

Red Wolf lunged out of the cell, grabbing the nearest guard and headbutting the man. There was a *crack* as his nose broke and he dropped soundlessly. Cassius swung a right hook at the other guard's head, stunning him long enough for Red Wolf to slam his face into the wall. They left the guards there and crept down the corridor to find Ettrias and Golmin.

"There, that's their cell," Cassius whispered, stopping near the stairs. Red Wolf peered into the cell to their right and found Ettrias and Golmin both asleep. Lord Cassius turned the key and let the door swing open.

"What kind of time do you call this...?" Ettrias yawned, rubbing his eyes and blinking.

"Time to get out of here. Where did they take your sister?" Red Wolf asked.

"Dunno, aren't you the ones who dragged her off?" Ettrias grumbled. He yawned again. "Wait. You're Red Wolf. Are we escaping?"

Red Wolf let out a long breath. "Come on. We're short on time."

Ettrias stumbled out of the cell, still looking half-asleep, Golmin right behind him. Red Wolf took the vial of Black Byur extract from Lord Cassius as they reached the top of the stairs and tossed it at the guards. It shattered against a wall and immediately released a thin, almost transparent cloud of smoke. The guards were quick to drop, weapons clattering to the floor. The four of them scrambled past and headed for the cellar.

"Ashera should be waiting by the passageway with Corvan," Cassius explained. "There is a hunting cabin an hour's hike from there, completely abandoned. We can shelter there while we plan how to get the queen out."

"What about weapons?" Red Wolf asked.

"Ashera and Corvan snatched all of your equipment from custody already," Cassius said. "If we can free the queen before the Hellhounds arrive, we might have a chance—"

Two more guards rounded the corner as they were halfway down the corridor.

"Damn it, they weren't meant to be patrolling here yet," Cassius hissed.

Ettrias and Golmin both lunged at the guards before Red Wolf could react. He watched as the prince slipped behind the first guard and tripped him without much difficulty, quickly wrapping his arms around the man's throat in a tight chokehold. Golmin threw the other guard and put him to sleep in the same fashion.

"The rest of the way should be clear," Golmin said. "Unless whoever is in charge at the moment has changed the night patrol..."

"I don't intend to find out." Red Wolf dragged the two unconscious guards into a nearby empty room and closed the door.

They met up at the cellar entrance without further incident, where Ashera passed around their weapons and equipment. Red Wolf was glad to have his sword back; the familiar weight of a weapon at his belt felt good. For a moment, he was tempted to return to the dungeons to find Talin, but that would waste precious time they needed to escape. Talin would never let him prioritise her over everyone else in the group. He lifted open the entrance to the passageway and waited for the others to duck through, then descended the ladder after them and slammed the entrance shut again. Emerging undetected outside the city, they quickly disappeared into Stormwood, led by Lord Cassius.

The hunting cabin was an old, decaying building deep in the forest, probably used once by the royal family but abandoned years ago. They found no supplies inside, but Corvan had brought maps of the city and a small bag of food. Red Wolf helped himself to an apple; after almost two weeks of eating slop and stale bread, he craved proper food.

"We know public executions are held in the city square, not far from the palace," Cassius was saying. "Getting there will be difficult, but I've managed to secure a permit from Hesar to enter the city. We will slip in undetected and find the guard holding the keys for the queen. Ashera, do you think you're up for some more stealing?"

"I can get the keys," the girl said.

"Good lass. Ettrias, you'll have to provide a diversion while Ashera frees the queen," Cassius continued. "As a safety measure, I will be keeping my dear brother busy so the guards can't alert him. Once the queen is freed, we'll slip into the crowd and return here."

"If something goes wrong—" Red Wolf began.

"We'll handle it," Golmin said. "You have my word that we'll keep her safe. It's not worth risking exposing yourself. Please, just...stay here. Shift in the woods where nobody will see. If the people find out what you are, there's no going back."

Red Wolf raked a hand through his hair. "I can't sit around *waiting*. I'm the Lord Commander of the Royal Guard. My *sole duty* is to protect the Crown."

"*Red Wolf*." Golmin's voice bordered on a plea. "This isn't worth your secret."

She's worth the world. He didn't voice the thought.

"I...can organise for my spies to guard the gates tomorrow evening," Cassius said carefully. "If something is indeed wrong, I can relay a message to them within a few minutes. You can wait by the gates if you wish, but do not go into the city unless you're certain you can help us get the queen out of there before you shift."

"If she's in trouble, I will not hesitate," Red Wolf said.

"I know. Promise me." Cassius met his gaze.

"You know I cannot promise anything, my lord," Red Wolf said.

Cassius sighed. "I understand. Consider this a request, then. Please. Stay put until we send word that the queen is safe."

"I'll try."

T alin was woken from her brief slumber by the sound of the cell door opening. For a moment, she was hopeful, thinking that one of the others had found where they'd taken her to and come to free her. But then she saw two guards standing in the corridor and her heart sank.

"Get up," one of them said. Talin considered firing a bolt of lightning at them and making a run for it, then decided against it. She couldn't hope to escape alone.

"Where are we going?" she asked.

"'Where are we going', she says." The guard laughed. "It's time for your execution. The whole world will be watching."

That's it? They'll just execute me like a common criminal...?

Talin kept quiet. The guards chained her hands and marched her out of the dungeons. She could feel eyes on her as she was paraded through the palace, past guards and servants alike. People once loyal to her, now serving Wormwood.

Part of her had always known there would be no trial, not with Wormwood able to bypass the High Court entirely. She would have no chance to plead her case. She had let this happen, in her own city, and now she was paying the price. She never should have gone west. The Drakels' reinforcements were unlikely to arrive in time anyway.

The palace's main gates swung open, and a huge, watching crowd greeted her. She remembered the welcoming crowd that had come to her coronation—a lifetime ago now—and knew that the same people stood here tonight. Folk who had cheered and waved when she walked through those doors as queen now watched her in utter silence. Guards lined the streets, keeping them back as she was led to the city square. She thought she caught a glimpse of a hooded man shouldering his way through the crowd at one point, keeping up with her, but he vanished a moment later.

Wormwood was waiting for them at the top of the wooden execution platform. He flashed her a humourless smile as the guards led her to the middle of the platform and unlocked her chains briefly, only to attach them again to a metal rod in the wood. She wasn't going anywhere.

"For conspiring in the murders of Anna and James Harrison, treason against the Crown, perjury against the High Court..." Wormwood began, reading from a long piece of parchment. Talin had never liked these formalities; it was bad enough to sentence someone to death without having to go through ten minutes of rambling that few could even understand.

There was a commotion in the crowd. Nothing unusual; there were always folk who wanted to get up close and jeer as criminals were executed. Wormwood continued reading, ignoring it all. Talin saw the hooded man again.

Ettrias.

Her heart almost stopped. Corvan and Cassius had freed the others. They were here to stop the execution now, no doubt. Ettrias was trying to cause a riot to interrupt Wormwood, but it wasn't working; the Master of Coin kept reading undisturbed. She saw the burly executioner sharpening his axe nearby.

Come on, just stop reading for a moment...

There was a tug against her shackles. She didn't turn to look; it had to be Ashera, having snuck behind everyone under the platform. The girl was jiggling keys in the lock, trying to find the right one.

"Don't rush it," Talin whispered. *More haste, less speed.*

Wormwood had finished reading from his parchment by now. More guards rushed to the front to subdue the crowd, leaving the back of the city square virtually unguarded. She saw the executioner lift his axe to his shoulder and stride towards the platform.

Gods, Ashera, we're running out of time.

"I can't get any of these to fit," the girl hissed.

Talin was focused on the executioner with his black mask and gleaming axe. He was at the edge of the platform now, walking towards her. The crowd pushed against the line of guards.

A single arrow sailed over the crowd's head and landed an inch from the executioner's foot. He halted instantly.

"The next person who so much as takes a *step* towards my queen will receive an arrow to the face."

The crowd parted cautiously as a towering figure strode forward, arrow nocked in a familiar-looking recurve bow.

Red Wolf.

"Arrest him!" Wormwood shouted. Red Wolf loosed his arrow at the nearest charging guard and shattered his kneecap. He spun without missing a beat, sword clearing its scabbard in an instant, slicing through another guard's hamstring. Two more came to intercept him. He head-butted one and sent the other tumbling away with a kick to the groin. The first guard came forward again with a swing. Red Wolf met it with a deft parry and opened the man's throat in retaliation.

The crowd parted again on his left, and Talin glimpsed a flash of steel as Ettrias and Golmin stepped out to cover his advance. Her bodyguard slung his bow over his shoulder and replaced it with his dagger. His gaze was fixed on Wormwood.

"Red Wolf, *don't*!" she yelled. *We need Wormwood alive to face trial.*

His boots drew to a halt in front of the execution platform instantly. Wormwood drew a guard's sword from its scabbard and jumped down to meet him.

"Surely you know what's happening tonight?" the Master of Coin said. Behind Talin, Ashera continued jiggling keys.

"I know. But the queen is innocent. I will not let you execute her." Red Wolf pointed his sword at Wormwood.

Tonight? What did he mean? Talin looked up at the darkening sky. *The full moon.*

"Now, let's not be too hasty..." Wormwood took a step back.

"Keep your mouth shut and let me talk, *abiyo*." Red Wolf scowled. "People of Belanore, Talin is your rightful queen! Whatever crimes this *traitor* has accused her of committing, she is innocent. Wormwood has orchestrated all of this to take power. He has been lying to all of you that you are safe, but the truth is, there are Hellhounds on the horizon, ready to march! We have to mount a defence before it's too late."

The shackles around Talin's wrists finally opened. She slipped them off quietly, and Ashera pressed a dagger into her hand. Neither of them moved.

"Nobody will believe the words of a common criminal, Red Wolf," Wormwood said. "That's what you are now. You have no power here. You're not even one of us. You are a Hellhound, which makes you an enemy of the state."

Red Wolf swung at him, but it was a wild swing, and the Master of Coin knocked his blade aside. Talin saw a guard behind him move and shouted a warning too late. The man's spear drove into Red Wolf's back, between his shoulder blades, and sent him to his knees. Ettrias cut the guard down before he could do any more damage, but it was too late; she heard the crowd gasp as her bodyguard stood. The guards around him took several steps back. Talin looked up again. *Oh no.*

"I must admit, Red Wolf, I've been stalling for time," Wormwood said. "But now..." He clambered onto the platform again and pointed at Talin. "She will die, and you will be helpless to stop it."

Red Wolf took a step forward but only managed to sink to all fours with a roar of pain. Wormwood smiled and nodded to the executioner, who raised his axe over Talin's head. Her bodyguard tried to move forward again, fighting his inevitable transformation, desperation building up in his eyes as he met her gaze.

Talin rolled aside as the axe came down and buried itself in the wooden platform instead.

Civilians screamed and scattered as Red Wolf shifted, bones cracking and reforming, clothes ripping free. Talin vaulted off the platform before the executioner could have another swing at her—not that she need have worried. The man had fled the moment he saw Red Wolf transform. Ettrias was at her side a moment later, along with Golmin, and they retreated towards the unguarded side of the city square. Ashera wriggled out from under the platform and joined them.

"Gods damn it, we told him to stay out of the city," Ettrias hissed.

"Good thing he didn't, or my head would be rolling around on that platform by now," Talin said. She saw the wolf leap onto the platform as the surrounding guards broke their formation and scattered. Civilians ran in every direction. The wolf pounced on Wormwood.

"He didn't go for the nearest guard..." Golmin mused.

"Wormwood called Red Wolf a Hellhound." Talin looked away. As much as she resented what the man had done, seeing the wolf rip him to shreds like that wasn't the punishment anyone deserved.

"We need to get him out of the city before he starts tearing into the civilians," Golmin said.

"Oh, great idea. Shall we whistle and see if he comes running?" Ettrias scowled.

"Ettrias." Talin glared at her brother.

"What?"

There was a shout from the square, and two crossbowmen turned to face them. Talin gave her brother a shove instead and he took off down the street without argument. Golmin flinched when a bolt struck the wall next to him. Talin turned to follow Ettrias, only to stagger forward as blinding pain lanced down her leg, sending her to one knee. She looked down, and sure enough, a bolt had clipped her thigh as it sailed past, tearing a deep gash in its wake. Golmin hoisted her back up with one hand and helped her get around the corner before the crossbowmen could reload and shoot again. He peeked around quickly and beckoned for them to continue moving.

"We'll get you to Corvan. He can have a look at it," the captain said.

Talin grimaced. "I don't suppose he's anywhere nearby..."

"He should be in the palace. There's a passageway not far from here that also leads to Stormwood. We'll get you out of the city, and Ashera can detour to the palace to find him." Golmin slowed a little. "I can carry you if you can't walk that far."

"I'll be fine." Talin glanced back as one of the crossbowmen rounded the corner after them. She saw the bolt in his crossbow a split second before the wolf appeared from behind, tackling him, razor-sharp claws slashing his throat open like paper. Golmin drew his sword.

"I really don't want to have to do this..." he began as the wolf bounded after them, attention focused on something over the captain's shoulder.

"Wait," Talin said.

The wolf launched himself over their heads and took two bolts to the chest as he landed. Talin looked past him and noticed the guards at the other end of the street for the first time. They barely had time to reload before he rammed into them, knocking one to the ground and clamping his jaws around the man's throat. The other looked at him, then at Talin, then dropped his crossbow and fled. The wolf glared after him.

"Red Wolf?" Talin let out a breathless half-laugh.

The wolf padded over and sniffed at her hand, where she was applying pressure to her leg. He looked up at her.

"I'll be alright," she said, and he bounded off again, vanishing down another back alleyway. Talin tried to get a glimpse of where he went, but he was already out of sight.

"Red Wolf—" she began.

"He'll find us again. I wouldn't worry too much," Golmin said. "Come on. We need to get out of the city."

They made their way through the streets slowly, alert to any more guards attempting to stop them, though the bodies they found littered along their route indicated that the wolf had been clearing the way for them. They met up with Ettrias and Ashera behind the butcher's shop, where they had met to set off on their journey west all those weeks ago. It looked different now, somehow. True to Golmin's prediction, the wolf also showed himself again here, sniffing once more at Talin's wounded leg before his tongue darted out to lick the blood from her fingers.

"He's with us?" Ettrias asked. The wolf growled at him.

"Don't ask. Just be glad he's here." Golmin opened the hatch to the secret passageway. Ettrias took his spot under Talin's shoulder while he jumped down to check the coast was clear. Ashera jumped down afterwards. Talin was about to follow her down when the wolf butted himself in front of her, looked up, and howled.

"Is something wrong?" she asked.

The wolf howled again at the full moon, louder this time. Talin strained her ears and heard a reply, then another. Then a third, followed by a whole pack of wolves responding to the call.

Except wild wolves didn't wander this close to the city.

Cloister bells tolled at the northern gate, followed by a long, echoing horn blast that seemed to quiet the entire city. *One blast for an invading force.*

While they were caught up in Wormwood's coup, the Hellhounds had marched south, and now the invaders were here.

And the city had no defences mounted to meet them.

XXXVIII

The four of them made their way through the city and to the tunnel that Talin had used for smuggling their horses out of the palace, keeping out of sight where they could and fighting their way through guards where they couldn't. With Talin's wounded leg and the wolf tagging along, climbing any ladders was out of the question, forcing them to change plans and head for a more accessible passageway instead. And given that the Hellhounds were no doubt swarming Stormwood by now, they had little choice but to return to the palace and seek refuge there.

"How's the leg?" Ettrias asked, glancing back briefly.

"I'll live." Talin grimaced. "Keep going."

"Ashera, run ahead and let Corvan know to expect us," Golmin called. The girl gave a nod and sprinted off, quickly disappearing down the tunnel.

"You sure you don't want one of us to carry you?" Ettrias asked.

"Please, I can still walk," Talin said.

Beside her, the wolf huffed through his nostrils and nudged himself under her free hand. Talin understood the motion; he was offering himself as a crutch to take her weight off Golmin's shoulders. She put a hand between his shoulders gingerly and allowed him to support her instead.

They emerged a few minutes later at the other end, where Corvan and Ashera both waited. Together, they made their way up to the old healer's tower. Most of the royal guards had been called to mount a defence, no doubt by Hesar, and those still left stared after the wolf and didn't dare get close. The wolf himself kept pace with Talin's slow limp, paws landing silently on the polished floors despite his huge form. At the stairs, Talin was finally forced to relent and allow her brother to carry her the rest of the way. Corvan began mixing a potion in his lab as soon as they arrived. Ettrias set her down on the sofa and took a seat in the corner. The wolf sat down at the door and refused to budge.

"We need to..." Talin squeezed her eyes shut as another wave of pain lanced through her leg. "We need to mount a defence. The Hellhounds..."

"Our walls will hold for now," Golmin said. "The Hellhounds have no siege weapons, Your Majesty. It will take them a while to get into the city, and we will have figured something out by then."

"I hope you're right." Talin tried to focus on something else, but the pain in her leg seemed to be worsening by the second now that the rush and tension from before had worn off. Corvan passed her a cup of clear liquid.

"This will put you into a deep sleep so I can close the wound properly," he said. "It won't wear off until morning."

Talin downed the potion in one gulp. It tasted vile. "We'll plan our next move tomorrow, then."

It didn't take long for the potion to take effect, and she felt herself falling into a blissful, dreamless sleep. She remembered waking briefly in the early hours before sunrise, but the potion hadn't worn off completely yet, and she quickly fell back asleep. This time, she dreamed of her coronation. Red Wolf was watching the crowd while she smiled and waved at them and silently wished it would all be over soon. He had hidden his true nature so well back then and for so long that nobody even questioned *why* he was different. And he'd thrown it all away in an instant to save her life.

Talin woke again a few hours later, still groggy from the effects of the potion, to find the others all asleep on the floor. Corvan had no doubt retired to his chambers. They'd somehow convinced the wolf to leave his spot guarding the top of the stairs and closed the door behind him. Red Wolf struggled to his feet now, having shifted with his back against the doorframe. He looked around for some clothes and soon found the trousers that Corvan had left for him. They were clearly too small, but he managed to fit into them all the same. Talin smiled to herself but closed her eyes again to spare his dignity.

"You awake?" he mumbled.

She thought she did a good impression of someone just waking.

"Mornin'," he said. "How's the leg?"

Talin looked at her bandaged leg. It felt fine now, but she suspected it would start to hurt again once the potion wore off completely.

"I'm fine," she said. "How did you know about my leg?"

"I..." Red Wolf blinked. "I don't know."

"The Hellhounds are here," Talin said. "They're already at the gates. They must have marched while we were trapped in the dungeons and Wormwood was busy taking over."

"Our gates will hold. They don't have the siege weapons to get through by force," Red Wolf said. "Is this...Corvan's study?"

"We were supposed to sneak out of the city, but then the Hellhounds came, and it was too risky," Talin said. "This was the next best place."

"Hmm." Red Wolf crossed to Corvan's bookshelves and dug through them until he found some maps. He spread them out on the desk and bent over them, blocking Talin's line of sight.

"What are you doing?"

"Planning." Red Wolf didn't turn. Talin leaned over as far as she could without falling off the sofa.

"Your plan involves looking at a map of the entire kingdom?"

Red Wolf sighed. "Do you know any places in Kies Tor by the name of Velnora?"

"No..." Talin said. "Why?"

"I would prefer not to talk about it right now." Red Wolf focused on the map again. Talin left him to it.

"You know, I think I understand," she said, after a while. "The Hellhounds have gotten this far because they hate everything that isn't like them. They channel that hate and anger. The wolf did the same at first."

Red Wolf paused looking through the map.

"Something changed, though. I'm not sure what." Talin did have a good idea of what it was, but it seemed far-fetched. "And I think that's why you remember more now."

"Maybe," Red Wolf frowned. He was silent for a while.

"I was right." He suddenly straightened. "Velnora, it's a village in the Highlands, right on the northern border. This could be where I'm from."

Talin swung her legs off the sofa and hobbled over to the desk to see. "That's right by the mountain pass." Her brow creased. She did have some recollection of that village name, way back when Corvan had tutored her in history.

"Velnora was the first village to fall when the Hellhounds invaded," she said quietly. "There's nothing left of it. Nobody survived."

"Wh—? There must have been someone outside the village, someone who knew the people there," Red Wolf said. His gaze was fixed on the map and the little dot that marked the village by the mountain pass.

Talin shook her head. "It was a bloodbath. The entire population was wiped out. Velnora was so remote that nobody from the outside ever really went there, and they had no way to defend themselves. The Hellhounds destroyed everything and burnt it to the ground."

"It's all gone?" A hint of sadness flashed across Red Wolf's eyes, quickly replaced with anger. "Then they really took everything."

"I've never seen you so focused on finding out where you're from," Talin said. "What's wrong?"

"Before, I'd...I'd given up. There was no point, I couldn't remember anything from before I was kidnapped," Red Wolf said. "But when I was in the dungeons, I remembered a name. Velnora. And I remembered...being told we lived there. I thought it was a strange name at the time, and I'd never heard it before." He gave the table a hard shove. "But the Hellhounds took that away too."

Talin took his hand. He looked at her and his gaze softened. "There's nothing you can do to change what's happened," she said gently. "Rage won't bring the village back."

Red Wolf sighed and rolled up the map, replacing it with a map of Belanore. "We should focus on the city. The Hellhounds are at the northern gates. Hesar has no doubt mounted a defence by now, but we need Highett to tell us where the Owls are spread."

Talin pulled up a chair so she could sit; her leg was starting to throb. "Lord Cassius? Where is he?"

"He was supposed to be keeping his brother busy during your execution, but I didn't see either of them," Red Wolf said. "Either he's planning something, or Lord Karl has caught on and arrested him."

There was a knock at the door. Red Wolf looked at it, then at Talin. Neither of them made a sound.

"Corvan, are you awake yet?"

Talin looked towards the healer's chambers. The old man was probably still asleep.

"It's Lord Cassius."

Talin breathed a sigh of relief and motioned for Red Wolf to open the door. Cassius stumbled in as soon as it opened and locked it behind himself. He certainly looked the worse for wear—his usually neat doublet creased, his hair tousled.

"Your Majesty, good to see you," he said. "Lord Commander."

"We need to know where Hesar's Owls are spread so we can assist," Red Wolf said, without skipping a beat.

"Ah, I thought you might," Highett said. "But I'm afraid we have another problem."

"Problem?" Talin asked.

"Wake Corvan, if you'll be so kind. The others, too. We have much to discuss."

Red Wolf crossed to the sofa and threw a cushion at Golmin. The captain jolted awake instantly, hand flying to his sword, then glared at Red Wolf's back as he went to wake Corvan.

"You two must have a great time in the barracks each morning," Talin said.

"He's an idiot." Golmin got to his feet and stretched. "How's your leg?"

"Better, thank you," Talin said.

"Corvan worked some wonders with his healing," Golmin said. "You should recover nicely. What's with the early wake?"

"Urgent business, Captain," Lord Cassius said.

"That so?" Golmin looked at Ettrias and Ashera, still sound asleep. He nudged them both awake.

"Go away, Rufus, it's too early..." Ettrias groaned. "Talin! Feeling better?"

"Fine. Take a seat." Talin gestured to the sofa. Corvan joined them not long after and gave Talin another potion to dull the pain in her leg.

"Good, we're all here," Cassius said. "My brother tells me he is to take charge of the city now that Wormwood is dead."

"And that's a bad thing?" Red Wolf asked.

"Yes. My brother might be good with civil affairs, but he knows nothing of battle or sieges," Cassius explained. "He knows this. Which is why he has begged me to find someone...more qualified."

"And you came to us?" Ettrias asked. "The city still thinks we're wanted criminals, in case you'd forgotten."

"I don't have many options. My spies at the front tell me the Hellhounds have siege ladders, and they're trying to make it over the walls. If that's true, it won't be long before they break through, especially if we do not establish a chain of command."

"Get me to the front. I can organise them," Talin said. "I might still be learning, but I do have years of tutoring and experience from El'Vane."

"There's no guarantee they'll listen at all," Golmin said. "I mean no offence, Your Majesty, but the City Watch and Royal Guard are hardly likely to follow someone who faced the executioner's axe less than twenty-four hours ago."

"They will listen," Talin said.

"You can't walk," Ettrias said. "Just reminding you."

"I can ride."

Red Wolf folded his arms. "I can't stop you, but I can accompany you." He looked at Lord Cassius. "Can you get access to the stables?"

"I can't, but...I can arrange for them to be unguarded."

Red Wolf nodded. "Do it. We need to start evacuating civilians in the meantime. Rufus, you and Ettrias will need to stay and secure the palace before the Hellhounds break through."

"How are we supposed to get everyone out of the city?" Talin asked.

"I'll talk to my brother," Cassius said. "He may see some reason in allowing all of you to take charge if only to stop the Hellhounds."

"Corvan, use the throne room as a medical centre. We'll transport injured troops back to you," Talin said.

Cassius stroked his chin. "My spies can find the other healers in Belanore and convince them to come here."

"A few extra hands would allow us to save more wounded, I agree. Make it happen."

"Ashera, I'll need your help, too, if you're up for it," Corvan said.

"I want to fight," Ashera said.

"No. Not out there. You're a good fighter, Ashera, but you cannot face off against those Hellhounds." Red Wolf lay a hand on her shoulder. "You can do more good here, helping Corvan. Saving people."

"But I..." Ashera's voice trailed off. "You all get to risk your necks fighting Hellhounds. Why not me?"

"Because you still have so much to look forward to, child," Corvan said. "Growing up. Joining the Royal Guard. Being knighted one day. Look at me, I'm an old man who can't fight any battles. But that doesn't make me less useful."

Ashera pouted but didn't argue.

"Oh, before I forget. I took the liberty of picking this up from the city square." Cassius held out Red Wolf's weapons belt. He took it with a nod of thanks.

"My lord, we'll need to know where Hesar has placed his troops," the bodyguard said, nodding at the map. The spymaster crossed to the desk, quickly going through what he knew from his spies and marking it all down. Red Wolf followed it all with an eagle eye.

"Alright, if there is nothing else, I think it's time we moved off," Talin said. "We've delayed long enough already and still need to gear up."

Corvan found a crutch for her, and she hobbled with the others from his tower, splitting up at the corridor to their different tasks. Golmin and Ettrias accompanied her and Red Wolf to the barracks for Red Wolf's clothes, then the armoury to don some mail and plate. Talin left her steel helmet behind; it would only obscure her vision when she needed to shoot.

"Hellhounds can only be killed if you destroy the brain. Aim for the eyes and temples; those are the easiest ways to pierce the skull," Red Wolf instructed. "Talin, your lightning should also work. Taking off their heads will kill them, but it's difficult to do so in one hit."

"I wish we could have gotten that torslek from the insurgents in time," Talin said. "A few barrels of that stuff would have been useful."

"We'll make do with what we have." Red Wolf put on his helm and buckled the strap, grabbing a tall kite shield on his way out.

The stables were unguarded as Lord Cassius had arranged. It was child's play to break in and saddle two horses. Red Wolf helped her onto hers and followed her lead.

"I take it you have a plan!" he said.

"Of course." Talin smiled. "I can get them to listen."

"Good."

XXXIX

The northern gates were in total disarray.

Red Wolf had never seen troops in such chaos. With Hesar trying to organise everything from his spot at the top of the wall, soldiers were running everywhere. He had to give the City Watch commander *some* credit, though; they'd held off the Hellhounds for now with the impeccable archery that elves were known for. One group of Hellhounds had managed to place a ladder, and they were trying to place more, but Hesar's archers and crossbowmen kept them at bay, dropping them before they could reach the wall.

The bodyguard exchanged glances with Talin. There was a beat, and then she steered her horse up the steps to the top of the wall. Red Wolf followed silently. She was up to *something*, no doubt about it. He was curious.

"Hesar, form all of your archers up along the wall!" she shouted.

Hesar turned. "I'm sorry, Your Majesty, but you're not in charge here!"

"Do it!" Talin said. "Your troops are all over the place! Band the archers together first, then we can talk."

Hesar cursed. "Archers on the wall, hold! I want any man wielding a bow to the front, now!"

There was a stampede of boots as the archers crammed themselves together at the edge of the wall.

"Loose!"

The archers resumed their shooting. A rain of arrows sailed down to stop a group of charging Hellhounds in their tracks.

"They'll get their ladders up eventually, Hesar, and half your men are running like headless chickens at the bottom of the wall," Red Wolf said. "Talin and I can get them into formation if you keep the archers organised."

"Keep shooting. Do not stop until the order is given!" Hesar shouted. He turned back to them. "What are you even doing here? You're still wanted criminals, and I could easily have you both arrested."

"This is my city. My people. I'm not going to abandon them," Talin said.

Hesar sighed. "Red Wolf said you were innocent back in the city square. Is it true?"

"I had nothing to do with my father's plans," Talin said. "And the rumours about me fleeing Kies Tor were spread by Lord Wormwood. Lord Cassius and Master Corvan can both vouch for me."

Hesar glanced over the wall and shouted for his infantry to form up. "And you, Lord Commander. You bear no love for the Hellhounds; I can see that. If you're not one of them, what are you?"

"Your ally—that should be enough," Red Wolf said.

"Aye, I suppose. We'll need every sword we can get," Hesar said. "Go, then, organise the men. I will keep the Hellhounds busy from up here."

Talin nodded and swung her horse around to face the city and the soldiers at the bottom of the wall. "All of you, listen up! The Hellhounds will get over the wall sooner or later. Anyone who isn't needed at the bottom is to form up behind the archers. Shields to the front. Form a wall!"

The soldiers stared at her, then looked at each other. Nobody moved.

"Get a move on and do as the queen says!" Hesar roared. "The Crown doesn't pay you to gawk!"

They all scrambled into action, forming at the bottom of the stairs and making their way to the top.

"Thank you," Talin said.

"I hope you know what you're doing, Your Majesty." Hesar turned back to face the Hellhounds and continued shouting orders at his men. The attackers were more wary now, having seen their organised movements on the wall, and teams of wolves were being sent out to place the ladders. It made sense; they were much faster on four legs than they were on two. Red Wolf left his horse with Talin and moved to the ladder that the Hellhounds had already managed to place, kicking it down. But more were coming, and he knew they didn't have the numbers to match them one on one.

"Think you can use your lightning to take care of these ladders?" he asked when he returned to her. "There are far too many of them for us to meet head-to-head. I know you'd rather keep your powers a secret, but..."

"I can't, not in my current state." Talin gestured to her leg. "I need to make physical contact with anything I want to use my lightning on, and I'm hardly going anywhere."

"Never mind, then, we'll make do," Red Wolf said. "Help the archers. I'll cover you when they get on top of the wall."

Talin limped closer to the edge of the wall and drew her bow. She loosed a handful of arrows in rapid succession and took out a Hellhound with each shot.

"More ladders are coming!" Hesar called. "You won't stop them all."

Red Wolf could see the wolves running up again, dragging ladders behind them. This time the Hellhounds were fitted with steel helmets that could withstand arrows.

"Target their ladders!" Talin shouted and switched her aim. But more were coming at once, having protected themselves from the volleys that slowed them down before. Red Wolf could see them inching ever closer.

It's only a matter of time.

The first ladders were being placed now, and the horde was gaining ground. It was the same thing he'd seen over and over; the Hellhounds' sheer numbers and brute force wore down even the strongest defences. Red Wolf wished he could get down there and lay waste to every last one of the *abiyoi*. But he knew his place was by Talin's side, keeping any Hellhounds off her back while she took out the ones yet to climb. He had to keep her safe above all else.

Hellhounds began to make their way onto the ramparts as more and more ladders were placed. Red Wolf shouted for the archers to fall back. One group of wolves placed a ladder directly below their position, and Talin was quick to blast it apart with her lightning. He saw a Hellhound charging with an axe and ducked under the blow, lopping the man's head clean off with his sword.

Another Hellhound came at him with his sword raised. Red Wolf blocked the hit with his shield before ramming the edge of it into his opponent's face, sending the man staggering. He followed through with a counter that ended with his sword buried in the Hellhound's skull. Out of the corner of his eye, he saw Talin reach towards the empty quiver at her waist, then curse and draw her sword. She limped away from the wall without turning and put her back to his.

"And how were you planning on fighting with a wounded leg?" he said.

"Well, you leave very little room for the horses," Talin said.

"Too cramped for you?" he asked.

"Just don't get stabbed in the head."

Red Wolf lifted his shield again to block an overhead axe swing. The blade buried itself deep into the wood, so he shook it off and drew his dagger instead, parrying another strike. He snarled at his opponent and plunged the smaller blade through the man's eye socket. Another Hellhound lunged at him, shifting as it did so. He sidestepped the wolf neatly and decapitated it.

Steel rang together behind him as Talin fended off a Hellhound from the other side. Hesar quickly joined them, lending his own sword to the fray and severing the head of his opponent.

"There's too many. We can't fend them off here forever," the City Watch commander said.

"Call a retreat. I'll destroy the gate mechanisms." Talin drove a dagger into her opponent's eye and whistled for her horse. Red Wolf headbutted a Hellhound, stunning the man long enough for him to help her up. He mounted his own horse and followed her to the bottom of the wall. Hesar shouted for the soldiers to fall back.

"How are you planning on destroying the gate mechanisms?" Red Wolf asked.

"I don't know—my lightning seems effective enough," Talin said.

"You'll spook the horse."

"Then I'll count on you to catch me if it throws me off."

Red Wolf sighed. "Can't stop you."

Talin sent a bolt of lightning into the gate mechanism as they rode past. Her horse whinnied and reared up, but she managed to stay in the saddle, much to his relief. The mechanism's gears cracked and crumbled, jamming against each other and destroying any way for the Hellhounds to crank open the gates. The only way they could break through now was by beating them down somehow. Red Wolf imagined it would be difficult without a ram.

"That ought to do the trick," he said. Talin nodded.

"Hesar!" she called. The Commander of the City Watch stopped halfway down the stairs to look at them. "Get your men to the palace! With any luck, my brother and Captain Golmin will have secured the defences there."

"Aye, we'll meet there," Hesar said. Talin turned her horse and took off at a gallop.

"Where are we going?" Red Wolf asked.

"The southern gate. I need to find whoever is in charge of evacuating the civilians."

"Lord Cassius said his brother could be persuaded," Red Wolf said.

"I'm not making any bets!"

They found some soldiers hurrying civilians down a main road near the market district, though they said their orders had come from their sergeant and they had no idea who was overseeing the evacuations. Another group of soldiers told them to go away before they arrested the queen. Red Wolf shot them a glare, and they quickly shut up.

"You don't need to threaten *everyone* who looks at me the wrong way," Talin said, as they moved off again.

"It makes me feel better."

They found Lord Cassius at the southern gate organising teams and moving groups of civilians back towards the city centre. He paused when he noticed them riding up.

"This gate is no longer safe either," he said. "The Hellhounds have circled to cut us off and kill anyone who tries to escape the city. We've been focusing all our resources on the northern gate—there's no way we can ferry all of these civilians to safety."

"The Hellhounds have already gotten over the wall," Talin hissed. "We need to get these people out of here *now*."

"They'll be ripped to shreds," Cassius said. "I'm sorry, Your Majesty. We're trapped in here."

"Maybe not." Talin looked at the waves of civilians being turned away from the gate. "How many are still in the city?"

"Thousands," Lord Cassius said. "We managed to evacuate some civilians before they cut us off, but I'm not sure if any of them made it to safety."

"Send them to the palace. We'll evacuate them through the tunnels."

"The tunnels that lead outside the city all go to Stormwood," Red Wolf said. "The Hellhounds are certain to spot them."

"No, I don't think so. They think they have the city. Belanore is about to be overrun by the entire horde. Nobody will be waiting outside the gates; they'll want to get in on the action," Talin said. "Organise some soldiers to clear the way. We'll keep the Hellhounds out of the palace."

Red Wolf considered it for a moment. She had a good point; the Hellhounds were unlikely to linger outside the city walls once they got the gates open. Sending some soldiers to clear the forest of any stragglers could very well be their best bet.

"We can have Hesar's men form a defensive line to protect the civilians until they get into the palace," he said.

"Can you get the word out?" Talin asked.

"Of course." Red Wolf hesitated. "What about you?"

"I'm going back to the palace to inform the others. We'll need to funnel the civilians into the passageways somehow."

Red Wolf nodded. "Look after yourself."

"You too. Don't go forgetting you can still be killed."

They parted ways at the market district, Talin taking a left to the palace while Red Wolf rode on to find Hesar. They had little time to work with and every second was crucial. He saw the bulk of the soldiers backing down the main road, pursued by Hellhounds, and rode in to lend a hand. There weren't many of them; no doubt the attackers at the wall were trying to get the gates open for the rest of the horde. The wolves could shift back and climb the ladders if necessary, but he knew it was faster for them to open the gates and let everyone through at once.

"Where's Hesar?" he demanded.

"Further down, Lord Commander!" one of the soldiers replied.

"My thanks." Red Wolf rode by and decapitated another Hellhound before turning to find Hesar. He spotted the man at an intersection down the road, shouting orders and directing his troops to cover their flanks as they retreated.

"Hesar, we need a defensive line around the palace," Red Wolf said as he neared. "The civilians are trapped in the city, and my queen wants to evacuate them through the secret tunnels under the palace."

"I can make it happen." Hesar nodded. "Lieutenant! Take your company and position them along Market Street. Nothing gets past it!"

"Yes, sir." The lieutenant he called hurried off to organise his men.

"I'll take half of my troops and put them along Bakers Avenue. Take the rest back to the palace. You'll need them there," Hesar said.

Red Wolf dipped his head. "Good luck, sir."

"Likewise, Lord Commander."

Hesar split his men and ordered half to follow him, placing the rest under Red Wolf's command. They parted ways at the next intersection.

"Listen up," Red Wolf called once they reached the palace. "Your job now is to defend the palace so all the civilians can be evacuated. Nothing, and I mean *nothing*, is to get past the drawbridge after them. I won't lie—the chances are we won't make it through this. But it is our job to defend the city and its inhabitants. You're all guards of the City Watch! This is your time to show the Hellhounds what you're made of!"

There was a collective shout from the men. Red Wolf split them into teams to guard strategic areas around the palace entrance and to block off the surrounding streets. They barricaded each street with whatever they could find, piling barrels and empty crates on top of each other to form a wall to slow the Hellhounds. It would buy them some more time, at the very least. Red Wolf left the lieutenant in charge and went to find Talin.

He eventually spotted her in the makeshift medical room, discussing possible routes to the passageways with one Lord Karl Highett. Perhaps his brother had convinced him to accept their help, after all. Talin had seated herself on the throne, no doubt to rest her leg, and they worked from a small desk dragged up there from elsewhere in the palace.

"...cellar passage would be riskiest," Lord Karl was saying. "It brings us closest to where the Hellhounds are positioned. If they're still outside the gates when you send the civilians through, they will spot us for sure."

"The cellar passage is the widest, correct?" Talin asked.

"It is."

"That will get everyone evacuated the fastest, risks aside."

Lord Karl shrugged. "I believe so."

"Then we will send extra teams to protect the exit. We cannot delay any longer."

Lord Karl bowed and moved off, passing Red Wolf on the way.

"Lord Commander," he said curtly, and then he was gone. Red Wolf continued up to the dais.

"Hesar's men are spread out," he said. "He's given us some more to guard the palace. I had them barricade the streets. The civilians?"

"Already arriving," Talin said. "Lord Cassius has been directing them here."

"Then I guess we're ready."

"Yes, all that's left to do is wait."

"Where are Rufus and Ettrias?" Red Wolf asked.

"At the outer wall. Once the Hellhounds break through the barricades, they will set the moat alight," Talin said. "Anyone on the other side of it will be trapped in the city with the Hellhounds. I hope to the gods we're all in the palace by then."

"We can evacuate them all, or as many as possible," Red Wolf said.

"I know." Talin turned her attention back to the palace blueprints. "I just...I wish there were a faster way."

"This is the only way out now," Red Wolf said. "The soldiers will defend these people with their lives."

Talin sighed. "We'll need to clear the ground floor of the palace as much as possible in case the Hellhounds break through. Lord Karl thinks it's best if we put the civilians on the upper floors and only use the bottom level for moving everyone into the passageways."

"It'll be easier to defend." Red Wolf nodded. "But the number of civilians we need to move into here could very well block off access to the inner walls and towers."

"That's what I said." Talin looked at him. "What do you think?"

"The Hellhounds will get into the palace eventually, regardless of what we throw up," Red Wolf said. "Keeping the civilians away from the fighting as much as possible would be safer, but we will need clear access to the battlements."

"We'll put as many in the upper floors as possible without blocking them off, then. The rest will stay on the ground floor."

Red Wolf took off his helm. "We're unlikely to evacuate all the civilians today. You'll lose access to your chambers."

"I'm aware. I am told, however, that there is plenty of room in the barracks."

"I...believe that's true."

"Good. I'm looking forward to your company," Talin said. "Go find Golmin and Ettrias. They'll probably have something for you to do in the meantime."

"Right." Red Wolf turned to leave, then had a thought and spun back around. "There are no extra beds in the barracks."

"I am also aware of this," Talin said.

"Well, now it would be rude of me not to offer you my bed," Red Wolf said. "The lord commander's quarters offers some privacy, at the very least."

Talin lifted a brow. Red Wolf quickly realised what he was suggesting might be misconstrued.

"I...meant..." He cleared his throat, feeling his ears burn. "Not...in *that* sense...I mean, you could take my chambers, and I would...find somewhere else...to..."

By the gods, there's no saving this one.

Talin laughed. "Go, already! I know what you meant. This palace isn't going to defend itself."

Red Wolf pulled his helm back on to hide his face and strode from the hall.

L ord Cassius was right about how many civilians there were still in the city. Far too many for them to spread out comfortably within the palace.

Talin cursed herself for underestimating the size of the city's population and overestimating how much space they had. They had managed to squeeze every last person into the palace by filling some of the tunnels with people, but still, there was hardly any space left for them to fight on the ground floor. Red Wolf had ridden out again at sundown to check on Hesar's soldiers at the outer line and hadn't yet returned. She suspected he'd taken the liberty of helping them thin out the Hellhound numbers to make the line last through the night. With the full moon having passed only yesterday, the attackers were still strong, and she guessed they would be at the palace gates by tomorrow night.

"Open the gates!"

Talin got up from her seat in the throne room and limped out to the balcony at the end of the corridor. Red Wolf had returned, it seemed, and without his horse. His armour was splattered with blood and gore and bore fresh nicks and dents, from what she could tell. He removed his helm as he passed through the main gates and out of sight, and Talin hurried downstairs to meet him.

"Hesar's line still holds, but not for much longer," he said when he saw her at the other end of the entrance hall. "All the civilians are inside?"

"Yes, but there's not much standing room," Talin said. "We've started moving everyone through the tunnels. I hate to put you to work again so soon, but I need you to escort the folk going through the cellar tunnel. They won't make it far if they run into any Hellhound stragglers."

"My place is at your side," Red Wolf said. "Those Hellhounds will reach the palace soon. I trust you to take care of yourself, but I cannot leave you in here alone."

"Your duty is to the Crown," Talin said. "And if that means protecting its people—"

"My duty is to protect you."

Talin pinched the bridge of her nose. The hour was far too late to be arguing about this. "Who would you send in your stead?"

"Captain Golmin and a dozen of the Royal Guard's best swordsmen," Red Wolf said.

"I need Golmin commanding the troops here. Round up your swordsmen and send them through," Talin said.

"Consider it done." Red Wolf moved off. Talin sent a runner to Lord Cassius to let him know the guards were coming and to make way for them. That done, she returned to the throne room to see if Corvan needed any help. The old healer was busy tending to a dying man when she limped in, holding his hand while he said his final words. Ashera was running supplies back and forth to the other healers who'd answered Lord Cassius' summons.

"So many wounded," she said, once Corvan had covered the man's body with a blanket.

"The Hellhounds leave more corpses than wounded, Your Majesty." The healer sighed. "Still, we must save who we can. I cannot say I approve of your walking around, but I understand."

Talin seated herself on the throne and allowed Corvan to change her bandages. He gave her another potion to drink when the pain returned. Red Wolf soon found her, too, having sent off the guards as promised, and he offered to escort her to his chambers.

"I doubt I can sleep at this rate," she confessed. "Part of me has been bracing for something to go wrong all day."

"You need to rest. We've gotten this far because of you," Red Wolf said. "I will wake you if there's an emergency."

Talin looked around at all the wounded soldiers. She could see some civilians, too—no doubt caught in the fighting. They would have to evacuate these people as well before the Hellhounds breached the palace walls. There was so much left to do.

"Very well," she said. *Maybe I do need a break.*

She allowed Red Wolf to help her to her feet and held onto his arm as a crutch. Being the giant that he was, he couldn't simply duck under her shoulder, though he probably could pick her up with one arm. They made their way downstairs to the barracks slowly, past the soldiers' lines to his chambers, where she let go of him to move to the bed that he'd given up for her.

"I'll...let you have your privacy," he said. "My chambers are yours for as long as you need them. If you need me, I'll be in the lines." He made a move towards the door.

"Wait. You're not staying?"

Red Wolf slowly turned back around. She could practically see the gears in his mind grinding to a halt as his gaze landed on the decorative swords hanging just behind her.

"What?" he finally said.

"You're not staying?" Talin asked.

"Wh..." Red Wolf blinked at her. "I...could...sleep on the floor here...if you preferred—"

"Gods, Red Wolf, your bed has space for both of us," Talin said. "You've been sleeping in the dungeons for two weeks. I'm not having you sleep on the floor."

Red Wolf opened his mouth as if to argue, then closed it again.

"Come on, I won't hold it against you if you steal the blanket," Talin said with a grin.

"Are you...sure?" he asked.

"We've been brushing shoulders on the road for two months. I'm certain," Talin said.

"...if you insist, then."

"I do."

Red Wolf let out a short exhale, but he stepped forward again anyway, unlacing his boots when he reached the edge of the bed. Talin moved over to make room for him. Her bodyguard hesitated, then kicked off his boots and pulled his tunic over his head, revealing the scars across his arms and torso. She tried not to stare.

"I could keep the tunic on, if it makes you uncomfortable," Red Wolf said, glancing at her.

"No, not at all," Talin said, perhaps a little too quickly. Red Wolf huffed a half-laugh and climbed into his side of the bed.

"Goodnight, Talin."

"Likewise."

Talin tried not to think about the Hellhounds, or the civilians being evacuated through the tunnels, or all the wounded in the throne room, and focused on trying to sleep. It was impossible. She remembered the dying man that Corvan had been with when she entered and wondered how many soldiers were dead on the battlefield with no one to hold their hand or listen to their final words. But maybe it was better to die quickly on the battlefield, instead of slowly passing away in a bed, knowing you were going to die. She fell asleep still pondering which she preferred and hoping neither option was imminent.

When she eventually woke, dawn had barely broken, casting feeble rays of light through the gaps in the curtains. Turning her head, she noticed that in his sleep, Red Wolf had wrapped an arm around her to pull her closer to him, and took a few moments to admire the lean muscle beneath his skin. He stirred when she traced a finger along one of the scars across his shoulder.

"Morning," he mumbled into the pillow.

"Good morning," Talin said.

There was a beat. Red Wolf lifted his head and sat bolt upright.

"I...that was..." He cleared his throat. "Apologies. I just..." His ears turned scarlet. "I didn't—"

"No, I'm sorry, I shouldn't have..." Talin began.

"Not your fault." Red Wolf rubbed his eyes with one hand. "I...need to think." He pulled on his tunic and boots and disappeared through the doors before Talin could open her mouth. For a moment, she considered catching a few more minutes of sleep, but then concern and curiosity got the better of her, and she slipped out after him.

She eventually found him on one of the upstairs balconies, watching the guards patrolling the inner wall. He didn't turn to acknowledge her presence, though she was sure he would have heard her.

"What's wrong?" she asked. "Bad dream?"

Red Wolf didn't speak.

"You can tell me."

"I know."

Talin joined him on the balcony.

"I wouldn't call it a bad dream," Red Wolf said. "More like a...good dream? It was..." His brow creased. "I don't know. I think it was before the Hellhounds took me. I don't know what to make of it. I've never been able to recall any good memories of that time. It was always flashes of...well, never mind."

"That's a good thing, isn't it?" Talin said.

"I don't...*know*." Red Wolf heaved a frustrated sigh. "That night at the Western Forts, when we were dancing, the bard played a song. I...remembered...a woman...singing that song for me. But that was it. I don't have any other information. It's like everything I *need* to know is hovering just out of reach. I don't know why I'm remembering these fragments now. It was better when I didn't remember. At least then I didn't have to wonder *why*."

"You don't remember anything else?"

"Just the woman singing. Beyond that, it's just...rage. They put that anger and hate into you until you can't take it anymore. I buried it instead and turned it on them." Red Wolf fixed his gaze on something on the horizon. "I fight them because I hate everything about them. I feel so much anger at them for what they did. Maybe they're right, and I am one of them." He scowled.

"You're not," Talin said.

Red Wolf scoffed. "You said it yourself—they're fuelled by rage and hate."

"You aren't, or at least that's not your main source of motivation anymore," Talin said. "I never really answered your question about why I wanted you to train me."

"Enlighten me," Red Wolf said.

"When we were first attacked on our way through Stormwood, I...was helpless. The rest of you could fight and risked your lives to protect me," Talin said. "It's my duty as queen to protect my people, but I couldn't even protect myself. And when you were stabbed in the shoulder..." She paused. "I should congratulate you on your acting there, you completely fooled me. Anyway, I knew then that I had to learn to fight, to be able to save my people, to lead my armies against the Hellhounds."

Red Wolf hummed. "I like that. But why tell me?"

"Because I think you're motivated by your duty too. The first time I met the wolf, he saved me by ripping out a Hellhound's throat. He challenged the other Hellhounds so I could escape. At the den, there was no danger, and he let me touch him. But his instincts told him to go hunt. But then, last night..."

"He followed you."

"Yes. He *knows*, Red Wolf," Talin said. "He knows your thoughts. Maybe he can't make sense of them exactly, but he tries. When he killed Wormwood, it was because he called you a Hellhound. And protecting me...you said that was your duty."

"It is." Red Wolf let out a long breath. "But before last night, I've never been able to remember anything he does."

"Maybe the fact that you can better control your emotions lets you control your curse more," Talin said.

"Maybe." Red Wolf turned back to face the inner wall, looking deep in thought.

"Can I ask you something?" Talin said, after a few moments of silence.

"Of course."

"If you can heal so quickly, where did you get all those scars on your body?"

"The...their experiments," Red Wolf said. "At first, they would cut you open and put their potions on the wounds, and it wouldn't work. So, they'd stitch you back together and try something else. For the potions we were forced to drink, they'd cut us to see if it had worked or to try to...trigger some kind of transformation. I don't know."

Talin winced. "I'm sorry."

"Don't be."

"If we get through this, we'll search the Highlands and find out who you were before the Hellhounds took you, no matter what."

"I appreciate it." Red Wolf straightened and looked past the walls, to the barricaded streets beyond the palace. "They're here."

"The Hellhounds?" Talin followed his gaze.

"No, these are Hesar's retreating men, but they'll be here soon." Red Wolf turned away from the balcony. "We need to prepare for battle."

Talin limped back downstairs after him to don her armour; with the Hellhounds on their doorstep, they were going to need every sword they could get. Red Wolf woke Golmin and Ettrias and sent them off to ready the palace defences.

"I hope to the gods the Highetts have made progress evacuating the civilians," Talin muttered.

"We'll hold them back until everyone gets through the tunnels, I promise," Red Wolf said.

"I certainly hope so." Talin grabbed a nearby soldier and sent him off to tell the Highetts to continue evacuating the civilians. Red Wolf accompanied her to the stables and helped her onto her horse. The soldier she'd sent returned not long after, looking shaken.

"Your Majesty, there's...there's a situation at the cellar tunnel," he said.

"Situation?" Talin lifted an eyebrow.

"The Hellhounds have found the entrance in Stormwood. Our men are holding off the attack as best they can, but they need urgent reinforcements."

Talin looked at Red Wolf and dismounted. "Go to the barracks. Tell them I sent you. Round up anyone who isn't at the wall and send them to the cellar tunnel. We'll be there right away."

The soldier bowed and sprinted off.

"Go help them, Red Wolf, I'll catch up!" Talin said. Her bodyguard lowered his visor and took off the way they'd come. She downed the potion that Corvan had given her to numb the pain in her leg and went after him. Pushing past civilians as she neared the cellar entrance, she found Lord Cassius in a suit of scuffed up plate armour, looking grim.

"We have no room to fight down there. I'm trying to back up the civilians, but—" he began.

"Keep moving them back out of the tunnel, I have reinforcements on the way," Talin interrupted. "Clear the ladder!"

A few civilians at the bottom jumped out of the way immediately.

Gods, I hope I'm not too late, she thought, and climbed down into the tunnel.

T he stench of blood in the tunnel was sickening.

Talin pushed her way through the crowd, trying to get to the front, but the sheer number of civilians stuck in the tunnel made it impossible for her to move anywhere. She managed to squeeze past the most crowded section of the pack before the people began to recognise her and scrambled to clear a path. She made it the rest of the way at a slow jog, Corvan's potion having dulled the pain in her leg.

As she neared the front, however, she began to see the carnage that the Hellhounds had already inflicted. Civilians were strewn across the tunnel and blood painted the walls and ceiling. A few wolves had stopped to feast on the bodies. Talin felt her stomach turn but managed to keep herself from throwing up. She spotted Red Wolf at the front of the line, holding back the attackers with what was left of the dozen guards responsible for guarding the passageway. He hacked off the head of a charging wolf as she watched.

"There's too many of them, just stay back!" he growled. Talin shot an arrow that brushed past his shoulder and buried itself in a Hellhound's eye.

"Not a chance."

Red Wolf turned his head and looked at her incredulously. "You almost missed!"

"I didn't miss." Talin sent another arrow at a charging wolf, this time letting it sail by his helm close enough that he could see it whizz past. He scoffed and slammed his pommel into a Hellhound's face, sending him staggering back. Talin followed up with an arrow into the man's eye. Two wolves pounced on Red Wolf at the same time. Her bodyguard sidestepped the first, took its head off, and thrust his dagger into the other's skull. Talin shot down a Hellhound behind him who'd snuck up to take a swing at his neck. He spun, dagger flashing towards his opponent, and was just in time to see the body fall. He looked at the arrow protruding from the attacker's face and frowned.

"I had him!" he called.

"Of course." Talin loosed two more arrows in rapid succession and took out another two Hellhounds. But more were coming through the tunnel now, far too many for them to fight off alone. She heard footsteps behind her and saw soldiers rush past her to defend the line. The reinforcements she'd sent for had arrived, finally.

But even with their new numbers, she could tell they were outmatched. One of the soldiers fell to a charging wolf who dragged him off and devoured him. Talin retreated a few steps as the rest of the line was pushed back.

There was a shift in movement beyond the line. She looked past Red Wolf to see what was going on and saw a heavily armoured knight pushing through the Hellhound horde, unarmed, trying desperately to reach their defensive position. Talin saw his red cloak as he spun and drove a stolen dagger through a wolf's eye. He was a member of the Royal Army.

"Help him!" she yelled. Red Wolf snatched up a fallen shield and slammed it against the nearest Hellhound's face. He cut down two wolves before a third latched onto his arm, trying to bite through his gauntlet. Metal crunched under its teeth. He cursed and stabbed the creature in the eye. It released him and crumpled, and he tore the crushed gauntlet off.

"Come on!" He reached the knight and stabbed a Hellhound in the chest, stunning him long enough for their new ally to escape. Red Wolf was about to free his sword when the Hellhound drove a dagger into his neck, under his helmet. He grabbed the blade to tug it out, but the man kept his grip on the weapon, cutting off his air supply. The knight spun around with a scavenged axe and lopped off the Hellhound's head. Red Wolf yanked the dagger free with a gasp.

"We need to collapse the tunnel!" the mystery knight shouted. "I've seen their numbers. There are far too many!"

Talin had been pondering the same thing. "We have nothing to collapse it with!"

Red Wolf turned briefly. "Lightning, Talin! Take out the supports!"

"Get back," she said. The mystery knight moved back, and she stretched out a hand, feeling wild magic in the air and concentrating as much of it as she possibly could. She put her hand against the nearest support and sent a bolt of lightning through it.

The wood blew apart with a thunderous *crack*, forcing her body-guard to flinch and peppering her with splintered shards and dust. Red Wolf grabbed her and pulled her away from the weakened tunnel section just as several tonnes of rock and dirt collapsed in front of them.

"That will buy us some time," the mystery knight said. "Come, Your Majesty. We must talk urgently." He removed his helm, and Talin's heart almost skipped a beat.

Behind that helm was none other than the battle-worn face of General Virion.

No word for months, and all of a sudden, you're back...

She looked to Red Wolf. He gave a barely imperceptible shake of his head, telling her to play along for now.

"Come, this way." She turned and headed back towards the cellar, back through the crowd. Her bodyguard followed close behind with his hand on his sword.

Inside the palace again, she explained the situation to Lord Cassius and told him to relocate all the civilians to the other tunnels, assuming they weren't overrun as well. She led Virion upstairs and into the war room.

"I'm afraid you'll have to wait outside, Lord Commander," the general said. "The information I have is rather sensitive."

"I go where my queen goes," Red Wolf said.

Virion looked at Talin.

"It's fine, General. I trust him with my life," she said. Virion pursed his lips but didn't argue. Red Wolf closed the doors after them.

"We've had no word for months—where have you been?" Talin demanded. "We thought we'd lost Vill's Crossing weeks ago and you and your army were wiped out, and now you turn up here?"

"We were completely cut off with no way to send a message," Virion explained. "They broke through our defences a month ago and took a handful of us as prisoners. I managed to escape but only barely."

"The Hellhounds take no prisoners," Red Wolf said.

"That's what we thought," Virion said, throwing him a glance. "But I...I overheard them talking. Saying something about...letting their alchemists run some more experiments, even though the last time it was a disaster."

Talin's gaze flickered to Red Wolf.

"Experiments?" he asked softly. "You're certain?"

"Absolutely, it's what I heard," General Virion said.

"Who are they experimenting on? Children?" Red Wolf asked.

"I didn't see any children, but I wouldn't put it past them. The conditions were awful. They kept everyone in cages like...animals. The northern horde is being led by a man named Kehlvor. He's the one overseeing the experiments."

Red Wolf fell silent. Talin didn't miss the flicker of panic across his face.

"You say you and a few others were captured," she said, trying to steer the conversation away from the experiments. "Are they still alive?"

"I don't know," Virion said.

"Alright. Did you at least return with anyone else?"

"Nobody, we were almost completely wiped out at Vill's Crossing," he said.

"I suspected as much. Go to Corvan in the throne room. He will treat your injuries," Talin said. "You're dismissed. I need to talk to my bodyguard."

"Of course, Your Majesty." Virion stood and bowed to her before leaving. Talin watched the door swing shut behind him.

"Something's not adding up," she said. "We've never heard any reports of Hellhounds taking prisoners before, and now this..." Her voice trailed off. Red Wolf looked like he hadn't heard a word she'd said as he stood there, gripping the back of a nearby chair so hard his knuckles turned white.

"Red Wolf?"

He didn't respond. She saw his chest heave as his breathing steadily quickened.

"Red Wolf." Talin came forward and put a hand over his.

Something's wrong.

Her bodyguard flinched at the contact and stumbled away from the chair, his back hitting a wall, breathing hard as if he'd just run a marathon.

"Easy," Talin said as he slid down against the wall, a distant look in his eyes. She crouched before him and cupped his face in her hands. "Red Wolf. Just...slow down. Breathe. It's alright."

It took a few minutes of careful movement and talking before he finally seemed to settle, eyes focusing on her once more. He blinked, reaching up to pry her hands gently away from his face.

"Are you—" she began.

"Fine." Red Wolf dropped his gaze. "I'm...fine." He took a few shaky breaths. "I'm sorry if I worried you. I just...Virion mentioned..."

"The Hellhound General," Talin said. "Who is he?"

Red Wolf ran a hand down his face. "Kehlvor? It doesn't matter who he is. If he's running those experiments again, we *have to stop him*." His voice shook ever so slightly.

Whoever he is, Red Wolf is spooked.

"I know," Talin said. "Slow down. You said it yourself, Red Wolf, there's a good chance that Virion tried to make a deal with the Hellhounds. Wormwood even confirmed that he was supposed to delay the northern horde for them. He could be working against us for all we know."

"But if he's...telling the truth, or he failed to make that deal, and the Hellhounds really are..." Red Wolf said.

"I know. I understand. We'll get to the bottom of this, I promise," Talin said. "We still need to check on our defences in the city and make sure they're holding. Give yourself time to think this through. I'll have Lord Karl keep an eye on Virion in the meantime. Golmin had mentioned that he was the one most suspicious of the good general."

Red Wolf let out a long breath. "Alright. Very well. Lead the way."

They returned to the stables, fetching the two horses they'd saddled earlier to ride out and assist the defenders on the streets. Talin stopped by the armoury briefly to fill her quiver, finding a messenger there to relay her suspicions to Lord Karl and ask him to keep an eye on General Virion. Red Wolf picked up another shield and spear.

"I still don't know about Virion," Red Wolf said, as they crossed the drawbridge. "*If* he's telling the truth—"

"As I said, give yourself time to think things through," Talin said. "Right now, we need to buy Lord Cassius and the others enough time to evacuate all the civilians."

"I can't argue with that." Red Wolf lowered his spear and readied it for a charge. "There's the first wall. They're already breaking through."

Talin grabbed a handful of arrows and loosed them one after the other. Each shot found its mark in a Hellhound's eye. Red Wolf zipped past her in a blur as he sent his horse into a gallop and rammed his spear through another man's skull. Leaving the weapon behind, he drew his sword, wheeling around to finish off whoever else had gotten past the barricaded street. Talin saw a wolf coming from the right and ducked.

The wolf pounced and shot over her. She sent an arrow into the back of its head.

"I'll stay here with this line. Go help the others!" she yelled.

"I won't leave you," Red Wolf said.

"Just go!" Talin said. "I'll be fine."

"We'll meet in the entrance hall," he said, and galloped down to the next barricaded street. Talin suddenly remembered the way the Drakel insurgents had bottled up the soldiers at the gate before pouring the oil.

"Red Wolf, give the order to retreat!" she called after him. He turned his head slightly to acknowledge that he'd heard. Talin pulled another half dozen arrows from the quiver and sent them off one after the other.

"Fall back!" she commanded. "Fall back to the palace! Man the outer walls!"

The soldiers glanced back quickly, recognised her, and began to move. She didn't stay to help them and moved to the next barricade. There, she gave the same order and moved on again, doing the same at each line until their entire defensive force was falling back towards the drawbridge. She didn't see Red Wolf in the chaos but knew she had no time to make sure that he'd made it back.

"Raise the drawbridge!" she shouted. Gears began to grind as the last of the retreating soldiers made it past. A few Hellhounds leapt the growing gap between the end of the drawbridge and the road beyond it. Talin looked up just in time to see a volley from the wall stop them dead in their tracks. Some of the bodies slid off the drawbridge into the water while the rest slid down towards them. She left her horse with a nearby soldier and went to find Red Wolf in the entrance hall. It was packed with soldiers rushing to man the walls and he was nowhere in sight. Talin began to panic as she pushed her way through.

"Red Wolf?"

No response. She continued pushing through the crowd, trying to spot his towering figure.

Gods, he'd better not have—

"Here." Red Wolf grabbed her hand and pulled her out of the crowd, down an empty hallway. She breathed an inward sigh of relief, lifting his visor to give him a quick kiss.

"I'm fine, what's the panic?" He huffed a half-laugh.

I thought I'd lost you. Talin didn't say it out loud. "Just glad to see you."

Ettrias had been right. She couldn't risk losing him.

And if you condemn Ettrias again, then what? Live the same lie as Red Wolf?

Talin pushed the thoughts aside. The alternative was to allow the court to sentence Red Wolf to death, or overrule the court entirely and risk losing what little support she'd regained after Wormwood's lies.

"The Hellhounds will try to swim the moat, yes?" she asked, trying to focus on the issue at hand.

"Yes. I take it that you have a plan," Red Wolf said.

"Remember when they lured the ram and some of the Draconian legionaries to the gate and bottled them there?"

"I like it. We need to light the moat."

"You read my mind." Talin led the way up to the outer wall and found the lieutenant in charge. A word from her and he gave the order. Barrels upon barrels of oil were poured into the moat, splashing as they hit the water. Talin watched the two liquids separate. Hellhounds had already jumped into the moat to swim across. This was perfect.

Red Wolf lit an arrow and sent it down.

The flames spread in an instant, crackling and roaring as the oil burned. The Hellhounds on the other side snarled and shrank back.

"I've always wanted to do that," her bodyguard said.

Talin watched the Hellhounds in the moat desperately struggle to crawl back out, but the oil had stuck to their skin and fur, burning them alive. She winced.

"Will the fire kill them?" she asked.

"Slowly. They'll try to heal, but the fire is faster." Red Wolf followed her gaze. "You don't approve."

"I may fight on the opposing side, but I don't want them to suffer," Talin said.

"I wish I felt the same way."

"I know. I understand." Talin turned away from the wall to talk to the lieutenant. "Shoot anyone who tries to swim through." She headed inside, Red Wolf trailing after her silently.

There was a commotion from the ground floor as they entered the palace again. Talin met Red Wolf's gaze briefly and knew he was thinking the same thing.

Gods, please don't let it be another attack on the tunnels.

They found Lord Cassius in the middle of a packed hallway shouting orders at soldiers to move the civilians. He saw them approach and wriggled his way free from the pack.

"What's with the shouting this time? Is there another attack?" Talin asked.

"No, no, nothing of the sort," Cassius said. He pinched the bridge of his nose. "The good general has deemed one of the tunnels too dangerous, says it's too close to the cellar tunnel and the Hellhounds might find it. He's ordered it sealed off and all the civilians to be moved into another one."

"And your brother? He was supposed to be keeping an eye on the man," Talin said.

"He was with Virion but didn't go down into the tunnel," Cassius said. "The general said it was 'too dangerous' and blocked all civilians from entering."

Talin hissed through her teeth. "We only *have* one tunnel left. Can you reopen the one he sealed?"

"No, he had some soldiers burn the supports and collapse the ceiling."

Talin cursed. "He's trying to trap us in here. Where is he now?"

"My brother seemed rather upset at him and demanded they speak in private," Lord Cassius said. "I've no idea where they went."

"We have to find him," Red Wolf said. "Gods damn it, you were right. We should have dealt with him before leaving."

"We were gone for less than an hour!" Talin strode off back the way they'd come, thoughts spinning. Wormwood had confirmed that Virion had struck some kind of deal with the Hellhounds to ensure their coup went off without a hitch, but given his unusual behaviour now...

One glance at Red Wolf's face confirmed everything she had suspected.

General Virion was working with the Hellhounds.

A lap of the palace's second level put them by the war room, where Red Wolf caught a whisper of conversation between General Virion and Lord Karl. He suggested they eavesdrop first before barging in. Talin hadn't objected. She put her ear close to the doors while her bodyguard leaned on the wall nearby, a scowl etched on his face, evidently still upset about buying into Virion's lie.

"This was not the deal!" Lord Karl was saying. "You were supposed to keep the Hellhounds at the White River until this whole business was dealt with!"

"And then what? You were going to 'save' the city when they arrived and be hailed as a hero?" Virion scoffed. "No reinforcements are coming! This is all we have left!"

"So, what happened? You made a different deal with them? One that ends with you in power?" Lord Karl asked. "The Hellhounds won't give you *any of that*. They hate everything that isn't them."

"They made me a promise."

"And you expect them to keep it?"

"I know they will."

"Then you're more naïve than I thought."

Talin looked at Red Wolf.

"I'm going to kill him," her bodyguard muttered.

"I think we've heard enough." Talin readied an arrow. Red Wolf pushed open the doors. Lord Karl jumped to his feet immediately, eyes widening when he saw the arrow pointing at his face. Virion's hand went to his sword.

"Take a seat, gentlemen," she said.

The two men looked at each other.

"I'd do as my queen says if I were you." Red Wolf crossed his arms. Lord Karl sat back down heavily. General Virion quickly did the same.

"Good, let's talk," Talin said.

"I can explain—" Lord Karl began.

"I'm sure you can. For now, you're going to stay very, very quiet."

Highett clamped his mouth shut.

"General, did you lead the Hellhounds to the tunnel?" Talin demanded.

"If you're asking, you already know," Virion said.

"Answer the question." Talin sent her arrow into the chair leg just below his knee and readied another one.

"Yes," General Virion said.

"Why?"

"I struck a deal with the Hellhounds. The original plan was for me to make a different bargain, allowing them to pass the White River without resistance if they waited until I received word from Belanore before marching on the city. This was to buy Lord Karl and Lord Wormwood the time they needed to take over and bring you down."

"But you decided not to work with them?"

"The Hellhounds had no interest in deals," Virion said. "Why would they strike a deal with us when they could crush all of Kies Tor with their hordes? I had to offer them something else. Belanore and you. In exchange, they told me the *truth*. The Hellhounds aren't here to conquer the world. They only want Kies Tor for what your ancestors did to them. I would help them and remake this kingdom as its new ruler. I was told to make up some story about their experiments to ensure my 'escape' would be convincing. I guess it didn't get past you. General Kehlvor sends his regards, by the way, Lord Commander."

Red Wolf started forward.

"Don't," Talin said. Her bodyguard stopped immediately.

"You're gods-damned lucky that my queen is here," he said softly.

"There won't be anything *left* once the Hellhounds are done," Talin said. "They don't want an empire, and they don't care about what *you* want. You're not one of them, so you're the enemy—just as we are. If we took you as a prisoner right now, they wouldn't even want you back."

"Am I your prisoner?" Virion asked.

"You are, yes," Talin said. "You turned on the kingdom, on me, and even on the people you conspired with to bring me down."

"And...what about me?" Lord Karl asked.

"You, I will deal with after this siege is over. If we survive." Talin lowered her bow. "Red Wolf, do me a favour and escort Virion to the dungeons."

"My pleasure." Red Wolf grabbed the general by the elbow and dragged him out of the room. Talin faced Lord Karl again.

"You and me, we're going to make a deal too."

"Anything."

"If we survive this, you will tell the people that Lord Wormwood lied and manipulated the truth to get what he wanted. You will give up this effort to bring me down, and you will explain to the High Court that Ettrias really did commit those crimes," Talin explained. "In return, I will tell the court that you were forced into this...disagreeable situation...by Wormwood, and you were threatened into keeping your mouth shut. If you're lucky, and I cannot guarantee anything, the court will allow your treason to slide and grant you an alternative punishment to the executioner's block."

"If I don't agree?" Lord Karl said hesitantly.

"I'll tell the court everything, of course, including how you conspired with General Virion," Talin said. "You've already lost, my lord. Wormwood is dead. The good general will not be of any help to you. Half the city has turned on you already after my failed execution."

Lord Karl nodded. "I'll do as you say. But I just need to know. Is your brother innocent?"

Talin felt a pang of guilt. "He is. But this is what he wants."

"Is it?" Lord Karl asked. "Or is it what you want?"

"I can't protect everyone around me."

"Then do the right thing, Your Majesty," Lord Karl said. "I will tell the court whatever you wish me to—if only to save my own skin. You must decide what to do."

Talin sighed. "Can I still trust you to hold off this siege?"

"Of course. I may have disagreed with you in the past, but I do not wish to see this kingdom fall to those creatures."

"Good. See to the evacuations. Your brother could do with some help."

He bowed and hurried off, leaving her alone in the war room.

He's right. This isn't what either of them would want. And it's certainly not the right thing to do.

Talin decided now was not the time worry over such niceties. She had a siege to win. If they all survived, she could decide what to do. Taking another dose of Corvan's potion, she headed outside, where she found Red Wolf again on the wall and joined him on the ramparts.

"They haven't made a move yet," he said, nodding at the gathered Hellhounds. "I think they're selecting a champion."

"A champion?" Talin looked at them. "They're going to challenge us to a duel?"

"I find it likely." Red Wolf's brow creased. "The Hellhounds have no way to cross the moat yet, but they know the fire will burn out sooner or later. They're giving us a chance to settle this with minimal bloodshed." He crossed his arms. "I suggest we funnel our forces towards the remaining tunnel. Just in case."

"In case of what?" Talin asked.

"An attack."

They were soon joined by Golmin and Ettrias, both having been alerted to the Hellhounds' uncharacteristically quiet behaviour. Red Wolf quickly explained the situation.

"So...are we choosing our champion, or is it going to be anyone who wants to get brutally killed in a Hellhound duel?" Ettrias asked.

"That depends on their terms of defeat." Talin watched the Hellhounds squabble a while longer before heading back inside to round up more guards for tunnel duty. It would no doubt be a while before they received the Hellhounds' challenge, and she had no intention of waiting for it on the battlements.

This is a losing battle.

She pushed the thought from her mind. They mustn't give in to despair now, not as long as they had any chance of fighting their way through this siege. She had to protect her people. Such was her duty as queen.

She was staring at the maps in the war room when Red Wolf entered, holding a piece of parchment. Ettrias and Golmin both accompanied him, looking grim. Talin suspected this wasn't going to be good news.

"The Hellhounds' challenge." Red Wolf set down the parchment in front of her. "Read it. It's...not good."

Talin unrolled it to read the neat scrawl. "'From the esteemed General Kehlvor...'" She glanced up. "Virion mentioned that he's the one leading the northern horde. Who is he to you?"

"The last man I would want to face in one-on-one combat." Red Wolf dropped his gaze. "He's...He trained me before I came to Belanore. Most of my skill with a blade comes from his training, not Brakis. Apart from that, he approved the experiments and even encouraged his alchemists to keep trying to perfect the artificial Hellhound blood, even though they were losing children so quickly."

"You believe he'll face us personally?" Talin asked.

"I don't know," Red Wolf said.

"The terms of defeat are such..." Talin muttered, reading on. "So, if we lose, we lower the drawbridge and keep it that way. If they lose, they allow us to evacuate the remaining civilians without resistance." She sighed. "These are not promising terms. I'm not sure whether I like our current odds or whether I want to risk everything on a single duel."

"We stand to lose our only escape. They lose nothing," Golmin said.

"If we refuse, they're likely to attack the tunnel," Red Wolf said. "Fighting on that front while evacuating civilians will be difficult."

"Well, then." Talin looked up. "Do I have a champion?"

"I'll gladly fight the Hellhounds for you, dear sister," Ettrias said.

"Fighting a Hellhound one-on-one is different from fighting them in the heat of battle, Ettrias," Talin said. "They only have to protect their neck and head while you'll need to be fitted in full plate. Good luck lasting more than five minutes in the Torrian heat in fifty pounds of steel. I won't risk your life like that."

"Then send me, Your Majesty," Golmin said. "I am merely a guard. If I lose this fight, so be it."

"If I might object to that..." Red Wolf began.

"Don't you go playing the hero, Red Wolf. Your duty is to protect the queen." Golmin fixed him with a glare.

"Well, I also object, so you're outvoted," Ettrias said, leaning past the bodyguard.

"In any case, the full moon has just passed," Red Wolf continued. "The Hellhounds will be faster than both of you combined. I'm the only one who can match their strength and speed and the only one who can heal like them. Let me kill this Hellhound champion for you, my queen."

"Kehlvor is looking for a fight to the *death*," Talin said. "If you lose—"

"I won't."

"Red Wolf."

"Trust me. Please."

How can I say no to that?

Talin sighed. "Very well. Send their messenger back. I accept their challenge."

A storm picked up just after sunset as Ashera was helping Red Wolf into his armour, washing the blood from the streets and cooling the weather somewhat. They had agreed to battle on the drawbridge. He knew the wood had poor traction in the rain and wouldn't be made any better by steel plate, so he'd taken his plate and mail and left the armoured legwear in favour of his usual guard's boots, knowing the worn soles had better traction. If he knew the Hellhounds at all, they would be unaccustomed to fighting in such slippery conditions.

"You're sure you don't want some armour for your legs?" Talin asked, as Ashera finished tightening the straps on his chest plate.

"Metal has no traction on that drawbridge. If I fall, I need to be able to get back up." He took his helmet from the girl and put it on.

"I'm surprised you decided to take the armour at all," Talin said.

"Well." Red Wolf shrugged.

Now is as a good a time as any to admit the truth.

"I won't be able to heal," he said. "The Hellhounds have their mages. They can manipulate their connection to the moon's magic, temporarily cutting us off completely. It's...tradition for such a thing to occur before duels to test the Hellhounds' raw skill in combat. I won't have my powers, and neither will their champion."

"Then, you..." Understanding flickered across Talin's face. "You lied. Before. I could have sent Golmin or Ettrias."

"I'm sorry," Red Wolf said. "But as I said, I've trained with the Hellhounds, with Kehlvor. I know how they fight. That should give me an edge—hopefully."

Ashera passed him his weapons belt, and he tightened it over his armour. *It's time.*

"You'll want to stay on the wall, my queen," he said. "It will be safer there—if I do happen to lose."

"You said you won't." Talin fell into step beside him as he made his way to the front gates. She was limping again now that Corvan's potion had worn off, and he slowed to match her pace.

"Well, you never know. Anything could happen," he said.

"You should have let me send Golmin."

"He will lose. I might not."

"You cannot lose."

"I'll certainly make an effort not to," he said with a half-hearted grin, trying to lighten the situation. Talin didn't look any happier about it. They stopped at the front gates, and two guards pulled them open.

Facing him in the middle of the drawbridge was none other than General Kehlvor.

The man looked much the same as when they'd last met at Castle Blackrun, sporting shoulder-length black hair tied back in a bun and a trimmed beard. He carried a heavy, ornate-looking helm in his hand and was fitted with mail and as much plate as the Torrian heat allowed.

Of course it had to be him.

One of his mages stood beside him, staff in hand, its tip glowing faintly with a purple light. Kehlvor's gaze landed on the bodyguard, and he rumbled out a laugh.

Red Wolf pushed down a surge of anger.

"Red Wolf." Talin grabbed his elbow before he could step out. He looked back at her. "Don't let your anger get the better of you. Fight to protect what you love, not to destroy what you hate."

"As you say." Red Wolf lowered his visor and strode forwards.

"The Traitor finally returns to his pack," Kehlvor said, motioning to his mage to begin the spell. Red Wolf felt his connection to the moon dim and fade completely.

"I never belonged in your pack. Not when your only goal was to use me as a weapon."

"You think you've found a sense of belonging *here*?" Kehlvor asked as the two circled each other slowly. "In Belanore, where the common folk shun your very existence? Serving a weakling queen who sends out a champion, a *weapon*, in her stead, instead of facing me herself?"

Red Wolf let out a soft growl and bared his teeth. "You know *nothing* about my queen. I serve out of loyalty, not slavery."

"Loyalty." Kehlvor lowered his helm over his head with a scoff. "Did your so-called *loyalty* apply when you betrayed the horde? Your pack? Your *brothers*?"

"I am not your brother."

"You are, and have always been, my brother."

Red Wolf heard a yell rip from his own throat as he lunged forward.

Kehlvor sidestepped his wild swing and spun around with a counter, forcing him back. Red Wolf parried the next hit and aimed a jab at his opponent's shoulder, aiming for a gap in his armour. Kehlvor knocked it aside easily and stepped forward. Red Wolf backed up again to keep the distance.

"It's not too late, you know!" Kehlvor yelled as the storm picked up, almost drowning out his words. "Swear your allegiance once more to me. Return to your brothers."

"My allegiance is to Queen Talin." Red Wolf came forward with another wild swing, hardly caring about technique and footwork, and Kehlvor quickly stepped around him to slash his shoulder. He hissed at the pain and pressed his attack again, backing the man up as he did with most of his opponents in training.

"Sloppy." Kehlvor parried and countered without skipping a beat. Blood splashed onto the drawbridge and was immediately washed away by the pouring rain.

Red Wolf ducked under his next strike. A pommel slam to the front of his opponent's helm had the man staggering back, dazed. He followed through with a thrust that glanced off the steel plate instead when the Hellhound general twisted aside. Red Wolf raised his blade to parry a strike from above.

He recognised the feint too late.

His parry met empty air as the general's blade came swinging in from the bottom, slashing at his exposed leg. He staggered with a curse. More blood dripped onto the drawbridge to be washed away by the rain. Standing again, he pressed his attack, ignoring the burning pain as rainwater splashed onto the cut. A memory flashed in his mind of pure, unbridled rage as he fought against leather restraints. He tried to push it down.

Red Wolf made a low growl in the back of his throat. He had closed the distance. Kehlvor stepped back too late. He stepped around the man and locked out his sword arm, driving his elbow into the back of his shoulder. There was a *crunch* as the joint dislocated. His opponent let out a hiss of pain and switched hands.

He used to fight you with his left hand, just to mock your skill.

Red Wolf ducked under a swing and slammed his shoulder against the general's chest, sending him staggering back. Kehlvor recovered just in time to parry and counter a strike that would have pierced through the shoulder gap in his armour.

The riposte that followed tore clean into Red Wolf's thigh and dropped him for good this time. He fell to one knee with a groan. Kehlvor finished with a kick to the face that sent him sprawling onto his back on the sodden drawbridge.

"You didn't really think you had a chance against me, did you?" The general kicked his sword out of reach and planted a boot on his wounded leg, forcing a roar of pain from his lips. "Living with elves has made you soft."

Red Wolf cursed himself for being so naïve. Talin had warned him before the duel even started not to let his rage get the better of him. And yet he had allowed General Kehlvor to goad him into doing exactly that.

I'm going to die here, and Belanore will fall.

"Look up, there is your queen," Kehlvor said. Red Wolf looked up at the wall and saw Talin standing there, huddled in a cloak, watching them. He lay back on the drawbridge and stared at the falling rain. Blood pooled under his wounded leg, mixing with the rainwater and turning it red.

"If I have to die for her, so be it," he said.

"Oh, you'd like that, wouldn't you? An honourable death. Loyal to the end." The general laughed. "I'm not going to kill you. Not right now."

Red Wolf glared at him. "Why?"

"Because, at the end of the day, we are brothers, try as you might to deny it." Kehlvor straightened. "I will spare you tonight. You have always been my alchemists' greatest achievement. We will give you until first light to prepare a final stand, and when dawn breaks across the eastern horizon, I pray that your death will be painless. Goodbye, Red Wolf."

In too much pain to stand, Red Wolf lay there instead, watching his blood swirl in the rainwater and drip down into the moat. He heard the gates opening a few minutes later and boots splashing in the rain as someone ran out. Ashera's face loomed into view.

"Can you walk?" she asked.

"I'm fine. I'll be fine." Red Wolf waved her off. He heard two more sets of footsteps. Golmin and Ettrias, no doubt.

"We need to get you to Corvan before you bleed to death on the drawbridge," the captain said.

"I'm fine. Just give me a minute." He squeezed his eyes shut. Talin caught up to the others not long after.

"Red Wolf?"

"Evening, Talin."

"Get him up. We need to find Corvan," Talin said.

"No, wait, I can..." Red Wolf cursed as Ettrias and Golmin dragged him to his feet and ducked under his arms to support his weight. Together, they managed to stumble inside, with Ashera carrying his abandoned helm and sword. He wriggled free and made his own way upstairs. Inside the throne room, he finally fell to one knee, and Corvan quickly found a spare bed for him to lie on. He swung his legs onto it and propped himself up against the wall instead, and Ashera helped him strip his armour off so the old man could tend to his injuries.

"Superficial cuts, mostly," the healer said. "Apart from the stab wound to your leg. That will require stitches to stop the bleeding until your powers return. My potions will not have any effect on you either, so you will have to keep still."

"Whatever you think is best, old man." Red Wolf leaned back against the wall to let him do his work.

"Are you injured anywhere else?" Talin asked.

"No, I'm fine. I'm sorry. I should have...listened to you. I let Kehlvor provoke me. Fought like an...angry child."

"He let you live—that's all I care about."

"So that I can watch as the Hellhounds tear through the palace thanks to my failure. It wasn't really an act of mercy on his part." Red Wolf closed his eyes. "You were wrong. I can't control that rage. He called me his brother and I just..."

"That doesn't matter now. We'll evacuate who we can and try to defend that last tunnel. When the Hellhounds break through..."

"We won't let them." Red Wolf opened his eyes again and looked at her. "We hold the gate for as long as possible."

"I only wish we could have returned from the Drakels with an army. Perhaps then we might have been more evenly matched in this siege."

"We will make do with the numbers we have. If Belanore falls, so too does this kingdom."

"I'm aware." Talin sighed. "I wish I wasn't the one shouldering the burden of this war. My father would have known what to do."

"Everything he knew, he taught to you. You have gotten us all this far. You will think of something."

"We don't have the numbers..." Talin's voice trailed off. "Maybe we could."

"I'm listening," Red Wolf said.

"If we can arm the civilians with weapons, that's...what? Thousands more swords to fight against the Hellhounds when they break through," Talin said. She turned to her brother. "I need you to gather up any civilians willing to fight. No children. Golmin, how many spare weapons do we have?"

"I don't know, but I'm sure Brakis does," Golmin said.

Talin nodded. "Find the quartermaster. Have him bring as many weapons as he can find." She looked at Red Wolf, who smiled.

You always think of something, Talin. I told you.

"Kehlvor has given us until morning," he said. "We should get moving. Corvan..."

"Yes, let me just finish up," the old healer said. He tied the bandage around Red Wolf's leg and wiped his hands on a towel. "There. You will be fine as long as you don't run around too much."

Red Wolf swung his legs off the bed and stood. "Excellent. Let's get to work."

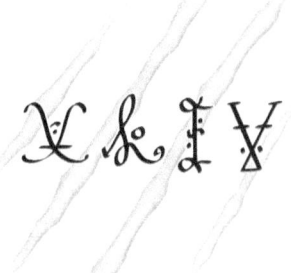

T he gates still held, thankfully, even after an hour's worth of battering from the Hellhounds. But Talin wasn't sure how much
longer they would last.

They had started their attack just after dawn, as Red Wolf had predicted, armed with no siege weapons of any sort at first. Lord Karl
had been quick to point out that if Virion had been in league with
the Hellhounds, he had probably supplied them with the siege ladders
they'd used to get over the city walls, and they were bound to have more
tricks up their sleeves.

And he was right. They had retreated briefly, giving the archers
on the wall a moment's respite, and then they had returned with a
battering ram. Red Wolf had quickly ordered the gates barricaded shut
with anything they could find. The ram had failed to break through so
far.

Talin doubted their luck would hold.

They had assembled as many civilians as they could and formed them just behind the gates. Talin saw them on her way up to the wall, fitted out with an odd assortment of weapons, some wearing used armour hastily hammered back into shape. Most were young men, no doubt determined to protect their families, but she saw a good number of women wielding swords and maces too.

Even this may not be enough.

The rain had stopped not long ago, and the ground was still slippery, slowing the Hellhounds as they tried to keep their balance while holding up the ram. Red Wolf joined her on the battlements.

"We need to keep the Hellhounds bottled at the gates for as long as we can," he said. "I've sent Rufus and Ashera to help guard the tunnel. You know where the entrance is?"

"In the back courtyard, by the training grounds," Talin said. Red Wolf nodded.

"You'll be glad to know Hesar made it back in one piece," he continued. "I saw Corvan treating his wounds in the throne room. He's in no condition to fight, but I think he'll live."

"I've started evacuating all the wounded. If we can just get all the civilians out of the palace, out of the city, we can delay the Hellhounds here. Make one last stand."

"You need to go with them," Red Wolf said. "Once this first gate falls—"

"I know." Talin turned her attention back to the Hellhounds below. "Come with me."

"We've been over this."

Talin sighed. Back at the war meeting several hours ago, she had given Red Wolf the choice between escaping the city with her and staying behind to delay the Hellhounds. He had gone with the latter. To redeem himself for losing the duel, he'd said, but Talin hadn't cared whether he won or lost, so long as he returned alive. She'd known they would lose the city either way.

"Please," she said. "Just come with us, help defend the civilians."

"I can't even protect them from myself," Red Wolf said. "The whole city saw me for who I truly am." He nodded at the attackers on the drawbridge. "At least let me die doing my duty. Protecting you."

"I don't...want to lose you. Not now. Not after all this."

"Those civilians will never make it far enough if I don't help hold the Hellhounds off."

"Red Wolf, please. Just for once, don't be a hero," she pleaded. "Come with me."

There was a deafening *crack* from below as the gates finally gave, letting the horde rush through. Talin picked off a few Hellhounds with her bow as they retreated towards the inner wall.

"Go, Talin," Red Wolf said. "There's nothing more you can do here."

Talin hesitated a fraction of a second too long. Her bodyguard lowered his visor and moved to the stairs leading into the courtyard, and she cursed herself for hesitating at all. Ettrias was by her side a moment later. The two of them made their way through the palace and towards the training grounds, their only escape route out of the city. She wondered if she would ever see Red Wolf again.

"There's nothing more we can do," Ettrias said when he caught her looking back again. "He's doing this so you can escape. So the whole city can escape."

"I just..." Talin began.

"I know. I know." Ettrias tugged on her arm. "Come on. The longer we delay here, the more time the Hellhounds will have to catch us."

Talin allowed herself to be led through the palace. At the back courtyard, they slowed, squeezing their way through the civilians gathered there. She saw Lord Karl standing at a hatch up ahead; the man had volunteered to stay and organise the evacuations. He would be one of the last to go through the tunnel.

"Clear the ladder!" he yelled as they drew near. Ettrias peered down to check for any civilians still on the ladder before descending.

"Careful, the bottom rung is missing," Lord Karl called after him.

"I'll keep it in mind." Talin swung herself over the edge and climbed down after her brother. At the bottom, they were greeted by another crowd, who parted as much as they could for her and Ettrias.

"Well, we can either help Rufus and Ashera fight the Hellhounds at the other end and join up with the crowd when Lord Karl comes through, or we can leave now," her brother said. "I'll leave the decisions to you, dear sister."

"We'll help them," Talin said. She wasn't about to abandon the fight when she had a choice.

"I thought you might say that. Here." Ettrias handed her a small vial. "Regards from Corvan. He figured you might need it."

"Corvan knows me too well." Talin downed the potion in one gulp. The throbbing pain in her leg eased a few minutes later, letting her walk properly.

"They'll try to flank us as we move the civilians deeper into Stormwood," Ettrias explained. "I had a look earlier. There aren't too many at the exit. No doubt they think most of us are still in the palace."

"We'll be out of here by the time they catch on," Talin said. "At least, that's the plan."

They emerged under one of the watchtowers along the outer wall, though it stood abandoned with nobody to guard it. Talin caught a glimpse of Ashera moments before she rushed at a wolf, jumping on its back and stabbing at its face with a sword until the blade finally pierced its brain. She jumped off it and went after her next target.

"That's one way to kill them, I suppose..." Ettrias muttered. Talin drew back her bow and shot an arrow through the eye-slit of a Hellhound's helm. Nearby, Golmin saw them join the fight and backed up to cover her while she provided ranged support. Ettrias moved further down the line of fleeing civilians to defend them as they made their way into Stormwood. She knew they would be much safer there; the wolves' huge bulk made it difficult for them to navigate the dense forest, and a Hellhound on two legs was easier to fight. Her people knew how to navigate the tropical forests in the south but the Hellhounds didn't.

She shot another half dozen arrows before a Hellhound stepped around Golmin and swung at her. She dodged aside, grabbed another arrow, and plunged it into his eye like a dagger. He dropped dead instantly. Up ahead, Ettrias appeared to be struggling with two more Hellhounds. She was about to lend him a hand when Ashera came darting into the fray, slashing at one of them. Talin seized the opportunity while they were distracted and shot them both.

More were coming. Golmin dodged an axe swing and took off his attacker's head. Talin reached for another handful of arrows and found her quiver empty. She yanked the arrow out of the Hellhound she'd stabbed and loosed that instead.

"I need more arrows!" she called. Golmin motioned to two nearby soldiers, and they formed up just ahead. The four of them moved together as she ran to scavenge arrows on the battlefield, shooting them as soon as she grabbed one. A wolf slipped past and launched itself at her. She dodged out of the way as one of the soldiers came up behind it and drove his sword into the back of its head. She gave him a nod of thanks before making a move towards the nearest arrow. Another wolf came charging past them and pounced on the nearest civilian.

"No—" Talin began. Her brother was on the creature in half a heartbeat, taking off its head. He kicked it off the civilian, and she saw that he'd been too late to save the man. A third attacker knocked him onto his back. He drove his dagger under its chin and pushed himself to his feet.

"Go! Keep going!" she yelled at the civilians who'd stopped to gape. They scrambled. Two weren't fast enough and fell victim to a wolf. Talin snatched up an arrow and shot him in the neck. He staggered back as his air supply was cut off and tried unsuccessfully to pull the arrow out. Ettrias took off his head to put him out of his misery.

She was running out of usable arrows; some had been lodged deep in wooden shields and were impossible to remove while others had splintered against armour when she missed an eye-slit. Golmin slammed his pommel into a Hellhound's face before decapitating him. A charging wolf knocked him down. Talin drew her sword, stabbed it in the neck and let it suffocate. Golmin had barely gotten back up when another wolf came charging at him, forcing him to roll aside and plunge his dagger into its skull. Beside her, two more Hellhounds had slipped past Ettrias and Ashera and had gone after the fleeing civilians. Talin scavenged two more arrows and sent them into the Hellhounds' heads.

"There's too many. You have to go!" Golmin yelled back.

"I'm not abandoning this fight until the civilians are safe!" Talin said.

Golmin shoved her aside to stab another charging wolf. "They will *kill you*. Go while you still can!"

Talin was about to protest when a wolf pounced on top of Ettrias and clamped its jaws around his sword arm. He drew his dagger and stabbed it in the eye. Another one took its place, pinning his arms, and he forced his knee up to try to keep the creature back. Talin rushed to help.

A Hellhound came swinging at her out of nowhere, forcing her to dodge. Steel glinted in the morning light as he swung again. She parried it just in time and one of the soldiers knocked him aside. Talin ducked past them both and kept running.

"Ettrias..." she began. The Hellhound's jaws clamped down over his armoured shoulder. She heard a *crunch* as metal dented. Ettrias punched the Hellhound in the face but it didn't seem fazed.

"Ettrias!"

"I'm fine, just..." Ettrias looked past her. "Behind you!"

Talin spun as a Hellhound swung his mace. She ducked under it and spied a fallen shield, quickly snatching it up to block the next attack. The weapon slammed into her with the force of a charging bull, knocking her off her feet, sending her flying back into the grass. She felt the impact ring in her arm and travel up through her shoulder and spine.

Gods, I think I broke something. Flat on her back and completely winded, she stared up at the Hellhound's swinging mace and resigned herself to her fate.

There was a blur of movement out of the corner of her eye. The Hellhound stopped mid-strike and fell with an arrow piercing his chest. Talin scrambled to her feet in time to see dozens of horses and riders charge past their struggling line and into the Hellhound horde. She looked over at Ettrias and saw a soldier helping him to his feet.

"Reinforcements...?" Talin stared at the horse riders, still too dazed to make sense of what was going on. Her leg hurt. So did her arm. She dropped the shield she'd been holding.

A war-horn rang out in the distance. A *Draconian* war-horn.

Kadis.

She saw then that these horse riders were Drakels, and more were streaming onto the battlefield. Behind the cavalry came scores of legionaries. Too stunned to move, Talin stood there instead, staring at their reinforcements as soldiers rushed past.

We're saved.

C lutching her injured arm, Talin watched as two of the Drakel
riders dismounted before her, one wearing a familiar-looking
helm and the other sporting red scales with no horns. Kadis and
Bo'Kata. She let out a half-laugh and limped forwards to greet them.

"Why is it, Your Majesty, that you appear to be at death's door every
time we meet?" the Draconian Prince asked, a grin spreading across his
face.

"I'm just glad to see you." Talin shook their hands. "We owe you our
lives. You came in the nick of time."

"Only upholding my end of the bargain," Kadis said. "You've been
keeping busy since we parted ways, I see."

"I'm afraid we'll have to catch up later, Your Highness," Talin said.
"Hellhounds have overrun the city. We must drive them out of the
palace and re-establish a command centre there."

"We'll meet at the palace, then." Kadis mounted his horse again and paused briefly. "Oh, before I forget. You'll be pleased to know that we brought as much torslek as we could get our hands on after Ked'Fald surrendered. I seem to recall the venom suppressed your bodyguard's healing."

Talin looked at the dead Hellhounds on the battlefield. "It seems to be working so far. Thank you again."

"No need!" Kadis threw her a mock salute and rode off, Bo'Kata close behind. Talin turned away and limped over to pick up her sword before retrieving what arrows she could still use.

"Round up the men and head back to the palace. Those Hellhounds have long overstayed their welcome," she told Golmin. The captain gave a nod and moved off, and Ettrias approached, clutching his shoulder.

"Now I know how you felt..." He winced. "And I was wearing armour."

"Come on, we should get you to Corvan," Talin said. "Ashera? You're unhurt?"

"I'm fine," the girl said. She bore some superficial cuts on her face but otherwise seemed unharmed.

"You've truly proven yourself today, taking on so many Hellhounds," Talin said. "Despite these odds."

"Red Wolf wanted to do the same," Ashera said. "He told me it's why he stayed back to hold the Hellhounds in the palace. He said that as long as there was a fight to be had today, he would never back down."

Red Wolf.

Ettrias must have noticed her expression change, because he slowed. "Go on ahead; we'll catch up. I'm sure he's fine."

Talin nodded and left them behind to finish rounding up the troops while she ducked back into the tunnel. It seemed the news had spread quickly; civilians were cheering left and right or simply holding each other out of sheer relief. She passed Lord Karl still at the other end of the tunnel and made for the front courtyard.

They'd been hit the hardest there. Bodies were strewn everywhere and piled on top of each other, and she could see heavy losses on both sides. The Hellhounds had retreated and the survivors now occupied most of the courtyard. She scanned the place for Red Wolf before looking up at the wall. No sign of him. Talin limped into the middle of the courtyard, checking the bodies, and praying to the gods that she wouldn't find him there.

"Talin?"

She spun around. Red Wolf stood at the gates covered in blood. His armour had been dented and scuffed in several places, and she could see a deep gash running across his arm where an arrow had no doubt nicked through the chainmail, but he was alive. He lifted his visor as he neared her and eased the helm off his head. She limped over and double-checked that he wasn't fatally bleeding from anywhere; his healing powers evidently hadn't returned yet.

"Thought you'd be deep into Stormwood by now," he said. "Guess you had to stay and help."

Talin kissed him. She didn't care that every soldier and civilian in the courtyard was watching. He was alive, and that was all that mattered.

"I told you I'd be fine," he said when they broke apart.

"The Drakels are here…" Talin looked up at him. "I never thought…"

Red Wolf glanced at her arm. "That needs fixing."

Talin realised that she'd been gripping her injured arm the entire time. She tried to flex her fingers gingerly but only succeeded in sending a jolt of blinding pain through the limb. They quickly agreed to find Corvan.

The old healer had set up again in the throne room to treat his patients, aided by some of the Draconian healers that Kadis had brought with him. Ettrias sat in a wooden chair in the corner with his armour stripped off and his arm in a sling. Talin took a seat on the throne again while Corvan splinted her arm and put it in a sling too.

"It's not a complicated fracture, thankfully," he said. "But you'll still need to rest it for a few weeks. Keep the splint on. You need to give the bone sufficient time to heal. That shield may have saved your life."

"Thank you," Talin said. "Kadis agreed to meet us in the palace, but I don't see him yet. I don't suppose I could trouble you to find him, Red Wolf?"

"Consider it done." Her bodyguard spun on his heel and disappeared through the throne-room doors. Talin waited until she was certain he was out of earshot.

"You were right," she said to Ettrias. "I can't...lose him. It's not a risk I could ever take."

"You'll go through with my plan, then?" her brother asked.

Talin winced. "I...made a deal with Lord Karl. If he...tells the court that Wormwood lied...Golmin can escort you to the border in secret..."

"Tell them I fled during the battle," Ettrias said. "That could work."

Talin glanced at the doors as if Red Wolf might return any second. "You're sure you want to do this? You and Golmin—"

"Rufus understands the situation, and he would rather save Red Wolf than have us both remain in Belanore," Ettrias said. "We'll be fine together. But if Red Wolf confesses to murder, Rufus loses him for good. You'll lose him too. *Ashera* will lose him too."

"And you? Am I to believe that parting ways with you again will be any easier?"

"You'd rather say goodbye to me than him."

"You cannot put a hierarchy on who I'd rather lose."

"Talin, I've...I got used to my exile, in a way," Ettrias explained. "Wherever I went, people didn't look at me like I was some sort of monster. Not like the way I've seen people look at Red Wolf. He belongs here, in Belanore, where there are people close to him who can accept him. I made a life for myself out there, just travelling. He might not."

"Just to be clear, I still don't like this."

"I know. But he's not a bad person. Father tricked him and used him for his own ends; he doesn't deserve death or exile for that."

The throne-room doors swung open at that moment to reveal Red Wolf, now accompanied by a slightly bloodier Kadis. The Drakel broke into a grin when he saw Talin and Ettrias.

"No need to worry—none of this is my blood," he said. "My men have been clearing the streets as best we can, but we keep running into each other. Belanore is like a maze."

"Come with me. The maps in the war room should help with organising your men," Talin said, getting to her feet.

"The torslek has been highly effective so far," he said as they walked. "I'm surprised you turned the throne room into a medical ward."

"We needed somewhere to put the wounded. The throne room was one of the few places here with enough space," Talin said. "Your legionaries were quick to secure the palace."

"Your lord commander had them bottlenecked at the front gates; it was quite impressive, actually," Kadis said.

"We learned from your attempt to breach the gate at El'Vane," Red Wolf said.

Kadis laughed. "I'm glad to hear it."

Red Wolf moved ahead to open the war-room doors for them, and they quickly gathered around the maps, where Talin briefly went over the city landmarks.

"Ah, I see..." Kadis flattened his palms on the table. "Here is the palace and the drawbridge. That means my legionaries have formed a perimeter here." He pointed along a nearby street running parallel to the palace.

"We need to push further," Talin said and pointed to Hesar's old defence line. "This was where we held the defensive when they broke through. It seemed to buy us the most time. If we could push them all the way back to here and establish a line..."

"Yes, that could work," Kadis said. "These narrow alleys must have been what slowed the Hellhounds' advance. If I leave my cavalry in the outer city, we can bottle them in these alleys and trap them there."

"From what I hear, some of the Hellhounds have retreated from the city entirely," Red Wolf said. "Shall I round up a team to pursue them?"

"No, I need you here," Talin said. *To stand trial and tell them you're innocent.*

"As you wish."

They finished their plans to take back the city and parted ways with Kadis, agreeing that he would take charge of the soldiers while she cleaned up the mess in the palace.

"Wait, one more thing, Kadis," Talin called as the Draconian prince reached the doors.

"Yes?"

"I've been meaning to ask—did you find your father? Is he alright?"

Kadis grinned. "Yes, he's fine. They did not treat him as badly as they might have during the years of his imprisonment. I suspect they thought he might make a good bargaining chip one day. He'll recover, though whether he wants to be emperor again is another matter. He's talking about abdication..."

"Oh? I might have to get used to calling you 'Emperor Kadis', then," Talin said.

"It does have a nice ring to it, don't you think?" Kadis laughed and disappeared through the doors, and Talin found herself alone with Red Wolf again in the dull light of the war room. She pondered over the maps for a while longer before turning away.

"Talin, I..." Red Wolf sighed. "I know you and Ettrias intend to clear my name. I didn't overhear your conversation, but I could guess what it was about. I can't let this happen."

"It'll be fine. I can have Ettrias escorted to the border in secret before the trial and tell the court that he must have fled during the siege," Talin said. "This is the only way to resolve things."

"You know that's not true," Red Wolf said.

Talin drew up a chair and sat. She had expected he would be stubborn, even at this perfect opportunity to clear himself of those crimes.

"I'm offering you a chance, a way out," she told him. "Just take it, please. For both our sakes."

"I can't let you involve yourself in this," he said. "As it stands, you're innocent in this whole affair. If you do this...you become part of it."

"The alternative is to let the court sentence you to death!" Talin protested.

"And *this* is what you want instead?" Red Wolf said softly. "Denouncing your own brother as a common criminal once again, *knowing* he's innocent?"

"I..." Talin felt her shoulders deflate. "I can't...lose you...because of what Father made you do. Not now, not after we've just survived this siege."

"I know." Red Wolf's brow creased. "If this is what you wish to do, I won't stop it. I just don't want you to live the same lie as I did."

"Red Wolf, promise me you won't do anything," Talin said.

"I...can't promise anything," Red Wolf confessed. "I understand. Believe me, I do. I stood in your position ten years ago, having to decide who to condemn, and there is no 'right' choice."

"I know. I guess it's too much to ask." Talin sighed. "Take a day off on the day of the trial. I'll find someone else to testify instead."

Red Wolf crossed his arms. "I assume this is an order from you as my queen."

"I've never been able to make you do anything," Talin said. "But yes, I would very much like it if you did as I ask."

"As my queen commands." Red Wolf dipped his head. "I should warn you, though. You might find yourself hard-pressed to find other witnesses who can testify against Ettrias."

"I know." Talin rubbed her eyes. "I'll think of something. If there's nothing else, you're dismissed. Go train Ashera or spar with Golmin, I don't know. I'd like to be alone for a bit."

Red Wolf bowed and left her with her maps. Talin stared at them for a while, mentally mapping out the route they took to the border and back. It wasn't until she looked at these maps that she realised just how far they'd travelled in such a short time. By all rights, it should have taken them at least a month and a half of travelling along the roads, but Red Wolf and Golmin's knowledge of the southern forests had allowed them to save precious time by going through the wilderness. Talin rubbed her leg absentmindedly. She had brought an army of Drakels from the west and saved the entire city, possibly the kingdom itself, but she couldn't do anything to save the people she loved.

Arnas had told her once that ruling meant putting the needs of the people before her own. She'd dismissed his words then, thinking that she couldn't possibly have to sacrifice *that* much to rule over the kingdom. Now, she realised that he'd been right all along, and had ignored his own words of wisdom in order to put her on the throne.

Now it's my turn.

She wasn't sure she was ready to choose.

T alin hadn't exactly specified what he should do on his day off.

Red Wolf considered this as he made his way to the city courtroom, where the six high judges were to decide Ettrias' and Lord Karl's fates now that the siege was over. He had convinced the exiled prince to remain in Belanore after revealing his plans, and he had told Golmin not to testify. Lord Karl would say all he needed to say to condemn Wormwood's actions, but he, too, would maintain Ettrias' innocence.

He'd spent most of the morning pacing and sparring with the royal guard, trying his hardest to respect Talin's wishes. She had made her choice. It wasn't his place to force the alternative on her.

Except he realised that he couldn't live with the knowledge that he could have righted a wrong and cleared Ettrias' name for good. And given that he'd done nothing more than promise to take the day off…why not walk into the court to observe?

Red Wolf took a seat at the back of the courtroom just as two of Hesar's men escorted General Virion out of the defendant's box and through a side door. Talin was nowhere to be seen yet, no doubt preparing for her next case against Lord Karl and Ettrias. He supposed that was a good thing; his presence here would remain unnoticed until the trial was well underway.

More people trickled into the courtroom as the minutes dragged on. Red Wolf prayed to the gods that his plan would go off without a hitch.

He spotted her enter eventually, wearing a light dress with long, semi-transparent sleeves. Lord Karl was soon marched in as well, hands chained together, flanked by two guards. The five High Court judges filed in after, followed by Branweyn, the Supreme Judge. There was a collective shuffling as the courtroom stood for his entrance. Red Wolf knew from his time in court ten years ago that Branweyn was in charge of deciding a split vote.

The courtroom was packed by the time they went through the usual formalities and began the trial proper; many of the common folk had gathered today to listen to the truth behind Wormwood's coup. *Talin's* version of the truth, if all went according to her plan. Red Wolf watched her pace back and forth as she read from her papers, long sleeves and elegant dress trailing in her wake, looking regal despite the sling that immobilised her left arm. Her hair had been braided and tied in an impossible-looking pattern to match the outfit. She threw an absent-minded glance towards the back of the courtroom as she paced and saw him, and he saw her falter for the barest fraction of a second before continuing. Red Wolf could already imagine her fuming at him silently and wondering what in the seven hells he thought he was doing.

"If all of this is true, then I expect Lord Commander Red Wolf is willing to testify?" one of the judges asked. "I see him in the back of the courtroom. Unless he is simply here to enjoy the proceedings...?"

"Red Wolf has refused to testify in this trial, your honour," Talin said. "No doubt he does not wish to have to condemn a friend for a second time."

"And your brother, Ettrias, you say he fled during the siege?" Judge Branweyn asked. He was a stern-looking southerner with silvery hair cropped to his shoulders and a stiff collar that marked him as the Supreme Judge.

"He has. I have dispatched search parties to look for him to no avail," Talin said.

I doubt that, but even if you had, they won't find anything, Red Wolf thought. *He's hiding in the city.*

"I see," Judge Branweyn said. "However, the trial that took place ten years ago largely hinged on the lord commander's testimony. I feel it would work in your favour to have him testify now, to confirm everything that has been said so far."

"I understand, your honour," Talin said. "There is another who can testify. The prosecution calls forward Lord Karl Highett—"

"I'll testify." Red Wolf stood. The courtroom fell so deathly silent that he was sure he would be able to hear a pin drop. The judges stared at him for a little while before having a hushed discussion amongst themselves.

"The court will hear your testimony if the prosecution enters it as evidence," Judge Branweyn said.

Talin shot him a subtle glare that went unnoticed by the rest of the courtroom. "Very well."

They went through the hassle of paperwork to enter him as a witness to the case before the judges agreed on a brief adjournment; Talin hadn't prepared questions for him, after all. She pulled him into an empty room, away from the main courtroom, and rounded on him.

"What in the *seven hells* are you playing at?" she demanded.

"You won't sway the judges without my testimony," Red Wolf lied smoothly. "I had some time to think this morning. What you're doing now...I don't like it, but it's your choice. I might as well make things easier for you."

Talin's shoulders deflated a little. "So this is you having a change of heart?"

"I'm doing this for you, not because I had a change of heart," Red Wolf said.

"Alright. Thank you. I'm sorry for doubting you." Talin let out a long breath. "Just...tell them the same thing you told them ten years ago. Please don't say anything unnecessary. We're *so close*..."

"I understand," Red Wolf said. "Anything else?"

"I'll ask for details. Again, just repeat what you said last time," Talin explained. She began scribbling on a spare piece of parchment, no doubt making notes for herself. "If I ask anything that might incriminate you, just say you can't recall the details."

"Of course."

"Then we're ready."

The two of them returned to the courtroom, where he took a seat closer to the front this time, and Talin stepped up to her table. Branweyn called for the session to resume.

"The prosecution calls forward Lord Commander Red Wolf," Talin said.

"I'm sorry," Red Wolf whispered as he passed her.

"Wait, what—" she began, but he had already taken to the witness stand and sworn to tell the truth, the whole truth, and nothing but the truth, or may the gods strike him down.

"Lord Commander, I'd..." She hesitated there, as if wondering whether she really should question him. "I'd like you to tell the court what you saw the night you caught Prince Ettrias ten years ago."

"Prince Ettrias is innocent," Red Wolf said. A deathly hush descended on the courtroom. "He never committed those crimes. Under King Arnas' orders, I was the one who killed the Harrison siblings and presented the bodies to him as proof. I was led to believe they were enemies of the state, but it was all part of a bigger plan to exile the prince and forfeit his claim to the throne." The courtroom erupted, forcing him to shout over the top of them. "King Arnas wanted his daughter to succeed him instead, but Queen Talin is innocent! She was deceived into thinking that her brother was a murderer, just as you all were!"

The look on Talin's face was enough to sell the lie. He didn't meet her gaze.

"You realise that this is a very serious confession," Judge Branweyn said, once the courtroom had quietened. "If I'm to understand correctly, you confess to the murders of Anna and James Harrison?"

"I do, your honour," Red Wolf said. "King Arnas and I framed Prince Ettrias for the murders in order to ensure his daughter's seat as heir, without her knowledge or approval. He had intended to reveal the truth on his deathbed, but he fell in battle before he could do so. It was my decision to remain silent until now."

"Red Wolf..." Talin's voice trailed off. If he didn't know better, he would say she looked like she was going to cry.

"My queen, with all due respect, I'd advise you to remain silent. Your involvement in this case may come into question at a later time," he said.

"I just want to know if it's all true," Talin said.

"It is. Every word."

Talin was silent for a moment. "No more questions, your honour."

"No questions either, your honour," Lord Karl said, standing briefly.

Red Wolf was dismissed and allowed to return to his seat with orders not to leave the courtroom. The judges went through the usual proceedings and overturned their verdict on Ettrias ten years ago, arranging for another session to formally convict Red Wolf. The courtroom slowly emptied until he was left alone with Talin and her guards.

"You..." she began, then hissed through her teeth and cursed. "I'll deal with you later. Golmin, escort him back to the palace and put him in the dungeons."

"I'd...prefer anywhere but the dungeons, my queen," Red Wolf said, as Golmin took him by the elbow.

"Of course." Talin's glare softened a little. "That can be arranged. Golmin?"

"I'll find a tower to lock him in, Your Majesty," the captain said.

"Thank you," Red Wolf said. A tower wasn't much of an improvement in his eyes, to be sure, but anywhere was better than back in that cell that reminded him of the Hellhounds' cages.

Golmin escorted him back to the palace at sword point to keep up appearances, though, in reality, Red Wolf was going along willingly. Word had spread quickly through the city, too. He could see people staring as he passed them or holding rotten food as if to throw it. They never got the courage to do it; he knew they were still terrified of what he could do.

"Friendly crowd," Golmin muttered as they crossed the drawbridge.

"I was always an outcast in their eyes," Red Wolf said.

"Why'd you do it?" Golmin asked.

"Are you going to get all worked up if I tell you the truth?"

"Depends on the truth."

"Talin never played a part in her father's plans. I'd like to keep it that way," Red Wolf said. "Ettrias' name needs to be cleared. And you two deserve some kind of a happy ending."

"Right, of course, protecting everyone." Golmin scoffed. "You didn't care about all that ten years ago. Just admit it—you're only doing it for her."

"Do you really believe that I think so little of our friendship?" Red Wolf asked softly. "I do this because *you* are the only brother I love and recognise. What I do now...I do to make up for my mistakes ten years ago. Mistakes that you and Ettrias had to suffer for."

Golmin huffed a short exhale. "You mean that?"

"Every word."

"Then I suppose I should apologise for doubting you."

"There's no need to apologise. You have every right to be angry at what I've done."

They climbed the steps to one of the tallest towers in the palace, Golmin leading the way. He had dropped his act now, and Red Wolf was certain he would be able to make a run for it and disappear into Stormwood, but that would be the coward's way out. He had to see this through to the end.

"I'll keep a guard outside the door," Golmin said. "Tell him if you need anything. They're still loyal to you, I'm sure."

"Thank you." Red Wolf stepped into the room at the top of the tower, and the captain locked the door behind him. He scanned the room before settling in an armchair near the bed. There was a window here, at least, but the sheer drop onto the inner wall fifty feet below made escape impossible, even with some sort of rope. There was a bookshelf by the door. He looked through its contents from his seat and found no titles of interest. A little round table stood in the middle of the room, though it looked rickety at best with uneven legs. After some contemplation, he snatched a random book off the shelf and moved to the bed to read.

It wasn't until dusk that the lock finally clicked in his door, and the hinges creaked to announce a visitor. Judging from the light tread and faint scent of perfume, he figured it was Talin, having finally finished her work for the day. He set his book down and looked up at her.

"I've been sorting out this mess," she said.

"I imagined you were," Red Wolf said.

"Red Wolf, the next trial is in two days. They'll ask for your plea and sentence you on the spot if you tell them you're guilty, which I assume you will," Talin said. "But I guess Ettrias has been proven innocent, so there's that."

"You don't approve," he said.

"Of course I don't approve." Talin scoffed and pulled up one of the chairs at the round table to sit. "They'll execute you."

"I'm comfortable with that," Red Wolf said.

"I'm not."

"I know. I'm sorry it had to end this way."

"What happened, anyway? Ettrias tells me you never knew about Father's plan until the trial," Talin said. "But if you killed the Harrison siblings..."

"Arnas came to me in the dead of night and told me that there was a matter of...state security," Red Wolf said bitterly. "Said that two 'fugitives' had fled the city through the southern gate and were trying to make it across the border to Astaria, to the Fae, to start another war.

He sent me to kill them before they could get away. In reality, he'd sent the Harrisons on an urgent but fake errand to the border patrol. It was a new moon; even I could barely make out anything. I'd never met the Harrisons before. I didn't know what they looked like and probably wouldn't have remembered their faces even if I had. But I saw the two of them riding at breakneck speed towards the border and believed they were the fugitives described by the king."

"So you killed them," Talin said.

"Given how close they were to the border, I couldn't risk them getting away, not when I believed I was the only chance we had of stopping them. But perhaps I should have known that something didn't add up."

"I understand. I think." Talin stared at the table for a while. "I told you the day the Drakels arrived that I didn't want to lose you. But now...what am I supposed to do with you now?"

"Do what you feel is right," Red Wolf said.

Talin pinched the bridge of her nose. "You keep telling me that. It doesn't help."

"I'm sorry."

She sighed. "The Crown has the power to pardon a convicted criminal. I could...let you walk free."

"You could." Red Wolf shrugged. "Your people won't be happy."

"Who cares what my people think!"

"You should."

Talin let out a long breath.

"I told you. The city will question your involvement in your father's plan," Red Wolf said. "If you pardon me, that is one more piece of evidence they can use against you. Think about what you stand to lose."

"I *am*..." Talin's voice cracked. "...thinking about what I could lose."

Red Wolf was silent.

There was a knock at the door. "Your Majesty, Prince Kadis requests an audience regarding the war effort."

"One moment," Talin said. She wiped her eyes and stood. "Call me selfish for it. But between losing my reputation and losing you for good, I would save you every single time. Don't you dare suggest that I would even consider doing otherwise."

She backed out of the room. Red Wolf heard the lock click again.

I have another option, Talin. You won't like it much more than what you have now.

He finished his book and thought about taking a nap, then decided against it. Thunder rumbled outside. Talin would be back later, no doubt, and they would be able to discuss things without interruption.

If this alternative doesn't work, I'm a dead man.

Red Wolf could accept that. Whatever happened, whatever punishment he received, he would have deserved it. Whether or not it was fair to Talin was...

It's not about either of us, he told himself. *It's about what's right.*

Could he really do it? Leave her behind? He wasn't sure. They were unlikely to remain in Belanore together either way.

But maybe he could accept that punishment too.

XLVII

Talin found herself distracted during Kadis' briefing.

They had gone through the usual planning and strategizing without issue, though she barely remembered any of it. She did recall, however, that he had said something about moving on to retake Illyris once Vill's Crossing was secure, with her permission, of course. She had agreed without giving much thought to what resources they would need to drive the Hellhounds out of a region that large. He'd also convinced her to agree to join them on the front once Illyris was retaken. She wasn't sure why she had agreed; the Highlands was a long way from Belanore.

But perhaps she needed something to distract her once the ordeal in the capital was over and she had figured out what to do with Red Wolf. Letting things play out as they were seemed unappealing. The High Court would simply order his execution.

Red Wolf was right about what might happen if she pardoned him, though, much as she hated to admit it. The city would speculate that perhaps she had been involved after all, which would only invite more people like Wormwood to question her ability to rule. In the end, her bodyguard's motives were to try to prevent a second coup in Belanore—and to protect her.

"You seem distracted today," Kadis remarked as they left the war room together. "This isn't like you. I could swear you barely paid any attention to my suggestion about retaking Illyris."

"I..." Talin sighed. "Am I that obvious?"

Kadis shrugged. "I wager it's something to do with Red Wolf."

Talin reluctantly explained the courtroom drama that had occurred today, how Red Wolf's confession to murder had set Ettrias free and how her bodyguard would now face the executioner's axe.

"I know you won't like hearing this, but..." Kadis paused there. "I'm inclined to agree with your bodyguard. Condemning your brother again fixes nothing. You must do what's *right*, not what's easy."

"I know." Talin winced. "I just...wish there was another way. One that doesn't involve losing either of them."

"I understand," Kadis said. "I cannot say I know much of your Torrian laws, so I'm afraid I won't be of much help. I wish you luck."

They parted ways there, her taking a right towards the stairs that led up to Red Wolf's tower. As she drew near the top, however, she could make out arguing; word had apparently spread quickly, and Ettrias had decided to confront Red Wolf. Talin crept up to the door to listen better.

"...can't believe I let myself be persuaded like that, *kust*, you're insufferable," her brother was saying. "I thought you had a plan to solve things without incriminating yourself!"

"I was under the impression that this was what you wanted from the beginning," Red Wolf said. "Your name cleared. Your father's crimes brought to light."

"Not like this!" Ettrias hissed. "Not at your expense! You'll face execution, and for what? You had no *choice*. The court will never recognise that. They'll treat you as if you'd played your part willingly."

"As I told you, I'm fine with that," Red Wolf said. "I wasn't going to let you throw away your one chance at remaining in Belanore."

"You lied to me."

"I'm sorry. For everything."

Ettrias huffed a humourless laugh. "I don't need your apology. What's done is done. I...*am* grateful. For what it's worth."

"I know," Red Wolf said. He raised his voice. "Your sister also joined us not long ago. Did you forget my hearing is good enough to pick up footsteps climbing the tower, Talin?"

Well, there's no use pretending any longer. Talin climbed the last few steps and motioned for the guard to unlock the door.

"You and I, we are talking about this later." Ettrias shot Red Wolf a glare before turning on his heel and striding off.

"Ettrias—" Talin began, but her brother had already vanished down the stairs. She spun back to face Red Wolf again.

"Please tell me you went into this with some sort of plan," she said.

Red Wolf frowned. "Yes and no. As I said, I don't care much what happens to me now."

"Red Wolf, my options are to let them order your execution or pardon you and deal with the repercussions," Talin said. "You *know* I can't lose you."

"I know," Red Wolf said. "I...do have a third option. An alternative if you like."

"Please, I'll take anything."

"Appeal to the High Court for my exile instead of execution."

Talin felt a weight drop into her gut. "That's not much of an improvement."

"No, it isn't," Red Wolf confessed. "But it's an improvement nonetheless."

"I could just pardon you," Talin said.

"You could."

"I could dismiss that guard outside and let you walk out of here."

Red Wolf cracked a faint smile. "But you won't."

"Why are you doing this?" Talin ran a hand down her face.

"Because I know what it's like to live with that guilt for so long. It eats away at your sanity every single day until you can't take it anymore. You never should have had to deal with this, and it's my fault that you do."

"I can't do this, Red Wolf. Send you away. We'd never see each other again."

"It's the right thing to do. And you're right; it's not easy," Red Wolf said. "But you are the queen. You have to understand, better than anyone, that doing the right thing means making sacrifices. When I condemned Ettrias ten years ago, it was out of a selfish desire to stay by your side. But I now know that to truly protect what we love, we must be prepared to let them go." He cupped her face in his hands. "Let me go, Talin."

"*Red Wolf,*" she said, almost a plea. "Please don't make me do this."

He brushed his thumbs over her cheeks, wiping away her tears, and offered her a half-hearted smile. "Show your people that you are better than Wormwood. Better than your father. Show them that you are worthy of being queen."

"I'll...alright. I'll talk to the court." Talin took a few shaky breaths. "But if they don't approve..."

"Then you will have tried," Red Wolf said.

"If the Court doesn't approve, I will pardon you," Talin said. "I can't let them execute you."

"I can't stop you."

"Thank you."

"You know, I am sorry for making you choose," he said.

"I understand." Talin made a move for the door. "I'm sorry it had to come to this."

"Me too."

T he lock in his door clicked again early that morning when he was still eating breakfast at the rickety table in his cell, though he could tell from the footsteps that it wasn't Talin or Ettrias. Red Wolf looked up briefly before returning to his meal.

"It's really alright if I go in?" Ashera's voice.

"Of course. You should be allowed to see him," Golmin said. "I'll be right here if you need anything."

Red Wolf finished the last few bites of his food and stood up just as Ashera stepped inside.

"The guards said you did some bad stuff, and that's why you're here," she said.

"They're not wrong."

"You know, before we left Belanore, way back…" Ashera began. "Well, the queen asked to speak to me. She said you'd been arrested for crimes against the Crown. Did you do something bad to her?"

"No, of course not. I would never," Red Wolf said. "But I did do something bad ten years ago. Something that I was never punished for. Now I'm making things right."

"What did you do?" Ashera asked.

Red Wolf hesitated. Was it appropriate to explain everything to a twelve-year-old child?

She deserves the truth.

He pulled up a chair and sat, gesturing for Ashera to do the same.

"I have to warn you that what I'm about to tell you is…not pleasant, to say the least. You might not understand all of it. If you'd like me to stop at any point or simplify things, let me know."

The girl nodded. "I'm not a little kid anymore. Tell me."

He told her everything, starting from the beginning, with Arnas' disappointment in Ettrias at every turn to the murders, the trial, and his own involvement. Ashera listened with wide eyes, completely silent apart from the occasional interruption to understand a complex word.

"But that's…that's not *fair*," she protested when he was done. "You didn't have a *choice*. The king knew that you wouldn't recognise them and used your loyalty to him to trick you!"

"The law doesn't recognise that," Red Wolf said. "At least not yet. In any case, I committed far more crimes than two counts of murder. I conspired against the Crown. Lied to the High Court. Lied to the head of state about my own past to secure a place as Arnas' squire. I'm…not the person you think I am, Ashera, and I never was. I'm sorry I lied to you too."

"Don't be stupid," Ashera said. "I've squired for you for over a year. If you were an awful person, I'd know." She paused there. "The only thing is...well, if you have to stand trial, and they find you guilty, what happens to me?"

"You won't be able to keep squiring for me," Red Wolf confessed. "Once the court accepts my guilty plea, my titles will be stripped. You can't be a squire if your master holds no titles."

"But...then...I won't be able to join the Royal Guard." Ashera's bottom lip wobbled. "I won't ever be knighted either."

"I'll talk to my queen," Red Wolf said. "Have her find someone you can squire for. She knows how important this is for you. I *promise* we'll figure something out."

Ashera sniffled and looked on the verge of crying. "Your trial is tomorrow, isn't it? They'll sentence you there and then...if you're guilty...they'll ask you to leave right away, won't they?"

"Yes," Red Wolf said. "If my queen can persuade Branweyn to exile me."

"Does...does that mean...we won't be able to see each other again after today?" Ashera asked.

Red Wolf felt a weight drop into his gut.

"Yes. I'll never be allowed to return unless I'm granted an official pardon from the Crown."

"The queen can do that, though, can't she? Pardon you?"

"Not without serious political consequences."

"But we'll never see each other again!" Ashera's tears were flowing freely now. He felt another stab of guilt. "Take me with you when you leave! Please..."

"You have a life here." Red Wolf stood up to wrap her in a hug. "Don't throw that away."

Ashera, for her part, continued bawling into his tunic, and he rubbed her back gently in an effort to calm her down.

Was this how Ettrias felt? Saying goodbye to everything you've ever cared about?

Footsteps sounded again on the staircase, followed by the lock turning. Red Wolf looked up to see the prince himself standing in the doorway.

"Come on, Ashera," Ettrias said. "You can come back tonight and say goodbye properly then. I'm sure you'll see each other again someday."

It took some coaxing, but Ashera was eventually persuaded to leave so the two men could talk in private, promising to return that night and making Red Wolf promise not to go anywhere.

"Not to say I don't appreciate having visitors, but why are you here?" Red Wolf asked.

"Talin's gone to talk to Judge Branweyn," Ettrias said.

"You don't approve," Red Wolf said.

"If Branweyn doesn't agree to this—"

"He's a reasonable man. And your sister is a persuasive woman."

"I wish you'd told me what you were planning," Ettrias said.

"I'm sorry," Red Wolf said.

"Stop...apologising." Ettrias hissed through his teeth. "I know why you did it. Rufus has already told me. Your motives are the same as mine. I only wish I'd known beforehand."

Red Wolf sat on the edge of the bed and said nothing.

"I don't want to sound ungrateful," Ettrias continued. "I am grateful. Of course I am." He stopped there as if he'd forgotten what he was going to say next, then let out a long breath and ran a hand through his hair. "Do you know what you'll do once you're exiled? Where you'll go, who can help you?"

"Bold of you to assume I know anyone outside Belanore," Red Wolf said. "As I said. I don't care what happens to me next."

"Kadis might welcome you in El'Vane."

Red Wolf sighed. "I'll think about it."

"I'll miss you."

"I'll miss you too," Red Wolf said. "I'm glad you returned—in the end. You gave me a chance to set things right."

"I'm afraid you'll have to forgive me for not crying on your shoulder as Ashera did. I won't miss you *that* much." Ettrias grinned.

Red Wolf snorted. "I'd rather you didn't anyway."

"Goodbye, Red Wolf."

"Goodbye, my prince."

The lock clicked again, and Ettrias was gone. Red Wolf heard him pause outside his door and strike up a brief conversation with Golmin, something about finding time to spar later, and allowed himself a brief smile.

They get their happy ending, at least.

He supposed it was worth it in the end. They both deserved better.

And Talin? Does she deserve all of this?

Perhaps not. But that was out of his hands now, no matter what excuses he might try to make for himself. She had to allow this if she wanted her people's support, and if she wanted to change the system, she had to allow his sentencing to go ahead. His fate was up to the High Court—and the gods if they did exist.

Red Wolf picked out another book from the shelf and settled on the bed to read.

XLIX

"With all due respect, Your Majesty, you came all the way to my courthouse to ask *me* to reconsider Red Wolf's sentence?" a perplexed Judge Branweyn asked.

They were seated in his office this morning, sipping chilled liquor while the humidity threatened to suffocate anyone who tried to set foot outside. Talin half-wished that she hadn't shown up at all and had simply pardoned Red Wolf instead. It would have saved her the trouble of having to explain her logic to Branweyn.

But she had made a promise, one that she was now obligated to keep.

"You're right. I could overrule the court and do it myself," she said. "That's what my father would have done. It's what Lord Wormwood would have done. I don't want that sort of power."

Judge Branweyn lifted his eyebrows.

"When my father established the new judiciary, it was supposed to act as a separate branch, not beholden to the Crown," Talin continued. "Yet what's the *point* when the Crown still holds absolute power over it? You could tell me that a man was wrongfully convicted, and I could tell you that I don't believe the presented evidence, and then have him executed anyway. Where's the fairness in that?"

"Then what do you propose?" Branweyn asked, refilling his glass.

"A new law for a new system," Talin said. "One that prevents the Crown's involvement in all judicial affairs. From now on, the judges' word is to be final. The Crown will only intervene if it truly believes that there has been misconduct on the *court's* behalf, and it must be able to prove such misconduct."

"I could agree to that," Branweyn said. "Still, I don't see any reason to change what's been a standard sentence for such serious offences."

"I wasn't done," Talin said. "In exchange, the court will recognise that I plan to abolish the death penalty, starting with Red Wolf's case. In its sentencing, the court will also recognise that there are mitigating factors to each case and act accordingly. Red Wolf didn't act of his own will; he was coerced."

The corner of Branweyn's mouth twitched. "I will admit, I like that line of thinking. I will consider his exile as an alternative, should he plead guilty tomorrow. However, I would ask that you have your official documents drafted as soon as possible."

"Of course. Thank you." Talin finished her drink and stood. "And thank you for hearing me out."

The city felt different now that she looked at it again. Perhaps it was the recent siege that left large parts of the city still in shambles...no. She was seeing the kingdom now for what it truly was and the flawed ideals that people held onto. People turned a blind eye when it suited them and shunned outsiders who were different in any way. Even the people close to her, people whom she'd thought were 'good', had done terrible things. Her father, driven to banish his own child in the hope of creating his 'ideal' kingdom. Red Wolf, tricked into following the king's plan by his blind loyalty and devotion. Even her advisors were corrupted by their selfish desire for power.

Ettrias too—he tried to have you killed twice.

She paused. The rest of the city didn't know that; it was a secret kept from her advisors and most of the royal guards. Perhaps it was best if things stayed that way.

"What did Branweyn say?" her brother asked when he met her in the main courtyard.

"He agreed to consider it. Red Wolf will be exiled if he pleads guilty," Talin said. "And it seems that your name has been fully cleared. No doubt people are still going to talk."

"That's alright." Ettrias shrugged. "Truth be told, I'd prefer the speculation about whether I'm innocent over being used as an excuse to defend real murderers."

"People will do that too."

"I'll be sure to give them my regards in a strongly worded letter."

Talin cracked a faint smile.

"I spent most of last night thinking things over. I could still pardon him," she said.

"You could." Ettrias shrugged. "You wouldn't be breaking any rules either. But you're not going to do that."

"No." Talin told him about her take on their father's and Wormwood's abuse of power and how it should never happen again.

"It's a good move. Stripping the Crown's influence over the law. I like it."

"Well, if it has Ettrias' seal of approval…"

Her brother snorted.

"You know, since you're staying…" Talin began.

"Yes?"

"I do happen to need some new advisors. And, I don't know, a new General of the Royal Army?"

"I'm flattered," Ettrias said, doing his best to look unamused.

"Oh, just say yes or no." Talin smiled and smacked his arm lightly.

"I would be honoured," Ettrias said with a grin. "No, really, I'm serious."

"I'm glad to hear it," Talin said. They had reached her chambers on the second floor, and the stairs to the upper level and Red Wolf's tower weren't far down the corridor. She considered going that way for a moment before stopping herself. There wasn't much to tell him that he wouldn't find out sooner or later anyway. She headed for her study instead.

"And here I thought you were continuing down the hall," Ettrias said.

Talin paused with her hand on the doorknob.

"I…shouldn't."

"I can't imagine he gets all that many visitors," Ettrias said.

"Look, if you want to talk to him, give him my regards." Talin ran a hand down her face. "I…don't know if…I can face him at the moment."

"We already said our goodbyes." Ettrias shrugged. "I'm going to find Rufus and break the news that the farm's on hold."

She watched him disappear down the hall and tried not to think about Red Wolf. The court would sentence him upon hearing his guilty plea, and chances were, he would be ordered to leave immediately. She would have to organise the guard escort that would take him to the border. Sending a messenger off with instructions for Golmin, she settled down to deal with her outstanding paperwork and begin drafting the new laws.

We might not see each other again after tonight.

Talin stamped the building permit to repair and renovate the city's outer wall. She knew she'd have a chance to talk to him briefly in the morning before the trial, then another chance to say goodbye at the gates. There would be time, surely.

Except she knew she couldn't bear to say goodbye, not tomorrow, and certainly not today. Once he was exiled, he would be no longer welcome in Kies Tor. And with her days soon to be filled once again with war meetings and battles, there would be no time for her to find him, wherever he was planning to go. She stared at the short stack of paperwork still to be completed and resigned herself to visiting tonight.

She was about halfway up the stairs to Red Wolf's tower when Ashera came sprinting down, almost barrelling into her, wiping furiously at her reddened eyes.

"Ashera—" she began, but the girl had already disappeared from view. She sighed and continued up the steps.

Inside the tower, Red Wolf appeared to be halfway through his supper, though he stood in the middle of the room with his food untouched. He jumped when he heard her enter; something serious must be occupying his mind for him not to notice her footsteps.

"I...passed Ashera on my way up..." she said.

"We said our goodbyes." Red Wolf worked his jaw. "I..." He drew in a sharp breath and rubbed his eyes with one hand. Talin could tell he was only wiping them dry.

"Branweyn agreed to consider exiling you," Talin said. "On the condition that you plead guilty. I assume that's what you're going to do."

"Naturally." Red Wolf dipped his head. "I need a favour."

"Of course, anything," Talin said.

"Ashera needs someone new to squire for," Red Wolf said. "I told her I'd ask for your help. I don't suppose that's too much to ask."

"No, of course not," Talin said. "In fact, I think I may already have a solution for you."

"Let's hear it, then."

"I'm riding north with Kadis after we secure the Western Forts. Perhaps...Ashera would like to squire for the queen. You squired for my father back in the day. It seems fitting that your squire takes on that same responsibility for me."

Red Wolf huffed a half-laugh. "Indeed, that would be fitting. Look after her."

"I will. Count on it," Talin said.

"Thank you."

They lapsed into silence. Red Wolf glanced over at his food and downed the rest of his ale.

"I actually came to—" Talin began.

"I know. I think it best if we did not say our goodbyes here." Red Wolf looked away.

"I...don't know if...I can bear to say them tomorrow," she said.

"I know." There was a hint of sadness in his eyes, though he was doing his best not to show it. "I'd hoped to avoid this conversation altogether."

"You think we'll see each other again someday?" Talin asked.

"Maybe. I'd like to have some hope." Red Wolf shrugged. "Your victory here in Belanore does not mean victory in the war, Talin. It could be years before you drive them back for good. And I...won't be here to see that day. My place has always been by your side, but now..."

His brow furrowed. "Truth be told, I would rather have let the court order my execution. I belonged here. With you, for a time. Beyond these walls, I've no notion of where to go. I've never belonged anywhere else."

"I could still pardon you—"

"You won't do that. You'll do the right thing, as you always have."

"I'd make an exception for you," Talin said. Red Wolf's mouth twitched into the faintest trace of a smile.

"Seeing as neither of us wishes to say our farewells at the gates, I take it this is our last conversation together," he said.

"Well, I..." Talin sighed. There was no denying it. "Yes. I suppose it is. I wish we could've had more time. I still can't believe I let you get close to me, despite my best efforts."

Red Wolf grinned. "Admit it, you didn't try hard."

"I don't regret it."

"I would hope not."

Talin couldn't help but laugh.

"I still owe you a drink," Red Wolf said. "If the guard outside were to conveniently fall asleep for a few hours..."

"I...I would love to, but I can't risk someone recognising you. Don't worry, you'll have the chance someday. I look forward to it."

He probably won't.

Talin pushed the thought from her mind.

"I won't forget, I promise," Red Wolf said.

"Then it's a deal. The next time we meet, you're buying me a drink," Talin said.

"Of course."

Talin settled in the nearby armchair while Red Wolf kicked off his boots to sit on the bed. "I...will admit, I have more questions for you.

About your time with the Hellhounds. If you were so inclined to answer them."

"Anything," Red Wolf said.

They talked till well past midnight, with Talin asking most of the burning questions she'd had about his past with the Hellhounds. Red Wolf answered them all, though she noticed that he dodged anything related to their alchemists and experiments unless she asked him directly. She didn't press him. Their conversation was finally cut off when they both realised that the trial would be first thing in the morning, and they needed to be well rested for it. Talin bid him farewell as if they were simply parting ways for the night and would see each other in the morning as usual. The guard outside had, indeed, fallen asleep, and quickly stood to attention with a mumbled apology when she passed.

You don't even need to be there. He's only in that tower because he doesn't want to escape. She didn't voice it out loud.

Now in the hallway leading to her chambers, Talin wondered if they should have said a proper farewell. Maybe it was better that they didn't; pretending they would see each other again soon was the only way she could cope. Perhaps it was selfish of her, when Red Wolf would soon be barred from setting foot in Kies Tor ever again, but he had gone along with it all the same. She was glad he didn't try to force her to say goodbye. And maybe he had seen through her façade earlier, but she refused to let him see her cry. She had to be strong in front of him, to show him that she would be fine on her own, that she could lead her people alone.

You'll never see him again. It's your fault that he'll be exiled when you could have pardoned him—

Talin brushed her tears aside angrily and walked faster.

The morning brought a drizzle that came and went during the trial, cooling the weather and gradually turning the roads dark with rainwater. For once, things seemed to go exactly as planned, though this time Talin wished they hadn't.

Anything to stop what's happening.

The gods, unfortunately, didn't see fit to supply her with a miracle of any kind.

"How do you plead?"

"Guilty," Red Wolf said, and that single word felt like a knife to her heart. She closed her eyes and refused to cry. Branweyn gave the verdict and sentence before ushering them all out so he could prepare for the next case. Red Wolf was ordered to leave immediately with his escort while Talin returned to the palace.

Now, standing on the balcony overlooking the entire city, she watched as the specks that were Red Wolf and his escort edged closer and closer to the northern gates. She had told herself many times that she would not go to farewell him; she still wasn't sure she could bear to say goodbye. He had understood. They had parted ways without saying anything, and now he was almost at the gates. Past the white walls of Belanore, she would never see him again.

Never is a long time.

Talin turned away from the balcony, threw on a coat, and raced down towards the palace stables for her horse. The stablemaster didn't question her rush, thankfully, and she was soon on the cobbled streets of Belanore, galloping for the northern gates. Red Wolf was already there when she caught up, having just ridden past the wall and left the city behind. He must have heard her approach because he stopped, forcing his escort to stop with him. She dismounted, but he remained unmoving, refusing to look at her.

"Red Wolf," she said quietly.

"I think it best...perhaps...if we did not say our farewells, my queen," Red Wolf said.

"I couldn't...not like this." Talin fought to keep her voice steady. "Not without saying goodbye."

"I understand." Red Wolf swung himself off his horse. "I didn't...I didn't want to make things any harder."

"There is no way you could make them easier," Talin said.

"I know." Red Wolf drew her away from the escort. "Talin, I..." He shook his head. "I can't. I don't know what I can say to you."

"No, there's...not much for me to say either." Talin swallowed. "I'm sorry..."

"Do not apologise. This was beyond your control. Your people would see me hanged or beheaded otherwise," Red Wolf said. "And I had my chance to make things right again. Clear your brother's name. Fix my mistakes. My only regret is that we must now say goodbye."

"I wish I didn't have to stay. You're right, this is my kingdom, and my people, and I have a duty to them," Talin whispered. "But after everything I've seen...I don't know that I want to lead them."

"You could pass on the crown to your brother," Red Wolf said. "Your people never deserved you, Talin, and you deserved so much better than them. But I know you better than that, or I hope I do."

"I must lead them. Change Kies Tor for the better, or at the very least, try to," Talin confessed. "Do you...no. Forget my father. If my mother were here today, do you think..."

"I think she would be *so proud* of what you've achieved," Red Wolf said, and Talin had to fight to keep her tears from falling. "Your father, too, for what that's worth, because you made the decisions that he never could."

"Don't go." It was all she could manage. "Please don't go."

"You have to let me go." Red Wolf reached under his tunic and pulled off a small necklace of a wolf's head. Its jewelled eyes stared at her unblinkingly. "I do not have much in the way of gifts, though I do have this. A trinket, of sorts, from the Hellhounds. They told me there was magic stored in this necklace, but I was never able to figure it out. Perhaps you'll make better use of it."

"I couldn't take this..." Talin began. "It's yours."

"A parting gift." Red Wolf pressed the necklace into her palm and curled her fingers around it. Talin looked down at it.

"Thank you."

"I have faith in you, Talin. If anyone can win this war against the Hellhounds, it's you," Red Wolf said.

"Wh...what will you do? Where will you go?" Talin heard herself ask.

"To the northern border, perhaps," Red Wolf said. "I'd like to find out who I am, if nothing else. Failing that, I'll go west again to the Drakels. I need you to do something for me."

Talin took a step closer. "Of course."

"Forget about me, Talin." Red Wolf took her face in his hands. "I need you to forget my face, my name, my existence. Move on, lead your people, and make this place better. Without me."

"Red Wolf, no. I can't do that. You know..." Talin's voice broke. "You know I can't do that. I won't forget you."

"Talin." Red Wolf silenced her with a kiss. She returned it almost desperately, knowing that this was their final moment together, that when they broke apart, she would lose him for good. His hands slid down to her waist, pulling her close as he deepened the kiss. It took every ounce of willpower to push him away. If she allowed herself to savour this moment, even for an instant, she knew she would never be able to let him go.

"Don't," she said, feeling more tears springing to her eyes. "Don't make this any harder. Please."

Red Wolf's expression never changed, but she knew he understood. "If you ever happen to need me again, send a bird west to El'Vane. It will reach me eventually."

Talin simply nodded; her throat had constricted too much for her to talk, and if she opened her mouth, she was certain she would fall apart. She looked up, into the rings of molten gold in his eyes, and tried her hardest not to cry.

"Until we meet again, my queen," he said. Talin watched as he turned his back and mounted his horse, and the escort moved off. She stayed there until his fading figure had completely disappeared into the distance, and she was certain she could no longer see him. Only then did she allow herself to climb onto the back of her horse and turn for home.

Later, as she retired to her bedchambers to change into a nightgown, she found a letter on her bed addressed to her in Red Wolf's familiar, elegant scrawl. She stared at it for a time, then broke the seal and read it. It wasn't much, but there was no doubt that her bodyguard had written it, perhaps sometime before his departure. She almost burned it afterwards because she couldn't bear to look at it again. In the end, she secreted it in a drawer in her study, and wore the necklace he'd given her.

She knew he didn't want her to forget.

My dearest Talin,

I wish I could offer some words of comfort, to tell you that all will be alright, but I cannot say this now with certainty. We walk separate paths, my queen, and difficult ones, to be sure. Yours perhaps will be the most difficult of all. I do not know if we will meet again, for my own road is perilous and dark. Be strong, be true, and above all, be brave. Your people will look to you in the times ahead. Give them hope. You may feel that you are not worthy to lead them, but know that you are the queen that Kies Tor needs. Instinct tells me that you'll not fail. And when the nights grow cold and bleak, and the days fill with fire and smoke, look up and look around, for my absence does not mean you are alone. The sun will rise each morning, the world will continue to turn, and though it may seem impossible, this war will be won.

Red Wolf

Acknowledgements

So, I wrote this book back in 2018. Left it for a bit. Came back and rewrote it. Rewrote it a few more times. Now I'm here, and I can still hardly believe this thing will actually be published for people to read. *Song of the Wolf* spawned as a standalone initially and only became a series through the wonderful power of the writing community, where I was able to bounce ideas off of fellow writers and yell about how much I love my characters. Truly, none of this would have been possible without the following people, so without further ado, let's get into it.

I would first like to thank my friends and fellow authors (you know who you are), who have always been there to provide support and encouragement while I was writing this book. In particular, I'd like to thank my fellow writers at the MelbNaNo Discord Server—the enthusiasm about Red Wolf and Talin was an incredible confidence boost when I felt like my stuff wasn't up to par. I hope none of you hold the ending of this book against me. For my old friends at the CitW Discord and the private Treehouse Discord (again, you know who you are), thank you for being there when I first started writing seriously and not being judgemental of my early awful prose—I don't think I would have taken my writing nearly as seriously had you not been there to cheer on my work. To all the people who have read one of my fanfics on AO3 and left kudos or comments, thank you for enjoying my content, and I hope this book also lived up to your expectations.

To the editing team at *The Expert Editor*, thank you for taking the time to go through my entire 120k-word manuscript line by line and offer suggestions for improvement. I know it was no easy feat; going through those edits took *me* almost a month. Your insight and expertise were incredibly useful in polishing this book and making sure it was the best it could possibly be.

I would also like to thank my family, without whose support I would not be able to publish this book. As embarrassing as it may be, thank you also for spreading the word about my book to everyone you know and helping with marketing in that regard. I would especially like to thank my brother's interest and enthusiasm about my story—your eagerness to read my manuscript as I was proofreading is appreciated, as is your eagerness to see my book cover before I'd even started making it.

To my schoolteachers over the years: Mr Stackpole, Ms Handesyde, Ms Hicks, Mr Walsh, and Miss Rowlston, thank you for recognising and encouraging my love for writing. I doubt I would be publishing a book all these years later without all of your support.

Finally, I would like to thank my cat, Athena, for always being there as moral support, and for not crashing my word processing app when she walked all over my keyboard while I was going through 500 pages of line edits.

Liked this book? Leave a review!